"*Playing the Witch Card* is an enchanting story of small-town magic, love, family, and friendship as delicious and captivating as Flair's tarot-themed cookies. It'll have you craving both witchy baked goods and a visit to your nearest swoon-worthy magical town."

—Lana Harper, author of *Payback's a Witch* and the Witches of Thistle Grove series

"A delightfully sweet, heartfelt novel about letting go of our fears to make room for magic, and the power of choosing our own fate. Utterly charming."

—Rachel Harrison, author of *Cackle* and *Such Sharp Teeth*

"KJ Dell'Antonia perfectly captures life in a small town in this delightful family saga. . . . It feels strange to say that a book about witchcraft and magic that won't take no for an answer is 'cozy,' but I really did get cozy vibes from this book! It put me in a fall, pumpkin-spice sort of mood and is the perfect read for curling up next to the fire."

—Jessica Clare, author of *What the Hex*

"Buckle up your broomsticks, people. *Playing the Witch Card* is an absolutely delightful wild ride that will leave you breathless at the end. This intricate and tightly woven novel is ultimately an exploration of identity, freedom, and the power of letting things go. This one will stay with me for a long time."

—Annabel Monaghan, author of *Nora Goes Off Script* and *Same Time Next Summer*

"KJ Dell'Antonia had me at 'magic cookies,' but then her story delivered so much more: a charming tale of second chances, family, and embracing one's true self, all set in an enchanting small town I'm ready to relocate to. This is a Halloween treat of a book."

—Elizabeth Bass, author of *A Letter to Three Witches*

"A magical, heartwarming, and hilarious story about embracing who we are, and women reclaiming their power. Set in a charming town with its own secrets and enchanted tarot cards, this book will cast a spell on you in the best possible way. I absolutely loved it!"

—Maureen Kilmer, author of *Hex Education*

"Witty, charming, and utterly unputdownable, *In Her Boots* is the perfect reminder that living life on our own terms might just be what it's all about. Once again, KJ Dell'Antonia has knocked it out of the park with a story that will work its way right into readers' hearts."

—Kristy Woodson Harvey, author of *Under the Southern Sky*

"[A] lively tale . . . Dell'Antonia offers an affecting take on damaged relationships, while keeping things light with descriptions of spunky farm animals and the quirks of rural life. The author's fans will love this."

—*Publishers Weekly*

"What can be better than a book that surprises and delights you on every page and yet at the same time speaks so clearly to the familiar joys—and challenges—of friendship, family, and self-discovery? . . . You'll gobble this one up and then push it on your best friend—and she'll love you for it!"

—Kelly Harms, author of *The Seven Day Switch*

PRAISE FOR
The Chicken Sisters

A Reese's Book Club pick

Instant *New York Times* bestseller

A *Country Living* Front Porch Book Club pick

"A delightful look at sibling relationships and the unbreakable bonds of family."

—*Real Simple*

"A pitch-perfect book with which to begin the new year, when the spirit of starting anew and putting aside baggage (no matter how many centuries old it may be!) is exactly what we need. Well, that and a plate of fried chicken, of course."

—*Country Living*

"If you prefer your family secrets served with a side of fried chicken, we highly recommend *The Chicken Sisters*. . . . [A] funny, heartfelt book."

—*HelloGiggles*

"A charming first novel about family, regrets, and second chances. Dell'Antonia deftly deals with issues of mental illness, marriage troubles, and dreams deferred, all the while telling a funny satire of reality TV. An utter delight from start to finish."

Booklist (starred review)

"Mae and Amanda are spirited characters, and their foibles are told with care and humor. Recommended for Food Network and HGTV watchers, this first novel is plucky, heartwarming, and a welcome distraction from the news of the day."

—*Library Journal*

"The comfort food of novels."

—Laura Zigman, author of *Separation Anxiety*

"Comfortingly quirky. A charming and satisfying story about family bonds that will make meat eaters everywhere crave fried chicken."

—*Kirkus Reviews*

ALSO BY KJ DELL'ANTONIA

FICTION

In Her Boots

The Chicken Sisters

NONFICTION

How to Be a Happier Parent

Reading with Babies, Toddlers & Twos
(with Susan Straub)

PLAYING
the
WITCH CARD

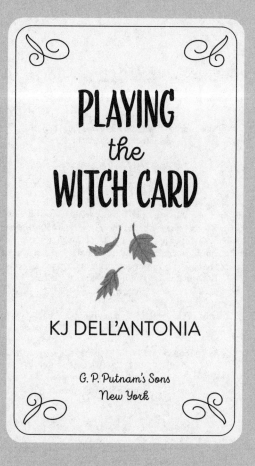

KJ DELL'ANTONIA

G. P. Putnam's Sons
New York

PUTNAM
— EST. 1838 —

G. P. Putnam's Sons
Publishers Since 1838
An imprint of Penguin Random House LLC
penguinrandomhouse.com

Library of Congress Cataloging-in-Publication Data
has been applied for.

ISBN: 9780593713792 (paperback)
ISBN: 9780593713808 (ebook)

Printed in the United States of America
1st Printing

Book design by Katy Riegel

This is a work of fiction. Names, characters, places, and incidents either are the product of
the author's imagination or are used fictitiously, and any resemblance to actual persons,
living or dead, businesses, companies, events, or locales is entirely coincidental.

For S and J, who know just when to ask

that all-important question:

"Are you a witch or not?"

PLAYING
the
WITCH CARD

CHAPTER ONE

Monday, October 26

OTHER PEOPLE, WHEN forced to start over, do so in appropriate places. New York. Los Angeles. Bozeman. Only Flair would wind up in Kansas, dragging a hand-painted, life-sized figure of Jack Skellington into her bakery and wondering where to hide it until the horror show that was Halloween in Rattleboro finally lurched to an end this weekend.

Flair hated seeing even the outside of her tidy space besmirched with the trappings of a ridiculous holiday that invited exactly the kind of chaos that she normally kept firmly at bay. But she'd had to accept it. From the skeleton on the now spiderweb-covered bench to the black-and-orange garlands and the wheelbarrow of painted pumpkins, her precarious new venture had become part of a Main Street so drenched in town-funded Halloween preparations that it was impossible to rest your eyes on a surface not wrapped in twinkle lights or faux-aged into flawless Gothic dereliction.

But Jack eating a slice of bloodred cherry pie was taking it a step too far.

Like nearly everyone, he was taller than Flair, making him difficult to maneuver, but Flair would not let that stop her from ridding her entryway of the blight. She wrestled him through the door and looked around the shop, wondering where she could stash him until the town's Halloween powers that be came to retrieve him in November. Or maybe he could meet an untimely and tragic end before then.

Lucie looked up from one of the white tables where she sat with her ankles wrapped around the legs of a turquoise chair, which she had—under duress—helped Flair to paint before Buttersweet Bakery's opening in August. Ostensibly she was doing vocab, but more likely she was staring into the phone Flair had given her when they moved. Flair's plan had been for Lucie to connect with (and feel appropriately cool next to) her new eighth-grade classmates, but Lucie preferred to use it to complain to her father and her friends back "home" in St. Louis about the cruelty of her mother's decision to move them both to the boondocks.

"Grand is having a show in St. Louis tomorrow," she said. "If we were there, we could go."

"Well, we're not," Flair said automatically. "And Grand's shows aren't G-rated, so we wouldn't be going anyway." Would Jack fit behind the hutch that was very nearly the only thing left of what had until recently been Marie's Teas, or was she going to have to find a place for him in her kitchen? "We'll see her soon."

"That's what you always say," said Lucie, who was clearly gearing up for another monologue on her favorite topic, *how you have ruined my life.* "But it's been since her birthday two years ago. If we were home, we would at least have dinner or something."

Maybe. Or maybe Cynthia would be so overrun by fans of the bewilderingly successful vampire-and-witch romances she wrote that—darn—she wouldn't be able to fit them in. Flair was relieved when the bells on the door interrupted her daughter before the pointless debate could continue. She tried but failed to hide Jack behind her as she prepared a welcoming, but not overwhelming, smile for what would be her first customer of the day. At 3:30 in the afternoon, but Flair wasn't counting.

Who was she kidding? Of course she was—and the count would still be zero, because unless Renee Oakes had abandoned her distaste for all things Flair and Flair-adjacent, the woman who walked through the door was not and would not ever be a customer. "He's supposed to be outside, Hardwicke," Renee said, pointing to the pumpkin-headed particleboard figure behind Flair. "We put him there this morning."

Flair drew herself up to her full height—which had to be at least six inches shorter than the stern blonde in front of her—and prepared to deliver a considered and logical explanation for why this decoration did not represent Buttersweet, even in the context of the all-encompassing town Halloween festival Renee directed with what should have been admirable dedication.

"But he's hideous," Flair said. "His eyes are seriously terrifying, and he looks more like an axe murderer than a friendly Halloween mayor dude or whatever he is. I mean, where did anyone even find this? The drive-in movie theater's dump?"

"I painted it," Renee said.

Oh. Flair turned to look at the creation leering back at her and could think of no way to backtrack over what she'd just said. Life, she thought, not for the first time, really needed some kind of rewind button.

"And you have an obligation to display the holiday decor provided to you by the decoration committee."

Flair knew that. Renee had already given her a "reference" copy of the building's covenant, which also required that she maintain the window boxes, whose riot of fall foliage and flowers threatened daily to overwhelm her entrance, as well as the paint and the trim (in approved colors only) and all the rest of the landscaping. She felt her resolve weakening. "But I don't even serve pie."

"I'll put it back outside," Renee said, taking the decoration from Flair and lifting it easily. She glanced around at the empty tables and the full pastry case before giving Flair a pitying look. "Maybe pie would help."

Renee marched out the door, Jack under her arm. Flair could see her through the windows, standing him prominently on the sidewalk in a way that would effectively deter any potential customers.

She looked at Lucie, hoping for some sympathy—Jack Skellington was truly dreadful—but Lucie was stuffing the worksheets Flair didn't think she'd so much as glanced at into her backpack. "I'm going home," Lucie said. "Unless you want to give me a ride."

"It's four blocks."

"Yeah, but it's not like you're doing anything."

Flair pointed to the door. Lucie went out as Loretta Oakes, the only member of the Oakes family Flair regarded fondly at this point, came in. At least Lucie managed to return Renee's mother's greeting politely. Either she did have some manners, or she was, like everyone else in town, both terrified by and in awe of Loretta. Flair would take whatever she could get.

Unlike Renee, Loretta embraced Flair, bringing with her a spicy, faintly floral scent that tugged at a memory Flair preferred to leave unpursued. Loretta also brought with her a comforting sense that here, at least, was someone who was happy that Flair was back in Rattleboro.

"My usual, please," Loretta said, taking a seat at the table closest to the counter. "And join me, if you can."

Flair appreciated the suggestion that she might suddenly be overwhelmed with customers, although Loretta must know as well as she did that it was unlikely. Obediently, Flair took up her place behind the case full of scones and cookies and flaky croissants, all lined up on their trays, swiveling the portafilter into place and waiting for the grinder's familiar growl.

Her occasional assistant, Callie, whose wages she really could not afford, had suggested renaming things "in the holiday spirit" and had gone as far as "Spooky Scones" and "Devilish Danishes" before Flair shut her down. Flair's baked goods weren't the kind of thing you bought in a plastic clamshell at Dillons. They were award-winning pastries that deserved better. On the cover of *Bon Appétit* once, she reminded herself. Featured in Martha Stewart's *Holiday Cookies* issue three times: see also the triptych on the wall. *Midwest Living* said, last year, that even if David's Table ran out of steak and couldn't fry another frite, it would still be worth the wait for Flair's Pavlova bars alone.

But after two solid months of effort, she couldn't seem to entice anyone in Rattleboro to try one. If today was anything like yesterday, Loretta would be her only patron. And she'd clearly noticed that not one thing on the carefully arranged trays had been disturbed.

"Slow day again?"

"Things will pick up," Flair said, repeating what she'd been telling herself for weeks. "Getting started is always tough."

"I think it's been more than tough," Loretta said. Flair hid her face behind the espresso machine while she prepared Loretta's favored macchiato so that the other woman wouldn't see how closely her words hit home, or how much her sympathy affected Flair. She'd grown up spending summers in Rattleboro. Her grandmother had run Marie's Teas in this spot for fifty years. It wasn't that she'd expected a parade, but she had thought she could make a go of it here. That she'd be at least sort of welcomed. Instead, other than her best friend and once-again next-door neighbor, Josie, Rattleboro seemed to have shut her out, and it was almost as if the shop were invisible.

"I'll be fine," she called. But when she looked up, Loretta met her eyes with an expression that made it clear she didn't buy Flair's cheery words.

"This is not fine," she said with a quick lick of her lips that Flair had learned was characteristic when Loretta spoke. "We need to do something to get you involved. And I have the perfect thing. You know about the Rattlebones Trail, of course."

It wasn't a question. No one could spend any time at all in Rattleboro without hearing about the Rattlebones Trail, and Flair was scarcely a stranger. Every summer she'd spent here had been punctuated by stumbling into macabre scenes in Nana's neighbors' garages and sheds in preparation for the event, an elaborate outdoor haunted attraction that had been a tradition for over a hundred years and had become famous not just in the Midwest but across the country. The trail, run by the League of Kansas Craftswomen, was legendary for its artistry and its scariness and for being something just a little bit more than what even the average horror fan was going for.

A few actors and performers had appeared as guests years ago, and a famous director had once taken it over, but for as long as Flair had known it, the trail had been masterminded entirely by Loretta, long the head of the league, micromanaged by Renee, and "haunted," in the town's parlance, by the same families again and again. Tickets, which sold out fully a year in advance, were distributed through a wildly complicated, untransferable system, and newcomers to town waited years to be initiated into the preparation.

"Of course," Flair said.

"Then you'll know what it means to become a part of it."

Flair stopped short, then quickly resumed adding foam to Loretta's drink, trying to hide her surprised dismay. She'd known she couldn't avoid the town's festival, with its crowds of costumed families. That was going to be bad enough. But the trail took place in an unusually thick wood just on the outskirts of Rattleboro, and given the competition to participate, Flair had expected the trail itself to be easy to avoid.

This was a hard no, and Flair was about to say so, delicately, when she heard a sharp rap on the door—the back door, which opened onto the alley that ran behind every building on this side of the street.

Nobody Flair wanted to see came to the back door without

letting Flair know they were here first. Loretta lifted her chin in the direction of the noise as the rap came again. "I can wait if you need to get it."

"No, that's okay." Flair didn't pause as she added a drizzle of chocolate over the drink. "Probably just a delivery." It wasn't, and she knew it. She wasn't expecting anything, and she could feel the urgency of the knock from here.

The knocking continued. Flair forced herself to move calmly as she placed Loretta's drink in front of her, the coffee beautifully serene in its white mug on an accompanying plate, tiny complimentary madeleine beside it. As much as she wanted to ignore the interruption, whoever it was, wasn't going away. "I'll just go take care of it."

She made her way through the swinging door into the kitchen quickly, intent upon putting a stop to this now. Teabag, the toy poodle who'd been the first thing Flair inherited from her grandmother, was up and staring at the door.

Flair yanked it open to a woman in a long coat, hood pulled up, hand poised to knock again. She peered around Flair.

"Where's Marie?"

If Halloween had arrived at the front door, its pagan sibling Samhain would come in through the back.

CHAPTER TWO

FLAIR SHOOK HER head, glancing over her shoulder to make sure the kitchen door had swung shut. "Not here."

"But I need her," the woman at the door said, stepping forward as if to charge past Flair. "And I'm out of tea."

Most people knew Marie was gone by now. Most people had already been convinced that coming to her granddaughter instead wasn't going to do them any good.

But Halloween had nearly arrived, bringing strangers to Rattleboro with it. For once, Flair wished that there had been more than the most minimal press coverage of Nana's accident. But her grandmother's fame was not of that kind, and this visitor was not Flair's first and wouldn't be her last.

"I'm sorry," Flair said, blocking the entrance. "Ms. Hardwicke died last year."

The woman stopped looking into the shop and stared at Flair instead. Marie had been small and quick, with long braids and blue eyes that had grown no less intense with the passage of time. Flair, with the same small stature, blue eyes, pointy chin, and pale cheeks, was obviously her kin, even though the wavy hair that fought to escape tight braids was blond rather than silver.

"Then you have to help me," the woman said, her voice rising as she reached for Flair's arm. Flair slid away with a practiced move, avoiding contact. Need surrounded her visitor, looking for a point of entry that Flair refused to give. Teabag barked once, a sharp yap of reproval, although whether for Flair or her unwelcome guest, Flair had no idea.

"I'm afraid I can't," she said, keeping her gaze firmly on the edge of the door between them, a metal door, red paint peeling. "We don't sell loose tea. Just coffee. And pastries." No tea except brewed, served only in bags. No candles, no tinctures, nothing to suggest Flair could, would, or might ever offer the services Nana had specialized in.

"Flair?" Loretta's voice, from the shop, and the click of her boot heels. "Is everything all right back there?"

Flair tried to shut the door, but the woman put out a surprisingly strong hand and bent just enough to force Flair to catch her eyes.

"But you are Marie," she said. "Or you could be. I can feel it. Can't you— I don't need the tea. I just need to know what I should do."

Flair heard the kitchen door open behind her. With a great summoning of her own will, Flair refused to see or feel anything in the gaze that so insistently met hers. She kept her voice carefully even, neutral. "I'm sorry," she said. "You've made a mistake."

Teabag brushed against her ankle and barked, startling the

woman. Flair used the moment to begin pushing the door shut, but she still caught the woman's parting words.

"I haven't," she insisted. "Maybe you have."

Flair slammed the door with more force than she had intended. The walls around it quivered in sympathy, and to Flair's dismay, a crack appeared in the paint at the corner of the doorjamb, the whitewash splitting to reveal the old wood underneath as Flair turned to smile at Loretta, who was peering into the kitchen.

"Everyone misses Marie," Flair tried to say brightly, but she heard a crack in her own voice to match the one in the paint.

"I have missed Marie for a long time," Loretta said. She stood for a moment, her eyes on the closed door. Flair held her breath, searching Loretta's face for any sign that she'd been aware of the second and probably more lucrative business her grandmother had run out of the shop. Thankfully she found none. Loretta couldn't have heard much from the other room. Maybe she wouldn't ask.

She didn't. Instead, she gestured for Flair to return to the front room, continuing their earlier conversation as though there had been no interruption. Teabag trotted after them.

"We do one stop on the trail that provides a 'treat' to give travelers a little breather. I've chosen you to provide the treats."

Loretta resumed her seat and took a sip of her drink. Flair hesitated as she took the other chair, looking for the most politic way to refuse. She had the faintest memories of standing behind a steaming cauldron while her grandmother ladled something into cups, delighted with the black lace and tulle that made up her costume, her hair hidden beneath one of Nana's glittering scarves. She remembered an evening that stretched on and on, people dancing, the night sky seeming to lower itself to meet them, a sense of anticipation satisfied that she had never experienced before or since.

But her grandmother had let go of whatever role she once played in the trail long ago, and Flair's single experience as a trail "traveler" was one she tried to forget. When she'd made the decision to return to Rattleboro, the trail—and all the Halloween madness that went along with it—was the one thing she hadn't looked forward to.

In the end, Flair hadn't had any choice other than to come back. This, though— "I can't," she began. Loretta didn't let her finish.

"This is your heritage," she said firmly. "There have been Hardwickes in the woods on Halloween for generations. Your grandmother was stubborn; your mother—" She waved a hand around, seeming to indicate that she, like everyone else, found it difficult to describe Flair's mother, and left it at that, instead looking intensely at Flair. "I know it's been hard to establish yourself here. Trust me that that will change, and this is how."

In her head, Flair disagreed. If anything, this would make people resent her more; it would be horning in where she wasn't wanted—

"*I* want you," Loretta said. "And when people see that, they will change their minds, and quickly. Your grandmother was once a respected part of this institution. Not just respected. Beloved. When people see that you are Marie's granddaughter in every way, they'll change their tunes. Give it a chance."

Marie's granddaughter.

Flair would prefer to be just Flair, but "Marie's granddaughter" was surely preferable to being "Cynthia's girl," a turn of phrase she'd caught being whispered behind her back over and over again whenever she returned here as a child. Being her mother's daughter had meant a hundred things that Flair had purposefully left behind, even when it meant abandoning her grandmother's teachings as well.

Flair avoided looking toward the back door, pushed aside intrusive thoughts of cards spread across what was now her worktable. She should have gotten rid of it, even if she couldn't afford to replace it.

But Loretta's Halloween happened in the street, not the alley. These revelers would dance in the square, pretend to scare themselves in the woods, savor their brush with darkness, and return the next day to their shops and offices without trying to impose any deeper meaning on what they'd seen. All Loretta was asking Flair to do was help create that illusion, not enter into it. She bit back her objections and focused on Loretta's words.

"Halloween is Rattleboro's biggest source of revenue and one of the reasons this town hasn't suffered the same decline as some of our neighbors. This year, with the black moon, will be bigger than ever. We're proud of our celebration, and you need to show that you are, too. This is your chance to prove yourself."

Loretta removed the sunglasses that held back her silver bob and shook them at Flair before donning them. "And"—her gaze included both sympathy and challenge—"it really isn't optional."

She took a folded paper from the handbag she'd set at her feet—a Birkin, Flair realized, incredulous—and handed it to Flair. "These are the details. You'll join us tomorrow morning with a sample of what you can do. Make it spectacular. Show everyone that you belong here, because you do. Marie knew it. I know it. I need you to know it, too."

She bent to pick up her bag, and Flair glimpsed its contents: keys, a lipstick, wallet—and a deck of tarot cards.

Flair stilled, her gaze caught. She glanced quickly up at Loretta and saw nothing in the other woman's face but the calm expectation that Flair would accede to her plans as everyone always did. Flair looked back at the bag and saw that she'd been mistaken.

It was a deck of playing cards, nothing more.

The transformation—or the mistake, because of course that had been nothing but Flair's mistake—was almost more disturbing than the idea that Loretta Oakes, Halloween queen, might also carry around an ordinary Rider-Waite-Smith tarot deck.

Anyone might have one of those. But if Flair began seeing that deck where it wasn't, she might begin to see others. And while the harlequin-like images in muted colors that Pixie Smith had created all those years ago were one thing, the deck that was most familiar to Flair, painted by her ancestor and far more vivid, was 100 percent not welcome here. Flair pushed aside the momentary intrusion of those images, brimming with an intensity that—according to Flair's mother—had been infused with all the magic of generations of witches and passed forward to Flair's mother for safekeeping.

A claim that, ironically, proved to Flair her mother must be lying. No one, witch or otherwise, would have handed over anything important to Cynthia Hardwicke for safekeeping.

Flair's mother had never kept anything safe in her life.

Flair looked up at Loretta. Playing cards, lipstick, wallet—ordinary things in an ordinary bag, and an ordinary request, really. Halloween was a thing people did, and Loretta was right—people all over the world had heard of Rattleboro and the Rattlebones Trail. Being part of it wouldn't be falling back into her mother's world. It would be proving that she had really and truly left it behind.

Plus, if there was anything Flair could do, it was spectacular baking. "Okay," she said, then regretted the informal word. "I mean, yes. Yes. I'll do it."

"Wonderful. We'll see you at the meeting." Loretta got up and swirled her way to the door as Flair watched, already running through options in her mind. It had been a long time since she'd been given an assignment like this, and ideas spun through her head like the leaves on the sidewalk as Loretta opened the door and offered one final piece of advice over her shoulder.

"I'm expecting magic," she said, and before she could register the look on Flair's face, she was gone.

Flair stared after her.

It was just an expression. Spectacular she could do. Magic, no.

Loretta's chair was out of place. Flair rose to adjust it, then went to each of the other chairs and tables, checking unnecessarily to make sure they were still where they belonged. She unfolded the sheet of paper Loretta had given her and forced herself to consider the requirements it listed—handheld, no utensils, one per serving, *a delight to the eye, the palate, and the spirit.*

That wasn't asking much.

Her own spirit rose to the challenge, and to the faith that lay behind it. She could do this. She could give Rattleboro's Halloween visitors something worth remembering, even amid the mayhem that was the Rattlebones Trail. And maybe if she did, Rattleboro would be forced to open up and let her in.

But Flair's momentary optimism dissipated as she looked at the empty shop. She just didn't get it. Even now, as she looked out the bakery's window, she could see people passing by without even glancing at Buttersweet, carrying to-go cups full of the weak brew available from the Keurig in Renee's bookshop. The only thing that stuff had going for it was the price—a dollar donation to the coffee-and-cats fund.

Flair had even checked in with Renee about the "competition" her bakery would offer said Keurig. Renee had barely looked up from the box of books she was emptying. *I don't care,* she'd said. *Do what you want.* She'd lifted a youngish cat out of the box and then watched, without even a trace of amusement on her face, as the cat jumped back in. *Coffee's not a moneymaker.*

Flair remembered her grandmother and a much younger Renee sweeping away a spread of traditional tarot cards as Flair came in through the back door of the tea shop. Renee's tendency to dismiss Flair even when she was in the room had always been irritating.

Renee had never liked her, and Flair in her turn had resented Renee for her part in those late-night readings—the only ones Marie didn't permit her to join. Until Flair became a teenager and decided to pity Renee instead, for never leaving Rattleboro, for the rigid and unchanging wardrobe of black turtlenecks and jeans that had turned out to actually just be ahead of their time, her apparent lack of friends, and of course her interest in the cards themselves, which Flair, so much wiser, had chosen to set aside.

But now here they were, and it was Renee who was at the center of everything in Rattleboro, who didn't just run the town's bookstore and the Halloween festival, but—at her mother's behest—essentially controlled the whole town. Loretta might hold the gavel at city council meetings and the purse strings of the League of Kansas Craftswomen, but it was Renee who did all the work. It was Renee who belonged.

Flair went to the door and stood holding it open, looking out at a street that was well populated with visitors even on a Monday. Teabag trotted up beside her and began dancing around on her hind legs, a request to be held that Flair granted.

She snuggled the little dog close as she looked out at the bright autumn leaves of the trees that lined the row of shops, galleries, and small restaurants that made up the core of Rattleboro, all transformed by Renee's iron hand into a Martha-Stewart-meets-Hogwarts display that everyone except Flair seemed to love. Buttersweet Bakery should fit right in, both with and without the loathsome holiday bling. Awful as he was, at least Jack and his luridly depicted slice of pie were on theme. Flair tried, and failed, to imagine Renee with a paintbrush, carefully shading the pie's latticed crust. Behind Jack, the window boxes were sprawling, blooming riots of yellow and orange interspersed with black feathers and dried seedpods to really pile on that Halloween motif.

Huge vines, the flowers like gulping yellow mouths, some

open, some closed, climbed up a trellis and over the door and hung down to the sidewalk as well, meeting the mums and marigolds that had been planted in the beds closer to the building. Maybe she should cut the vines. They were a little daunting, and if they got any bigger—could they get bigger? They were already gigantic—they'd block the light from the windows.

But the thought of attacking them with scissors was daunting as well. She'd consult Josie, whose gardening prowess far exceeded Flair's.

Even Flair's smiling presence in the doorway didn't encourage anyone to consider coming in. Maybe she was the one who was off-putting. Flair returned to the empty shop and opened her laptop, meaning to brainstorm ideas for her trail treats and saw instead her spreadsheets. She opened a new document to cover them, quickly tapping in ideas, but the unwelcome truths they contained bled through her notes and her thoughts.

She massaged her hands, pressing the tips together to stretch them out and release the tension. If she didn't get some customers in here soon, she'd be icing cakes for Walmart. Loretta was right—doing the Rattlebones Trail would help her finally find her footing here.

Flair spun away from the computer and paced the shop instead, unnecessarily lining up flatware so that all the tines and bowls were even and straightening sugar, sweeteners, and straws, contemplating petit fours and tarts before finally settling in her mind on iced sugar cookies. Unlike most, Flair's cookies were both beautiful and delicious, sought after as party favors and a moneymaker for Flair when things got tight. She lacked shaped cutters for this particular holiday, but rectangles were easier and more efficient anyway. She'd ice them to look like retro Halloween cards; they'd be beautiful and no one would ever know how easy it actually was to create the dramatic swirled effects people loved.

Two hours later, with the cookies baked and cooling and the icings made, Flair found herself contemplating the sketches she'd made with distaste. The Victoriana-style beaming pumpkins, black cats, and green-faced witches were so smarmy, so jolly and naive. She would hate re-creating them again and again, even if it were just for a week.

What could she make that she wouldn't loathe?

Flair couldn't think of a thing.

Outside, it had begun to rain, driving torrents accompanied by thunder and wind. She needed to get started if these were going to be dry before tomorrow's meeting, needed to get home to Lucie, who would not like being alone in a storm. Teabag, disturbed by the pounding of raindrops on the tin awning over the back door, huddled under her feet as she sat in front of her worktable, glazed blank cookies and piping bag in hand, and thought about her grandmother, beside her in the shop, packing dried tea leaves, spices, herbs, and flowers into metal tins, and then in the kitchen back at the house, helping her to frost wonky black cats and jack-o'-lanterns that Flair's grandmother said only a mother could love.

That younger version of Flair had thought of her own mother, who never so much as got out of the car in Rattleboro, and whether her grandmother loved her. She'd been afraid to ask, but Marie answered anyway, as she often did. *Hush. Of course I love your mom.* More nights, mostly summer nights, brewing tea, talking, the lights flickering off and on as Flair and her grandmother lifted and lowered their hands and Marie clapping happily when Flair caught on, a memory that Flair shut off instantly.

The lights in the shop flickered, too, echoing her memories. Her head nodded over the table, the result of not enough sleep and far too much of everything else, and when she tried to force her eyes open, she saw, instead of her tidy white walls, the cluttered wood of Marie's tea shop, jars on every shelf, dried flowers hanging from every beam, a woodstove behind the table where Nana held the hands of the women who came in and whispered to them, then spread the cards before them.

But it wasn't Nana's shop anymore. Flair knew it in the way you know things in dreams and because she saw her window boxes, but then she saw her grandmother there, too, tearing at the yellow clematis that was growing faster than she could hold it back, shutting Flair in and her grandmother out until finally Nana ripped it all away.

And then her grandmother was laying out the cards, but their faces kept shifting until it was not one of Marie's many decks but *the* deck, the family deck, in front of Flair, with the skeletal baby bird fool, the raven of strength, the tree house tower. A voice pressed her to read the cards, and she almost felt as if she could, but then it was her mother's voice, asking her what she saw, and then it wasn't, it was some other voice, and always the Ferris wheel of fortune turning, turning, and at its center the symbol on the back of every card, the eye within the triangle, blinking furiously at Flair and demanding her attention. Flair shook her head just as furiously because she did not want to give that eye her attention, not when there were so many other things to do, and she didn't need the eye and it didn't need her, and it needed to go away, she'd made it go away a long time ago—

And then she was really shaking her head because she was sitting at her worktable, and honestly, there was so much to be done and she was better than this—she did not doze off in her shop when the sign was turned to *Welcome*, like some apprentice just waiting to be fired so they could go into hotel management. She tightened her grip on the pastry bag and turned her attention to the cookie in front of her.

But it had already been iced. That one, and all the rest. Every cookie she could see drying on every surface of the kitchen, on every set of stacking racks, every counter and every windowsill, had been decorated to perfection with Flair's distinctively precise piping work and lettering lightly dusted with black-and-gold edible glitter. Images she recognized instantly, horrified. The Fool. The Hierophant. The Hanged Man. Death.

These were not the designs she'd planned earlier. These were images she knew, had always known, down to their tiniest detail and right down to her very bones.

She'd stolen the originals of these tarot cards almost thirty years ago and hidden them, with good reason. She didn't want them back.

CHAPTER THREE

FLAIR STARED AROUND her, frightened by what she'd done. At the sound of the bells on the door jingling, she leapt up and ran into the front of the shop, tearing off her apron and flinging it on the floor behind the swinging kitchen door, half expecting to see more cookies on every surface, but the café was as tidy as she'd left it. Teabag, who'd run after her, now stood waiting for her walk, perfectly composed, as though she'd never cowered from a storm at Flair's feet. Josie stood in the doorway, bemused.

"You look like you've seen a ghost," she said. Flair ignored her, grabbing her jacket and keys from their hooks behind the counter and practically pushing her friend back out onto the sidewalk, clucking at Teabag to follow and grateful that the rain had stopped. As she slammed the door and locked it, she realized that Josie was looking at her oddly. "What's wrong?" Josie asked.

"Nothing." The only ghost Flair had seen was of her own past.

If Flair even could explain what had just happened, she wasn't sure she would, wasn't even sure, now that she was outside, if it had happened at all. If she went back in the kitchen, would she see nothing but bare cookies and hastily strewn bags of unused icing?

She hesitated, hand on the door, and saw the icing caked under her fingernails. She knew the truth. She'd decorated every single cookie as her family's tarot cards, a deck she hadn't looked at in years and wasn't going to look at now, no matter how hard it seemed to be knocking on the inside of her own head.

There was no need to worry like this, she told herself. Of course she'd think of that deck when she was back in Rattle-boro. When she was stressed. When she was at a decision point. That was what she'd been trained to do.

But she didn't have to listen. Flair decided then and there: she'd be damned if she was going to Loretta's meeting, or anywhere near Halloween. The cookies she could dispose of in the morning, a failed experiment that would cost nothing more than the price of the ingredients and her time. These things happened.

Josie was waiting for Flair to expand on her response. She shook off all thoughts of Chariots or Temperance.

"You know better than to joke about ghosts here," Flair said, gesturing around her. In the weird post-storm light of a sunset under dark clouds, the cornices and parapets of Rattle-boro's turn-of-the-century main street would have looked a little ominous even without their ghoulish embellishments. "Someone will just think they missed a spot."

"Impossible," Josie said, hooking an arm through Flair's. "There is not one single square inch of this town that isn't fully on theme and then some. Even the final holdout here." She surveyed Flair's transformed business. "Your day," Josie demanded. "How was it?"

"Bad, very bad, and then worse," Flair replied. She was gripping her keys so tightly that the teeth had bitten into her palm. She shoved them in her pocket.

"Customers?"

"One. If you count Loretta. Maybe it's too Halloween-y. Look what Renee added today." She pointed to Jack Skellington, and Josie burst out laughing.

"He's maybe a bit much, yeah. But you know that's not it. That's what people are here for. My customers prefer the alley, though. You know, part of the mystique."

The alley. Yet another thing Flair wasn't going to think about. "Yes, because tattoos are so rebellious. Only, like, every third person you see has one."

"Except you." Josie had her own designs all up and down her legs and left arm, while her right arm, for obvious reasons, was largely bare. Flair could remember when her friend had inked her very first one, a series of shooting stars, with a needle she'd bought from a shop in this same alley, and how angry Josie's mother had been when she found out what Josie had done. Josie had followed her mother, who was a nurse, into medicine, training as an EMT, but the art never let her go. Now appointments at her own shop, just a few doors down, booked out months in advance, especially this time of year.

"As soon as I think of anything I want tattooed on me forever, you'll be the first to know." Flair was walking quickly, glad to put distance between her and the bakery. The awnings on the newer fifties-style buildings of the next block had been replaced by seasonal ones in an orange-and-black scheme. Banners advertising *The Darkest Night of the Year* hung from every light post. A few businesses had even replaced their signs and names with Halloween versions, but Flair knew that behind the Scare Salon lay Posh, where Lucie had had her hair trimmed in August, while Terror Wreck-ords hid Vivi's Vinyl. The boba shop had simply gone all in, named itself Bubble, Bubble and kept up a mad witch-chemist display year-round.

"That's part of my job, you know. Helping people figure out what they need and where it should go. Want to know what you should get?"

"I do not." Flair was afraid of needles, and permanence, and Josie's too-probing insights. She changed the subject, pointing at one of the banners. "I keep meaning to ask. What is this black-moon, darkest-night-of-the-year stuff? Just this year's slogan?"

"Hardly. We're leaning in on this year's astronomical oddity. You know what a blue moon is? Second full moon in a month?"

"No, but now I do."

"A black moon is the opposite." Josie pointed to the sky, where a fat, C-shaped crescent moon was just visible under the clouds in the fading daylight. "The moon is waning now. Getting smaller. There's one day in every cycle when there's basically no moon visible. When that happens twice in a month, it's a black moon. Thus, the darkest night of the year."

"But not really. Because that's in December."

"That's longest. Fine, so technically no night is darker, at least moon-wise. It's poetic license. If you were into this sort of thing, you'd know it was a big deal." But they both knew that Flair was not, and they knew why.

At least Josie would understand Flair's decision. "Loretta wanted me to bake the treats. For Rattlebones. But I'm not going to."

Josie stopped, forcing Flair to stop as well. "Get out. Of course you're going to. Nothing could possibly be better for business. You tell people you're part of the trail, and they'll line up."

Flair shook her head hard enough to make her braids bounce. "No, no, and no." She should have said no from the beginning.

"I know you hate Halloween. Whatever. But you do not hate customers, and you do not hate the lovely, lovely money they bring with them. Seriously. I charge three times as much this time of year. You're going to have to suck it up, buttercup."

"Not like that. There has to be another way." Flair looked back at Buttersweet. "The shop just isn't pulling people in for some reason. Fine—it's not Jack. Maybe people don't like the plants, or the window boxes. Too *Little Shop of Horrors*. I can't go in or out without feeling like those yellow things are going to eat me."

She was joking, but Josie turned to stare up the street, where the Buttersweet Bakery storefront was still visible. Her eyes widened slightly. "Of course," she said. "I can't believe I didn't see that."

Flair waited for her to say more, but instead Josie tugged at Flair's arm and they started walking again. "I can't deal with it now. But we'll tear those down tomorrow. You'll do the trail. It will get better," she said. "You'll see."

Flair didn't bother to argue—she wasn't doing the trail,

although she wasn't averse to getting rid of those creepy vines. She'd have to think of something else to improve business.

The town's Halloween vibe faded slightly as they turned the corner onto more residential streets, although many homes were equally decorated or in process. Another corner, and they could see Josie's Victorian, where an elaborate trick-or-treat haven filled the porch and overturned toys took the edge off of a graveyard of politically themed tombstones. Flair's house lay just beyond it, nongrass plants all cut back for winter—Josie said Flair had done it wrong—and the porch free of furniture or decoration except for the hanging bench. Flair had sanded and repainted that porch herself, and she'd find a way to do the whole house next summer if she couldn't find someone to do it for her.

Josie's door flew open. Travis and Declan burst out, one demanding Popsicles, the other brandishing art made in preschool. Her mother, who took care of the boys after school when Josie's partner was away on a tour of duty, waved from Josie's porch. Flair had about half a second to envy the enthusiastic greeting before her own door slammed into the wall. Lucie stalked out and struck a dramatic pose, no doubt inspired by the unexpectedly larger audience.

"I am never going back to that school," she said loudly. "Ever."

Teabag barked, in greeting or possibly agreement. Internally, Flair sighed. They'd had this conversation. Many times. In her first weeks in her new school, Lucie had managed to alienate more than one teacher, and probably most of her fellow students, with her descriptions of how much better school was in St. Louis, how far behind Rattleboro was in math and science, how she had already read *Romeo and Juliet* (in second grade) and, obviously, *Great Expectations* (duh, that was last year).

Lucie put her hands on her hips and glared at Flair, waiting for a response.

"What happened?" Flair tried to infuse some sympathy into her voice. Lucie had seemed at least relatively resigned to her fate that afternoon. This had to be some small eighth-grade drama. As much as she'd envied the Rattleboro schoolkids when she was younger, dreaming of what it would be like to live here full-time, Flair could concede that showing up in the final year of middle school might be a little tough.

"How big a baby do you have to be to have an actual Halloween birthday party? And put actual invitations in people's mailboxes? Who even does that?"

Flair had a pretty good guess at who did that. "I take it you didn't get one."

"I wouldn't go anyway. I hate Annabel Anderson. She's a bitch."

Language, Flair thought but didn't say. Teabag pranced up the porch steps and let out a small, demanding bark. Lucie bent down to scoop the dog up and then plunked herself down on the bench.

"Teabag's offended," Flair said, climbing the stairs. "She can't believe you'd compare her to Annabel."

Lucie's only response was to bury her face in the little dog's curls.

Not the time for joking, then. "It takes time to get used to a new place." Flair had been hopeful things would get easier for Lucie, but the truth was, after all her own moves, she knew it was unlikely.

"I don't need to get used to it," Lucie said. "I talked to Dad today. He'll come get me for Halloween—he said he would. He says Carly is gone and he has to work, but I'm old enough to trick-or-treat by myself. Unless you want to come, too." She looked at Flair, a challenge in her eyes.

Unable to keep her thoughts from showing on her face, Flair went to stand behind Lucie, twirling her fingers in her daughter's red hair, which was nearly as curly as Teabag's. She'd been counting on David staying uninterested. He'd been sending casual texts to Lucie telling her to keep her chin up, stick with it—the kinds of things you said when you didn't want to have a real conversation or actually tell your kid you had no intention of bringing her home to live with you, or explain your new girlfriend, Carly, who had been Lucie's nanny. "Gone" meant that Carly had been discarded, like all of David's flings, with the predictable result that David wanted Flair back. Flair knew David well enough to know that his supposed willingness to come get Lucie had nothing to do with Lucie and everything to do with Flair.

But Flair was finally done. Lucie hadn't known what it meant when she found Carly's sweatshirt under Flair and David's bed. And maybe Flair wouldn't have thought anything of it if she hadn't recognized the look on her husband's face when Lucie brandished the sweatshirt cheerfully, saying how glad Carly would be that she'd found it.

Josie, who knew the whole story, shooed the boys back into her house but paused herself, leaning on the railing at the bottom of the steps. "You won't want to miss Halloween here," she said. "Parties are nothing. Your mom's doing the Rattlebones Trail."

Flair, from behind Lucie, had begun shaking her head frantically the moment she realized what Josie was going to say. Lucie looked up instantly. "What?"

Josie sounded smug. "Yep," she said. "The trail itself. Loretta Oakes asked her to do treats. Tell Annabel to put that in her pipe and smoke it."

Lucie jumped up, dumping an annoyed Teabag to the porch. "Seriously? Everyone wants to do that. Can I help?"

Flair could have slugged her friend. "I'm not doing it," she said.

"Mom." Lucie dragged out the single syllable in an elaborate moan of frustration. "You have to."

Flair glanced at Josie and saw a knowing smile on her face. She'd backed Flair into a corner, and she wasn't going to help her get out.

"Do we get costumes? What do we do?"

"I don't even know," Flair said weakly. "I still have to bake something." Something different. She'd have to clean up everything she'd done, pull herself together, and bake something else, anything else. The thought exhausted her. "She might change her mind."

"She won't!" Lucie ran into the house, the screen door banging behind her.

"I might change my mind," Flair said to the closed door.

"I already changed it for you," Josie replied cheerfully. "Halloween, here you come."

"I'm not doing it," Flair said.

But if it meant keeping Lucie happy, she knew she would.

CHAPTER FOUR

THEY'RE JUST COOKIES.

Flair repeated it over and over like a mantra as she drove to Loretta's house, a short trip as the crow flies made longer by the need to drive out to the edge of town, past the riverside woods where the trail would take place, and around two corners of a huge cornfield before doubling back to the driveway of what had once been a simple farmhouse but had long since grown enough guest wings and outbuildings and landscaping to turn it into something far more glamourous.

Cookies. Butter and sugar and flour and salt.

The tarot card cookies were beautiful, though, and when she went back to the shop after dinner, leaving behind an excited Lucie looking up everything she could find out about the Rattlebones Trail, Flair couldn't bear to start all over. Cookies were cookies. If the decorating process had been . . . strange, that was on her. She needed to change the atmosphere of the bakery. Add music, maybe. More lighting. And get more sleep.

She wouldn't let it happen again. Meanwhile, she had cookies, and she had a mission. If the Rattlebones Trail was what it took to keep Lucie happily in Rattleboro, Flair would make it happen.

Inside Loretta's house, she avoided looking at the images on the tarot cookie spread before her in exactly the same way she avoided meeting the curious eyes of the women around her. She would not be nervous. There wasn't any reason to be.

She refused to take the measure of the enormous dining room—hall, really—lined with portraits of Loretta and every matriarch who'd owned the house before her. At least Renee wasn't here. That would have been enough to make Flair hide beneath the long wooden table. She'd never been to the Oakeses' home, not even during that one summer when Loretta's son, Jude, had been the center of Flair's life. She didn't belong here, and they'd both known it.

But now Loretta had asked her. Jude was long gone. Lucie had wanted her to come, and Josie practically dared her, and now she was here.

Cookies arranged, Flair pulled herself up to her five feet two inches and looked around, trying to ignore the impulse to straighten her presentation one last time. She greeted Pamela, Loretta's loyal chief of staff and the mother of the envied Annabel, as well as the other women who would build and "haunt" all the trail stops, in many cases women who'd done so for decades and even generations. Their husbands or partners might help, but the league was and had always been a strictly women's realm, the crafts produced by its members valued both as art and as useful products for sale. Rattleboro had been founded by women, run by women, and supported by women since the beginning. These were the people who could take Flair and Lucie into the very heart of this town.

Or, as they'd been doing so far, shut them out in the cold.

Loretta swept in and made the rounds, pressing her cheek against those of each guest in turn, and her energy raised the excitement level of the room. Flair could see maps of the forest strewn across the table with scrawled notes and arrows— *scarecrows, spider lair, laboratory*—and found her interest rising in spite of herself. She'd walked half of the trail, once, holding Jude's hand before they snuck off just after a scene involving a vampire's coffin that still occasionally appeared in her nightmares. This meeting, this crowded room, was her first real glimpse into the effort that lay behind the single-night endeavor, and she knew that this year's trail, for the much-advertised black moon, was meant to outshine all the previous ones.

When Loretta reached Flair, she embraced her warmly before turning her attention to Flair's tray, and Flair knew instantly that Loretta loved her creations as much as she herself disliked them. The other women gathered around, silent until Loretta expressed her approval.

"These are a delight," she said, turning her head to examine the cookies more closely. "The idea, the execution—you've captured the intersection of artistry and the occult. Wonderful."

Now came the murmurs of agreement, the compliments, but none of them mattered as much as Loretta's. And Loretta was right—Flair knew it. The cookies were stunning, the best she'd ever made. Even if she didn't know exactly how she'd made them.

Loretta went on. "They aren't based on the Rider-Waite-Smith deck, or any deck I've seen." She laid a manicured finger under the bottom row. "Very intuitive, yet historical. Did you create the designs yourself?"

The obvious question, and one Flair should have been prepared to answer. Instead, she stumbled.

"They're . . . my own interpretation. Just a lot of things mixed up, a little of this, a little of that. Not from anything I've ever seen. Not directly." She was saying too much, but she didn't seem to be able to stop. "Sometimes you see old decks in antique stores, and of course, my grandmother . . . had some." She snapped her mouth shut. That was exactly where she didn't mean to go. She wanted to be part of Main Street Rattleboro, not its kooky back-alley fortune teller.

Even as she thought it, she felt the disloyalty of the description. Her grandmother had been far more than that. Flair, however, would be making her own very different way.

And the cookies were different. The real cards her mother had consulted for so long were intricate and elaborate, far beyond what Flair could do with a piping bag. She'd created something much simpler, although to anyone who'd seen the originals, there could be no doubt about where they came from.

Fortunately for Flair, there were only two other living souls who'd ever seen the original deck: Josie and Flair's mother. And if Cynthia hadn't even bothered to come to her own mother's funeral, she certainly wasn't coming back to Rattleboro now.

Loretta was still surveying the tray in front of her. "Only the major arcana?"

Flair nodded. She hadn't chosen to make tarot cards and never would have, but if she had, she would certainly have chosen only the more well-known images. "It's easier," she said.

"I prefer the subtleties of the four suits myself, but for

our purposes, I agree." She looked at the women around her, as though contemplating them. "Sharon, would you like to be the first to try one?"

As Sharon paused, looking to her, Flair suddenly understood.

"Oh," Flair began, "they're not— I can't—"

But she could.

This was why she shouldn't have come here with tarot cards. Even if they were just cookies. Even for Lucie. Flair glanced down at the too-familiar images in front of her and as she did, all the stories each one encompassed rushed through her mind, as though she'd glanced at a shelf of much-loved books. Of course she could read them. It was impossible to remember a time when she couldn't.

But she didn't. Not anymore.

Yet with Loretta and Sharon and everyone else watching her expectantly, Flair found herself unable to say no. After all, to most people, tarot cards were a game, a parlor trick. A seasonal entertainment, like the Rattlebones Trail itself.

If Flair made a big show of refusing to hand over a cookie and explain the meaning—a meaning, she reminded herself, that anyone could find a version of on their phone—that would attract more attention than just lightly complying. Putting too much weight on the cards and their meanings would place her firmly in the back-alley camp.

Almost before she had time to understand why she was doing it, Flair reached for one of her bakery papers and then quickly selected a cookie, letting herself believe she was choosing at random. Flair Hardwicke, human Magic 8 Ball. In for a penny, in for a pound.

Besides, this was the part she had never minded, had almost enjoyed. Her mother's friends would bring their decks, and Flair, prodigy of tarot from the moment she first touched a card, imbued with a power that she refused to acknowledge, would read.

"Strength," she said to Sharon, a woman wearing the sweatshirt of the local high school, her hair, face, and stance suggesting that she'd like to have worn something better but no longer had the energy to care.

Once someone was in front of Flair, it was always very simple.

Sharon looked confused, maybe a little worried, but Flair paid no attention, waiting for the cues that told her if her words were resonating: a softening of the eye, a movement of the shoulder.

"You have strength. You don't know it. But you have it and you will use it and it will stay with you."

Flair ignored the stirring around her, concentrating on Sharon. "It's not what you think; it's not some big thing that moves mountains. It's patience and fortitude and doing the right thing and not turning back." Flair handed her a cookie, one of Flair's favorites, if she was to allow herself to have favorites within something she handled with such reluctance. "The raven signifies resilience."

Applause and slightly uncomfortable laughter followed her words, and Pamela wrapped an arm around Sharon and pulled her aside. "We all know you're strong," she said. "I think you forget."

That was exactly right. Flair smiled, suddenly at home and

pleased to be surrounded again by people who wanted what she had to offer, both her delicious cookies and the words she'd grown up sharing. She offered Temperance to a woman beside her, saying don't laugh, it almost never means alcohol—but what was she doing too much of? To another she delivered the Hermit, suggesting to the mother of five that some solitude might be just what she needed.

This would be fine. Unexpectedly, Flair found herself feeling grateful to the cards for coming back to her in this limited way, giving her something she could offer to this insular little town. She could be Marie's granddaughter on her own terms, and it would always be better than being Cynthia's girl.

Loretta watched, seeming pleased, and began to gather a few women forward to discuss details and plans. As Flair picked up another cookie, there was a commotion as the double doors at the head of the room swung open.

Her eyes fell first on Renee, an unwelcome sight, pushing a bar cart into the room with the help of a man in chef's whites. Then the man at the front of the cart, after pulling it fully through the doors, turned to face them. Flair snapped the cookie she was holding in two.

Jude Oakes.

Flair very much didn't want to be here anymore.

Loretta turned, appearing surprised. Renee spoke before either her mother or brother could.

"This is what I was trying to tell you this morning," she said to Loretta.

Renee glanced at the tray in front of Flair, then at Flair herself, and even as distracted as she was by Jude's unexpected arrival, Flair could swear she saw a slight wariness in Renee's eyes as she took in the cookies before Renee looked up and dismissed Flair's efforts with a few words.

"I'm sure what Flair has brought would be fine. But"— Renee gestured to the array of candies on the cart, orbs of what looked like chocolate dusted with edible glitter, invitingly wrapped, the sparkle evident even from where Flair stood across the room—"to have a unique Jonka creation that's only available in Rattleboro, and only once? That's spectacular."

She was right. Nothing Flair could make could compete with treats offered by the professional version of the boy she hadn't seen since they were teenagers, and Flair knew it.

"Famous" and "candymaker" weren't a Venn diagram that usually intersected, but Jude was known by both foodies and big-box shoppers for his chocolate-candy creations, which even in their non-Halloween guises always held a trick or surprise. Willy Wonka had been imaginary, but Jude Oakes—Jonka— was not, and nothing could be more perfect for a Rattleboro Halloween. Flair might as well pack up and go home.

Ideally before Jude noticed her, because if he hadn't wanted to see her again after their last adventure together as teenagers, he definitely didn't need to see her now, and not like this, a supplicant in his family seat, the crumbs of acceptance that had been momentarily extended about to be swept away. She set down the broken cookie she was holding. The Lovers.

She hated it when the cards tried to be funny.

Jude saw her, and there was nothing she could do about it. He was, in fact, sidling through the group toward her, avoiding the arm of what must be his assistant, who'd followed the cart into the room, and brushing by at least one extended hand with nothing more than a quick nod. He barely seemed to notice the people around him—except for Flair, who was on the receiving end of a glow of wonder and interest and even delight, an expression that seventeen-year-old Flair would have recognized as a trap that she'd already fallen into.

It had been so long. She searched her feelings, looking for a vestige of the hurt and anger and even hate she'd once felt, but all she found was nostalgia for the version of herself that had believed Jude's promises.

He reached her, arms out as if to scoop her into an embrace, but stopped when she took an unconscious step back, maybe remembering that this was not exactly a first meeting of old friends.

Aware of the women around them, Flair managed a smile and extended a hand. "Jude," she said. "It's been a long time."

"Too long." Thank goodness for the scripts of Midwestern manners. He took her hand and she squeezed quickly, barely touching his before dropping it, refusing to feel anything between them. If he meant it—well, she'd never been hard to find. Not that she'd wanted him to find her. Her grandmother had made Flair's choices clear, in the aftermath of that long-ago Halloween when she last saw Jude: stay, with all that staying meant, or go, and leave Rattleboro and everything and everyone in it behind.

Flair had never regretted her choice.

Jude stared into her face as Flair held her careful neutral smile. Probably they would have to talk about that night. He'd have reasons he never called, never came looking to see if she was all right. She'd shrug them off and pretend to have forgotten all about it. For now, they'd be friendly and professional.

He played his part well, looking at the cookies on her tray, admiring.

"But these really are fantastic," Jude called to Renee as though there were no one else here. She had remained on the other side of the room with the bar cart next to Jude's assistant, a young man who was watching his boss with evident bewilderment. Not, Flair guessed, what he had expected to happen. That made two of them.

The resemblance between Jude and Renee, which Flair hadn't noticed when Jude was a teen and Renee a seemingly distant elder in her twenties, struck her now. They were both tall, looming over Flair. Renee's blond hair hung straight and gleaming over her black turtleneck, while Jude's flopped over his blue eyes as he ran his hand through it. Both had strangely compelling angular faces and a way of laser-focusing their interest.

At the moment, Flair and her cookies interested Jude. "Gorgeous. The edges, the piping work, the gold accents. They're perfection."

It was the assessment of a fellow chef, a famously finicky one at that, and Flair should have preened. But Jude's disturbing proximity, and the way the women around them were watching him, made her uncomfortable. She'd never fully felt worthy of his notice. And the cookies—were they even hers? The way they'd come to her now seemed unfair, wrong.

She looked around, but there would be no support for Flair in this group. Even the paintings on the walls made her feel unwelcome—paintings, she suddenly saw, that looked eerily like the faces on the original cards, those elaborate, detailed miniature works of art she'd somehow re-created, simplified, on her cookies. They were painted at the same time, she reminded herself, tearing her gaze away from the depiction of a woman who might have been the model for the empress only to have it land on another with a distinct resemblance to the high priestess herself, both imperious and uncaring. She was imagining things.

Jude was watching her, looking anxious himself. Flair didn't want to be rude and managed a wobbly smile. She would be polite, and then she would leave and that would be that. She should be grateful. She hadn't wanted to do Halloween in the first place, and now she wouldn't have to. Lucie—she'd manage something for Lucie.

But Jude had different ideas.

"Come on," he said to his sister. "Why not do both? Cookies and candy. All the sugar. What else is Halloween for?"

Loretta came to stand next to Jude, possibly to agree, but Renee spoke first. "Too complicated," she said firmly. "And no one will know what those mean unless she stands there and tells them, and I can see that that might seem magical, but it will take way too long." A faint sneer crossed her face. "Halloween in Rattleboro isn't magic. It's business."

A sentiment Flair could get behind, if only it came from someone else.

"It could be both," Loretta said. An energy Flair couldn't quite interpret seemed to flare up between mother and daughter, with Jude on the outside.

"It could be," he agreed. "I'm not opposed to working with someone else if it's Flair. Not at all."

Renee sighed. "We don't need to create unnecessary complications."

Loretta waved her off. None of them seemed interested in what Flair thought. "We'll discuss it later," Loretta said.

She addressed the larger group. "I'm delighted to see Jude back, of course. As you can all tell, it's the perfect surprise. After all, most people want their family together for the holidays, and for us, this is the most wonderful time of the year."

Jude caught Flair's eye, his expression apologetic. She tried not to care.

"Meanwhile," Loretta declared, "we adjust." She came to stand beside Flair and held a hand down to Flair's tray, her eyes still on her audience. Before Flair could say anything, a cookie seemed to leap from the tray and into Loretta's hand. Flair blinked, reaching out after her creation and then stopped herself as Loretta displayed the Wheel of Fortune to them all, licking her lips quickly before speaking. "The only constant is change, and we must welcome it."

Flair, startled, did not feel very welcomed. She felt Renee glaring at her over the heads of the other women and resented it deeply. Flair hadn't asked for any of this. And Jude stood at her side, watching Flair as though he had any right to, anger in his face, too, although not at her. At who?

And there was Loretta, a card in her hand that Flair had not chosen for her—no. Cookie. Not card. Cookie, and Flair didn't need to have chosen it; it was a cookie. But Flair couldn't restrain the sense that what Loretta had done was a wrong far greater than taking a cookie, and the room seemed to be blurring around her.

Flair's Wheel of Fortune was a simple Ferris wheel, meringue powder, water, confectioners' sugar, coloring—nothing more. A cookie, not a tarot card, with just enough sparkle to catch the eye, as it caught Flair's now.

And moved.

The Ferris wheel began to turn, and then to spin wildly. Flair looked around, frantic, and saw no change on anyone else's face, no indication that they could see the cars on the Ferris wheel moving, people tumbling out, images no one could create in icing moving in ways icing could not move. No one else appeared to see what Flair saw.

She looked down at the table, trying to steady herself, but the images on those cookies were moving as well, death's mouth opening, the skeletons of judgement dancing, the high priestess somehow larger than them all, shaking her head at Flair. No.

Flair backed away, crashing into the wall behind her, knocking a painting askew. Jude moved to her side, but she backed away from him as well. She put her hand over her mouth as everyone's eyes turned to her, Renee's full of contempt.

"I'm sorry," Flair said quickly, barely able to get the words out. "I'm so sorry. I'm ill. I have to go."

She pushed her way past people, unseeing, hearing Renee's voice as she opened the dining room door and cooler air greeted her. "So much drama. Just like all that family."

There was no one in the hall. No one outside on the grand porch, no one to see her slip and almost fall down the stairs and then run to her car and lean on the side, trembling, gathering herself. She was fine; she was safe. But she wouldn't be. Not if she let this keep happening.

There was only so much Flair could attribute to dreams and a lack of sleep. She needed to face what she'd done. She'd come back to Rattleboro, and the cards were trying to come back to her.

She wouldn't let them. She'd return to the bakery and crush every last cookie, and then she'd take the original deck from where she'd hidden it and destroy the tarot cards, like she should have done a long time ago. She had choices. She would not yield to the fate the cards chose.

She reached for the door handle and realized as she did so that she had a cookie in her hand.

The Fool, naive and unknowing at the beginning of an unstoppable journey.

Flair's own illustration, a baby bird staring up at an unreachable nest, mocked her. She barely hesitated before she bent down and tucked the cookie under the driver's-side tire before she took her place at the wheel and backed squarely over it, then drove forward over it again for good measure. She could see the splotch of crumbs against the black asphalt in her rearview mirror as she pulled through the circular driveway and drove off.

CHAPTER FIVE

LAIR DROVE STRAIGHT to the bakery, found her single parking spot in the hated alley taken, cursed the owner of the beat-up Toyota Yaris, and, with difficulty, found a metered spot amid a slew of out-of-state plates. Teabag, who'd resisted being left at home that morning, stood up in the passenger seat, and Flair scooped the little dog up in her hand and tucked her under her arm as she left the car, the dog's legs dangling, a position the six-pound poodle was used to. Flair often thought she appreciated the view.

Marching down Main Street, caught up in her plan to destroy the remaining cookies and not leave her house or shop until this stupid holiday was over, she didn't even see Josie stuffing the last of the clematis from her window boxes into a garbage bag until her friend called out to her.

"I don't know who planted this stuff, but this is your problem," she said. She waved an arm at the interior of the shop. "It's better already."

Flair didn't like the yellow flowers much either, but they

were the least of her worries. Still, she followed Josie's gesture and almost stumbled. Buttersweet Bakery wasn't just open (how could it be? She wasn't even here yet)—it was crowded.

"I'll come by later," Josie promised, heaving the bag up over her shoulder. "I have to go."

Flair walked through her front door, making the bells jingle, and set Teabag on the floor automatically, staring at the line of customers. Teabag wove through legs and made the kitchen door swing as she trotted off to her bed. Callie, her hair bright orange today, stood behind the counter, looking harried. Flair made her way past a group of cyclists, helmets dangling from their fingers, many in the special seasonal bike jerseys of the rental company— *Rattlespokes: Tour the Heart of Halloween Country*—that geared people up and sent them out on local mini tours.

Callie hailed her with relief.

"Oh my gosh," the younger woman said. "It's never been this busy. I don't know what I would have done if you didn't get here."

"But—" Flair started to ask her why she was here at all when Flair hadn't scheduled her, then stopped. She'd ask her later. Right now, it didn't matter. Callie had opened up somehow, and they were busy. Flair wasn't going to look a gift horse in the mouth.

"Coffee," bellowed one of the cyclists.

"Espresso," said another. "Civilization." A group from one of the coasts, then.

The tables were full, the line long. Flair shed her jacket quickly and pulled her apron over her head, her catastrophe of a morning disappearing into the familiar, beloved rhythm of a busy bakery.

Orders came quickly. Lots of almond milk in this crowd,

but some of them were looking at the pastry case. Flair glanced in as she began prepping the drinks alongside Callie—and knocked the portafilter into the side of the espresso machine, spilling the packed grounds in her surprise.

The case was full of tarot card cookies.

"Where did those come from?"

"What?"

Flair pointed. "Those. The cookies."

"Oh, I love those," Callie said. Her high, anime-style pig-tails bobbed as she followed Flair's pointing finger. "Did you just start making them? They were in the case when I came in."

One of the cyclists had already called over her friend. "Look at these," she said, and the friend clapped her hands together.

"I definitely need two of those," she said. "Can we choose which ones we get?"

Flair thought, for an instant, about telling her they weren't for sale. How had they even ended up in the case? But the friend wanted one, too, and the person behind her wanted one and also a chocolate croissant, and Flair's service instincts took over.

"Of course not," she heard herself saying. "That would ruin the fun."

The cyclists weren't from around here. They would eat their cookies and go, and Flair would take the rest of the cookies out and smash them, just as soon as she had time. She had scones in the freezer—she'd bake those to fill in and it would be fine.

But business never slowed down. Flair sold plenty of cookies, and everything else, too. Callie was beginning to make noises about needing to go home at three, and Flair was realizing she'd have to call on Lucie to help out, when the door jingled again, and Flair immediately recognized Pamela, Annabel's mother.

Flair saw the other woman's face light with pleasure at the sight of the tarot cookies as she approached the counter.

"I was hoping for one of those," she said. "I didn't get one earlier. And an oat-milk latte, please."

"Of course," Flair said, because she had to. She wanted to get away from the pastry case and its contents, so she gestured to Callie to switch places, but Pamela looked up quickly, stopping them.

"Hi, Callie," she said. "Don't stop what you're doing. Flair can get it." Her tone was friendly, casual, but Flair felt the base of her skull tingle.

Pamela didn't just want a cookie.

"You gave Sharon strength this morning. Do you remember? She literally put her husband's stuff out on the lawn when she got home from the meeting. Everyone from here knows he's been sleeping with his dental assistants for years. Did you know? How did you know?"

Flair shook her head. Go, Sharon. Flair herself was guilty of putting up with that sort of thing for a whole lot longer than she should have. But it wasn't like Flair had known what Sharon would do.

She'd only known what Sharon needed. Just like she always knew what people needed when the cards were involved.

Flair had handed cookies out all morning without letting them or her customers intrude beyond what it took to put a cookie on a plate, pointing anyone who asked to their phone for an interpretation.

But Pamela's face was full of anticipation. She wanted the Flair she'd seen at the meeting. And the cookies, shimmering in the case, wanted the same.

"Coincidence," Flair said lightly. "I'm happy for her, though." Although Flair also hoped Sharon had longed for that strength. Sometimes you didn't want what other people thought you should.

Pamela waited, undaunted. "Sure," she said. "I'll take some of that coincidence if you have it." She laughed. "Not that I'm worried about my marriage. But I never got it together to come see your grandmother, you know? And I always wished I had. Everyone says she was special."

"She was." No disagreement there. "But I'm not my grand-mother," she said. "These are just cookies. Seriously."

Pamela held up her hands. "Just for fun, then."

Flair couldn't tell if she meant it, but she couldn't say no again without offending the mother of the queen bee of the eighth grade. She dropped her hand into the case. She would simply hand her the first cookie she touched, she thought. She wasn't choosing. But she hesitated over the first and took the one behind it, her hands knowing exactly what they were doing. She put it on a plate and handed it to Pamela.

"The Wheel of Fortune," she said, and her stomach shifted. The cookie from this morning. This one, though, remained still. It was only Flair's mind that began to spin.

Pamela raised an eyebrow. "Does it have a meaning?"

Flair appreciated her careful selection of words, but she still didn't want to reply. That you have a sweet tooth, she could say. That your deepest late-morning snack urges are about to be satisfied.

But her tongue got ahead of her brain. "Traditionally, the wheel suggests the beginning of a change. A shift. It's a card that suggests a need to get ready, to brace for something."

"Something good, or something bad?"

The right answer, Flair's mother would have said, was always "something good." No one wants to hear anything else. But Nana didn't do things that way. And Flair was, as Loretta had said, Marie's granddaughter, whether she wanted to be or not. "The card doesn't place a value on it. Every change can be good. Or bad. Or both. But change is coming." To Pamela, or to Flair? Flair didn't know. But as long as the cookies were here, she didn't seem to be able to stop it.

Pamela nodded, picked up the cookie.

Callie handed her the coffee she had ordered. And for the first time that morning, there was a small lull. Pamela leaned on the counter, speaking a little loudly to be heard over the conversations going on at every table.

"Annabel would love these," she said, gazing at the cookies and taking a cautious sip of her hot drink. "My daughter." A thoughtful look at Flair. "You have a daughter in her class, right?"

"Lucie," Flair said. "She's new."

Another sip, this time accompanied by a small smile. "I'll tell Annabel to look out for her," Pamela said. "It can be tough coming into a school where the kids have been together since before kindergarten."

Flair smiled back, the churning worry in her head slowing down for an instant. If Annabel reached out to Lucie, it might make up for the disappointment of Flair's decision to keep their family Halloween as small and far away from the Rattlebones Trail as possible—a decision that Pamela's attraction to the cookie cards only made feel more pressing.

The girls were thirteen. Young enough that a push from a mother—as long as it wasn't Flair—might help and couldn't hurt. "That would be great. She hasn't been here as much as I was when I was a kid. She loves it, though." A lie in the service of a hoped-for future truth.

"I'll tell Annabel to stop in after school. She'll want one of these cookies. Maybe she'll see Lucie then."

Flair would make sure she did, and she felt pretty sure Pamela knew it.

Pamela's words added emphasis to the text Flair sent her daughter asking her to report for duty after school. Lucie would be surprised—Flair hadn't needed her help yet, but she would show. It was a good thing, too, because the shop's invisibility cloak seemed to be gone, and Flair stayed busy up through and after Callie's 2:45 departure.

Lucie appeared at three, and Flair greeted her with the same relief Callie had shown at her own appearance that morning. It was hard being the only one behind the counter. Lucie ducked into the back, braiding her hair as she went. As she darted by, Flair realized for the first time that her daughter was taller than she was. Lucie reappeared with an apron over her ripped black sweatshirt before Flair could quite recover from the shock and took over at the espresso machine just in time for a big group of students to appear.

Things moved quickly. Flair disliked handing out the cookie cards but found herself even more reluctant to let Lucie handle them, especially given Lucie's enthusiasm for the cards.

"I knew you couldn't really hate Halloween," Lucie said, peering in through the back of the case and ignoring the customer waiting for his Devil card, while Flair tried not to wonder what had him in its grip. "This place still sucks"—far be it from Lucie to give her mother any credit for Buttersweet, or admit that working there was better than sitting at home—"but these are amazing."

It was a sentiment echoed by everyone who ordered one, and Flair didn't need to hear it from Lucie. She wanted to get rid of the cards, but she was beginning to wonder if she could, when customer after customer arrived saying their friend or their sister or their cousin had told them they *had* to see these.

Lucie put out her hand to reach into the case, and Flair pushed it away.

"What?"

"You can't touch things we're serving," Flair hissed, knowing that wasn't what had stopped her.

"Fine. But these are so cool." Lucie paused, licking her lips nervously, a habit Flair hated. "They look different from most tarot cards. I've looked it up. Where did you get them?"

Where did she get them? Flair had been pushing the real tarot deck her cookies sprang from out of her head so fiercely that it was almost a shock to be reminded that her family's cards existed. Though, as far as Lucie was concerned, they didn't. Flair silently vowed again to destroy them as soon as she got home. She should have done it years ago.

Flair shook her head and handed the waiting customer his plate so quickly that the Devil cookie almost slid to the floor. "I made them up," she told Lucie. "Just a mishmash of a bunch of designs. I probably couldn't do it again if I tried."

And she wouldn't, either. It looked like she was stuck with this batch of cookies, but there wouldn't be any more.

Lucie seemed about to say something else, but a waiting customer cleared his throat, and Lucie had worked behind the counter enough to know what that meant. Back to work.

"How can I help you?" Lucie gave the customer a wide, genuine smile, and Flair felt something between relief and pride wash over her. She'd had Lucie at her side so often, here or at bake sales or other events back in St. Louis. When Lucie started resisting Flair's company in every way after the move, she'd missed this simple togetherness, being so in sync with her daughter that they didn't even have to talk. Her Lucie was back. Even with the cookies leering out at her from their case, this felt good. She had to keep it going somehow.

Flair worked the pastry case and tried to encourage people to take croissants and scones as well. It was hard, she pointed out to a hungry-looking teenaged boy, to fill up on cookies.

But the cookies remained the bestseller by far. The students dove merrily into the interpretations available on their phones, filling the little shop with talk and laughter. Lucie was brewing her lattes with a determined focus, her eyes firmly on the cups and the counter, until a slightly older girl said her name.

"Lucie, right? From cross-country?" The eighth graders did their training with the high school, and Flair was grateful for her insistence that Lucie run, citing fresh air and exercise rather than meeting people, although obviously her hope was for both. Lucie nodded and handed over the girl's cup.

"Ooh, a swan!" Lucie's latte art skills had always far exceeded Flair's, and Flair was delighted by more proof that as much as her daughter claimed not to want to be here, she wasn't phoning it in.

"She made me a hummingbird," said a girl from a nearby table, and in spite of Lucie's neutral expression, Flair could tell she was pleased. Flair turned back to the customer in front of her and realized it was Annabel, with a girl on either side.

"Hi," she said cheerfully. "My mom told me you'd give me and my friends cookies."

Flair didn't remember saying that. A loud thump from the vicinity of the espresso machine told her that Lucie didn't want her to argue. "Sure," she said, hoping the crowd of other kids didn't hear and start expecting the same. Hopefully the three of them would pay for their drinks. "Do you want a tarot card? Or something else?"

"Tarot card, please," she said. She didn't seem so bad. The girl looked at the cookie Flair gave her curiously, and Flair was grateful that it was one of the most beautiful in the case.

"The Sun," she told Annabel. It was a card with many possibilities, and Flair realized, as she stood there, that she held those possibilities in her hand. She'd already broken her resolve to leave the cards and their meanings alone. It couldn't hurt to offer Annabel a little extra insight. "A card for leaders, who welcome new friendships and encourage others to do the same."

Annabel smiled, startling Flair slightly with a mouthful of bright-blue braces. "Cool." She turned to Lucie, who was staring at them both but quickly busied herself making a drink Flair wasn't sure anyone had ordered. "Can I have, like, a Frappuccino?"

Flair waited for Lucie to pour on the scorn she reserved for anyone who tried to place an order off the too-familiar Starbucks menu, but instead Lucie crossed her arms and looked at Annabel thoughtfully. "I'll make you all something better, okay? Do you like chocolate and marshmallow?"

Ugh. Flair knew what that meant: a concoction Lucie called Unicorn Poop that involved a jar of marshmallow Fluff and a shaker of purple sugar glitter she kept under the counter for just this purpose. Flair refused to let her put it on the menu, but maybe Annabel and her friends would love it as much as Lucie did. The line had dwindled for the moment, and the three girls lingered at the counter, all enthusiastically endorsing both chocolate and marshmallow as they watched Lucie.

"I can't believe you work here," one said.

Lucie shot Flair a glare, but there was admiration in the girl's tone. "It's my mom's shop," Lucie replied. "You can work at thirteen if it's for your family business."

"Cool," the other girl said. "I wanted to get a job this summer, but my mom won't let me do anything but babysit."

"My mom won't even let me do that," said Annabel. "She says I have to focus on grades and soccer."

"My mom doesn't care about that stuff," Lucie said. Did she think that was good or bad? Of course Flair cared. But she didn't know how to show it without adding to the pressure Lucie already put on herself.

Lucie whirred her horrible mixture in the blender, where it gelled into a sort of slithery texture that Flair found repellent, then poured it into three glasses and began topping them. Flair was about to tell her to make a fourth and join her friends when she realized that Lucie was taking extra care to both make the drinks beautiful and show off her skill in preparing them, sticking out her tongue just a little in concentration the way she always did, swirling the whipped cream to perfection, drizzling the chocolate sauce from a dramatic height, and applying the sprinkles with a flick of her wrist. Showing that here, at least, she mattered. She was in control. She belonged.

Flair stopped herself just in time.

Annabel and her friends each took their drink with admiration as Lucie—the very picture of someone with an important job to do—began cleaning up. The two friends turned to go, but Annabel waited to catch Lucie's eye.

"Hey," she said. "I'm having an early Halloween birthday sleepover this Friday. The night before. Do you want to come?"

Flair slid out from behind the counter to quickly bus a few tables, delighted by the unexpected success of her machinations and not needing to wait for Lucie's reply.

By five, Flair was thinking only of flipping over the *Closed, but Still Awesome!* sign, and she was sure Lucie felt the same. She leaned against the door she'd just locked from the inside, and they exhaled in tandem, and then Lucie put her arms up above her and stretched, grinning. They'd never had anything even approaching such a rush, and Flair savored the return of the accompanying jolt of adrenaline she'd felt in other jobs. She could see that her kid felt it, too, along with the camaraderie that came with getting through it together.

"You're going to have to hire more help," Lucie said from behind the counter. "I was dying over here."

"I know. I'd try to come froth the milk or something, but then I'd have to get another cookie, or let someone pay—wow."

They smiled at each other, and Flair reveled in it.

"Is that the busiest you've ever been?" Lucie asked.

"Yep. I didn't even notice when your friends left."

"Neither did I." Lucie's smile grew even bigger, probably remembering her invitation, or maybe even recognizing that it was good to be the one who didn't have time to say bye.

"Kind of fun, wasn't it?"

Lucie's expression shifted, and she ducked her head away,

hiding her face as she moved past Flair to begin their nightly clean-up. Flair watched her. They had had fun. Lucie didn't have to admit it. They'd been a team. They would be again. Mothers and daughters, Flair reminded herself, not for the first time, weren't only one way or another, fine or not fine. Real relationships were complicated. She spoke again before Lucie could.

"You go on home," she said to her daughter. "I'll clean up."

That was always a winning offer. Lucie dropped the chair she'd been setting on a table, getting ready to sweep and mop, then pulled her apron over her head quickly. "I want to take some cookies to school tomorrow," she said, ducking behind the pastry case with one of Flair's signature turquoise boxes. "Is that all right?"

Flair followed her, then leaned on the case from the customer side. She wanted to say no, but she couldn't ruin this moment with Lucie. All she could do was hope the cookies behaved themselves. As soon as she had that thought, she wanted to put her head down on the counter and moan because until she'd come back to Rattleboro, she'd never had to worry about the antics of her baked goods.

Lucie stood up and headed for the door, Buttersweet Bakery box in one hand, backpack in the other. Flair replaced her behind the counter—she'd start her clean-up in the kitchen—and then stopped Lucie just as she reached the door. "Wait! Your phone."

All phones went on a single shelf in the shop during business hours, although Flair had stopped following that rule when she was alone with no customers. The screen of Lucie's phone lit up as Flair handed it over, and she saw her mother's name among the notifications.

"Have you been texting with Grand?"

Lucie looked far guiltier than anyone who'd just sent their grandmother a casual greeting should, but she shrugged. "She's in St. Louis," she said. "She wanted to know why I wasn't there, too."

Flair's mother knew perfectly well why Lucie wasn't in St. Louis. Her pleasure at Flair's decision to finally leave David had been immediately eclipsed by her dismay over Flair's planned move to Rattleboro, and nothing could convince her that Flair—who had no savings and no intent of asking David for help—really had no choice but to embrace the inheritance her grandmother had left her.

"There's always something else to try," Cynthia had said with her usual lack of practicality. Even thinking about her dismissive attitude made Flair clench her teeth. It could have been her life motto—Flair's mother never met a moving truck she didn't love—although the truth was, things were finally going well for Cynthia. She'd turned her genius for what she called creative living into a genius for creative writing. Stories about how she wished the world worked spilled out of her, stories with glamorous witches and devoted vampires and loves that transcended time.

She rarely changed a thing once she'd written a full draft, and it turned out that what she wanted was exactly what hundreds of thousands of readers wanted, too. She narrated them herself and described the covers she imagined to a designer who made them happen. The one piece of luck life ever brought her mother was when she fell in with an honest independent publisher who did all the hard stuff for a small percentage of the cash. That independent publisher was now the biggest thing going in the genre because for them, it was finding Flair's mother that had been lucky.

Flair knew that her mother was doing one of her shows in St. Louis, strange events where fans came to hear her read and to see some sort of small theatrical production Flair tried to avoid knowing too much about, because her mother's novels were steamy, which was fine—who didn't love a little heat in a romance? But not when part of you kept imagining your mother dreaming it up. Flair didn't even open the packages her mother sent anymore, just dropped them straight off at the doorstep of the used bookstore down the street. Apparently, the shows were popular, just like her books. Flair hoped Cyn wasn't giving Lucie too many lurid details. Her mother had zero filter.

She walked with Lucie to the door, grabbing the opportunity to slip an arm around Lucie's waist and snug her in close. Lucie didn't return the hug, but she didn't resist it, either, and Flair shut her eyes for a second, savoring the feeling of having her girl so close. Something was clearly up between Lucie and Cyn, but she didn't need to worry about it now. As she gave Lucie a final squeeze, someone tapped on the door in front of them, startling her. At the sight of Jude in the window, she rushed to open up again, unable to suppress a smile of welcome, and Lucie glanced at her, surprised.

But when Flair saw Loretta and Renee behind him, she admonished herself. Why would she be pleased if it was him, anyway? Ten minutes of politeness in his mother's dining room didn't erase the fact that he'd thought he was too good for her twenty-six years ago and probably still did. She shouldn't have cared then and definitely didn't care now.

Jude, followed closely by his mother and sister, strode into the shop. Lucie stood with her box, uncertain, watching Jude, who was approaching Flair with a warmth in his expression that Flair could tell Lucie didn't like.

"We're closed," Lucie said pointedly to him.

Jude must have caught the hint that he was unwelcome, because he stopped and tried out a charming grin on Lucie. "Right, but we townies have to stick together," he said. "Closed to tourists, but never to each other."

Flair could tell that Lucie had several responses she wanted to make to that, so she spoke before her daughter could. "You get on home," she said. She pointed to the phone still in Lucie's hand. "Tell your grandmother I'm letting you off easy tonight."

Loretta smiled at Lucie. "Your grandmother will remember Halloween in Rattleboro," she said. "She always loved it. Give her my regards."

Lucie gazed at Loretta, a little awe creeping into her expression. "I will," she said, momentarily stopped in her tracks. But when Flair started to speak again, Lucie shoved her phone in her pocket with undue speed and gathered up the backpack she'd let fall to the floor. "I'll tell Grand," she said quickly to Flair, raising Flair's suspicions even further before she ran out the door, Teabag romping after her. There was no way Lucie and Cynthia were texting about anything so dull as Lucie's work at the shop, even if it involved complaints about Flair the micromanaging stickler.

"Nice kid," Jude said. Flair sighed.

CHAPTER SIX

THE PRESENCE OF the three Oakeses made Flair aware of the disarray that pervaded the shop after the busiest day she'd had yet, and she found herself itching to sweep the sugar and sweetener wrappings from the tables and the windowsill. But she'd learned that drawing other people's attention to the things that bothered her only made them worse. So she shoved her hands in her apron pockets and looked resolutely away—and right at Jude, who was leaning against the counter, staring at her intently.

He smiled a little when she caught him. "This invasion was my idea," he said. "I really would welcome your help on the trail. And your cookies. My chocolates are going to be a little wild. Not everyone will be a fan."

He couldn't have said anything that would pique Flair's curiosity more. "What are you going to do?" She herself did relatively little experimenting with flavors, preferring to expend her effort on perfecting simplicity and making it beautiful. But she admired people whose culinary efforts were further out on the edge.

"Before he tells you his plans," Loretta said, with a small, slightly dismissive nod in Jude's direction, "which might take a while, let me add my encouragement. I—we—would really like you to join us in the woods this year. I've missed your family's contribution."

Flair couldn't resist a glance at Renee, who leaned against the door as if she couldn't wait to leave, her slouched posture echoing her brother's. If Flair hadn't known, she would never have taken her for ten years older than Jude. But then, Loretta also looked far younger than her seventy-some years. Like good looks and an even better opinion of themselves, it must run in their family.

Renee gave her an even stare without saying anything. Two votes from the Oakes family, and one abstention, then. But Flair's was the voice that mattered, and the decision she'd made that morning hadn't changed. "I'm going to put my full effort into the shop this year," she said. "I hope you understand."

"Excellent choice," said Renee briskly, straightening. She glanced around. "It does look as if there will still be a learning curve before you can handle the business."

Jude cleared his throat. Flair fumed silently at the unfair aspersions. She'd like to see the bookshop at the end of a busy day.

Although, with Renee likely to materialize in front of anyone who so much as slid a book out of place, oozing disapproval, maybe it did look perfect.

"Come on," said Jude. "We'd have fun; you know we would."

"I feel certain you would enjoy it," Loretta said. "Or, at least, appreciate it in a way few can."

"She doesn't want to," Renee said. "And we don't need her. There's more than enough going on."

"There's something about the woods on Halloween," Loretta said, ignoring her daughter. "The travelers, each with their own singular experience. The anticipation, the buildup, everyone working on their own creations and the way it comes together. There's nothing like it. And this year, with the black moon, will be the best yet."

Flair knew very little about the trail's tradition or history, but she knew what Loretta meant about the trail's excitement—although she had a feeling her own experience had been a little different than the one Loretta intended. She glanced at Jude to see if he, too, remembered.

But Jude wasn't looking at her. The shop was growing dark—Flair hadn't yet turned on the bright light she'd use to get everything clean before morning—and he was watching Loretta's fingers, which were tapping on the marble of the little table.

Tapping. And—sparking. A tiny pop of light at each tap.

Before Flair could be sure of what she'd seen, Jude slid between her and his mother and put a hand over Loretta's, lifting it and gently inviting her to rise.

"I'll work on changing Flair's mind," he said. "Renee, maybe you want to take Mom home?"

Renee sighed, sounding, for a moment, like Lucie being asked to put a dish in the dishwasher.

"I don't need an attendant," Loretta said, standing up quickly.

"Sorry." Jude smiled at his mother, a full-wattage barrage of charm. "Maybe I'm just trying to get rid of you both so I can talk to Flair."

Loretta did not look won over, but she stepped toward the door as Renee opened it, speaking to Flair as she went. "We'll revisit this tomorrow," she said. "I feel sure we can convince you." She walked out the door, and Renee started to follow but then paused and turned her head so that only Flair could see her face. She smiled, a slow, insincere smile completely lacking in Jude's charm.

"I see you changed the plantings," she said. "It's looking a little bare out there."

The first thing Flair thought of was the stupid building covenant. The second was what Josie had said that morning about the clematis. *I don't know who planted this stuff, but this is your problem.*

Renee was watching her carefully. "Perhaps you thought they were a little overgrown," she suggested, her tone unreadable. "I can come fill them back in tomorrow."

Flair blinked. Had Josie seriously been suggesting that Renee's plants somehow bewitched the shop? Mentally, she shook away the notion. She really was letting the tarot cards get to her. But still . . . "No thanks," she nearly shouted, before moderating her tone. "I'll take care of it. I'm trying to—take more of an interest. In plants."

Right, because everyone took up gardening at the end of October.

Renee's perfectly groomed eyebrows shot up her forehead as she stared into Flair's face, which Flair—still trying to figure out what was happening—kept carefully neutral.

"Suit yourself," Renee finally said. She slid silently out the door, shutting it behind her.

Flair, suddenly aware that she'd been standing rigidly in the center of the room, sank into a chair. That felt like a close call, although she had no idea why.

A look of worry crossed Jude's face. "I'm sorry," he said.

Flair looked at him blankly. He might not be her favorite person, but he wasn't at the root of her many problems. "For what?"

"I know they're a lot." He smiled, a hesitant, tiny just-for-Flair smile that she definitely preferred to his usual barrage of charm. She wasn't sure she could handle a full-on blast of confident Jude tonight. "Halloween is really important to my mother. But I don't want her to force you into something you don't want to do."

"She won't," Flair said lightly. Jude sounded strangely intense, and just for a moment Flair remembered him promising her teenaged self that the trail would be fun, pushing her to join him, and she almost hoped he didn't give up so easily on persuading her to try it again. In one way, at least, he was right. The trail had been fun, at least the first part. Fun, and full of exactly the energy Loretta had just described.

Flair thought of the sparks from Loretta's fingertips and wondered if they were just another thing that only she could see—an effect, not of Loretta, but of all the energy that was still in her grandmother's shop, no matter how much Flair painted and cleaned.

Which was what she should be doing right now. Cleaning, going home, breaking the news to Lucie that they wouldn't be on the Rattlebones Trail and enduring the resulting storm, and definitely not letting Jude try to talk her into changing her mind. She got up and started briskly popping chairs and stools on tables. Jude, to her surprise, joined in. "You don't have to—"

"I know I don't. I want to. Don't worry. I've closed a restaurant or two thousand in my time."

A little reluctantly, Flair showed him where they kept the broom and other cleaning supplies. The Jude she'd known years ago had been largely a stranger to physical work. This one seemed right at home sweeping away while she broke down the espresso machine and pretended not to be watching him, trying to figure out why he was here. Eventually she couldn't take the silence.

"So what are you going to do? For the trail?"

"Oh." He stopped sweeping and went to the jacket he'd hung off an upside-down stool. He took one of the wrapped chocolate globes he'd wheeled in this morning from the pocket and presented it to Flair with a flourish. "One Rattlebone Surprise," he said. "I'm still perfecting them, but this is pretty much it."

Flair unwrapped it and popped it into her mouth in a single bite, making Jude smile. She'd known a lot of chocolatiers, and none of them liked it when you bit their work in half and peered dubiously into its center. An explosion of sweet but peppery flavor fizzled into her mouth with an accompanying series of pops before sliding into an echo of cherry soda and then the taste of chocolate once more. "Wow," she said. "I like it. Pop Rocks, right?"

He nodded. "But you see what I mean. Classic, flawlessly iced sugar cookies would be the perfect complement, don't you think?"

Flair laughed. "Not this year. Or any year." She kept her face firm and disinterested, aware that he was watching her. After a moment, he seemed to let it go.

"That's okay. My mom will be disappointed, but she'll get over it."

Was it wrong to wish Jude were the one who was disappointed? She found herself saying to Jude what she'd yet to say to anyone except herself. "I'm feeling a little overwhelmed by all this Halloween."

Halloween—and being taken for her grandmother, and the way she'd re-created a set of tarot cards she thought she'd safely locked up years ago. And images on cookies that moved, and sparks at Loretta's fingertips.

She would stick to lumping it all together as Halloween. "And I'm tired," she said, gesturing around her. "Moving back has been a lot." How much did he know?

"Renee told me."

"Oh, so you only know the bad stuff, then." Espresso machine taken care of, Flair moved on to mopping, which she preferred to do herself. Jude, with a gesture, offered to wipe the counters.

"You're divorced, you came back with your kid to live in your grandmother's house and take over her shop. What's bad about that?"

Flair was not divorced—yet—but she let it go. "I'm sure she made it sound bad."

Jude didn't deny it. When Flair was growing up, Renee had been largely a mystery, a frequent presence in Marie's shop who never spoke to Flair, barely acknowledged her. Cyn, when asked, had dismissed Renee with a few rude words, but Marie seemed to respect her, and Flair had resented it, then resented it even more when Renee clearly didn't care what Flair thought about her at all.

But not being noticed by Renee was better than whatever attention Renee had been paying Flair since her return to town. She'd ask Josie about those window boxes as soon as she had a chance. Meanwhile, the front of the shop was as ready for to-morrow as she could make it, even with Jack Skellington loom-ing in front of the windows. She returned the mop to its place and took the rag from Jude's hands as he put a final polish on a faucet that even Flair would call shiny enough.

"Done," she said, and then felt sorry. Done meant she went home to disappoint Lucie about Halloween; done meant he went off to wherever he was staying. She hadn't even asked. She was a terrible old friend, if that was what they were. And what else would they be?

But then Jude said, "Walk you home?"

A warm, contented feeling spread through her, followed by a spark of excitement, not unlike the sense of biting into the Jonka chocolate he'd handed her moments ago. She nodded and watched him grab his jacket. That was how it had all started then, too, that last summer.

If Renee had been a dark horse, unknowable, Jude was the brightest star of Rattleboro during Flair's childhood. He was the boy with the newest bicycle and the darkest tan from summer camp, always the center of a group Josie described as "the socials" and shrugged off as "basically totally out of reach." Flair and Josie spent summers when they were together drawing (Josie) and reading (Flair) on plastic lawn chairs, doing chores to pay for occasional admission to the pool. Jude and his friends always had a full summer pass.

The summer Flair turned seventeen, she took a job serving up frozen yogurt on Main Street. Flair worked full-time while Josie did the same at the diner at the end of the block, and neither the lawn chairs nor the pool saw much of either of them.

Jude had gone to Italy with his mother and sister that summer. When he returned home, he had an ACT tutor and a very part-time gig caddying at the only nearby golf club—and a new interest in frozen yogurt, especially when Flair was working. Small cone, twist, every night, just Jude and none of his friends. The whole thing seemed so unlikely that Flair couldn't bring herself to tell Josie about it until the night Flair closed up and found Jude waiting outside, saying these exact words. *Walk you home?*

That had been the beginning of nightly walks that got longer and longer, of hours spent with their legs stretched out in front of them on the benches along Main Street. Of Jude telling Flair that he'd been watching her for years, of her admitting the same, and then the two of them listing everything they loved about Rattleboro: the way that at the edge of town you could tell a car was coming by the dirt that rose up behind it, the way the clouds trailed out endlessly until they finally met the horizon, how sneaking up the fire escape to the top of the old Sumner County bank building made you, at three stories high, the tallest thing for miles.

They'd talked about everything. Their childhoods, their mothers. What they loved about school (English for Jude, math for Flair, chemistry for them both) and what they hated (Jude:

eating in the cafeteria; Flair: moving from school to school and never knowing anyone, although she'd been unable to keep herself from making it sound far cooler than it was). Their hands had hovered close to one another on the bench, night after night, until one day Jude hooked a pinkie around Flair's and they'd sat for another hour, Flair not wanting to move.

That night was the first time he kissed her. On the corner, in the dark spot, between the streetlights. By then, she'd been wondering for weeks if he ever would, doubting herself. But that kiss had left no room for doubt.

When she brought her own jacket to the door and then locked the shop behind them, she could tell he remembered, too. "Same old walk," she said.

"Yep." He seemed about to say something more, then let it go. "Yogurt shop was closer to your house. But I'll spot you the extra couple hundred feet."

The minute they stepped outside, Flair felt as though Rattleboro's eyes were on them. Most of the people who passed them were strangers and tourists, but before they'd so much as left the block, Flair lifted her hand to a parent she recognized from Lucie's class, and Jude greeted a woman she knew worked at Renee's bookshop.

The twinkling lights and festivity of Main Street faded away behind them as they talked more companionably than Flair would have believed possible. Jude's past twenty-six years, in four blocks: law school, jobs he hated, chocolate competitions, surprise success, never married, no family, assistant and sous-chef bunking in the room next to his at Loretta's house.

Flair's: waitressing, bartending, waitressing, scrounging, culinary school, line cook, pastry school, David, Lucie, an interval she glossed over because who wants to hear about someone else's marital failures, the surprise of her inheritance, and now Lucie waiting for her on the porch as though she hadn't been hiding in her room every night to avoid Flair's apparently odious presence.

One look and Flair knew Jude was why Lucie was swaying back and forth angrily on the porch swing. In Lucie's mind, Flair was the one who'd torn up their life and brought her to Rattleboro for no good reason, and unless Flair was willing to throw David under the bus, Flair was stuck with that. But she had a feeling Lucie's loyalty to David was about to make things very awkward, and she was right.

Lucie ignored Jude, extending her phone to Flair.

"Dad wants to talk to you," she said, emphasizing that first word. "He wants to talk about us visiting. He says you don't answer his calls."

Flair didn't. She had, at first. But she'd answer "a quick question about the restaurant" and find herself listening to him bemoan his inability to find a good manager, let alone a pastry chef, and hang up to keep herself from screaming in frustration. He'd had both, and she'd had a safe job and a solid if not always happy life. He was the one who'd thrown that all away. With Carly now gone, he'd be trying to get it back, and that was a game Flair didn't want to play.

Lucie was waiting. The look on her face told Flair that she knew she'd played a strong card. Flair took the phone, then turned to lift a hand to Jude in farewell. "This will probably take a while," she said. And she didn't want him listening.

Jude nodded, waved to Lucie, who didn't respond, and then wandered back down the street.

As Flair joined Lucie on the swing, she realized that in her nostalgic walk with Jude, she'd completely forgotten about her car.

"Damn it," she said, forgetting, too, that she'd just lifted Lucie's phone to her face.

"Nice to talk to you, too," David replied. His voice, with its always forced-sounding good cheer, irritated her instantly.

"That wasn't for you. I forgot something. But it could have been." She stopped at that.

"Lovely. I talked to Lucie."

"Obviously."

"She says you'll never admit it, but you clearly miss me. I'm sorry, Flair. You know I'm sorry. Why don't you and Lucie grab a flight up here and we can talk about it? I'll get you tickets. You know she wants to come home."

Flair glared at her daughter, hampered by her presence from saying what she wanted to say, which involved icebergs and hell, and then regretted it when Lucie's face seemed to crumple. What did she want Flair to say to any of this? What did she think was going to happen?

"I'll bring Lucie to see you at Thanksgiving," she said. "That's what we planned on."

"I want to see you sooner," David said. "Both of you. Lucie doesn't like it there. She says there aren't customers, either, and of course there aren't. It's a tiny town in Kansas. You're better than that, and so is she."

"There are," Flair began, angered into defending herself, but before she could go on, David interrupted her.

"Hang on," he said, his voice as casual as though she'd called him, as though she wanted to talk to him and he, busy man that he was, was indulging her. "I have another call. Why the hell would your mother be calling me?" His voice was annoyed.

"I have no idea," Flair said. And she also didn't care. She'd been bullied into this conversation. "Why don't you go find out?"

She hung up and handed Lucie her phone. "Your dad and I aren't together for good reason," she said to Lucie firmly, allowing a little of the anger she felt to show in her voice. "If I want to talk to him, I'll talk to him. When you want to talk to him, you talk to him. But you don't get to make me talk to him."

"I made you talk to him because you don't listen to me," Lucie said. She seemed close to tears, and Flair moved to put her arms around her daughter, because of course Flair would listen, but instead of crying, Lucie stood up, sending the bench swinging into Flair's thigh. "Did he tell you that I want to move home? He said I could, too. He says it's not too late in the school year. They'll take me."

Flair breathed in sharply, the sudden pain in her leg forgotten. This was exactly what she'd been afraid of the minute Lucie mentioned that David had offered to bring her to St. Louis for Halloween. But she and David had an agreement. Lucie stayed with Flair, and Flair didn't call lawyers, or demand her share of the restaurant or anything else. He couldn't do this. She wouldn't let him.

"You might have reasons for being here," Lucie said, mocking Flair's words. "But I don't. I love Dad, and I miss St. Louis. I'm going home."

CHAPTER SEVEN

FLAIR FOLLOWED HER daughter into the house, scrambling for words she didn't have a chance to say. Lucie ran up the stairs, stomping hard on each one. Teabag looked up from her bed in the corner of the kitchen as if considering following, then put her chin back on her paws with a tiny doggish sigh. Flair thought Teabag had probably made the right call.

The cookies Lucie had brought home from the bakery were strewn across the table in total disregard of the *we don't touch what other people will eat* rule. She'd brought a lot of them home, very nearly one of each, giving Flair a glimpse of her daughter's hopes for what Annabel's offer of friendship could mean. Next to them, an empty frozen pizza box suggested that Lucie intended to hide in her room all night.

Lucie was so up and down now. It was impossible to predict what kind of mood she would find her daughter in at any given moment, and Flair hated it. What had happened to them? She turned away from the table and went to the sink, automatically washing the dishes Lucie had left there. No matter what, David couldn't take Lucie. If Flair had to, she'd make good on her threat to involve lawyers and everything else. They'd had an agreement.

An agreement that did absolutely no good if Lucie didn't agree with it.

Flair had never considered what would happen if Lucie wanted to go back to St. Louis without her. She and Lucie had always wanted the same things. They had always been a team, her and her little girl. She'd never gone in for the matching clothing or mini-me jokes of some of the mothers around her, because she hadn't needed to. She was the one who picked Lucie up after school, who taught her to read and to cook, who snuggled her up for Disney movies and made sure her every Christmas and birthday wish was granted. And Lucie was her sunshine, making Flair laugh with her sudden precocious bits of snark and reminding Flair to have more patience with the world around them, from the checkout clerk whose bad leg Lucie's sharp eyes spotted instantly to the downstairs neighbor who, Lucie always reminded Flair, was trying his very best to soothe his crying baby. Lucie was everything to Flair, and Flair was everything to Lucie. Until now. Until they came to Rattleboro.

This little Kansas town, with its history as a haven for artisans and artists alike, had always been a haven for Flair as well. From the minute her mother pulled into the driveway and told Flair to scoot on out and grab her bag, Flair knew what to expect. Her bed would be fresh and the bathroom all her own. She'd be able to do her laundry. Her grandmother would cook meals, at normal times, times when other people ate. Flair wouldn't have to wake up in the middle of the night and pack up her things or knock on a neighbor's door and ask to borrow an egg she knew she would never return.

Rattleboro was predictable, even if some of the things that happened here like clockwork—the knocks on the back door, the lessons in herbs and tea and tarot, the steady voice of her grandmother reading the cards every night when Flair had learned that other grandmothers might read from books instead—might not have seemed normal to everyone; they were the closest to normal Flair had ever had. In Rattleboro, she was safe.

But for Lucie, it was life in St. Louis that had always been safe and predictable. She didn't know that it was Flair who kept it that way, who shot down David's wilder ideas and plans in order to make sure that the restaurant and apartment didn't get lost in his shuffle, who disguised David's frequent absences from both Lucie and the restaurant staff, and who let David come home no matter what he'd done as long as he put Lucie first.

Even though she knew David never really put anyone ahead of himself.

Flair, having started to clean, kept going, returning Lucie's jacket to its hook and her shoes to their place by the door. The table she avoided, but she couldn't keep the images spread across it from intruding into her thoughts.

She'd loved learning to read the cards. Loved how easily it came to her, loved her grandmother's praise. Still remembered the first time her grandmother whispered her out of sleep and brought her downstairs and the face of the mystified woman asking Marie if she was sure.

"Flair is better at this than I am," Marie had said. "Trust me."

And Flair had seen in the spread what was confusing her

grandmother, the cards that seemed at odds with one another, that didn't fit. "There are two of you," she'd said.

Her grandmother had laughed and the woman had cried and Flair knew now what had been so odd and what she hadn't understood at the time. The woman had been in her midforties and had never had a pregnancy end in a baby. That one did, though.

Marie called on Flair rarely, but once Cynthia understood Flair's talent, she dragged it from her greedily. Cynthia taught Flair the things her grandmother left out, complex, intricate spreads of cards representing influences and reversals, arrivals and exits. Under her mother's instruction, Flair learned to search the faces of her mother's friends for what they hoped for as much as for what they felt and to find those dreams within the cards, and then to do the same for "friends" who made "offerings" that helped out with the rent and groceries. Flair never found out if Nana Marie knew, but she suspected her grandmother wouldn't have liked it.

Flair did, though. She felt the bitter delight that came from knowing things other people didn't, sharp and almost painful, like her favorite candies before the sugar overwhelmed the sour. And she'd especially loved reading for her mother, from the one tarot deck that was for them and them alone, until she didn't anymore.

That was the day she was thinking of now. Not the cards she read, or what came after. Those were things she rarely allowed into the front of her mind. Instead, she thought of her grandmother's words when Cyn arrived in Rattleboro with Flair and a smashed-up face and arm that took all of Marie's and Josie's mother's combined skill to put right before Cyn drove away in search of revenge and the return of what was hers, leaving Flair behind. That was when Flair produced the cards from her backpack.

Had she expected her grandmother to be surprised? Flair couldn't remember anymore. But she remembered holding out the cards and telling her grandmother that she wanted Marie to take them, that she didn't want her mother to have them anymore. The cards caused all the trouble in their lives, and the cards gave Cynthia the powers that enabled her disdain for the kind of safe and predictable life Flair craved. The life that Flair knew—especially after that night—would be better for them both.

"She shouldn't be magic," Flair had said. "It hurts her."

Flair had wanted her grandmother to ask for details, to take the cards, to make everything right somehow, but instead Marie had come to stand very close to her, then put a finger under Flair's chin and tilted her face up until Flair was forced to look into the older woman's eyes.

"Do you think that's your choice to make?"

Flair had felt herself squirm, felt the sharp edges of the wooden box that held the cards press into her hands as she gripped it close. She thought of Cyn with the cards, reading them, accepting what they said, and how it never, ever went right.

"Someone has to," she said, and pushed the cards into her grandmother's chest. "You take them."

But Nana had backed away.

"I can't do that," Nana had said. "They're yours now. That's the way they work. We have the cards, and we have our daughters, and when it's time, our daughters take the cards and they leave." She'd smiled, and Flair had seen that her eyes were also full of tears. "That's our fate. The way it always ends. They leave."

Flair hadn't thought she was leaving Cyn in that moment. She was thirteen years old, and Cyn had come back for her the way she always did, and they'd continued to live in much the same way they always had. A little steadier, maybe. Without the cards that gave her the ability to light a candle or turn on a faucet or send the wind to blow open a door, Cyn's wilder urges had seemed subdued. No more charming someone into hiring her by making sure they felt warm and comfortable whenever she appeared. No more distracting shop owners or sparking the ignition on cars Cynthia felt sure no one would mind if she "borrowed." The tiny tricks and movements of the elements had many uses beyond lighting the occasional candle, and Flair had just begun to understand the way they helped Cynthia avoid doing what Flair thought of as anything real.

With the cards unused and untouched, the magic had slid out of their lives. Flair had been happy to see it go. She didn't want to be like Cynthia, and she never would. She'd never seen her grandmother use magic in that particular form again, either. No more candle lighting or warming Flair's sheets with a touch, no more shifting the clouds just enough to let the sun shine on the clothes that flapped on the line, although Marie continued to read for her customers as she always had. Flair didn't know if her grandmother's elemental magic had faded as the cards fell out of use, or if Marie simply chose to hide those powers from her granddaughter, and she didn't care. By now it all seemed like a childhood dream to Flair.

It wasn't until much later that Flair realized that her

grandmother had been right. From the moment she took the cards away, it had only been a matter of time before Flair, too, was gone.

But that wasn't because of fate or a curse or the cards. It was because Flair's mother made her crazy. Because even without magic, Cyn never stayed put, couldn't hang on to a job or her credit rating. She always considered a few weeks of good times with whatever man had conned her to be worth any heartache that followed. She was the Cat in the Hat and Thing One and Thing Two all rolled up together. Flair liked her mother best when she was far, far away, and Flair intended to keep her that way.

Because Flair didn't do fate or curses or magic. She made choices.

Flair put down the sponge she was surprised to discover in her hand—why was she cleaning counters that were already clean?—and opened the front door, grabbing the flashlight she kept on the table in the entry. It was time to destroy the family tarot cards and the trouble they caused. If they hadn't shown up, she'd have iced a bunch of black cats and jack-o'-lanterns that wouldn't have caught Loretta's eye. Lucie wouldn't be spreading them all over the table, calling who knows what into their lives. Flair and Lucie might still be struggling to find a place in Rattleboro, but they'd be doing it on their own terms. Flair should have gotten rid of the cards long ago.

"You stay here," she told Teabag.

The night was warm, too warm for October. Flair glanced up for an instant as she always did. There was Mars, below the moon's tiny crescent. The moon was in Pisces—a mystical time, Flair's mother would tell her. Nana, too, would have noted the moon—and told Flair that it was always a good idea to stay on your toes in Pisces, prepping for the Aries energy that was to come.

She made her way around to the back of the house and pulled up the double cellar doors, securing them so that they wouldn't close and trap her, then used her flashlight to make her way down the unfinished wood stairs.

Other people's cellars might be scary places, inhabited by spiders and full of dark shadows and dusty corners, but not Flair's. When she pulled the string on the single bulb, the light illuminated neat shelves that held blue Rubbermaid tubs and a floor and walls as clean as dirt and concrete could be. Flair had a very low tolerance for spooky.

She put her hand on the tub she wanted instantly, the one labeled *Taxes, Receipts, Misc.*, and set it on the dirt floor. She lifted the top off and took out the first accordion file and set it aside.

It wasn't until the cardboard of the second file flattened at her touch that she realized something was wrong. The cards were gone.

Flair scrambled through the other boxes, knowing she wouldn't find anything but unable to stop, emptying them all in turn until the basement was awash in files, holiday decorations, and Lucie's preschool masterpieces. The box where the cards should have been she tore apart, as if by looking again and again she could make them reappear.

When she finally gave in and went back upstairs, leaving the contents of the boxes to the mercy of damp and gnawing rodents, she found Josie coming across their shared lawn, clearly surprised to see Flair emerging from her own backyard. And then she saw Flair's face in the porch light.

"Okay," she said slowly. "You look like you've seen a ghost. Again. What is it with you all of a sudden?"

Flair couldn't think of a response. Possible explanations for the disappearance of her cards churned wildly in her brain, and none of them were good. She couldn't figure out what to do next, which way to go. In the house? Somewhere outside? If Lucie had them, she would have said something. David—the whole reason she'd labeled the box as tax forms was because of David's allergy to all things involving numbers, paperwork, and unpleasantness. He left those to her.

But there wasn't anyone else. Where were the cards?

Josie grabbed her elbow. "We're going to walk very calmly into the house, and then I am going to make you some tea, because tea is very good for people who keep showing up with pale faces and their eyes practically spinning. And then you are going to tell me what's going on. I can't just go ripping enchanted clematis out of your window boxes and pretending nothing is happening."

Tea sounded reasonable. Flair let Josie lead the way inside. Teabag yapped at them both, because sometimes she preferred yapping at things she knew were in no way a threat, and Josie scolded her, then stopped speaking the instant she caught sight of the cookie tarot cards Lucie had left spread across the table.

"Whoa," she said softly at the sight of images she must recognize, now casually strewn around like Pepperidge Farm's finest. "When I said you should do Halloween, I didn't think . . .

These are amazing. They look just like—" She stopped stumbling around for words and spread both of her hands out on the table, surveying the cards.

Flair watched her, numb now to the sight of the cookies, while Josie appeared to think and then turned, her expression serious. "You made these. Does that mean . . . Are you back?"

She looked at Flair carefully, and Flair returned her gaze. She knew what Josie meant. She just didn't know how to answer. After a pause, Josie, eyes never leaving Flair's face, flicked one finger in the direction of the pillar candles Flair had placed in the kitchen fireplace.

The wick of the tallest candle quivered to life.

It had been so long since Flair had seen anyone do that, felt that spark appear where one had only been possible before, that she had to hold back a gasp. But she knew what Josie could do. Had known for as long as she could remember, for as long as she'd known what she could once do herself. But Josie knew that Flair's powers depended on the cards, and that Flair had packed them away along with the deck long ago. Her action strengthened Flair's resolve without making her feel any less panicked.

"No," Flair said. She collapsed into a chair, and Josie sat across from her. "The cards aren't even here. The real cards. Only these. I made them for Rattlebones, but then Jude showed up and now I'm not doing it, and then I wasn't going to use them, but they were already in the pastry case and people started to see them and . . . yeah." She'd read from the cookies. But they still weren't the cards. "It's not the same."

"It's pretty close," Josie said. "Maybe you could—" She looked meaningfully at the candles.

"I don't want to," Flair said. "I don't want it back. I don't want any of it."

"Including Jude?"

Flair shot Josie a look. There were bigger problems at hand. Josie should understand how bad it was that the cards were missing. Josie had seen the real deck once. Cyn brought her into the family secret on an outing to a Taco Bell in Ark City in a uniquely Cyn fashion. Josie knew some of what had happened to make Flair take the deck for herself. And she knew what it had meant to them all that Flair had hidden the deck away. But the cards were the past, even if they didn't seem to be able to leave Flair alone; and even though their disappearance stunned and worried her, what Flair was more worried about at the moment was the immediate future.

"Lucie hates me. She wants to move to St. Louis with David."

"Whoa," Josie said again. "I'm sorry. That's big."

"Huge. Huge and I can't fix it and I hate these stupid cookies. I hate them and I hate the cards and I hate Halloween."

"Because Halloween and the cookies are . . . why Lucie is leaving?"

"No," Flair said. It was ridiculous to sound cross at Josie, but she couldn't help it. "Halloween was why she was staying. But then she changed her mind."

"Well, change it back. If I can make you change your mind, you ought to be able to take on Lucie."

"She thinks I've ruined her life."

"Of course she does. She's thirteen. But you haven't. And she doesn't really want to leave you. You know that. She's just unhappy right now."

Josie was probably right. But with everything that was happening, unhappy right now might be enough to make Lucie try to ruin everything for both of them.

"She has David lined up to come get her. I think she thinks I'll go, too."

Josie gave her a sharp look. "But you won't."

"I won't." Flair could only say that because every time she thought about the possibility of Lucie leaving with David, she realized again that she would never let it happen.

No matter what any cards said.

She got up to make tea, filling the kettle angrily, taking out bagged Earl Grey. Josie rose to help and Flair waved her back to her seat, not wanting to deal with the mess Josie would leave in her wake.

Josie was still looking at the cookies. "Have you considered . . . that this is what you do? You read the cards, and things happen."

"But not things I want to have happen. Not with those cards and not with these cookies." She set teacups in front of both of them, properly on saucers, and brought over the sugar and two spoons while she waited for the water to boil. "Never. I should have burned them a long time ago. I was going to do it tonight. But I can't find them."

"You can't burn them," Josie protested. "Those are old. They've been in your family forever." And burning them would change her family forever, which was exactly what Flair wanted.

They stared at one another, all of that unspoken between them. Finally, Josie shook her head. "So the real cards are gone, and I don't blame them, not if that's your plan. But these are yours. You made them. Maybe . . . for you—"

"Maybe for me what?" Josie, of all people, should know better. When Flair swore never to touch another card, never to let any of it touch her ever again, Josie was the one she swore it to. "Maybe for me, the cards will suddenly stop bringing their patented doom and destruction? Because everything else is going so well?"

Josie was looking at Flair now, her expression sympathetic, and Flair couldn't take it. This was why Josie only knew part of it—the easy parts. The parts that really hurt, Flair kept to herself.

The kettle began to clatter and Flair snatched it up before the whistle, filling up both of their cups before she sat down again. She took the nearest cookie and placed it carefully between them. The Tower, of course.

"Fine. I'll read for myself, shall I? Past, present, future. Past: chaos and disaster. That's the Tower, all right." Flair paused, surveying all the cookies in front of her. "Let's give me a better present than the real one. The Emperor. I get power over everything. Much better."

Oh, the number of times she'd thought to herself how great it would be if you could just pick your cards. Well, she was doing it now. Even if these were just cookies.

When she did this reading for real—past, present, future— that last card was always the one that came with the flash of premonition Flair had grown to hate. The knowledge of what was coming. Knowledge she didn't need or want.

But this time it didn't matter. She'd already decided what was going to happen. Or at least what she wouldn't let happen.

Flair closed her eyes against the faces of the cookies in front of her only to see the real cards in her mind. The Five of Cups:

loss, desperation, fear—a card she hadn't even iced into being. The Hermit: herself, alone. The Hanged Man: Lucie, trapped, struggling.

Those were definitely the wrong cards. She opened her eyes to survey the cards of her making and reached out to push away the Devil, the card of danger and lies and energy run amok, but instead her hand tightened around it. If the Devil was in front of her, she could work with that.

"This is all David's fault," she said. "So that's the future. I'm the devil, and I will crush him into submission and get him to do what I want for a change."

She crunched viciously into the cookie, and as she did, the single candle Josie had lit in the fireplace flickered out. Josie looked at it. "Well," she said, "that was way less dramatic than you'd expect from the special effects for a spell that dark."

"It wasn't a spell." Flair finished the Devil cookie and licked the crumbs off her fingers. "It was a wish. And you know how much use those are."

"Maybe you should talk to David."

"Talking to him doesn't do any good. He's the worst. She can't go live with him."

"Agreed. But you know what I think."

"I know." Josie thought Flair should have left David a long time ago. "I'm enabling, and my own worst enemy—I got it. But I'm done with him this time. As long as he's done with Lucie."

"Yep, that sounds like a totally healthy co-parenting relationship." Josie surveyed the cookies. "These do look good. Which should I eat?"

Flair pushed the cookie of Judgement in her friend's

direction, considering the possibility of transferring her anger from David to Josie. People were so annoying when they might be just the tiniest bit right. She took another cookie, not at all surprised to find herself holding the Death card with her grandmother's voice loud in her head. *We cannot outrun death, and we cannot outwit change.*

Words of wisdom, but not ones she needed to hear right now. Flair glared at the sugar skeleton dancing on the cookie in front of her and then bit its head off.

Josie watched, laughing. "Okay, Morticia. Maybe we leave the nice cards alone now. I think you've had enough."

CHAPTER EIGHT

AFTER JOSIE LEFT, reminding Flair that David was famous for saying he was going to do things and then doing something completely different, Flair let Teabag out while she cleaned up the tea, stacked the cookies neatly, covered them loosely with a towel, and then went upstairs.

Josie was right. David was infuriating and unpredictable, but she'd been dealing with him for years. Lucie would listen to her. She'd be angry about the trail, but she'd get over it. There had to be fun, nonrisky things they could do for Halloween, without tarot cookie cards that seemed determined to predict her terrible fate and then seal it.

Flair brushed her teeth and managed to persuade herself, as usual, that she wouldn't regret skipping her nightly skincare routine that was really more like weekly. She crawled into bed, pushing Teabag off her pillow. When sleep finally came, it was haunted by Lucie painting impossibly intricate arcana on lattes and a series of people demanding Flair read the results, cards she'd never heard of—the Swan, the Dragon, the Bird. And then the birds were all caged, bird after bird after bird, and then the client she was reading for—no, she didn't have clients; she had customers; she didn't read—started to pound on the table, hard, spilling her drink, the caged bird sloshing and disappearing as Flair's mother's voice shouted her name.

Flair couldn't tell if she was fighting to stay in the dream or get out of it, but she was struggling through the murk of sleep, and the banging didn't stop, and the voice didn't stop either, because, she realized, sitting up suddenly and slamming her feet to the floor in a single motion, the voice was real.

Her mother was banging at her front door.

"Why would you lock it?" Cynthia demanded angrily when Flair answered, as if she'd barged through this door every day of her life instead of walking out of it at seventeen and swearing she'd never come back. "My mom never did."

She pushed past Flair and into the house, leaving Flair holding the door, gazing out into the street where the car her mother had just left was still running, its headlights blazing. Flair blinked in confusion.

David's car. A Lincoln Town Car, old, big, bulky, ridiculous, and gas-guzzling, and something no one could possibly love, as she'd argued with David every time she paid the bill for its insurance.

Why would her mother be here in David's car?

She could see no sign of her soon-to-be ex and turned to find Cyn glaring at her, hands on hips, waiting for Flair to ask her what was going on, waiting to produce whatever litany of blame and woe and anger she'd stored up against Flair this time. Flair wouldn't give her the satisfaction.

Instead, Flair pointed at the car. "Go turn it off. You're going to wake up the whole neighborhood."

Her mother looked down at Flair, making the most of her significant height advantage, her entire being a cloud of wild red-and-silver hair and frustration. Flair was used to this standoff, though, and she put her hands on her hips and tilted her chin up, not giving an inch.

Cynthia hesitated, then marched out the door and across the grass, yanking open the car, leaning in to turn the key.

"There," she said, but the keys were still in the ignition, the lights still on, the door open, the pinging reminding Flair of a dozen nights in her childhood trying to sleep in the back seat while they drove to one guy's house or another, listening to her mother hurl accusations, then drowsing for hours on the road, exhausted from the sound of Cynthia arguing with people who didn't want her to go and people who did.

Flair sighed and walked out to slide into the driver's seat herself. She knew this car. She hated this car. And she could not come up with a single reason for her mother to have it.

She turned off the lights. Took out the key. Slid back out of the car and quietly but firmly closed the door. She started to return the keys, then thought better of it. She didn't know why Cyn was here. But it was always a good idea to make sure she couldn't suddenly run away.

Cyn laughed. "Keep them," she said. "It's yours, after all. All yours." The anger returned to her face, and she resumed the theatrical stance she'd taken up in the house, as though she'd rehearsed it. "Unlike the last thing you took from me."

She reached into the slouchy bag she wore over her shoulder as though to pull something out with great drama, only to realize that she couldn't find it. She rummaged for a minute while Flair watched.

Her mother couldn't have what Flair was thinking.

But when she finally tugged the wooden box out from whatever flotsam it had been hidden beneath in a grand, anticlimactic gesture, Flair knew she'd been right.

The tarot cards were back, and Cyn had them.

"So now I know. My perfect little daughter is a thief." Cyn's voice rang out into the night. Flair knew for certain that she'd been planning the line for the entire drive, stewing over the past.

Coming from someone known for writing melodrama, Flair thought her mother's words fell a little flat.

Flair glanced around and caught at her mother's arm and pulled her inside before she defended herself. People did not have loud arguments in the middle of the night in their yards in Rattleboro; it just wasn't done.

"You couldn't keep using them," Flair said. "You know you couldn't. I saved your life. I saved both of our lives."

"You had no right," Cyn said, fully releasing the fury she'd been barely suppressing. Flair saw her mother then as she had the day the cards disappeared from their life: desperate, beaten by the cards and her choices but ready to follow them again.

"Someone had to do something."

All through Flair's childhood, her mother never made a move without consulting some form of oracle. Tea leaves, dreams, palms—all held more reality for her than any sensible advice from a human source. If a friend offered her a nice, steady job answering the phones and running an orthodontist's office, with health benefits and free braces for her gap-toothed teen, but she ran into a guy in a shirt with thirteen stripes on the thirteenth of February who had a bar she could tend called Bitter Eleanor, which had thirteen letters, she would be working for tips and an under-the-table paycheck before Flair could even make an argument about the many benefits of straight teeth and social security.

Flair was thirteen when that happened, which she hoped hadn't contributed any weight to her mother's dubious numerology. By then she knew the cards were making things harder for them. Every time Cyn made Flair read, she turned whatever Flair saw into an excuse to do exactly what she wanted to, no matter how Flair or anyone else felt about it, and if Flair refused to read, Cyn looked for messages everywhere else. Because if it was fate, it wasn't her fault, and Flair had nothing to complain about.

Flair tried, but while she could insist they buy tea only in bags and beg to go to the grocery store that wasn't around the corner from Cyn's favorite astrologist, she couldn't stop dudes who owned bars from walking around in striped shirts, and she couldn't stop her mother. As long as there was a universe, Flair's mother would look for its signs, and those signs never said what Flair wanted them to say.

She'd read for Cyn, the day she finally took the cards. The day she finally decided that even if she couldn't protect her mother from her fate, she refused to be the voice of it anymore.

They'd been settled, or as settled as they got. Her mother had been with Rodney for a few months by then, had quit the job tending bar and taken one answering the phone at his auto body shop. She worked normal hours, came home, cooked, spent evenings watching TV even when Rod went out. Her life wasn't filled with her friends and their needs—in fact, her friends hardly came around at all. She'd only asked Flair to read her cards once in months.

Rod was good to Flair, paid for her to join the drama club, picked her up after rehearsals for *Up the Down Staircase*, brought her chocolate.

But sometimes he didn't like the way Flair's mother dressed. Or he thought she'd taken too long at the grocery store, or she stopped in the bar downstairs to say hi to her old boss, and his eyes would get small and piggy and he'd refuse to eat what Cyn had cooked or sit close to her on the sofa. Flair wanted to believe that if her mother would just do what Rod wanted, he would be nice to her the way he was to Flair. This was the closest to a normal life they'd ever had.

That particular night Rodney and Cyn had an argument that ended in silence. Scary, horrible silence after familiar words, like *Bitch* and *What was he doing here?* and then Cynthia, her voice high and scared and nothing at all like the fierce mother Flair knew, *He just came by to see how I was; I didn't ask him*, and then the sharp thwack of a chair falling over and the screech of the table scraping across the linoleum and a thud, soft but ugly, the sound of a body hitting something. Maybe her mother screamed, maybe she didn't.

From the door of her bedroom, Flair could see the light in the kitchen. She'd walked into the hallway, keeping her feet quiet, holding her breath—and then she saw him, bending over her mother's stillness. Flair was frozen into stillness herself, staring until he started to turn around.

She didn't know what he'd do if he saw her. If he knew what she'd seen.

She'd ducked into the closest room and rolled under her

mother's bed, where she found herself curled around the shoe-box where Cyn kept the tarot cards, in their old wooden box with rusty hinges and a clasp on the front like a bird's claw hooking through a ring, along with a bunch of concert ticket stubs and pictures, a watch that didn't work, and any money she was trying to save, although that never stayed in the box long.

The minute Flair touched the box, her heart slowed, but the calm only lasted an instant because Rodney slammed into the room and began to tear it apart, a flurry of clothes being yanked from hangers and drawers overturned, looking for something.

There was nowhere she could go, nothing she could use to defend herself. Flair slid her hand into the shoebox and pulled out the cards in their own small box, slid them up under her shirt to hide them close, watching his feet, pressing herself up against the wall, wondering if he could reach her, if he would drag her out, and what she would do if he did.

They should have left the night before. Packed up while he was still at work instead of sitting around the table, reading the cards.

"One question," Cynthia had said lightly. She sang the words. "Should I stay or should I go?"

Her brittle voice hadn't fooled Flair. It was a real question. And when Flair had turned over the cards, she'd seen the an-swer. The Five of Swords. Danger might loom, retreat might be the strongest choice, but the Five of Swords signifies both a need for caution and the recognition that its warning will not be heeded.

Cyn would stay. But with that knowledge, Flair had felt, in a rush, some part of what was coming. Not the details. She never got details. But the crash. The anger. The pain, the regret.

And she hadn't said anything.

At the time, she'd told herself there was nothing she could say or do. The cards said Cyn would stay, and whatever followed would follow. But huddled there, under the bed, Flair had wished desperately that she had poured out that vision to Cynthia and somehow dragged her away. And she'd been so afraid that she knew why she hadn't, because all she wanted was a normal life. Flair had failed her mother, and the cards had failed them both.

Rodney's steps had slowed. He'd stopped throwing things around, and Flair began to hope that he would leave, go to buy flowers. Instead, he knelt and looked under the bed.

His face didn't change when he saw Flair, and that was the most frightening thing. He looked at her, through her, as though she didn't matter at all. Silently, he pointed to the shoebox.

Flair pushed it to him.

He pulled it out, turned it over. All Flair could see were his boots and his knees as he knelt, pawing through. He took the money, crushed the pictures in his hands, put the watch in his pocket.

Flair heard him go, heard the door shut and his feet on the stairs, and she still couldn't move. She stayed hidden, taking tiny breaths, as small and as quiet as she could be, until she heard her mother move. Push a chair aside. Curse. Then walk, her steps sounding all wrong, until the bedroom door slammed into the wall as she leaned on it, and Flair could see, from under the bed, her kneeling in exactly the same spot Rodney had just left, picking up the box, the pictures, breathing heavily.

Flair could picture her mother's face when she first looked under the bed, could remember the sound of her own cry at the sight of her mother's cheek, cut and still bleeding, her nose smashed to the side, half of her face the dark red of a bruise that had barely begun. One of her eyes swollen shut. She had looked at Flair through the other with the same dead expression Rodney had worn.

And then she looked everywhere else. Past Flair as she crawled out. Sweeping her arm under the bed as far as it would go. Throwing the covers aside, muttering and then shouting. *No. No.*

She should have been looking at Flair. Instead, she'd looked for the cards, and if Flair had thought she hated the cards before, she'd hated them more in that instant than she'd ever thought possible.

The wave of memory and emotion rose, visible to both Flair and her mother as red and gray smoke, its tendrils snapping between them until it vanished as suddenly as it had appeared and they were alone.

"You," Cynthia said now. "You took them. I begged him—do you know that? I found him and begged on my knees. But the minute the cards were gone, he didn't want me anymore."

"I had to. They told you to stay." Flair told her to stay. "I just wanted them gone." But the cards would never leave. How could Flair have imagined anything different?

The cards had betrayed them. They'd put them at odds, turned them against each other—and even so, Cynthia had still wanted them. She would still have asked Flair to read. Still listened to what they said. Flair had known that if that was going to change, she would have to change it. So she had. She'd always known that someday she would pay the price.

"You kept them," Cynthia said. "All along, I felt them, and I thought what I was feeling was you. That you had them inside you somehow, the way I should. That I was feeling the power you refused to use. But it's not that, or it's not only that. They were there."

"I never touched them," Flair said again. Somehow it seemed important, that she had not taken them to use. She only wanted them gone.

"You never gave them back."

"You have them now," Flair said, and as she spoke, all the questions that had faded away when she saw the cards came back, loud and insistent. "How? They were supposed to be here."

"David had them," Cyn said, and a look came over her face, a little nervous, a little fearful. "I was in St. Louis for a show. I went to your apartment and he had them spread out across that ugly table of yours."

David's words, right before Flair had hung up. *Why the hell would your mother be calling me?* David, with his unerring instinct for seeing what she did not want him to see and finding what she did not want him to find, digging through her things. Cyn showing up, taking the cards away.

If that was what she had done. Suddenly everything about this felt wrong.

Cynthia had the cards back. Which meant she had her magic back. She didn't need Flair. So why was she here?

Flair realized she was still holding David's keys, an old-fashioned set with a key for the ignition, a fob for the locks and trunk. She felt their sharp edges against her hand as she shook her head. "And then what happened?"

Cynthia opened her mouth, then closed it. She crossed her arms. "I don't know."

"What do you mean, you don't know? You said David had the cards. Now you do. Something came in between."

"Fine." She turned on the point of a ridiculously high heel and walked back out the door, down the porch steps, and out to the car.

Flair followed, increasingly sure she wasn't going to like this.

Cyn pointed to the trunk. "But remember, you asked me, okay? So this is on you."

In spite of her grandiose and rather ridiculous words— whatever was wrong, Cynthia had clearly sought Flair out—she could tell that her mother's primary emotion wasn't irritation, but fear.

A lot of it.

She could feel the heat from the car's muffler as she approached the trunk, and something else, too—a pressure around them, holding them in, encircling her and her mother and the car and demanding their attention.

Flair shook it off, forced herself not to hesitate. She'd dealt with so many of Cyn's problems over the years. How much worse could this one be? She pressed the button and the trunk's lock popped open. She put out a hand and lifted the lid all the way up.

Inside, curled up around the spare tire, eyes shut, wearing his usual jeans and old concert shirt, was David. And everything about him suggested very clearly that he was dead.

CHAPTER NINE

Wednesday, October 28

DAVID. DAVID, WHO was horrible and a cheater and never listened. Who was always so, so sure that Flair would take him back no matter what he did, and who was only threatening to take Lucie because he knew then Flair would come, too. David, who was Lucie's father, who had carried her around the house when she was a sick little baby and sang to her—his mood, Flair later learned, greatly improved by banging the pastry chef who'd taken over Flair's job, but Lucie didn't ever need to know that. David, who mansplained and gave Flair directions to places she'd been a thousand times and offered helpful tips on baking. Who only wanted Flair when she didn't want him. Who had destroyed her over and over again but didn't deserve to be folded up like a carpet in the trunk of his old Lincoln.

What had Cyn done?

Her mother pushed her aside then leaned in and started prodding David's body with her hand.

"No," Flair said, cringing away. "Don't do that. Stop it."

"What?" Cynthia turned, but not before she gave David what amounted to a punch in his upper arm. "You have to know the worst."

Flair felt certain she already did. "Just leave him alone," she said, her mind racing.

David groaned and flipped over, and his arm flopped out of the car.

Flair leapt back with a scream. "He's not dead."

Cynthia stared at her. "No," she replied in the tone of someone who'd had a lot more time to get used to this than Flair had. Then she looked at Flair thoughtfully. "Did you want him to be?"

"No!"

The only thing worse than David alive in the trunk of his car would be David dead in the trunk. Flair was trying to figure out what to do next when she heard a window thunking open behind her.

"Mom? Are you out there?"

Flair pushed Cynthia out of sight behind the open trunk and stepped closer to the house, hoping it was too dark for Lucie to see anything, glad for once that Rattleboro only had streetlights on Main Street.

"Yes . . ." She let her voice trail off, because what could she say next? Lucie's next question sounded more awake.

"What are you doing? Is that Dad's car?"

"No!" Flair glanced at the car, which was undisguisable. "It's . . . it's . . . Remember Jude? From earlier? He has a car just like it." Oh, why had she said Jude? That wouldn't help, and what were the odds—

But Lucie didn't know anything about cars. "What are you doing?" Now she sounded mildly disgusted. Maybe invoking Jude had been the right choice.

"Going to get my car." At four in the morning. "I left it in town earlier."

"I don't want to know," Lucie hissed. "Just be quiet. People are trying to sleep."

"Thanks, Mrs. Kravitz," muttered Flair's mother from behind her.

"Shut up," to her mother. "Okay, sorry," to Lucie in a hushed singsong. "It's nothing. I just . . . didn't want to walk—"

Cyn tugged at the back of Flair's sweatpants. "Who's Jude?"

Flair kicked at her to silence her, and David groaned again, but softly. At least someone understood the need to get Lucie to shut her window before they did anything else. "We're leaving!"

Lucie slammed her window shut, possibly to shut out Flair, and it was hard to blame her.

"Who's Jude?"

"Loretta's son. Loretta Oakes. Why are we talking about this?" Flair tried to stuff David's arm back into the Lincoln. They had to move the car—

"He's Flair's ex-boyfriend." Josie came up behind them. "Flair? Who are you talking to— Cynthia? David?" Josie's voice went from casual to surprised to panicked as she took in the scene and then took a step back as if she'd thought better of coming outside at all. David struggled and began to try to sit up, and Flair was sure she saw relief in her friend's face. At least Flair wasn't the only one who thought her mother was capable of showing up with her ex dead in the trunk of his own car.

Josie looked from Flair to Cyn. "What happened?"

"I don't know," Cynthia said again, and at her tone of out-raged imposition, Flair realized she had had enough.

"No one knows," Flair hissed. "But we need to get him out of here. Josie, Lucie's awake. Can we take him in your house? Please? And we have to hide the car."

Josie was looking at David, her mouth open, eyes wide. "Does he . . . want to go in my house?"

Flair turned to the car, where David, on his back now, seemed to be making himself comfortable by stretching his legs up to meet the interior of the trunk door.

"It doesn't matter what he wants," Cynthia said. "He does whatever you say. Or whatever I say. Except leave."

"What?" Flair and Josie spoke at the same time.

"Watch. David, get out of there and come with me."

David began to struggle his way out of the trunk, and Flair panicked. "Not where Lucie might see him," she said, moving to block any view of the back of the car from the house.

"No problem." Cyn pulled a blanket out of the back seat. "This is how I got him out of the apartment, anyway." She put it over David's head as he stood up and then started to push his covered form toward Josie's house. Flair shot Josie a wor-ried look.

"Is this okay?" Flair asked her.

"I guess it has to be?"

Flair felt a rush of gratitude for her best friend. She looked at the Lincoln and then at her mother, shuffling David across Josie's lawn. "We have to hide the car," she said. "Lucie already thought it was David's."

Josie, her mouth still open and her eyes still wide, nodded

and then shook her head, quickly, as though finally joining the party. "Fine. I'll move my car out and put this one in the garage. You go with your mother."

Flair pressed the car keys gratefully into her hand.

Inside, Cynthia directed David to sit on a chair in Josie's formal living room, blanket still over his head, which was fine with Flair. Josie came in while they were still arguing over what to do.

"We can fix him," Cynthia was insisting, while Flair asked if she was sure it wasn't a hospital that David needed. It would be just like Cynthia to assume magic instead of an allergic reaction or a heart attack. Not that the figure who was humming to himself on Josie's settee seemed sick. It would just be so much easier.

"But what happened?" Josie seemed to be avoiding looking David's way.

"I was doing a show in St. Louis," Cynthia said.

Josie glanced at Flair, questioning.

"She does shows. For her books. I'll tell you later."

Cyn kept talking over the interruption. "I went to Flair's apartment, and David buzzed me up, and when I went in, he had the cards spread out everywhere. My cards. That Flair took." Her voice rose, as if ready to tackle that again, and Flair stopped her.

"She knows, okay? You can be mad again later."

Josie pointed at the ceiling. "Sleeping kids, too. Life will be much easier if they stay that way."

Cynthia snorted through her nose like a horse being calmed against its will and went on more quietly. "I told him he needed to give them back to me, and he said they were Flair's. And then he scooped them up and kind of threw them around, which was so disrespectful. I picked up what I could, but he had the rest and he didn't want to give them to me. But I was holding cards."

Her voice took on a reminiscent tone, and she smiled a smile of deep satisfaction. "So I told him he had to listen to me. And he did. And I took the rest of the cards back." She crossed her arms, and Flair realized that her mother was still holding the box of cards in one hand. "That's what happened."

Josie pointed at David. "Yes, but why is he here?"

Cynthia heaved a dramatic sigh. "Because he wouldn't stop listening to me. Everything I say, he does. Except leave me alone. He followed me, and he wouldn't stop." She walked over to David and yanked the blanket off his head.

David wobbled a bit, then smiled broadly. "Flair," he said, his voice distant and oddly content. "Flair, Flair."

It seemed rude not to respond. "Hi, David."

"Oh, I like Flair. I like saying Flair. Flair, Flair, Flair . . ."

"Stop," said Cynthia briskly. He did. "Now, stand up." David stood. "Sit down." He sat. "Sing." David started to sing, an old School of Fish song.

Strange days—he had that right.

"Enough."

"Oh, but I like to sing." He kept going, and Cynthia put a hand up to her forehead.

"Damn it. I did this earlier, and he didn't want to stop. It's how he ended up in the trunk."

Flair spoke over David's song. "So you told him to listen. And then he did."

"I didn't even realize what I was doing—but I should have

known. Once I had any of the cards in my hand, I could get him to do whatever I needed him to do, at least temporarily." In spite of the trouble with David, it was easy to see Cyn was pleased by that. "I'm out of practice, though. And something went wrong."

"And this happened earlier tonight?" Josie glanced over at Flair, who avoided her gaze. She knew what Josie was thinking, and Josie was wrong. Flair had just been messing around, not casting a spell. This was exactly the kind of thing her mother's magic did.

Cynthia nodded.

"You tried to undo it?" Josie sounded far calmer than Flair suspected she herself did.

"Of course I did. I just wanted my cards; I didn't want this! I tried three times, but nothing changed. I took him out to his car and started driving to see if it would go away after a while, too, but it didn't. And then he started singing with the radio, and I'd tell him to stop and he'd start again, and finally I just pulled over and made him get in the trunk. He seemed perfectly happy."

"And then you came here." No matter how hard Flair studied her mother's face, she couldn't figure out why. To dump David? To yell at Flair?

"Right." Josie didn't seem worried about Cyn's motivations. She pushed the coffee table to the side of the room and gestured to Flair to move the ottoman, then disappeared toward the kitchen, leaving Flair alone with her mother.

"Are you sure you can't get him to stop?"

"If he does stop singing, he starts talking. I promise you that's worse."

They stared at each other. Flair had no idea what to say.

Fortunately, David's singing covered any awkwardness.

Josie returned, a box of salt tucked under one arm and a small cauldron looped over the other. In one hand, she held a pair of scissors, which she handed to Cynthia, in the other, a cluster of Tootsie Pops, which she extended first to David. "Red or purple?"

David took purple, and Josie handed a red one to Flair before she could ask, unwrapping one for herself. Flair, catching the longing look on her mother's face, handed the red to Cyn and then held out her hand to Josie for the remaining purple. There was a moment of blissful silence after David put the Tootsie Pop in his mouth before Flair, who was trying to take all this in, pointed her Tootsie Pop at Josie's cauldron.

"I'm sorry, what?"

"Welcome home, cupcake. I don't think I have time to catch you up." Josie turned to Cynthia. "Can you make a poppet?" Cyn nodded and turned to David.

"Sock," she said. He lifted a foot and she yanked off his shoe, then his sock. She pushed the shoe back on, then leaned over and used the scissors to cut off a chunk of David's hair, which she shoved into the sock. Josie gave her a look.

"What? It has to take on his energy."

"With a lock of his hair, not a giant clump off the side of his head."

"He wasn't nice."

"He never is." By now, Flair had begun to think further than the next five minutes, forward to David waking up, or coming to, or whatever you would call it. Here. In Josie's living room, with Lucie angry at Flair a few hundred feet away and a car all lined up that Lucie would be delighted to hop into. Lawyers weren't going to be able to help her bring a thirteen-year-old back to Kansas who didn't want to come.

Josie was still talking to Cynthia. "If you don't want to reverse the spell, the spell won't reverse."

"I've been putting up with him all night," Cynthia said. "Believe me—I want it to."

Flair wasn't sure she did. But when Josie directed her to sprinkle the circle of salt around David, she did as she was told. Josie placed a pillar candle in each of the four quadrants, and Cynthia, who had returned her attention to the poppet, looked up at Flair with a triumphant smile and then lit each one with a twitch of her finger.

Flair ignored her and concentrated on the circle. "Wait—do we have something to open it with?"

Cyn reached into the bag that had held the cards as well as whatever she was stuffing the poppet with and took out a dagger, holding it by the jeweled handle and pulling the long blade out of its suede case with a flourish.

Flair took it gingerly. "Okay, then," she said around the lollipop in her mouth. Great.

Josie urged David farther into the middle of the circle, and Flair closed it behind them all, then placed the dagger on the floor at her feet.

Josie extended a hand and took his Tootsie Pop stick, then, after apparent thought, held the cauldron out for everyone else's. Cyn crunched a last bite of candy. Flair held out hers, which was still round, the Tootsie Roll showing through the candy coating.

"Oh, for God's sake, Flair," her mother said. "Just bite it."

"How many licks . . ." began Josie.

"Okay, okay." Flair bit off the candy. Now she'd be picking it out of her teeth the whole time. Another bite or two, and Flair handed Josie the stick, which she dropped into the cauldron. With a flick of her hand, Josie lit its contents on fire, and the smell of sage and lavender and burning sugar filled the air.

"It's just regular sage," Josie said, as if Flair had asked. "We don't use the white kind anymore."

That explained why it smelled more like Thanksgiving than the circles of Flair's childhood.

Flair's mother turned to her. "It's so trendy now it's practically endangered," she said. "And it's an Indigenous thing—"

"I know," Flair said, too loudly. They weren't here to discuss appropriation. The ritual had begun, and they all knew what to do.

The more than two decades that had passed since Flair had last stretched out her arms to create the circle disappeared as she took Cyn's hand on one side and Josie's on the other.

"Who's starting?"

"I will," said Cyn. "Three stalwarts live true," she began, and Josie and Flair joined in.

"Three ready and willing. Three in need, three in communion, ever prepared to embrace the power and take the journey."

And the wheel of fortune began to turn. Five. Seven. Or even, in a pinch, three. Odd numbers for a ritual that never had a chance to feel odd to Flair, since her mother made Flair one of her circle as soon as she could stand and attempt to say the words. Cynthia was always looking for the perfect third, or better yet fourth and fifth, but she tended to attract women who were more interested in what was immediately on offer than on being stalwart and true or taking a journey. Flair's mother didn't tend to keep friends. Except for Josie, neither did Flair.

Josie, who'd clearly stayed a part of this world long after Flair left it behind. Their chant of invocation finished, Cynthia pulled both Flair's and Josie's hands to her chest, drawing in their power, and Flair felt that heat and pressure of something shared between them coming through the circle, through her, to her mother in a way she hadn't felt in over twenty years.

She turned her attention to her mother, who was looking from David to her poppet and reciting the first part of her spell.

"Because we say so once, this is you." Josie and Flair joined in again.

"Because we say so twice, this is you. Because we say so a third time, that which is in you shall also be in it. Because we say it a fourth time, that which is in you shall leave you. Because we say it a fifth time, that which is from you shall stay with it."

Cynthia's eyes were shut, her face intense, and Flair knew that she was enjoying her return to the real magic she had lost rather than the stage magic that she had mastered. As Flair watched, the connection between her mother and David became clearer, the strands of power stretching thinly from Cynthia's hands out into a web of glowing light that laced around him like a thin, barely perceptible veil. Cyn felt the connection, Flair could tell, and beneath her mother's worry over what she had done was a strong undercurrent of delight that she'd been able to do it at all.

Flair didn't agree. As bonkers as her mother's current career choice was, it was far safer than the way she used to be. And

Flair already had enough problems. The return of the family magic meant she would now have to add an unbewitched soon-to-be-ex-husband sitting in her best friend's living room surrounded by salt and missing half of his hair, his intent unknown and almost certainly unwelcome.

As the many possible outcomes of David's reemergence into full awareness crossed Flair's mind, she saw the faint glow of another web beneath her mother's. Clear, almost invisible until it deepened to a rich, pulsing red under her scrutiny, the second lattice covered David so completely that it almost seemed to be a part of him. As the threads connected to Cyn began to unwind, their energy returning to her, they suddenly tangled as though caught by the bloodred strands.

Flair shook her head, doubting what she'd seen. Her abrupt movement seemed to spur a response in David, and a flicker of cunning replaced the placid look on his face. At the sight of it, Flair, without entirely meaning to, loosened her hold on Josie's hand, and the magic flickered out of her sight as though she had flipped a switch.

Josie, sensing the change in Flair's focus, held Flair tighter, and Flair, regretting her momentary lapse, returned her squeeze. Whatever it was she had seen, she had to help undo. Whether David stayed enchanted or not, there wasn't really any way this ended without more problems for Flair.

Cynthia was speaking her own words now, reversing what had been done, gathering her magic back into her hands. "Return," she said. "Return, return."

She opened her eyes as they looked at David, who seemed to be sitting straighter, and at the poppet, which hadn't moved. They raised their hands, together, then lowered them, carrying the cone of the circle down into all of them and the work they'd done.

Flair took up the dagger again, and she who had closed the circle now opened the circle, cutting a door in the air above the place where she had last sprinkled the salt, then gently clearing it away before stepping out. They waited—David should leave next, and then the explanations could begin.

But David looked up at them with the same gaping, loose smile he'd worn before. He tilted his head, appearing to wait for instructions, then blinked a few times and spoke.

"Could I have another Tootsie Pop?"

CHAPTER TEN

B UT IT WAS working," Cyn said. "I felt it. Didn't you feel it?"

Flair nodded, avoiding Josie's eyes. It had been working. The bright strands had been peeling away, their hold weakening even as they became visible. Cynthia's magic had been returning to its source.

It was Flair who had hesitated. But if this wasn't her spell, her hesitation shouldn't have made a difference. She'd given her energy to the circle, and the circle had held.

But nothing had changed, which could only mean one thing. This wasn't Cynthia's spell—or at least, not only her spell.

That red web had to be Flair's.

Flair sat very still, trying to hide from the realization as it spread through her. The family magic had returned at exactly the wrong moment, and while Cynthia had named the curse, it was Flair whose wrath had fueled and created it. The result was a snarl of malice that they had been unable to release.

David waved, and Josie handed him another Tootsie Pop

while Cynthia stared at him in consternation. "If I wanted a manservant, he's not who I'd choose," she said.

She should tell her mother what she knew, but Flair could not find the words. Cynthia pulled the coffee table back over and took up the cards, which she'd set at her feet in the circle— always, Flair had noticed, out of Flair's reach. Cynthia slid the cards out of the box and put the box on the table, still holding the cards tightly in her grasp.

"I don't want them," Flair said. That, at least, she knew for certain. Her mother looked at her, and Flair saw the disbelief in Cynthia's eyes. Flair held her hands up, trying to show how very much she meant it. "Seriously. I wanted them gone. It's different."

Cynthia loosened her death grip, maybe to show that she was at least trying to take Flair's word for it. The cards slipped through her fingers, or possibly leapt from them. The three women exclaimed in dismay as they landed all around room, somehow reaching every corner, David watching with evident pleasure.

One of the cards had fallen at Flair's feet. Flair bent quickly to retrieve it, made instantly anxious by a sense that the cards themselves had panicked. She could no sooner have left them where they fell than she could have left the infant Lucie wailing in the street, and the compulsion to gather them was so powerful that in that moment, Flair couldn't believe she'd left them untouched for so long—even if they had tricked her into using powers she'd never wanted.

But the minute she touched the card, she felt her mother beside her, picking up the other cards nearby, frantic, scrambling in her rush to gather as many as she could. Josie stood watching them both, not moving.

"Mom." Flair grabbed her mother by the shoulder. Cyn shook her off, and Flair grabbed her again. "Mom. Here."

It was an unexpected effort to part with the card, but Flair placed it firmly in her mother's hand, resisting the urge to pick up any others until Cynthia allowed it, hoping to demonstrate how little she wanted anything to do with the magic they contained.

Her mother looked down at the card Flair had given her. The Queen of Wands. A card of abundance, declaring that there was plenty to go around. A card of trust. "Let me help," Flair said. "I never wanted anything else."

She drew in a breath to calm herself and Cynthia, and to calm the cards. The cards had flown apart with their own energy, urgent, alive, full of their own wants, pushing everything else aside. They needed to be gathered together, made to feel safe, before Flair could even begin to think about what to do next.

After a minute, Cynthia nodded, and Flair nodded at Josie as well. They began to pick up the cards—and every card Flair took up, she handed to Cynthia.

At first, they didn't want to go. But the more cards Flair's mother held in her hands, the more easily Flair was able to hand them over. The Knight of Swords, the Three of Pentacles, the Empress, the Moon.

Maybe her mother was meant to have her magic back. And Flair was meant to let it go.

At the thought, Flair sped up, barely pausing to look at the cards. There was nothing she wanted more.

She'd loved these images once. Copied them, studied them,

pored over them with her mother, listening to her tell their stories as though they were a book. Our family, she called them, and when Flair asked Nana Marie about it, she'd hesitated and stared at her for a long time before agreeing, then settling in to tell the story of the cards themselves.

"Your"—Nana Marie had paused to count—"great-great-great-grandmother painted them. Alice. Right before she died." Alice, as in Alice Hardwicke, Flair knew now. Alice, who along with an ancestor of Loretta's and three others, had helped to found Rattleboro. "She learned the art in Paris, when she traveled there after the Civil War. That's really when tarot became big. And a lot of the images are her and her friends, and probably other people around here."

"Then why does my mom have them? Why don't you have them?" Flair must have been eleven or twelve by the time they had this conversation. By then, she'd already begun to hate the cards a little.

A shrug from her grandmother, an expression she couldn't interpret. "She needs them. I don't."

Flair picked up the King of Wands, grandly gowned, knees spread, taking up space with his intricately decorated throne and encouraging success, drive, action. She held it for a moment as she picked up the card beside it, the Two of Wands, the start of a creative journey full of opportunity. She turned them both over. The backs were nearly but not perfectly identical, as though hand-printed or stamped, with colors that didn't match precisely. On each was an elaborate medallion, a fleur-de-lis with an eye inside a triangle made of a floral vine. A pattern covered the rest of the card out to a frame that reminded Flair of the piped shell border around a cake.

Flair turned the cards back over and added them to the ones in Cynthia's hand.

Slowly, carefully, she moved around the room, gathering the remaining cards and the memories that went with them. The time her mother threw a party they couldn't afford after the appearance of the Four of Wands, saying it would bring them good luck, and the way everyone who came brought something— food, wine, flowers, desserts—so that they really did end up better off than when they started. The way the Six of Pentacles encouraged her mother to empty her wallet again to help a man and his dog on the street. Money went through her mother's hands like sand, and Flair had resented it, but holding the cards again reminded her that Cynthia had always managed to hang on to joy much longer.

With three of them working, all seventy-eight cards were picked up quickly. Flair looked around, thinking they were done, until Josie pointed. A single card stuck out from under the sofa, faceup. The Fool.

Flair knelt to retrieve it and sat back on her heels, examining the card. The beginning of a journey, yes. Opportunity. Energy. Forward motion. But there was also chaos and recklessness, the impossibility of being prepared for what lay ahead.

She did not want to be the Fool. She delivered the card to her mother, and Cynthia, seeming more confident already, tapped them against the coffee table and then shuffled them between her hands before looking at Flair. "Do you want to read for me?"

To her surprise, Flair found she did. She took three cards from the deck her mother extended and laid them out on the table: The Ten of Swords. The Page of Cups. And then the Magician.

"You know the cards as well as I do," she said to her mother, but Cynthia was already shaking her head.

"Knowing them and reading them aren't the same," she said.

Flair knew that. And these cards were different. They always had been. Other decks held possibilities, the reader only a conduit. These cards held answers for Flair's family alone. Answers Flair didn't always like to questions she didn't want to ask.

But this she could read. She touched the Ten of Swords, among the bleakest cards in the deck—but at least a card suggesting that the bottom had arrived, not that it was yet to come. "We move from suffering and loss," she said of the card before going on to the Page of Cups, "through a swirl of possibilities." The Magician, easy. "So that magic can return to your life."

Flair wanted Cynthia to have her magic back. And she would be happiest if Cynthia kept it.

"Thank you," Cynthia said, and Flair thought she meant it. She returned the three cards she'd drawn to the deck and pushed it toward her mother. "There you are," she said. "All yours."

Josie put up a hand as if to draw their attention. "That was very touching," she said, "but he is also all yours." She pointed to David, who hadn't moved from the floor at the center of what was now a very messed-up circle. "And you need to figure out what to do with him."

David didn't seem to notice their scrutiny. He was the perfect vision of someone existing only in the moment, with no worries about the past or fears for the future. It wasn't as great as advertised.

"What *are* we going to do with him? I can't let Lucie see him," Flair said.

"No one can see him," Josie said. "Look at him. And if he's supposed to be at his restaurant or something—"

"Dang." Flair stuck a hand out to David. "Phone," she said.

David fished it out. Flair held it to his face to open it, then turned off the passcode so she wouldn't have to do it again before opening up his texts.

The messages were from Lucie mostly, and she left those. A few from Carly, who seemed not quite as gone as promised. Flair would ignore those. She scrolled down until she found Jorge, who'd stepped up as manager when she'd left. "Dude," she read as she typed. "Flu. Bad. Gonna be out all week."

Josie looked incredulous. "Someone will believe that?"

Flair laughed. "No. But they'll believe he thinks they'll buy it. Who knows where they'll think he actually is." She put the phone in her own pocket. "But that only solves part of the problem."

Josie nodded. "We're going to have to try something else," she said. "And we're going to have to really want it to work."

Josie had her arms wrapped around her cauldron, and suddenly Flair got a glimpse of who she might have become if she'd made a different choice when her grandmother offered all those years ago. *Stay, and learn to use it. Or leave, and leave it all behind.*

In every other part of her life, Flair was in charge. But now she was at a loss, and she didn't like it.

She didn't like the way Josie was looking at her, either. "I do want it to work," she said to Josie. "I just need to—"

Josie glanced at Cynthia, engrossed in her phone as though the appearance of David's had given her permission to essentially leave the party. "Crush him into submission, and get him to do what you want," Josie said softly. So Josie had guessed, too, why Cynthia's effort, even with their support, hadn't worked to lift the spell.

Flair shook her head fiercely, her eyes indicating her mother. She might have to tell Cynthia the truth eventually, but she wasn't ready. Not yet.

Josie nodded.

"We want to fix him and send him back," Flair repeated for her mother's benefit, then realized Cyn still wasn't listening and nudged her. "Mom. We're not done here."

Cynthia looked up. "I know. I do have a life, though. People actually will wonder where I am tomorrow."

"Speaking of tomorrow," Josie said, getting up and stretching not very subtly. "Maybe that's all we need. A little time. Daylight. Why don't we sleep on this? Figure it out tomorrow."

Flair was about to object when Josie shot her a look. *I need to talk to you alone.* "Cynthia, Flair has a guest room. We'll put David somewhere," Josie said. "Why don't you go ahead and go home?"

So, so not subtle.

At least her mother hadn't noticed. "It's your old room," Flair said.

Cynthia looked around, and for the tiniest of seconds, Flair thought she might offer to clean up, or help with David—but no. Like Lucie, when given a chance to get out of an unpleasant task, Cynthia wasn't going to start asking a lot of questions. She scooped up her bag and returned the cards and the dagger to its depths, then, after a moment, the failed poppet.

"I'll see you in the morning, then," she said to Flair.

"Lucie will be delighted."

For a minute, Cynthia looked uncomfortable, and Flair was reminded of her texts on Lucie's phone, but there was no time to follow up with it now. Her mother shrugged. "You're right," she said. "She will be."

An unnecessary swirl of her jacket, a slam of the door, and she was gone.

"Teabag will bark at her," Josie said.

"She'll deal."

"Think she'll stick around?"

"For a while," Flair said. "Maybe."

"Until she figures out you're the problem."

Flair took a deep breath, acknowledging the truth of what Josie had said. "That would be pretty typical," she finally replied. "What are we going to do with him?"

"As long as he does what we say, we'll manage. For tonight, we can stick him in the cellar. I'll drag down a beanbag or something. It's not cold."

Flair had never before fully appreciated the depth of her friend's ruthless practicality, but she wasn't going to argue. Instead, she put her head in her hands and indulged in a little crying over spilt milk. "Could she not have gone chasing the cards yesterday? Or tomorrow? Instead of right when I was frosting them here and cursing David all over the place? The timing was terrible."

"It's not like it was all a coincidence," returned Josie. "These are the cards we're talking about here. The timing wasn't terrible; it was perfect. You got what you wanted. Now you just have to figure out how to deal with it."

"I want to fix him up and send him home," Flair said slowly. "Without Lucie."

"That's what's stopping us right there," Josie said. "You, me, your mom—we could undo whatever double whammy the two of you pulled off if you wanted to. But you want something more, and I don't know how to tell you to get it other than to let us unravel him and then sit down with him and with Lucie and unravel that, too."

Flair was shaking her head before Josie even finished. "I can't," she said.

She could tell Josie was unsurprised by her answer. "Then you need someone who can help you figure out how to get him to really do what you want, and there's only one option there." She grinned. "I think you need to talk to Loretta Oakes."

Flair hadn't expected that. "Loretta?"

"If you haven't already figured it out, she's all the power in this town. And when I say all the power, I mean all the power."

"Loretta." Josie's mother's teas. The long-forgotten faces of the other women in her grandmother's coven rituals. She should have known that there was more magic in Rattleboro than she'd thought. That didn't make the idea of going to Loretta easy, especially now.

"What am I supposed to say?"

"You won't be the first person in town to come to her with magic that went overboard. Trust me." Josie paused, as though considering what she'd said. "Just . . . don't show her all your cards." She grimaced. "Or maybe not any cards. But if she wants to, she can help."

CHAPTER ELEVEN

How did one ask the town's most powerful witch for help unenchanting one's future ex-husband—but attaching a few strings in the process?

Sadly, as sure as Josie was that Loretta could help, neither of them had any idea what that might look like. They'd decided Flair should maybe take her a little something—not exactly an offering but something that would be traditional—and also, avoid Renee, which, duh. Flair avoided Renee as a matter of principle.

Avoiding Jude also seemed like a good plan. Actually, avoiding everyone. Josie might claim that Loretta's side gig was fairly well-known around here, but that didn't mean Flair wanted to be known to be a part of it. In fact, she affirmatively did not want to sign up on the Rattleboro witch mailing list. Nothing about her determination to keep all such magical activities out of her life had changed, but extraordinary circumstances called for extraordinary measures. And your ex showing up under a spell in the trunk of his own car driven by your mother certainly qualified.

Flair packed up two mochas and a cookie for Loretta. She greeted Callie and thanked her for coming in on such short notice before setting out in the car she'd finally retrieved from Main Street with two tickets on it for meter violations. Her mother had often bemoaned how ineffective magic was with regard to traffic tickets, and Flair found herself agreeing. That was thirty bucks she wouldn't get back. Plus, whose idea had it been to put little black cat stickers on the envelope? That was just obnoxious. Flair was sure she saw the fine hand of Renee in that one.

Yesterday—how was it only yesterday?—she'd marked each turn in the road that drew her closer to Loretta's mansion-like farmhouse. Today she zipped along, far more worried about what she would say when she got there than anything else, especially if the sleek red electric car she'd seen Jude driving (nothing like David's Lincoln at all) was in the driveway.

But there were no cars, and if Flair hadn't called to ask Loretta if she could come by, she would have been afraid the house was empty.

Knock or go in? These were not currents you had to navigate in St. Louis. Flair had just raised a hand to choose the former when the door opened to reveal Loretta herself, which was unexpected. Flair had envisioned her with a maid, or better yet an ominous butler, but instead there she stood, accepting Flair's proffered coffee with pleasure and looking with interest into the white bag stamped with the turquoise Buttersweet Bakery logo.

Flair followed her through the entry and past the formal dining room of yesterday's meeting into a bright modernized kitchen with latticed floral wallpaper in between large windows. Loretta set her coffee down, then reached into the bag to take out the cookie and set it on the table between them. "The Devil," she said. "Is this me or you?"

Flair stared at the cookie, flustered. She'd meant to bring the High Priestess, a cookie and also a compliment. "N-neither," she stuttered. "It's . . . a problem. The Devil is. And I have a problem. That's why I'm here."

A smile spread across Loretta's face. "Interesting," she said. "I thought perhaps you'd changed your mind about joining us on Halloween."

The Loretta of old had appreciated directness, or at least bravado. "The devil turned up at my house last night, in a way."

"That I want to hear. Sit."

Flair launched into the version of the story she'd decided on. "My mother—do you remember her? She experiments with things. Takes chances."

"I remember."

No one ever forgot Flair's mother.

"She tried to do . . ." Flair searched for another word, came up empty. "A spell."

She risked a glance from the pale grain of the wood table to Loretta, to see how she was taking this. It would be easier if she said something.

She didn't.

"She ran across my personal devil. My ex. And she wanted to teach him a lesson. Or something. And now he's—"

Finally, Loretta tried to help her out. "Dead?"

"No!"

"Good," Loretta said. "Dead is hard to fix."

Flair hadn't been aware of how tightly she'd been holding herself until she felt a release in her shoulders at Loretta's words.

She should have known. From the minute Loretta first walked through the door of Buttersweet, Flair had felt the same shift in the air that came when her grandmother entered a room, but multiplied. The scent of biting sweetness, plum and pepper, the palpable thickness in the air that Flair had locked up with the cards when she'd taken them, the thing Cynthia wanted as much as she wanted all that came with it.

Power. Magic.

Whatever was at Rattleboro's center, whatever made Flair's grandmother the woman everyone came to with their problems, whatever had David so firmly in its grip was something that Loretta had.

And Flair needed. She just wasn't sure how much she needed to tell Loretta in order to get it.

"He had something of hers. And he was going to take something important away from me," Flair said. "She stopped him. But now he's here, but he's not. He's like a puppet and we hold the strings. He's utterly cooperative, physically, mentally. Whatever we want, that's all he can do."

Loretta looked pensive. "Your personal devil at your command? For the right woman, that might be very appealing."

Ew. "But it's not real. This isn't the way he is. I have to put him back."

"Do you?"

"Of course I do." This was not the way Flair had imagined this conversation going. "But when we tried, nothing happened."

"And your mother is the one who did this. Cynthia." Flair

nodded. If her mother had had some help, what difference could it make? "You tried to undo it with . . . who?"

"My mother and my friend. Josie."

"I see. Who suggested you ask me about this?"

Was she going to be angry? Never had anyone looked so witchy without a hat, cape, and wart as Loretta did in this moment. She even had her long, pale fingers tapping together at the tips as she watched Flair intently, the Devil cookie still on the table between them.

"It was Josie's idea. But I'm the one who decided to do it."

"I suspect that was hard for you. How long has it been?"

"What?"

"Magic. How long has it been? Your grandmother thought so highly of you. You had everything your mother lacked. Steadiness, a willingness to learn, an understanding that the mysteries of the tarot and the gifts that come with their understanding cannot be expected to come easily. She hoped you would follow in her footsteps, and here you are. But these cookies are the first sign I've seen that you remember anything at all."

So she knew about the people in the alley. Knew what they'd asked of Flair and that Flair had refused.

"I don't read," Flair said firmly.

"You create cards this elaborate but don't listen to the messages they bring?"

Flair had been a tarot prodigy once, and the hubris that came with listening to the cards had led her to risk her mother's life and her own soul. "I don't believe in fate."

Loretta waved away Flair's words. "I'm not asking you about fate. I'm asking you about the tarot. You don't have cards of your own?"

Josie's words came back to her. *Don't show her all your cards.* But Flair wouldn't have anyway. The cards might have led them into this, but Flair had no intention of risking their chaotic powers again. She was glad to be able to tell the truth in this at least. She didn't have cards. Cynthia did, and Cynthia was keeping them.

"Not anymore," she said. "Not for years."

"So you threw it all away. Why?"

Loretta did not, in most ways, look like Flair's grandmother. Marie had been tiny, a quicksilvery fairy of precision and grace. Loretta was imposing, majestic, with an unnerving stillness about her. But Loretta's words were the accusation Flair had always expected her grandmother to make someday, and Flair found herself responding with the words she'd imagined hurling at Marie but never needed.

"Because it ruins everything. Whenever anything magic appears in my life, it's like the cautionary part of a fairy tale. Everything's great, and then I make a wish, and bam—there's a sucker punch hidden behind the rainbows and unicorns."

"You're afraid, then."

"With good reason, don't you think? My mother wasn't exactly the best example of the many ways magic could change your life for the better." And magic's return to Flair's life was no bed of roses, either.

"You are scarcely your mother. I asked you a question. Earlier. When was the last time you used magic?"

When she was seventeen. When she'd thought that maybe she'd been wrong and should give it one more chance. Halloween, which seemed fitting. Just an ordinary Halloween. Only

Flair had thought it might be special. "A long time ago. When I was a teenager."

"I take it it didn't end well."

"No. It did not." That was all she planned to say about that.

"And whatever's happened with your ex also hasn't gone well."

"That's right."

"Well. Maybe magic just isn't for you, then."

Wait. That was supposed to help? Flair sat up straighter in her chair, her face hot. Lucie was texting David, begging him to take her away. David was here, and the only thing keeping him from doing exactly that was a curse she hadn't planned and couldn't control. And all Loretta had to offer was *Well. Maybe magic just isn't for you.*

"I'm sorry I bothered you," Flair said, starting to get up. This was a mistake. She picked up her drink, hesitated over Loretta's—the urge to bus the table was strong.

"Sit."

"I'm going to go." Maybe she'd go home and find that it had all worn off overnight.

"Sit." Loretta's voice was commanding.

Flair sat.

Loretta laughed.

Laughed.

"I'm sorry," Loretta said. "But if you could see your face, you'd understand." She took a sip of her drink, her smile wide enough to be seen around the lid of the cup, while Flair watched angrily. Nothing about this was funny.

"Clearly you disagree. Which should tell you something.

Magic is power, Flair. And you have it. But you can't use it if you're putting all your energy toward fearing it."

Flair understood Loretta better than she wanted to admit. But all her life, that power had done nothing but turn against her. It wasn't until she locked it away that she was able to take any kind of control over her own life.

Now—she still didn't understand how—it was back. And she was stuck with it. It was time to admit the truth.

"I wouldn't hate it if it worked."

Loretta tilted her head to the side, a faint smile on her face as though she had won. "It works," she said. "You just have to let it. What is it—exactly—that you're afraid of?"

What wasn't Flair afraid of? But one thing loomed above all the rest. "If David wakes up and understands any of what happened, he'll make things hard for me. And Lucie. My daughter."

"People are usually quite willing to forget this sort of oddity. You know that. So far what you're trying to do—break your mother's spell, which was probably quite messy and impulsive, without his remembering what's happened—should be simple."

But it wasn't. Flair twisted her ankles around the legs of the chair as her fingers twined together in her lap.

Loretta leaned forward, placing her elbows on the table. The silk gray shades of her striped shirt shimmered as she put her chin on one hand and stared straight into Flair's face. "What do you really want from me?"

"I want to take off the spell. I want to send him back."

"And?"

And.

Flair was not someone who talked about her problems. This was private. Personal. Between her and Lucie.

"He wants to take something that's mine," Flair said. "I want him to let it go."

Flair felt a familiar frustration. When she'd said she'd like magic if it worked, she'd meant it. Why couldn't Loretta offer specifics? Perform an action, combine this and that, set a timer, await results.

But magic wasn't baking.

Loretta's eyes didn't leave Flair's. "And you're sure your mother did this? Because what you're describing—a bind this powerful—would normally require a deep shared connection. Magic can do a lot. But it can't create something that isn't already there."

Flair couldn't help it. She looked away. "I don't know what happened." Her voice shook a little, and she took pains to even it. "I just want it to go away."

"So there is more between you than you'd like. Isn't that always the way it is with the devil?"

"He's not the devil," Flair said, hating the way her mistake with the cookie had resulted in them giving David a greater role in her life than he deserved. "He's just my ex, and I want to keep him that way."

"Fine," Loretta said. "Where is he?"

"With my mother."

"Call her. With video. I need to see what we're dealing with."

Cynthia's greeting came against a background of salsa music, and behind her, Flair could see the wreck of her own kitchen counter, flour open and spilled, milk beside it with no lid, an open carton of eggs, shells tossed into the top. A bowl, batter dripping down the side, sat too close to the waffle iron.

As if this morning weren't bad enough, now she would have to go home and clean. She wanted to scream. Instead, she called on every reserve of patience and held the phone so that her mother could see who she was with.

"Mom. I'm with Loretta Oakes. She wants to see David."

Loretta leaned forward and spoke in the slightly louder voice older people seemed to use when video calling, revealing herself to be human after all. "Loretta Oakes, Cynthia. It's nice to see you again."

Cynthia turned quickly, the background changing from messy kitchen to white wall. The music shut off. Apparently even Flair's mother wasn't immune to the pull of Loretta's authority.

"Of course." This situation might be beyond even her mother's gift for filling the air with light conversation.

But no.

"He's right here. We have to feed him, and I'd never expect anyone to go without coffee. So. Here he is. He's eating. I told him to eat."

"Mom, just let us see him."

The image on the screen flipped to David, in his syrup-stained Pearl Jam shirt, mechanically eating, then back to Cynthia again.

"I was feeding him," she said. "Then I remembered I could just tell him to eat."

She would have had to insist. Cynthia was a terrible cook.

"Just let me see him again," Loretta said evenly.

David sat chewing, fork lowered, expressionless.

Loretta looked at Flair. "Say something."

Flair didn't want to. Earlier that morning, when they'd told him to go to sleep in Josie's basement, David had seemed harmless. A pleasant and obedient drunk. But when she'd retrieved him after Lucie left for school, his acceptance of the situation seemed to have soured along with his breath, and she'd been relieved to leave him, a sulky, ominous presence, with the reluctant Cynthia. "Good morning," she said, for lack of anything else to say.

His eyes shot to hers through the phone, still blank but without hesitation, as though he'd been waiting for her voice.

"Does he talk?"

An expression that might have been irritation crossed David's face. "Good morning," he said in flat tones.

"Finish your waffle," Cynthia said cheerfully. David stabbed a piece off his plate and lifted it to his mouth just as Cynthia turned the phone back to her face. At least they wouldn't have to watch him suffer. "So, what do you think? Can you help? I've never had a result like that before, but then, it had been so long—"

Flair cut her off. "My mom doesn't usually have to put spells on men to get them to do what she wants," she said. It was entirely possible that Cynthia would spill their entire history with the tarot cards, unnecessary and unhelpful.

"I can imagine," Loretta said. "Thank you." She pointed to the phone. "Can you ask her to give us a moment?"

Flair put her mother on mute, holding up a finger to indicate that they'd be right back.

"Your mother may have set that off," she said. "But what's holding him is not your mother's magic. It's yours. And if you don't know its source, it's going to be difficult to undo."

"I didn't mean to do anything," Flair protested, relieved that at least her mother couldn't hear this. She knew Loretta was right. But if Cynthia could shift the blame for David onto Flair, she'd be gone before Flair even got home.

"So you say. Which only makes it more difficult to free you. Both of you." She looked annoyed for a moment, then smiled to herself in a way Flair wasn't entirely sure she liked.

"This will have to be done in the right way, and at the right time."

With a sinking feeling, Flair realized she knew what Loretta meant. "You're going to tell me we have to do this on Halloween, aren't you?"

"If you want it to work, yes. Bring your mother back."

Flair took her mother off mute. Cynthia had carried the phone with her to peer into the refrigerator, and Loretta called out to her to regain her attention. "I hope you don't have plans for Halloween," she said. Cynthia looked up, and Flair waited for her objection.

But Cynthia had a cagey look that suggested she'd be willing to put aside whatever she had going if she received a better offer. "Nothing I can't change," she said.

"Perfect," Loretta said. "We've had one of our usual families drop out of trail preparations this year—for Rattlebones, of course—and it occurs to me that you used to be quite a presence out there. If you'll join me again, with Flair, we can put this right. In fact, we'd be putting quite a few things right."

Cynthia squealed. "Of course," she said. "Anything." Like so many kids who'd grown up in Rattleboro, Cynthia had done classroom art projects based around the Rattlebones Trail since grade school, worked on it for anyone who would hire her every year as a teenager, and imagined herself out there as an adult, part of the show. Flair knew that not because her mother had told her but because her grandmother had. Cyn herself did not like talking about things that had not worked out the way she'd hoped.

"If you put together your own stop, I'll be able to join you after the final travelers come through. The timing and the energy will be perfect."

A stop. An entire scene on one of the most famous Halloween experiences in the country? Flair touched Loretta's arm. "I thought you wanted me to help Jude—"

Loretta shook her head. "That was different. For this, I need you to be fully immersed in the experience. Plus, your mother is here. I've seen her work. It would be a shame to waste this opportunity."

Cynthia's work? Loretta knew what her mother did?

Ordinarily that was a revelation that filled Flair with shame—it was very hard to have a normal conversation with someone once you knew they'd not only read something like *The Bite That Stopped Time* but also knew it had been written by your mother. Now, though, she was struggling to figure out what Loretta could possibly mean.

"But . . . I can't. We can't." It was Wednesday. Halloween was Saturday. That gave them three days, four if you counted today. People prepared for these things for months. There was no way. She looked to her mother for backup but quickly realized her mistake. Cynthia looked—there was no other word for it—thrilled.

"Shut up, Flair," she said.

"I understand your reluctance," Loretta said. Her tongue shot out of her mouth in the familiar, slightly snakelike gesture. "It's a big undertaking. But you need to be out there." Flair could see her mother listening avidly. "People talk about the magic of the date, the thinning of the veil between the worlds—but that's not all it is. We need the raw emotion, all of that fear and excitement and willful submission to the darkness. Learn how to use that power, and you can control anything."

She took Flair's phone from her hand and ended the call, then turned to her, both perfectly groomed eyebrows raised. "Looks as though I've changed your mind about Halloween after all."

Flair was starting to get tired of hearing that. "I'll do what I need to do—" she began.

Loretta interrupted. "You said you don't believe in fate. I do. But it's always possible to push fate around a little."

It was a dismissal. But Flair wasn't ready to leave. "But how am I supposed to get a trail stop ready in three days?"

"Not you. Both of you. Listen to your mother."

CHAPTER TWELVE

FLAIR WOULD HAVE liked to have gone straight home and remonstrated with Cynthia, but Callie could only fill in for so long. And Flair was supposed to train two theater students who were home to help family members with their trail efforts but were free during the day and in need of extra cash. They'd fill in for a couple of days until the crush associated with Halloween and the surprising success of the tarot cookies faded and Flair could assess what she really needed.

Cynthia, after some persuading, agreed to stay with David at least until Josie came home.

"Someone has to keep him out of Lucie's sight."

Flair's mother had tried to dismiss her concern. "Maybe she'll like him better this way. I certainly do."

Flair's shriek of frustration had been unusually effective. Possibly even Cynthia could see Flair was at a breaking point.

"Okay, okay. I've got it."

"Tell him to go to the bathroom," Flair said, and hung up.

She parked her car back in her driveway and ran to the shop without even glancing at the house. She didn't have time. Cynthia would have to deal.

Having help—and enough customers to really need it—meant Flair was finally able to feel some pride in Buttersweet Bakery as well as find time to replenish the pastries in between turning away Marie's former patrons. As a result, five o'clock came surprisingly quickly. When Jude knocked this time, she had already cleaned up and was looking, she hoped, less like someone who'd been through a hurricane and more like a successful business owner at the end of a good day.

"You got my note?"

"I did."

Jude's assistant, again in his chef's whites, had come in for coffee and ham-and-cheese croissants at lunchtime and to deliver Jude's "formal invitation" that Flair permit him to walk her home. The assistant had done this with a general air of expecting Flair to eat him alive, and Flair got the idea that Jude might not be the easiest person to work for. "Do you let that kid wear anything else once in a while, or does he just travel with two sets of whites and a jug of bleach?"

Jude, who was waiting for Flair to lock up, looked at her somewhat blankly. "He can wear whatever he wants, I guess. But we were working. I took a space down the block for the time being."

"Does he know he can wear whatever he wants?"

Jude raised his eyebrows. "He could ask. I don't bite."

"I'm not convinced he knows that, either."

Cynthia had reported earlier that she "made the handoff" to Josie, who'd texted that David, back on his beanbag in her cellar, was watching *Ratatouille*. Lucie had taken herself home after track practice and was apparently with Cynthia, who claimed to have "called in the troops" in the name of planning a trail stop. Those three, at least, were taken care of. The list of additional things Flair needed to worry about was long and varied and truly so overwhelming that she found herself strangely happy to let it all go for the moment and focus on being with Jude, even if he presented his own set of challenges. But he seemed to have set that all aside, so she would, too.

Last night they'd walked at a careful distance, but tonight Jude extended his arm. "Since this is an official walk," he said.

Flair glanced at him, hesitant. There was only so much ignoring the past she felt capable of. "What is an official walk, exactly? I might need to know what I'm committing to." Against her better judgement, she felt a flicker of something that wasn't just the pleasure of an attractive man's interest. Something that felt a little like . . . hope.

Which was not a thing Flair permitted when it came to Jude.

But Jude was charming, and he would be gone after Halloween. And Flair really didn't want to think beyond the next ten minutes.

"You mean, 'to what I am committing'?" His tone of mock grammatical correction was appropriately arch. "I assure you I have only the most honorable of intentions."

"I'm pretty sure I can translate that in Regency terms, but I can't even imagine what it might mean today."

"Exactly the same thing—I guarantee it. Didn't you watch *Bridgerton*?"

"Until Lucie started to blush, yes." And then she'd switched to the books and gobbled them up in a matter of weeks, because why not?

It was surprisingly delightful, ambling down Main Street with Jude for the second time that week, making jokes about how she should have taken his offer first, before she ended up stuck haunting the woods with her mother.

The town itself was looking as haunted as it was possible for a lively streetscape filled with visitors to look. There had been more crews out today, amping up the already extreme Halloween display to the nth degree. Every last detail of the towers on the two old bank buildings—one the headquarters of the League of Kansas Craftswomen, the other its shop and classroom space—had been outlined in lights. The flawlessly restored old movie theater advertised showings of *Hocus Pocus*, *Little Shop of Horrors*, and, at midnight Saturday, *The Rocky Horror Picture Show*. On the small median that ran along the two blocks of Main Street, a tiny Halloween market had been erected, consisting of a row of shedlike kiosks offering everything from hot minidonuts with cider to knitted hats and extravagantly beaded bracelets.

The sun hadn't set, so they couldn't yet see the full effect, but with lights wrapped lightly around every tree, pole, or sign and dripping with glittery black fringe, Rattleboro was truly impressive. Flair couldn't help but admire what had been done. "I still can't believe this place."

"Renee really built it up," Jude agreed, looking around. "It was always pretty amazing, but now—"

"It's incredible." It really was. Disney, Universal Studios—Flair had never seen anything like this, and it was hard to hate it as much as she'd intended. She turned back to look at her own shop and realized that even that had been further transformed, with lights in the form of tiny cakes and treats now outlining her windows and sign, interspersed with the black and purples that lined the whole town and pulled it all together. The taco shop had even more skulls; the bookstore, stars and moons; the craft emporium, black cats and bats that seemed to have been quilted or crocheted. Even the streets and sidewalks sparkled.

Jude followed Flair's gaze downward. "She has them spray glitter on them every morning," he said. "People say they go home with the stuff on their shoes and find it for weeks."

Some magic happened. Some magic, it was clear, had to be made.

They turned the corner off of Main Street, and as Flair contemplated the ring of ghosts set up in front of one house and the jack-o'-lanterns lining the porch of the next, she smacked her forehead in a pantomime of dramatic realization. "We're going have trick-or-treaters! And I'll be out on the trail—"

"They do a big candy collection from all around town at the bank, and you can go get a few bags of that and put a bowl out. As long as you decorate a little and leave a light on and ask a neighbor to refill it, you'll be fine."

Flair smiled, picturing little kids in costumes. Their apartment building in St. Louis had allowed kids to trick-or-treat the hallways, and they had lived near a few row houses, but it wasn't the same. "Lucie could answer the door. Or she should dress up. She's still young enough."

Jude shook his head. "She's in eighth grade, right? That's not what they do. They come work at the party at our place with the high schoolers, helping out, making sure no one sneaks out on the trail before they're supposed to, and then the church has a big party for them. You were only here that one Halloween, or you'd know."

That one Halloween. The one where Jude talked her into walking the Rattlebones Trail, and got tickets, and then talked her into slipping off the trail into the night. She looked over at him and saw no sign that he remembered. Suddenly their walk didn't seem nearly so pleasant. "The church? Has a party?"

"I know, right? They actually used to run the trail out of the church, too, a really long time ago. It's a community thing."

"That's both very surprising and pretty cool."

They walked on in silence. In just a few short steps, Flair had gone from enjoying herself to fuming, and instead of a ten-minute break from reality, reality was being rubbed in her face.

Flair had used a big chunk of what she'd saved from her frozen yogurt job to get herself back here that Halloween, and when she'd arrived unexpectedly via bus, Marie had not been sympathetic to Flair's declared desire to see Halloween in Rattleboro for herself.

She had to have guessed why Flair was really there. It had been Flair's idea to keep her growing relationship with Jude as hidden as they could. They saw relatively few people on their nearly nightly walks, and by turning down Jude's suggestions of movies or parties in favor of hikes and bike rides outside the town limits, Flair could at least pretend no one knew. She could imagine what people would say if Cynthia's girl showed up holding hands with Jude Oakes, and she didn't want to hear it.

But, as her grandmother was fond of saying, love and a cough can't be hidden. Flair had seen Marie looking out the window after Jude's retreating form when he walked her home. And Josie knew all, which meant that Josie's mother knew all, no matter what Josie said. Marie could probably see how Jude never missed a chance to see Flair, or Flair him, and could easily have guessed that he was the one who left flowers on the porch and, that one time, the box of chocolate that had melted disastrously in the heat.

Flair had been going to tell her grandmother, she really had. But when summer ended, she'd been too sad and too afraid that everything else would end with it. And when she came back, Marie didn't seem to want to listen.

Instead of embracing Flair as she always had, Marie had doubled down on everything Flair had been avoiding on her visits to Rattleboro since she'd taken the family tarot cards and declared her intent not to use them. "Halloween is Samhain here," she'd said harshly. "You can join in, or you can get that bus back home."

So Flair, for one last time, joined her grandmother's ritual, standing next to Josie. Flair raised her arms and chanted, avoiding the curious looks of women she hadn't seen in years, because even covens have their gossip. She led the many visitors who wanted to consult Marie into the back room of the tea shop and watched her grandmother read while the family cards sat in Flair's backpack as they always did, because as much as Flair didn't want to touch them, she was never quite able to leave them behind.

Flair didn't know what she would have done if her grandmother had demanded that she read. She would have done a lot to stay in Rattleboro in that moment. But Marie never did.

On Halloween, Jude had come right to the front door, like they'd planned, and asked Marie if he could take Flair out to the Rattlebones Trail. And Marie, with a doubtful look at Flair, said yes—and then whispered in her ear to be careful. Most of what was out there was people playing, she'd said. But some of it wasn't.

Flair had enjoyed the hay wagon ride out to the torchlit start of that year's trail and the wait to begin, hearing the shrieks of the delighted groups and couples who went ahead of them. And then Jude had taken her hand and they'd walked out into woods lit only by glow lights and occasional lanterns and scared themselves silly guessing when something might happen until something did.

A hooded figure had approached them, beckoning. They'd drunk from chalices and solved riddles and had a net fall on them from above, and if once in a while Flair could sense that the pretend tricks were being helped along by someone who could encourage the branches to move or darken the night sky, it only made things better.

Even more fun had been the kisses Jude slipped in as they walked between trail stops, on her hand, her cheek, lifting her hair up and brushing his lips along her neck. They'd been told to keep moving, and Flair knew they should—there were groups behind them and ahead of them, and to change their pace risked ruining someone else's trail. But when Jude pressed himself tightly against her from the back, Flair wanted to stop more than she'd ever wanted anything, and when she turned to face him and he wrapped his arms around her, she'd let him guide her off the trail without a single protest. She didn't care what came next on the trail. All she'd known was that she didn't want Jude to stop.

They wouldn't have, either. As soon as they'd gotten far

enough away that they couldn't see any lights, Jude had pulled off his jacket and thrown it on the ground and pulled her down, whispering, stroking more kisses wherever he could reach, and she'd done the same, so much so that he hardly needed to ask if it was okay when he unbuttoned her shirt because her hands were already pressed against the skin of his back.

They'd been idiots.

The woods weren't that big. And they'd been full of people, although why it had to be Renee who came calling into the clearing, shining a light on the ground, hissing that whoever was there had better come with her and get off the trail and they absolutely would not be allowed back, Flair didn't know.

What she did know was that she'd scrambled to her feet, pulling her shirt around her, and Jude did, too, cursing and grabbing his jacket, and as Renee came closer and they realized who it was, Jude had pushed Flair away.

It would have been embarrassing to be caught making out in the woods by Renee, but it wouldn't have been that bad. Flair would have survived. But Jude had been frantic. *Move*, he'd said. *Hide. Just get out of here.*

When Flair realized why, she'd elbowed him in the gut as hard as she could. He didn't want Renee to know who he'd been with. He was embarrassed. Fine. Flair would make sure she didn't know.

Flair had spun around and told the wind to blow up the leaves around Renee, and around Jude as well. Held her hands out in a way she hadn't practiced in four years and swirled up angry circles until she couldn't see Jude anymore between the dirt in the air and the tears in her eyes. She could have stopped there. She'd thought she had stopped there. But as she ran toward the nearest light, she'd heard a tiny crackle of flame behind her, and then she'd really run.

Marie had shaken her awake from a fitful sleep and dreams of robed figures caught in flames. Flair had convinced herself she'd imagined that crackle, but one look at Marie told her she hadn't.

"You started a fire in the woods," she'd said angrily.

"It was an accident. I'm sorry."

Marie released Flair's shoulders and sat on the edge of the bed, looking away, not speaking. Flair had huddled behind her, waiting, and finally reached out to touch her grandmother on the arm. "I'm sorry," she whispered again.

"Sorry isn't enough," she'd said, turning back to Flair. At the look of fear on Flair's face, she'd sighed. "Nothing happened. No one was hurt; someone put it out quickly. It's easier to put out your own fire than someone else's, but it can be done."

It was her grandmother's next words that Flair remembered most clearly. "You can't have it both ways, Flair. You can't only make magic when you want magic. You have to decide. Stay, and learn to use it. Or leave, and leave it all behind."

For Flair, that night had cemented the choice she'd made at thirteen. She left and never intended to come back. Jude was far from the only reason, but he'd been more important than she wanted to admit.

She hadn't given up magic because of him. But if he'd stood by her, maybe she would have made a different choice.

And to Jude it apparently meant nothing at all.

She felt her footsteps growing heavier and angrier as she

snatched her hand from Jude's arm. He turned to look at her. "What?"

"What?" There were so many things Flair had been saddled with since she came back to Rattleboro that she couldn't talk about. So many men, since Jude, whose various transgressions from the small to, well, David, that she'd decided it was easier to not mention.

She didn't want one more. "That one Halloween? That's all you're going to say about it? When you pretended we were going to be some big thing and then totally ran out on me? It was a long time ago. But I'm not just going to pretend it didn't happen, and neither should you."

The look of shock on his face was far too dramatic for someone who'd just been called out for being a seventeen-year-old asshole, and suddenly Flair didn't even want to hear his side of the story. "Whatever," she said in exactly the tones of her own seventeen-year-old self as they turned the corner onto her block. "Just don't let it happen again."

She walked faster, intending to run up her steps and leave Jude behind. She'd said her piece, she'd have to listen to whatever apology he would come up with, but she didn't have to do it now. She needed to find her mother and—

That was when Flair saw the giant tour bus idling in her driveway. As she watched, stunned, the door opened and the sound of the bus lowering to allow the steps to descend filled her ears, unexpectedly loud on the quiet street. *Enter the World of Cyn Starkley*, the ad on the side read, her mother's pseudonym in grand and scrolling script across images of book covers featuring shirtless tuxedoed werewolves and vampires in low-cut gowns.

Flair's lawn was filled with an assortment of camp chairs and people. Josie was watching her boys in Flair's driveway, Hula-Hooping with someone Flair didn't recognize, and behind them were three people on stilts. Someone else was leaning out one of her top-story windows, tossing a rope to someone on the ground. Strings of tiny paper lanterns in Halloween colors dangled from the porch where someone stood on a stepladder wielding a staple gun.

Her eyes returned, as if drawn there, to the bus and its open door. Her mother descended the stairs, waving and calling to her and then, cheerfully, to Jude behind her. Flair thought she couldn't make out the words, but after a moment she realized that they were simply so ordinary that she hadn't taken them in.

"We started up the grill out back," Cyn Starkley, the current and most successful evolution of Cynthia Hardwicke, was saying. "Come and eat."

Flair always thought of her mother as a metaphorical traveling circus. This was the first time she realized that she'd been right.

CHAPTER THIRTEEN

C YN STRODE OUT to meet them, her wildly patterned wide-legged pants swishing above chunky boots, silvery red hair tied back with multiple scarves, ruffle-edged hot-pink sweater completing her extravagant ensemble. She greeted Flair with a brief surprising embrace and Jude with delight.

"Loretta's youngest—I've heard all about you. And of course I love your chocolate." She turned and hollered to the occupants of Flair's lawn, some of whom looked up. "Jonka in person! Someone make him something fizzy." She turned back to Jude. "Of course you're staying. You have to stay. My team will love to meet you, and you'll love them."

She took Jude's arm and pulled him over to begin introducing him around. "I prefer Jude," Flair heard him say, and even though she was still fuming, she caught Josie's eye and had to laugh. Jude being trapped by her mother was not sufficient revenge for anything in their past, but it was better than nothing.

As was knowing she looked good. Flair ran inside to take

out her braids, fluffing the resulting blond mane, added some lipstick, and took a moment to appreciate the way the black button-down she'd chosen that morning tucked into her jeans and emphasized her curves in the right places. Flair loved the way she looked and the fact that she didn't feel the need to change out of day-to-day choices to impress anyone. Not that she had any interest in impressing Jude. But finally telling him off had felt good, and she wasn't above hoping he might feel some regret over how he'd screwed up.

She came back down to find Josie in the kitchen, finger on her lips. "David is back in my house," she said softly, an eye on the door. "I get that you don't want Lucie to see him, but I can't keep him forever. What did Loretta say?"

"Halloween," Flair said, then, as Josie stared, repeated it with more conviction. "Halloween. She said we have to get him out there with the whole black moon thing, on the Rattlebones Trail, and all the energy and power and . . ." Flair felt her voice trail off. Loretta hadn't really told her what they were going to do.

But she could guess. Her grandmother had taught her, as Loretta had pointed out. "It's a classic binding spell," she said. "It's just stronger than usual."

"Because of you," Josie said. "Because you can't let him go until you're sure you know what he's going to do. Which is never." She looked frustrated. "If that's what it is, we don't need the power of Halloween. We need the power of Flair-finally-figures-out-that-sometimes-she-can't-control-everything. Did you tell her that you're afraid Lucie will go back to St. Louis with him?"

Josie said it so casually. As though it weren't the end of the world.

"Not everyone needs to know everything," Flair said too quickly, too loudly. They didn't. She was used to coping by herself. And also, talking about Lucie leaving to Loretta felt like it might make it real, and that was one thing Flair could not take. She let herself imagine the house without Lucie slamming doors and stomping down the stairs, and felt a clench deep in her gut, the same feeling she would get when toddler Lucie slipped from the jungle gym, or an older Lucie took a tough tackle during a soccer game. Lucie's current grumpiness was temporary, a blip. She would come around. Hurt Lucie, and you hurt Flair. Take Lucie, and Flair would have to go, too, or she wouldn't have anything left.

Flair sniffled. The smoke from the grill must be getting into the kitchen, because her eyes were starting to water. She wiped at one, and then the other.

"Flair?" Josie's voice was suspiciously tender.

"I'm fine. It just isn't going to happen—that's all."

Josie came around the kitchen table to where Flair had turned to face the sink full of dishes from her mother's morning cooking attempt, including the waffle iron. The dishes looked a little wavy, like she was looking at them under water. Or tears. Which would just be dumb, because there was nothing to cry about.

Josie took Flair by the shoulders and pulled her into a hug. The beaded tail of the black cat on her orange sweatshirt, a choice that only Josie could make look punk rock rebel, pressed into Flair's cheek.

"It's going to be okay," Josie whispered. "We'll do it your way. I'm sorry. If it seems like I'm not taking it seriously, it's because I know this isn't really what Lucie wants. She's angry at you, and the move. And she's thirteen. You just have to let her figure some things out."

"I know." Flair sniffled again. And then—because she hated crying and needed to lighten the mood—she grabbed Josie's sweatshirt and pretended to be about to wipe her nose on it.

Josie yanked away, laughing.

"That's a very ugly sweatshirt," Flair said.

Josie preened, flouncing around in a circle that showed off the sheer black tights that let her tattooed legs show through under cutoff denim shorts, with knee-high thick black socks and black motorcycle boots. "You're just jealous," she said.

"Of the way your butt looks in those shorts, maybe. Of the sweatshirt, never." Flair turned on the water. "I have to clean this up."

"Or you won't be able to stand it. I know. But you also have to come get David, because I do not need a new roommate. What if I ask Lucie to help me put the boys to bed and you hide him up in your attic?"

"What if he gets up in the night? And Lucie sees him?"

Josie grinned. "I can fix that. My mom left me some tea when I was having trouble sleeping last year. And you know my mom's teas."

"Dangerous to the uninitiated."

"I woke up ten hours later to Declan and Travis building a fort with all the drawers from my dresser," she said. "I brew that stuff very weak now. Put a full cup in him and we won't see him until noon."

"Okay." Flair gestured to the party going on outside. "When this dies down, give me the signal, and we'll make a trade."

She followed Josie out the kitchen door. Most of her mother's team had moved into the backyard by now, and they turned out to be experts at the traveling meal over a grill. Forget burgers. There were skewers of marinated gnocchi and vegetables, of shrimp, of mushrooms, of sausages. Bread and salads. Oatmeal chocolate chip cookies that must have come from a bakery somewhere along their route, and that were so delicious that Flair made a mental note to ask where it was.

Jude chose to stay. Flair could tell he hoped to pull her into a discussion of what she'd said on their walk, to get out those apologies he was probably practicing in his head, and she enjoyed thwarting him. Eventually he settled into a discussion at Flair's one picnic table with Cynthia and Alto, a person Cyn described as her chief of staff. Flair's mother was plotting out an elaborate scene for their Rattlebones Trail stop that Flair would previously have argued vehemently was overreaching. But after seeing that someone had hung a trapeze from the tree in her yard and was spotting Lucie's flips in a very professional manner, she conceded that her mother and her team could likely pull it off.

"Giant puppets," her mother said, waving her hands at the vision. "The big-head kind. Towering over people."

"Too much," argued Alto. "I like the puppet idea, but we're in the woods, right? Puppets in the woods is more weird than scary."

"Marionettes that come down from the trees?"

Alto appeared to contemplate. "Maybe."

Jude leaned in. "The simpler it is, the scarier," he said. "What if y'all made the marionettes from the trees? Like stick figures. Big ones. That move. That would be scary as hell."

Cynthia and Alto paused, Alto with a forkful of salad poised halfway between plate and mouth. They looked at one another. "Genius," said Alto as Flair's mother clapped her hands.

"Magnificent." Cynthia stared off at the trees, and at the little boys now wobbling on stilts in the driveway, surrounded by a team of spotters while Josie Hula-Hooped nearby. "Piles of sticks," she said slowly.

"That rise up," said Alto, hands mimicking the words.

"So you approach," Cynthia murmured, her tone gathering them all in, "and it's a still clearing. Barely lit. Empty. You don't even notice the piles of sticks under the trees until suddenly, they move, and before you can run, they've become animate, surrounding you, menacing you—" She and Alto acted out her words and Flair had a visceral sense of the chill that would come over the travelers on the trail. Then Cyn dropped her hands to the table and clasped Jude's.

"Perfection. Do you need a job? There's always room on my team."

Jude laughed, and Flair, who had pulled a lawn chair up beside the table, shrieked like a teenager. "Mom."

Lucie left the trapeze, probably drawn by the spectacle of her mother and grandmother having a normal, civil conversation. She leaned against the back of Flair's chair and played with her hair, putting in a tiny braid at the top, and Flair reveled in the closeness. Once, they'd taken turns doing exactly this. Flair could make any braid imaginable, could pull off nearly any vision Lucie came up with (except for the time she wanted to look like Princess Jasmine, because smooth and black and gleaming was outside the realm of possibility for either of them). But Lucie hadn't let Flair touch her hair in months.

Cyn beamed at her daughter and granddaughter. "Lucie can help," she said. "Learn a few tricks of the trade."

"That would be so cool," Lucie said, even as Flair straightened and glared at her mother.

"No," she said automatically, realizing immediately that she had taken the wrong tone. Lucie and Cynthia both glared at her, matching expressions of pique. Flair tried to salvage the situation. "There's a high school thing everyone does," she said, remembering Jude's words. "It's really cool. You won't want to miss it." Lucie could not be with them while they tried to restore David.

But Lucie must have already absorbed a lasting truth of teenaged life in Rattleboro—the coolest possible thing to do on Halloween was to get a job working on Rattlebones. "I'll have lots of time to do that," she said, looking at her mother with a face full of hope. "This would be so fun—and we could do it together. What if this is the only year Grand does a trail stop?"

Cyn's eyes lit up, and Flair could see that it had not occurred to her that she might do this again. She could almost see her mother's mind working, envisioning a role in the annual Halloween institution that grew over the years. Even Flair couldn't resist letting the vision of a family trail tradition take over, all of them out there, every year, making magic—but not the real kind. And *we could do it together* had to be the most beautiful words a thirteen-year-old girl could say to her mother.

Except that they couldn't. Not this year. Not while they were trying to channel energy into David and return him to his own life, a life without Lucie or Flair in it. She suddenly felt exhausted and irritated with her mother for destroying the first moment of closeness she'd had with Lucie in months. "You should do the town thing this year," Flair said. "Then we'll see."

Lucie started to argue and Flair gave her the maternal we'll-talk-about-this-later expression, with a pointed glance at their guests, and Lucie stomped back to the trapeze, a return to their new normal. Flair felt Jude's eyes on her and gave him what she hoped was a resigned shrug. "Teenagers," she said.

"It probably would be more fun for her to do the trail."

Not helpful. At least he waited until Lucie was out of ear-shot. "I'll think about it."

Someone produced a fire pit from the bus, and Flair tried to gather the shreds of her earlier pleasure in the evening as they cracked beers over s'mores. She seized a moment while Jude practiced juggling with Alto to pull Cynthia aside.

"The whole reason Loretta asked us to do the trail stop is because she thinks Halloween is the only time we can fix David," she said. "Lucie can't be there. I don't want her out there while we're messing around with magic."

"She has to learn sometime," Cyn said.

"You can't mean that. She doesn't even know he's here. Or . . . what you did. Or anything." Flair didn't expect her mother to understand. Flair had never had to learn about magic, because she'd grown up steeped in it. Steeped in Cynthia's world, where rituals took precedence over school and Flair's most important qualities were those she couldn't let most people see.

Her grandmother had shown her a different version—a relatively safe and normal life that embraced their family magic as tradition, heritage, something to be proud of, though it still placed them firmly outside the norm. In the end, Flair had chosen (c) none of the above, and her choice had become Lucie's, too—which was the safest choice.

Josie, ready to leave, caught Flair's eye. They'd firmed up their plan—Josie had David in her back room now, and as soon as she had Lucie giving the boys a bath, Josie would walk him over.

Flair sat down on her porch steps, feeling the rounded edge of the step behind her press into the small of her back, tilting her head back to stretch. It had been a day. It had been a lot of days. It wasn't going to get better.

The sun had set long ago, and the glow of the fire pit around the side of the house had become the only light. In its shadows, members of Cyn's team moved around, cleaning up, bless them, and Flair had left them to it. The party was coming to an end. Cyn sat down beneath her and stretched her arms out, indicating the admittedly fairly tasteful Halloween décor that Cyn's team had applied in Flair's absence.

"You can't be part of Rattlebones and not do up the house, too," she said. "It wouldn't look right. What do you think?"

"It's fine," Flair said. It *was* fine. But the absence of the moon—she'd noticed the tiny crescent in the sky before sunset— reminded her that Halloween was only three nights away. As if she needed reminding. Cyn looked hurt, but Flair was out of enthusiasm for decorations or anything else. "It's good. It's all good."

"It's better than good," her mother said. "It's fantastic. And our trail stop is going to be the best one Rattleboro's ever seen."

Flair only nodded. Cyn watched her for a moment and then

shrugged and waved one arm again. Three taps in the air with her hand, and three tall torches Flair hadn't even noticed, planted along the edge of the porch, sprang into light.

Flair sat up straight. "Mom." An irritated warning. "You can't do that."

"A little pre-Halloween magic is all. There's automated stuff going on everywhere. No one will notice."

But Cyn was wrong. Someone had. Flair looked past the torches and saw Jude coming around from the side of the house. She stood up quickly, hoping to draw his attention away, but he was already staring at the three bright flames Cynthia had just drawn from thin air with a look of total understanding on his face.

CHAPTER FOURTEEN

FLAIR HAD NO idea what to say. Cyn rose, oblivious, and called a cheery good night to Jude before going into her bus to say good night to her team. Other than Flair and Jude, the now well-lit yard was empty for the moment.

Jude strode forward, the angles of his face even sharper in the light of those damn torches. Flair came down the steps, and he caught her by the arm, blue eyes staring down into hers with an intensity that couldn't be explained by the sight of a little, fully explainable pyrotechnics. "Did your mother just light those torches?"

Flair pulled her arm away but couldn't bring herself to stop looking up into his face. He'd looked at her like this once for a very different reason. She felt a quiver down her back like a drop of sweat at the memory. "She had a remote."

"She didn't. She lit them herself. And you tried to keep me from noticing." Flair felt her eyes grow wide as she scrambled for a response and found nothing. She only had a few minutes, max, before Josie brought David over.

She walked as quickly as she could back around the side of the house, counting on Jude's following her.

"And you remember the night in the woods."

Flair's heart stuttered. "Of course I do." Sometimes she wished she didn't—but that wasn't the kind of thing you forgot about.

"But you shouldn't. Because Renee told me she fixed it so you wouldn't remember. So you wouldn't get hurt."

Nothing Jude was saying made sense, and she seized on his last words. "Why would I get hurt? Other than the obvious, that you were embarrassed to be with me. Which definitely hurt." As had the days of thinking about it after and trying to forget. "And Renee . . . I don't understand."

"I wasn't embarrassed." Jude sounded furious, frustrated. "I didn't want Renee to see you because . . . I knew better. I wasn't supposed to go out with anyone, and I knew she'd be really upset. I didn't want her to catch me, but if she did, I didn't want her to see you. Because then I knew I'd really be in trouble."

"Why weren't you supposed to go out with anyone? And why would it matter if it was me?" Flair forgot about Josie and David for a moment, caught up in Jude, in memories.

"Because she knew I cared about you." They'd reached her back steps again, as far as Flair could reasonably get from the inevitability of Josie walking David from her house to Flair's, and stopped, with Flair unable to think of any other way to keep Jude from seeing anything out of the ordinary.

Anything else out of the ordinary.

Jude stepped closer. Flair remembered the way the full

length of his body filled her field of vision when he stood this close, the way she had to turn her face up to see anything beyond his checked shirt. She flushed in a way that couldn't be accounted for by the heat of the fire pit behind her.

"I've been trying so hard to hide this from you. My mom making cookies leap into hands, sparks in your shop—I didn't want you to see. I didn't want them to scare you. But you knew all along. Why didn't you tell me?"

Flair stared up at him, still confused, although maybe she shouldn't have been. If Loretta was the head of Rattleboro Magic Inc., as she seemed to be, and Renee could wield what Josie had described as enchanted clematis, how could he not know?

"I don't know," she said. All she could offer was the truth. "It's not something I talk about. But I still don't understand what you mean about that night."

"I've never told anyone this before," he said so softly that she had to strain toward him to hear it. "But in our family, we don't . . . care about anyone. Because if we get too close to someone . . . they get hurt."

His voice shook just enough to keep her from throwing a hand on her hip and joking that it sounded like he'd watched *Practical Magic* one too many times. He was serious.

And he was standing so, so close. "Renee loved someone once. He rolled his ATV right in front of her and broke his neck. And our dad—she was the one who got the call the night he crashed his car. Our mom was thrown clear, but he didn't make it."

Flair put a hand on his arm. She'd never heard him talk about any of this.

•

"Renee warned me. I meant for us to just be friends. But it was so hard not to want more. And she made all that wind and the fire—I was afraid she'd hurt you. By the time she put it out, you were gone. And then she got to you before I did and made you forget."

Flair felt herself on the edge of understanding. "I don't know what you mean about Renee getting to me. I never talked to her after that. But the wind, the fire—that wasn't Renee. That was me."

Jude was nodding slowly, his eyes never leaving hers. "You're a witch, too."

Flair heard herself give a disbelieving gasp at his bluntness. Even with everything she'd seen and been a part of, she didn't think anyone had ever looked at her and put it quite so plainly. Jude was still lost in his own discovery.

"Your mother lights torches. You made the fire and the wind. And Renee couldn't have made you forget, because that wouldn't work. Which means . . . you thought—"

"I thought you didn't want to be seen with me," Flair said. "I was so angry. I was the fire and the wind, not Renee. I don't understand why she'd tell you that."

"She must not have known," Jude said. "She wanted to protect us both."

Flair was still caught up in what had happened to her—to them both. "My grandmother was furious at me because of the fire. I didn't mean to start it—but I was mad. At you, for pushing me away. And when you didn't even try to call me, or come after me, that made things worse." She took a deep breath, remembering. "But I left you a note. In your mailbox."

"I never got it."

Flair felt a return of the same fury she'd felt earlier, remembering that night, but now it was entirely directed at Renee. She didn't care what Renee had been trying to do. What mattered was what she had done. "I absolutely wanted to be with you," she said. "And I remember everything. Everything."

They stood together in the light of the fading fire pit, as close as two people could be without embracing. Flair felt his breath on her face as she held his eyes, and his mouth came closer to hers—

She heard a crashing noise from the front of the house, as if someone had tripped over a step, and then a muffled curse.

Josie. And David.

Jude looked toward the noise, the moment broken, and started to turn to investigate. And Flair did the only thing she could think of to do. She reached up and pulled his face closer to hers.

"Flair . . ." He breathed her name as her lips touched his, and then she kissed him, and with any luck, he forgot about anything else.

Because she certainly did.

She pulled him in close, her hands sliding to the back of his neck, and felt the hint of his tongue between her lips and the heat of his entire body pressing against hers, one arm holding her firmly away from the fire, the other encircling her shoulders. She didn't want to move, didn't want to stop—until the side yard light flicked on.

And then off and then on again.

They broke apart and Flair looked up at the window and saw Josie, pointing into the kitchen. She was in. With David. And Jude hadn't seen.

Because he was looking at her, gazing at her with the same light in his eyes that she remembered from their summer together, when she'd wondered for so long why he hadn't kissed her and once he finally did, how she'd possibly last until he kissed her again.

"I missed you," he said softly.

Flair wished desperately that missing him was the only reason she'd kissed him, because then she could do it again. Instead, she made an apologetic face, pulling away.

"I have to—"

He laughed, not letting go. "Is that your mom?"

"It's Josie." She sighed. "And she's doing that because my kid is with hers and will be back any minute."

He tucked a strand of hair behind her ear, clearly not wanting to let her go, and she felt an answering pull. "Well, I can't argue with your kid," he said, as if he wished he could.

"Believe me—you don't want to." The light flicked again, and Flair got it. Not a moment for dalliance. "I'm coming," she called over her shoulder, in case Josie could hear.

Jude dropped his hands and stepped back, gesturing her into the house. "To be continued?"

"Definitely." She turned and ran, stopping on the step to wave, loving it when he turned back to look at her, glad he didn't know that she partly just needed to make sure he was gone.

When Flair shut the door, Josie was waiting. Waiting with her arms crossed and a butter-eating grin on her face.

"If you'd told me that was what you had planned, I might have agreed to keep David," she said.

Flair collapsed against the door. "I didn't. We were talking, and he heard you. I had to distract him."

"If I need distracting, you can just point and yell, 'Over there.'"

"Maybe he's smarter than that."

"Maybe you were waiting for an excuse to grab your first love around the neck and start making up for lost time."

"Shh." Flair widened her eyes and tilted her head in the direction of the kitchen. "Is he in there?"

"Do you think he understands? And seriously, if anyone should be able to date, it's you; it's not like he shouldn't expect that."

The idea that David might remember this was enough to blow away any lingering clouds of romance.

"It doesn't matter," Flair said. "He'd still be upset. Especially now, he'd be all *I'm sorry, you know you're the only one for me, how can you do this when I just want us to make everything right?*"

She'd gone on one date, once, after the first time she'd caught him cheating and thrown him out. She'd thought it would bring him running, and it had. She'd never bothered to do it again, though. He always came back anyway.

Josie's lips were pressed together, as if she wanted to say more, but Flair was glad when she dropped it. "T minus half an hour to Lucie, max. Get that tea in him and get him upstairs."

"Will do." Flair leaned forward and hugged her friend. "Thank you," she said. "For having my back."

"Always," Josie replied. "Call if you need me."

"I'll just blink the porch light like crazy until you show up."

Flair sighed and dropped her head forward, then shook herself all over and walked into the kitchen to find David sitting with a book that Cynthia must have left for Flair in his hand.

He set it down, and Flair's mother's airbrushed face gazed out at them.

"I know her. She's magic." David looked from the book to Flair. "You're magic, too, I think."

"What was your first clue?"

Not surprisingly, David ignored Flair's sarcastic response. "I want to go home," he said. "I don't want to be magic."

She patted him on the arm. At least this version of him wasn't too bad. "You and me both, bud."

She found the container of tea Josie had left for her, its cover painted with two closed eyes in Josie's signature style with a Post-it stuck to the top: *2 spoonfuls should do it. Steep 2 minutes.*

She'd already switched on the kettle, so she added tea and water to a mug from the shelf as David sat watching her. Other than his unaccustomed silence, this whole situation felt familiar. Too familiar. It wasn't just that she was getting his tea. It was David sitting in front of her with a problem, waiting for her to work it out.

He wasn't usually quite this docile. Maybe it was the absence of his customary soliloquy that made her able to see things clearly now. Or maybe it was spending a few minutes with Jude and seeing how quickly two people who wanted to clear away the confusion between them could achieve exactly that. Now that clarity had arrived, Flair couldn't believe she'd never seen the way David was playing her before.

Flair had picked out their apartment. Taken him to places where they could afford the furniture and let him make appropriate choices. Managed the restaurant—and chosen the site and overseen the build-out. Planned their one child and all the scheduling around her. When things were good, she booked caterers and made dinner reservations. When they weren't, when money was tight and time scarce, Flair had set the limits. He'd let her. He'd made her.

And that was why this stupid spell was working so incredibly well. Irritated with him and with herself, Flair took her eyes off the kitchen clock's second hand and strained the tea. "This is what you want from me," she said to him as she set it in front of him. "You want me to tell you what you should do."

He took a sip of the tea and winced.

He'd made her his authority figure so he could rebel against her and then delight in coming back. "Drink," she said firmly, watching him as he took a sip, then another. "I can't believe you," she said. "I can't believe I didn't see it sooner, either."

She snatched a cookie up from the box of slightly damaged pastries she'd brought home and forgotten to share with the traveling circus. After a glance at the cookie, she took out another and set them on a plate. These she'd be happy to read.

"The Devil," she said, sitting down across from him. "Go ahead. Eat it. That's your past. Giving in to a lot of temptation, playing out a nice, unhealthy addiction to me. Then we have the present, Justice, which you're finally being served."

David picked up the Devil cookie. She didn't know if he wanted to say anything, or whether he could, and she didn't care.

"Don't talk," she said. "You don't get to. This is my time to have my say."

She thought he looked sullen. His slightly robotic movements seemed faster and jerkier as he held the cookie to his mouth and then set it back on the plate, untasted, so hard that the cookie broke and the second cookie leapt into the air.

"I told you to eat it," she said, suddenly angry. "If you want me to be the one who tells you what to do, you got it, only you can't get away from me now. Can't decide when you'd like to come and go."

She'd made his life so easy, and he made hers hell. It didn't matter that she didn't want him anymore. He'd forced her to give up everything she had built, and now he wanted to take the one thing she had left.

"I can't believe you slept with Carly. Or did I pick her for you, too? Put her right in front of you? Lucie loved her. But you can't let anyone else have anything."

He still didn't speak, but now his hands were clenching and unclenching, as though he wanted to throw the plate at her, or something worse, but was held in place by a spell he'd been a part of creating.

Magic was always worse when you brought it on yourself.

She looked into his eyes, every ounce of the fury she'd hidden for so long fully on display, expecting to be met with the same blank gaze he'd presented for days. Instead, he blinked and the vacancy disappeared, replaced by a churn of resentment and desperation. When he raised one hand, unbidden by her, she gasped and froze, poised to react, uncertain how.

He moved his hand just slightly, an inch, maybe two, and flicked half of the Devil cookie toward her. It spun and landed directly in front of her, one head of a beautiful snake with sparkling scales, forked tongue mocking Flair. Then he picked up the Justice cookie and took a bite.

He'd understood what she'd said. Maybe better than she had.

Flair turned the Devil over in her fingers, watching David eat. She'd had enough cookies already, maybe enough for a lifetime, but she knew what David was trying to say. If he'd needed someone to take charge, she'd wanted someone who would let her. Someone who wouldn't ask more of her than what she could give on the surface, who never got too close. Someone she could tend and blame all at the same time.

That was what held them together, but that wasn't all.

"I know Lucie is your daughter, too," she said. "But she still needs me. We can't mess her up just because we messed up."

She put the second half of the Devil cookie back on David's plate. She couldn't tell if he was still listening. His intensity was gone, as though the effort was too much to sustain. His forlorn look returned as he finished the second cookie and licked his finger to pick up the remaining crumbs.

She wanted to hate him. She almost could.

"Finish your tea," Flair said.

CHAPTER FIFTEEN

Thursday, October 29

FLAIR WENT INTO the shop before daybreak to do the next day's baking, leaving Lucie's lunch behind on the table with a list of reminders for her day. Cynthia dozed in a chair on the landing at the top of the stairs in case David's tea proved less potent than expected. The rest of Flair's evening the night before had not improved even after getting David stowed away in the attic bedroom. Lucie had come in still arguing for her right to work on the trail stop and gone to bed angry. Flair was hoping she could make up for it with a breakfast delivery.

Callie arrived at 7:30, just in time for Flair to slip out, Teabag at her heels, and head home to make sure Lucie got out on time. They found her heading up the street, walking, to Flair's delight, with one of the girls she recognized from Annabel's visit to the shop days before.

Lucie fluttered a hand, possibly waving her mother off, but Flair was set on handing over the fresh croissant and then assessing what Lucie had with her. Backpack, lunch—"Do you have your sneakers? For gym?"

Lucie looked irritated. "We don't have gym today," she said. "It's Wednesday."

"It's Thursday," Flair said, pointing to the house. "You have just enough time to go back."

Lucie looked at her new friend, who had bent over Teabag and was trying unsuccessfully to pet her while Teabag—who thought every new person planned to pick her up—danced away to hide behind Flair's legs. The girl straightened back up and shrugged. "I can't wait," she said. "I promised Ms. D'Amato I'd talk to her about my report before class."

Lucie gave Flair a look that would have melted a hole through glass before heading back to the house, while the other girl kept going. She could easily have waited—it would only take Lucie a minute if she ran—but that would have made Flair's life too easy. Instead, Flair had ruined Lucie's morning, croissant or not, and would almost certainly hear about it later.

Flair made her way back to the shop, urging Teabag along while the little dog insisted on stopping to sniff the exact same spots she'd stopped at on the way. She could hope for another day as busy as yesterday, but she probably didn't need to rush. She tried to enjoy the walk, the morning sunlight illuminating the colorful leaves of the sweet gum trees that lined the road, the scarecrows leaning in all directions in the yard she was passing, a *Country Living* cover come to life.

Even with Lucie's teenaged angst burning a hole through the ozone behind her, Flair managed to feel almost confident with the situation. David's phone revealed that his irritated colleagues had accepted the reason for his absence, and Flair somehow couldn't feel too bad about the increasingly pissed-off missives from Carly, who seemed to feel she'd been ghosted.

Halloween was in two days. Thanks to the miracle that is overnight shipping, the seasonal clothes Flair had grudgingly ordered after being reminded that Halloween in Rattleboro really wasn't optional had already arrived. Her flowing black maxi dress over a purple-and-black-striped leggings-and-shirt set (really pajamas) was working better than she'd expected. She had a second identical dress and green-and-black-striped pj's to alternate.

Lucie, offered the chance to throw in an order for her own take on Halloween, had shaken her head. "I'm going to be Lydia," she said. "From *Beetlejuice*." Flair didn't really expect her to want matching mother-daughter Halloween looks, but her refusal did mean Flair was debuting her Halloween style solo. She felt even more self-conscious after Jude's words last night.

You're a witch.

And now she looked the part. She adjusted her new witch's hat, nicer than most, with a crown in alternating satin-and-velvet stripes, over the long, loose braids she'd put in her hair. Blondes were always expected to be sexy witches, but Flair had gone hippie instead, more Joni Mitchell than Samantha Stephens.

She felt ridiculous but also pleased. If she had to be a witch hiding in plain sight, at least she made it look good. Flair liked dressing up, always had, and it had been fun to be able to carry the costume to its extreme, which also meant a pair of very practical yet also wildly expensive black boots that zipped up to her knees: waterproof, with comfortable barefoot-style soles suited for the woods and described on the website as for nights on the town after days on the trail. To Flair, they looked like something Billie Eilish might wear to Burning Man, which was pretty much the aesthetic she was going for.

"Flair!" She turned to see Josie, dressed as Catwoman, running up behind her.

"Ooh, I love it." It took an extensive wardrobe of black leather and an amazing figure to pull this off as well as Josie was.

Josie twirled her cat tail and preened. "Thanks. Tomorrow I'm the Black Widow and on the big day, Buffy."

"You put me to shame. I'll be recycling this. I may be sad on November first when I have to pick clothes again." But with any luck, she would also be very, very happy that all of this was over.

"In December you can go full elf."

"As long as I'm still here and everything's okay in December, I just might."

They'd reached the alley behind their shops and Josie pulled Flair into it. "How did it go? Did the tea work?"

"As far as I know, he's still asleep."

"Perfect. Now I need more scoop than you dished last night. What really happened with Jude, and when are you going to see him again?"

Josie alone knew the full story of Flair's last Halloween in Rattleboro. When Josie and Flair had realized that Marie truly meant what she said—she didn't want Flair back in Rattleboro—Flair had been afraid that her friendship with Josie would end. Instead, they'd begun making a point of meeting up in other places—Flair joining Josie when she spent a week studying biomechanical technique with an artist in New Mexico, Josie coming to stay with Flair during the summer she spent at the Culinary Institute of America in upstate New York. If Josie had wished Flair had made a different choice when Marie gave her that ultimatum, she'd never said so.

Flair had spent hours last night turning over what Jude had revealed, imagining the ways things might have been different. If she and Jude had somehow found their way to the truth. If she'd accepted Marie's invitation to stay in Rattleboro for good.

But then she wouldn't have Lucie.

For the past thirteen years, Lucie had been the sun Flair orbited around. Not that she spoiled her daughter—far from it— but where David needed Flair to provide stability he could fight against, Lucie needed that same stability for a different reason, and that was the kind of need that Flair thrived on. She loved creating a safe world for her daughter, loved having her to come home to, loved the way her schedule had to fit around Lucie's. Loved sitting with her to color and draw or finding classes in painting or ceramics they could do together. Loved the way, if Lucie's little soccer team played against a team across town, Lucie was always ready to find a new taco stand or bubble tea shop together. As much as Flair didn't believe in fate with a capital *F*, she couldn't imagine her life without Lucie.

And she couldn't imagine how it would have felt to bring the cards out of hiding and open herself up to their predictions once again. Predictions that led inexorably toward a single end, the one her grandmother had described to her long ago, before she'd had any idea what kind of pain the words held. *We have*

the cards, and we have our daughters, and when it's time, our
daughters take the cards and they leave.

Her striped leggings and witch's hat aside, Flair certainly
wasn't accepting that.

Kids left—of course they did. Parenting was the job where
you were supposed to create your own obsolescence and all
that. That was life. But Lucie was only thirteen. And what
Flair was trying to avoid was fate. Fate with all its crashing
swords and drama and special effects, as produced by the cards
whenever she gave them the slightest chance.

She told Josie everything that had happened last night, from
Jude's complete lack of surprise at Cyn's antics to everything
he'd shared about Renee and their family's supposed curse.
When Flair was finished, Josie put her hands on her hips.

"Renee."

Flair nodded, eyebrows up and lips pursed. "Yep. And I'm
sure she'd be terrified if she saw you like that, Miss Kitty."

"I am a very threatening Catwoman." Josie poked Flair, and
Flair felt a tiny pop, as if Josie had shocked her.

"Did you do that on purpose?"

Josie did it again, and Flair squirmed away. "I don't think
you should do that. You're misusing your power. I can't even
imagine what your mother would say."

"I can't even imagine what we would have been like if we'd
known we could do this when we were kids." Josie put her
pointed finger up to her lips and blew on it, gunslinger style.
"And the person who is misusing her power isn't me. It's Renee. Unless we believe in her family-curse story."

"I'm sure Jude believes it. But I think the only one cursed in that family is her. She's the one who planted the window boxes, too," Flair said.

Josie smacked herself on the forehead. "Of course. She's plants."

"What?"

"When you dropped out of ye olde summer magic school, you missed a lot. I did know Loretta and Renee had magic. Everyone descended from one of the original coven witches might have powers, and what we can do varies. Renee has plants. My mom, too—thus, the magic and amazing teas, and if you ask me nicely, I will share the one that gives you very good dreams. Jude—does he do magic?"

"He didn't say."

"You mean, before you stuck your tongue down his throat and prevented further confidences? Gotcha. There aren't many men with magic. My mom says it skips them, but I think . . . maybe they just never needed it. Never stopped to listen."

"What about you?" Flair had been meaning to ask ever since she'd realized that for Josie, magic had never stopped. Part of her was ashamed that she'd never thought of it, the other part glad that magic hadn't had a chance to mess with their friendship.

"I didn't think I had anything special until I started with the tattooing, and then I realized—the cards are special for you; tattoos are that for me. You know what people want, what they need. I know what they need to remember. Sometimes it's the way a person makes them feel; sometimes it's a moment when they felt most like themselves. Whatever it is, it's a symbol of who they want to be, what they want to keep with them. And then I ink it on them. Boom."

Flair shook her head. "I'm not trying to do anything with the cards," she said. "I don't want to do any of it."

"I'm not sure you have a choice." Josie looked at the time on her phone. "Shoot, I have to go. But you know who does have a choice? Renee. You should tell her to quit it. Tell her you know."

Flair thought of Renee—her scornful look, the disdain with which she looked down, literally, on Flair and always had. And of her clematis, which, even before Flair knew it was enchanted, had seemed as though it might choke her like a boa constrictor just for the hell of it. "I might be scared of Renee," she admitted.

"Renee should be scared of me. Us. I don't know why she has it in for you. But now that we're on to her, she's going to have to stop."

Flair tried to channel Josie's Catwoman attitude when she rounded the corner of the alley and found Jude on Main Street, helping Renee to roll the carts of books she put outside her bookstore every day. A quick glance at Jude and an answering shake of his head told Flair that he hadn't talked to his sister yet, but— as though remembering Flair's hurt when she'd thought he'd been embarrassed to be seen with her in front of his sister—he greeted her warmly. Maybe not as warmly as they'd parted last night, but that was definitely for the best.

Renee didn't greet her at all.

Jude thought Renee was trying to protect him. But the more Flair thought about it, the less likely that seemed. Renee knew Marie. She'd known Flair, too, even if she never talked to her. Which would have meant she knew Flair was a witch. And decided, for reasons of her own, to let Jude think something different.

Flair could only think of one reason for that. Apologies to Teabag, but Renee was a bitch.

Renee rolled her book cart a little too close to Teabag, who leapt back and barked. At that, Renee straightened and seemed to resign herself to conversation.

"Nice familiar," she said, taking in both the dog and Flair's costume. "Maybe you should have gone as Dorothy."

Flair met Renee's eyes. She wanted to tell Renee to back off. She wanted to tell Renee that she knew what Renee had done. But she didn't need Jude to know that she was putting all the blame on his sister. Not yet, anyway.

She put on a bright smile. "I'm all grown-up now," she said. "I don't need a flying house or a bucket of water to handle my fellow witches."

It wasn't the suavest comeback, but the look on Renee's face told Flair she'd been understood.

Jude caught up to Flair as she walked on toward Butter-sweet. "Renee and my mother have me all booked up today," he said. "Now that she has me here, my mom has all kinds of ideas for me. She's kind of walking us around and doing the 'someday all this will be yours' thing."

It was a reminder that Jude, like Flair, had never intended to end up in Rattleboro and that, unlike Flair, he didn't intend to stay. "Well," she said, trying not to sound too invested in it, "maybe she's hoping to get you here more often."

"It's definitely more than that. She has visions of Rattleboro becoming the next Hershey. Jonka factory, Jonka-land. The whole nine yards."

Flair could only imagine that Loretta had been trying to get her son back here for years. "That can't be new," she said.

"No." He tilted his head to look sideways at her as they walked beneath the taco shop's giant sugar Day of the Dead skull. "But it's the first time I've been willing to listen."

Flair looked away, at the glittery sidewalk beneath her feet. When she didn't look at him, Jude hooked his pinkie finger around hers, and a slow warmth spread through her, making her want to lean into him and see what happened next instead of behaving like a proper business owner just steps away from her respectable establishment.

"Some of my memories around this place are changing," he said. "I thought it might be time to consider making some new ones."

She squeezed her pinkie lightly around his, still staring down. "That's about where I am, too," she said.

They reached Buttersweet, and Flair wondered who had added the garland of what looked like classic dotted-icing spiders, ghosts, and bats. She had to admit it was a nice touch. "This is my stop," she said.

"Okay. Today's taken—but I'll look for you tomorrow. Same bat-time?"

"Same bat-place."

A man who could make dumb jokes from an old TV show they would both have seen only in reruns. And who looked better in his jeans than any man had ever looked in a Batman costume. She had to force herself to open the door so she didn't stare after him as he strode away.

CHAPTER SIXTEEN

THINGS MOVED QUICKLY in the shop throughout the day until Flair called to one of her new assistants to suggest that she bring more tarot cookies out from the back and the assistant returned empty-handed.

"I thought we had one more tub," Flair said. The young woman dramatically pulled the lid off the white lidded container Flair had thought held a few dozen cookies.

Point made. Flair spent the afternoon baking rectangles and then, thinking of the last time she'd decorated these cookies, packed them into boxes and headed home after they closed up shop. For this, she'd rather be in her nice, safe kitchen.

She'd just begun to set herself up for work when Teabag hopped up, barking as the door opened and Cynthia pushed David in, then came in after him.

Flair paused as she filled a bag with royal icing. "I thought you were keeping him in the bus for a while?" According to

Cynthia, no one on her team asked questions, ever, about any-thing. If David was weird, well, David was weird, and they would roll with it. Flair, after a brief hesitation, had elected not to argue.

"He's getting annoying," Cynthia said

"I'm getting annoying," repeated David. His expression was cheerful, but Flair thought she detected an edge of something else in his smile.

"He keeps doing that."

"I keep doing that."

Flair, possibly even more annoyed, set down her tools. "Well, he can't be here. Lucie will be home any minute."

"He has to be somewhere. And it can't be the bus."

"I have to be somewhere," said David. This time he didn't smile, and Flair felt a growing nervousness in her stomach.

"Every time he finishes doing whatever I've told him, he gets up, but he doesn't seem to know where to go." She paced around Flair's kitchen, picked up a catalog and moved it to a different place on the counter, shuffled papers around, then, catching sight of the electric teakettle, filled it and switched it on while she talked. "He keeps walking around the table for no reason and messing with things, anything we haven't told him not to touch."

"Who does that remind me of?"

Cyn ignored her. "He goes in and out of the bedroom. Or he stands at the window. And there just isn't room."

"There's a bedroom on the bus?"

"Two, but they're small."

As if that made it less remarkable.

Now that he was here, David wasn't showing any signs of the fidgeting Cynthia had described. He just stood there, looking at Flair. Staring, really.

She watched him for a moment, looked away, then back.

His eyes were still glued to her.

Flair would have been unnerved if she hadn't heard footsteps on the front porch. She leapt up and took David by the hand, looking around frantically before pushing him out the back door in front of her and then pulling it shut quickly in Teabag's annoyed face. Inside, she heard Lucie come in and her mother deny any knowledge of Flair's whereabouts—despite the fact that there were undecorated cookies and icing bags spread out across the table—while Lucie's voice rose in complaint, demanding to know if Cynthia knew why Flair was "so mean all of a sudden."

"This is your fault," Flair muttered in her mother's direction. David repeated her words, also softly. "This is your fault."

She turned and found him still looking at her. "Oh no," she said, staring him down. "This is *your* fault. You told Lucie you'd come get her. You told Lucie she could come home."

"Come home," David repeated, gazing at her.

She shook her head, no longer sure who was talking to who.

"I'm not coming home," she said. "And you're not taking Lucie. You wouldn't have the faintest idea of how to take care of her." And she didn't have the faintest idea what to do with him. She looked around and her eyes settled on Josie's garage, which had David's Lincoln in it.

"Look," she said, unsure how much he understood. "I'm going to put you in your car, and Cyn's going to bring you a laptop, and you're going to watch all of season three of *Master-Chef*, and then you're going to go to sleep in the back seat. And you're not going to repeat any of that. Or say anything."

He didn't say anything, but he didn't look happy, either.

"It's just two more nights," Flair said, as much to herself as to him as she tugged him along behind her. "Two more nights."

By the time she had David settled, Lucie had disappeared upstairs. Cyn objected to giving up her laptop, so Flair brought David hers, ignoring his disgruntled expression, then returned to the kitchen and settled in to decorate cookies. Without magical intervention, the work took a lot longer, but as usual, she got into a groove, her earbuds in and an audiobook on. When Lucie came up behind her sometime later, Flair jumped in her chair, hitting her leg on the table and sending a strand of black icing shooting across the Sun card.

Lucie, well trained in this if nothing else, waited for her mother to lift off the mistake with a toothpick before plunking down in a chair.

"I keep texting Dad," she said. "And calling him. And getting nothing. And I know he gets busy, but . . ."

Flair, who had already taken another cookie and begun piping in the frame, started to reply flippantly—Lucie's dad had never been the most reliable of correspondents—when she looked up at Lucie's face and saw real concern and disappointment there.

She should have thought of this. She lifted the piping bag, stopping for a moment, then continued. She didn't want Lucie to think there was a reason to worry. "I've heard from him. He's probably just busy." She pointed to the stove. "I made mac and cheese."

Lucie wrapped her arms around herself and stared down at her lap, not answering, and Flair thought she was going to say something else. Instead, she leaned forward and looked at what Flair was doing.

"Which one is that going to be?"

"The Hermit. The one that's just the one person in a robe."

"Oh."

Flair returned to her work, but she could feel Lucie's eyes on her. She looked up at her daughter. "What?"

"Will you teach me? What they mean?"

Flair stared down at the cookie in front of her again. She'd mostly convinced herself that the cookies she'd made, while prone to luring her into reading them for people and possibly trying to get her attention in strange ways, were harmless, a manifestation of her return to Rattleboro that she could live with. But that didn't mean Lucie needed to be contemplating the many things the arrival of the High Priestess could signify in your life.

But why not? Flair had never asked herself what she would do if Lucie showed up with a box of normal tarot cards, and she probably should have. Even kids whose mothers and grandmothers were nice, ordinary lawyers and doctors dabbled in such things, and Lucie would probably have been no different even if she'd never left St. Louis.

Lucie was staring at her, waiting for an answer, and Flair made up her mind. She'd loved reading tarot cards once, and there were all kinds of tarot cards in the world besides the particular set whose determined presence in Flair's life was causing so much trouble. Regular cards didn't give anyone magic and couldn't predict anyone's fate. It was her family's tarot cards, painted by Alice Hardwicke, that she wanted to avoid—and Cynthia was probably happiest if Flair never touched them again.

As if summoned by the thought, Cyn put her head around the door. "I need tea," she said. "We're out." She came all the way in and looked at the hundreds of cookies spread out on the table and Flair's drying racks. "What's going on?"

"Lucie wants me to teach her to read tarot cards," Flair said.

"Cool!" Cynthia put the kettle on and then sat down at the table, picking up a perfectly executed Devil card and biting into it before Flair could object. "These are great. Lucie told me about them, but I hadn't seen them yet. Like a blast from the past."

Flair glared at her over the reference to their history, and the waste of a cookie she could have sold. "There's a whole tray of mistakes over there," she said, pointing.

"The pretty ones taste better," Cynthia said, licking crumbs from her fingers. But she got up and took a smudged Judgement from the tray. Flair savored the tiny irony. Judgement, the card that reminded you to think before acting, crunched between the teeth of someone who would have *I leapt, then I looked* on her tombstone.

Lucie shifted her gaze from her grandmother to her mother. "So you will?"

"I will," Flair said.

Lucie smiled at her, the first genuine smile Flair had seen from her in days, and hugged Flair, carefully avoiding the cookies. Flair reached up from her seat to return the hug. This was definitely the right call. "Take a bowl of pasta and sit."

"We will," said Cyn, sitting down herself as Flair groaned. "This will be fun."

Lucie looked at her mother anxiously, as if guessing that Cyn's presence might put Flair off the project—but this was exactly why she should be the one to teach Lucie how tarot cards—ordinary tarot cards, the ones Lucie could find anywhere—worked before Cyn took it on herself to demonstrate the many ways they could be used to justify messing up your own life. And Lucie was here, in the kitchen, glad to be with Flair again. Flair would have agreed to almost anything for that.

"The first thing you should know," said Cynthia before Flair could stop her, "is that the cards aren't directions. They're possibilities. For example, the Wheel of Fortune"—she pointed to the cookie Flair had just finished—"reminds us that change is the only constant. Or it suggests that change is coming into a person's life, or maybe encourages us to welcome inevitable change, or accept it, or stop resisting it."

Flair stared in surprise at the woman who had definitely once used this exact card as a specific demand that they go spend the money that carefully-budgeting-Flair had allotted for groceries to buy lottery tickets instead. And then when they didn't win even enough to cover their cost, claimed she and Flair had been meant to be in that gas station parking lot, because Cyn met a trucker who bought them dinner and told her about a club that was hiring in Phoenix.

Flair reminded her of that now, and her face lit up. "Jerry! Do you know I still know him on Facebook? He listens to all my books on audio."

Flair pushed the thought of her mother's more extreme sex

scenes as audio out of her head along with the certain knowledge that her mother had not been this judicious about her
readings back in the day and jumped in.

"Grand is right," she said, as much as it pained her. "We
share the meanings we see in the cards, and the person we're
reading for interprets. Like this."

She moved some cookies out of the way with her gloved
hands and set a clean piece of parchment paper in front of Lucie, who lifted the bowl of pasta she'd taken from the pot on the
stove and held it in her hands, out of the way. "Past, present,
future," she said as she picked cookies to represent each for her
daughter. The Fool, for beginnings. The Chariot, for overcoming obstacles. And the World, for a joyful and successful future.

She laid her choices in front of Lucie, put her finger above
the first cookie, and blinked.

That was not the Fool. Cynthia was looking at her in surprise as Flair's hand hovered above the Tower. She swallowed
and looked at the cookies beside it, the cookies she had set out
to represent Lucie's past, present, and future.

The Tower. Upheaval, change. The Moon. Secrecy, anxiety,
fear. The Hanged Man. A surrender of all that was familiar to
accept an uncontrollable fate.

Those were not the cookies she had chosen.

The words on her tongue stuttered as a stillness overtook
Flair and Cynthia, while Lucie watched them both, looking
down at the cookies, then back to them.

"Did you forget? I could look them up—"

"No!" Flair and Cynthia both spoke at once, and Flair
pressed her shaking hands into her lap. Lucie couldn't do that.
And the cookies—why had this happened? Flair wasn't trying

to do a reading. She didn't want to do a reading. And these were her cookies. The tarot cards—the real cards—were safely with Cynthia.

Except that apparently they weren't. They were here, trying to get their claws into Lucie, and Flair wasn't going to let them. But she needed to say something.

"You never look the meanings up," Cyn said, and although normally she disagreed, Flair nodded gratefully. Lucie should not look these up.

"Exactly."

"But you told people in the shop to look them up. There's a website."

"There are lots of websites," Flair said. "And most of them are wrong, and awful. And . . . we don't look the cards up. In our family. We just read them."

"But how do I know what they mean?"

"You look at the names," Flair said. "And the pictures. Then it just comes to you."

It had better not come to Lucie. Flair glanced at her daughter, taking a bite of pasta from the bowl in her hand, and saw that at least she didn't seem to see anything amiss in the cookies in front of her.

Lucie looked at the cookies spread all around them. "But I don't even know what a"—she stumbled over the word—"hierophant is. And the Moon could be anything. What do these even mean?"

Flair stared down at the cookies that had appeared for her daughter. As she watched, the icing moon blinked itself out of the sky, leaving nothing behind. As frightening as it had been when the cookies first revealed their tendency to be more than just cookies, what was in front of her now was terrifying.

But she couldn't say that. Wouldn't say that. Wouldn't accept it. She shut out the emotions and impressions the cards were trying to force on her. Chaos, loss, fear. The kind of fear that eclipsed everything else.

She thought quickly, scrambling for words. "The Tower." That was easy, at least. "It's a card of change and upheaval, and you've had plenty of that this year."

Lucie nodded. Flair struggled to keep her voice light. "The Moon . . . suggests you're looking at both sides of things," she said. "Day and night. Light and dark. It's an openness to new ideas."

She felt Cynthia's eyes on her at that questionable interpretation of a card that even at its best demanded a reckoning with the shadows, but she kept her own eyes resolutely fixed on Lucie, avoiding the sight of the cookies arrayed in front of her daughter. "The Hanged Man seems awful, but it doesn't have to be," she said. That at least was generally true, but even without looking, the image she'd seen didn't leave her. The hanged man choosing to give up. Surrendering, letting fate make the next call, and entering the darkness.

No. Flair rejected this, all of it. She would not be ambushed in this way by her own creations. She forced herself to laugh.

"It's not a very exciting card for the future—sorry. A lot of the time, the Hanged Man just means waiting for things to happen. I should have grabbed something else for an example."

"Okay." As Lucie considered the cookies, Flair asked herself again if Lucie saw anything other than icing. She didn't think so. How many times had she looked at her daughter and wondered if Lucie could do the little things Flair and Josie had been so delighted to learn, and desperately hoped not? You could light candles with matches instead of magic. But once you could see the kinds of things the cards insisted on showing Flair, you couldn't unsee them.

Flair was an adult now, though. Maybe she couldn't unsee, but she no longer had to accept the demands and pronouncement of any cards, not even these. She didn't have to just watch things happen. She could change them. Like Cynthia said, what the cards revealed were just possibilities.

Possibilities she could protect Lucie from if she tried. As if reading Flair's thoughts, Teabag left her bed and came to lie under Lucie's chair with a possessive snort.

"I wanted to take cookies to Annabel's party, though. And kind of, like, read for people. Like you did when Annabel came into the bakery." Lucie set her bowl on the floor, and Teabag bounced up and began licking it happily.

Flair blinked as she pulled herself out of her thoughts and back into the present moment.

"Every card has a lot of meanings," Flair said, willing herself to believe it. "There is no fate that the cards foretell. It's all up to you."

"Mom." Lucie dragged out the word, clearly frustrated. "Nobody wants to hear that. That's no fun."

Fun. Right.

Cynthia, who had been watching Flair with the same worried expression Flair was trying to keep off her own face, took over.

"They do have some symbolic meanings," she said. "Most of them aren't hard—like, the Sun is a bright new dawn, Justice is wanting justice or feeling like you can't get it. Just try to remember the weird ones. Like, the Hierophant can represent someone very conventional, or suggest that someone is avoiding convention."

"So every card can mean what it means or the opposite?"

They could, thought Flair. Of course they could.

"Pretty much," Cynthia said after Flair didn't respond. "That's the fun of it. You're the conduit. The translator. You watch your friends and see how they react, and then you lean into whatever resonated."

That sounded more like the old Cynthia. Flair managed to agree. "The idea isn't that we tell anyone what anything means. Even when it's just for fun. The idea is that they find meaning themselves."

They spent the next hour coaching Lucie through the major arcana, quizzing her, encouraging her to see both sides of tough cards like the Devil and those that seemed to bring only glory, like the Magician. Lucie took up a piping bag and helped Flair finish the last of the cards with a steady hand, while Cynthia made her usual comments about never being able to do anything that required that much patience, and Flair found herself less annoyed by them than she usually was. Lucie might remind Flair of her mother in many ways, but at least she could sit still long enough to ice a cookie.

The remaining cookies behaved, the images as flat and stylized as they should be, the only movement coming from the toothpicks they used to add swirls to the icing. Flair was grateful for that small favor. Flair's hands steadied as well, soothed by the familiar motion. The strings that had tightened around her heart released, and her mind stopped spinning.

She felt as if she'd been warned. Alice's tarot cards wouldn't rest until they had all three Hardwicke women under their spell again. Flair was not going to let that happen.

When they finished, Lucie hovered over the cookies, admiring their work, then grinned mischievously.

"I think I've got this." She pulled down the Hierophant, the Wheel, and the Empress with her gloved hand. "There you go, Mom. You were bossy and demanding. And now you're realizing that your kid is growing up! So here you are in the future, treating her as an equal. Oh, and buying her a car."

Flair laughed, and her mother did, too. "Sure, manifest your destiny," Flair said to her daughter. "If you build it, they will come."

If only it worked that way.

CHAPTER SEVENTEEN

LUCIE WENT UPSTAIRS when Flair tackled the dishes. Cynthia watched her go, waiting until they heard the sound of a door shutting upstairs before she spoke.

"That's not what you saw," she said.

Flair scrubbed hard at an already-clean frosting bowl. "It is," she said. "You said it yourself. Even cards that look bad can have perfectly fine meanings."

"They can, yes. But perfectly fine meanings don't make you turn puke green and sound like someone's strangling you. Why did you even pick those cards?"

Flair put the bowl down and stared into the sink, wondering how much she was going to regret sharing this. "I didn't."

She looked up as Cynthia, who'd wandered back to the tray of cookie mistakes, turned to stare at her. "What do you mean, you didn't? You picked them. I saw you."

"When I picked them, that's not what they were. I picked the Fool, the Chariot, and the World. And then they changed."

Cyn looked thoughtful. "Okay," she finally said. "That makes sense."

"Does it? Then we are using a very different definition of that phrase."

"We always were," Cynthia said. "Of course you chose happy cookies for Lucie. But you don't choose. You know that."

As upset as she was, Flair couldn't let that pass without comment. "You chose all the time," she said. "How about when you picked the Six of Wands and got promoted to manager at the Bubbler? Or when you used the Four of Swords and we moved down to Saint Thomas? Or how about the Lovers? I think you wore that card out."

"That's different magic," Cynthia said. "And it never really works."

True. That promotion had cost Cynthia the only friend she'd made in Wisconsin. Getting to Saint Thomas had been one thing, but getting off the island took months of both of them cleaning hotel rooms. And Cynthia's romantic history was a thing best left undiscussed.

Playing with the cards in that way always backfired, and it had backfired on Flair, too, when she'd invoked the Devil on David. Before she realized her cookies, like the cards they came from, had their own power.

"I know that," Flair said. "I didn't realize you did."

"It's just so tempting. But no."

"Okay, you've grown up. Point made. But I wasn't trying to choose Lucie's cards. I was just making an example. With cookies."

"The cards wanted to be read," Cynthia said. "They always do."

"They're cookies," Flair said loudly. "Cookies."

"Are you talking to me or them?"

Flair gave up on her dishwashing and made herself a mug of tea. "I don't even know," she said.

"What did you see? Really?"

"Nothing." Lucie confused and torn and making desperate choices out of fear. Lucie letting herself be taken away. But Flair wasn't going to speak those possibilities into being.

"Bad nothing, I take it."

Flair nodded.

Cynthia turned her mug in her hands, looking down into it, although thanks to Flair's insistence on tea in bags, there was nothing to see. "You should tell her."

"Tell her what? That my cookies change into other cookies? Or that I see predictions in cards we just told her don't foretell the future? Not helpful. None of it."

"Not that specifically," Cynthia said. "But just . . . about things in general. The cards. Marie. What the cards let us do."

"None of which I can explain," Flair said.

"Not everything has an explanation. Maybe if you'd understood that better when you were younger, you wouldn't be so frightened of it now."

Or maybe she would be even more frightened. "Don't you think that was exactly my problem? That I was always surrounded by things I didn't understand, and you were always telling me to trust you right before you packed up and dragged me off somewhere?"

"I was figuring myself out. Was it really that awful?"

Flair thought of her younger self gradually realizing that whenever Cynthia said, "Trust me," it meant that she shouldn't—and also that she didn't really have any choice. "It was," she said firmly.

Cyn stared down at her hands. "I was where I was. I did what I did." She brightened. "And here we are. So that can only be a good thing, right?"

There was no point in getting into it. "Here is a mess," Flair said. "Telling Lucie right now would only make things worse."

"She has to know sometime."

Maybe. "I'll tell her. Later. When everything is back under control."

"When will that be?" Her mother laughed. "It's much better to learn to ride the surf than try to tame it."

"That is your motto, not mine. How about we keep Lucie out of the ocean entirely, okay? She's thirteen. Middle school is deep enough."

"Which is exactly the age when you should start figuring out how to swim."

Flair groaned. "Enough with the metaphor. I'm not worrying her. Not now."

"Fine." Cynthia had chosen a slightly wonky Magician cookie, and she nibbled at the edge. After a moment, she gestured to the three cookies Flair had put out for Lucie, still where they'd left them.

"How bad was it?"

As bad as anything the real cards had ever shown her. Flair separated the three images and sorted them back where they belonged, hoping the vision she'd seen would dissipate, but her fears remained. The more Flair thought about what she'd seen, the worse it seemed, and the harder to understand.

"Bad," she said simply. She sat back down, dropping her hands into her lap. "Really bad."

Cynthia's expression was sympathetic as she waited to see if Flair would go on, for once not seeming as though she was going to rush off or chide Flair further for her failure to surf the waves or whatever. As much as Flair wanted to believe tonight had changed something between her and Lucie, helped them to get back to where they belonged, she couldn't. Lucie still wanted to leave her, and Lucie could—and there was something about the whole situation that called that dark, foreboding series of cards into place. Even Cynthia wouldn't want to just roll with that.

"Lucie wants to go live with David," Flair said. "And what I saw—if she does, it will be awful. She's in danger." Flair gulped back a sob, which came partly from her fears for Lucie and partly from admitting to her mother that she, too, had failed. That to Lucie, the life Flair had given her was awful enough for her to seize any alternative, just as Flair had once done. "She hates me."

Cynthia gazed at her daughter, and Flair thought she saw the glitter of tears in her mother's eyes as well. "Oh, Flair," she said. "I'm sorry." She put her cookie down on the table and started rummaging through the pocket of the embroidered duster she was wearing over her usual flowing pants and tunic.

"Here." She set the box containing the deck of tarot cards in front of Flair.

Flair recoiled, leaning back so hard that the front legs of her chair lifted slightly and came down with a thump that made Teabag jump up from her bed. The cards scared her.

And Cynthia had wanted the cards, and the magic they gave her, for so long. If she was willing to give them up for Flair, she must sense how bad things were becoming—and feel guilty about it.

Flair didn't want what Cyn was offering, but she couldn't let her mother go on thinking this was all her fault. "I can't take them," she said. "I don't even want to. And this thing with David isn't just you. I had my cookies, and I was pretending to read for him." Her eyes filled with tears of frustration. "He wasn't even there. And they weren't cards. But you had the cards at the same time—"

"Of course." A look of understanding crossed Cynthia's face, and she reached out a finger to trace it along the box of cards but didn't pick them up. "I should have known."

Flair heard the disappointment in her mother's voice as Cynthia went on.

"This whole time, they've wanted to be with you. Ever since I took them from your apartment. Whenever I try to read them, I can only see the Wheel." Her expression grew stern. "You have to take them, Flair. They're yours. They want the cycle to continue."

Whatever the cards thought they knew about her future, Flair didn't want to hear. She wanted the cards to stay with her mother. And she wanted her mother to stay with her.

"I don't know what to do," Flair said, and a hiccupping sob came out with the words. "They're yours. I won't read them."

"Then don't read them. That's not all they're for."

"I don't want their help," Flair said fiercely, pushing the box away. "I want yours."

Cynthia's expression softened. She hesitated, as though considering reaching for Flair, and Flair wished that she would, but instead Cyn straightened her shoulders and took a step backward, away from the cards and from Flair.

Flair tensed, fearful. This was it. She was going to be on her own.

But Cyn smiled, and in her voice, Flair heard more understanding than she ever had before. "You have it," she said. "I'm not going anywhere. Neither are they." She pointed to the deck. "I know you blame the cards for the past," she said. "But you need them now. I don't think either of us fully understands what's happening. With David or Lucie. The cards will give you the power to protect what's important to you."

Those were not the cards Flair knew. "But when you had the cards, that's not what happened. Not at all."

For the first time, Flair thought she saw some regret in Cynthia's face. "You have to know what's important first," she said as she walked to the door. "I hope you do."

And then she was gone, leaving the cards on the table along with her tea and the half-eaten cookie.

Flair stared after her for a moment before she picked the mug up and carried it to the sink, then returned for Lucie's bowl, still under her seat. Teabag looked at her, hoping for more pasta, but put her head back on her paws as Flair put bowl and pot into the sink as well. The cards sat on the table quietly. The box didn't glow, or clatter against the surface, or try to draw Flair's attention. In Flair's mind, the tarot deck it contained had become the bogeyman.

But according to her mother, it was something entirely different.

She took up the little wooden box. It was clearly handmade

by someone, its sides a little uneven, the gloss worn away in precisely the spots her hands landed as she cradled it. She used one thumb to push aside the tiny iron claw that held it shut, then eased it open, tilting the cards out. The Wheel of Fortune, faceup, was on top.

Flair slid her mother's card into the deck but didn't turn over one for herself. She wasn't sure she was ready to. And she had no urge to call fire from the air or draw water from the ground.

But she did know what was important. Lucie. Their life here. The peace she felt when the shop was buzzing with people enjoying what she had to offer them. Even the hope she felt when she looked into Jude's eyes. If the cards could help her protect all that, she had to give them a chance.

She replaced them in their box and slid it into the pocket of the long black dress she was still wearing. She'd never imagined a time when her mother would be willing to give her the cards. Or when she would be willing to take them.

The kitchen was a mess. She returned to the sink, washing and drying the dishes, returning them to their places. The cookies had to dry, but she could at least tidy up a little. Line up the drying racks. Wipe away the crumbs.

Flair picked up the cookie her mother had left on the table. Cyn had eaten away most of the magician's gown, leaving a face and the hand holding a rather smeared wand. There was magic there, yes. But also determination. Resourcefulness.

Flair had those. And in her own way, so did Cynthia.

Flair would use the cards to protect her world if she had to. Even if it meant using magic. She gazed at the cookie. *Are you with me, Magician?*

The slightly wonky wand, at Flair's invitation, waved, and Flair felt just slightly less alone.

Two more days. Two days of cookie tarot cards and David and Halloween madness and then all this would be over.

She climbed the stairs to her room, Teabag at her heels, and tapped on Lucie's door, calling her name as she opened it.

Lucie had fallen asleep sprawled on top of her covers. Her collection of stuffed animals and her beloved doll were lined up against the wall, except for Lizzy the green lizard that had always been her favorite, which was tucked under her cheek. The sight made Flair sigh for tiny Lucie, who'd carried Lizzy everywhere. The one thing David had always been good at was knowing when Lizzy had been accidentally left behind and producing her like a genie when Lucie noticed the toy's absence.

Flair pulled the covers out from under her sleeping daughter and rolled her away from the edge of the bed, retrieving Lucie's phone from where it seemed to have fallen from her hand, which was just slightly less charming. Unlike Lucie, the phone hadn't gone to sleep yet. Flair glanced at the screen and saw that Lucie had been texting David.

Lucie's lonely texts filled two screens. She seemed to have stopped asking David where he was and instead to be checking in, hoping for a response.

someone named Annabel asked me to a party and I'm going

this is funny, followed by a picture of one of Josie's yard tombstones: IF YOU ARE READING THIS, YOU SHOULD GET A LIFE

mom and grand taught me to read tarot cards tonight it was fun

miss you

David had never been the greatest dad, but he wouldn't

leave Lucie texting him funny pictures without at least replying with a thumbs-up. Once again, Flair felt Lucie's sorrow over all her dad couldn't give her—except now it was partly Flair's fault. She wanted to keep Lucie in Rattleboro, not crush her spirit.

She plugged Lucie's phone in, which was probably more than Lucie would have remembered to do, and went into her own room, where Teabag was already asleep. She looked out the window and saw that Josie's garage was dark and silent. Either her mother had dealt with David, or he'd fallen asleep, and it was fine either way. She took the tarot cards out of her pocket and put them on the bedside table, next to David's phone.

David would have answered Lucie. This wasn't fair, and while Flair wasn't overly concerned about being fair to David, Lucie didn't deserve to suffer. She picked up his phone and added a *haha!* to the picture of the tombstone and a heart to *miss you.*

I miss you too, she typed. *I am in the Ozarks. No reception*

That was better than nothing.

She put the phone down. Picked it up again. Put it down.

She probably shouldn't.

She picked up the phone again.

glad you're going to a party, she wrote. *have fun*

She pressed send. But that didn't seem like enough.

it's good you're settling in. I think you'll be happier there than you would be here

This was how he was going to feel when he woke up—Flair would make sure of it. He was going to be a fine weekend dad. Saturdays, anyway. During the day.

It wouldn't hurt to ease Lucie into it.

She thought about that for a minute.

you belong with your mom

There. That would help. She was sure she'd read somewhere that when kids were going through a divorce, they needed the security of knowing what to expect. Of course Lucie was probably feeling a little fear. Not like the fear Flair had seen in the cookie cards, but some. They'd changed things up on her, and even if it turned out for the best, nobody liked change.

It would be easier when all of this was over. For all three of them.

CHAPTER EIGHTEEN

Friday, October 30

AFTER LAST NIGHT, Flair thought she was ready for anything. Or at least as ready as she could be. She had a plan; she had—warily—the cards and their power. She had her mother on her side and her kid once again under her wing, she was wearing her tough-girl witch costume, and she felt ready to rumble.

But she was not prepared for this.

At any other moment it would be funny. And definitely charming. When she was young and still reading tarot, she'd always liked it when she helped people find some happiness. But if handing someone the Lovers was always going to result in the kind of PDA going on at the corner table now, Flair was going to purge the case of that card.

The couple, who'd come in as friends, seemed to have discovered that they'd harbored a hidden passion for one another for years. Many years, since his Kingsman costume came with a cane he evidently needed and the vintage Chanel she wore with her Anna Wintour glasses and wig fit her too perfectly to have come from the RealReal.

But if they didn't stop gazing into each other's eyes—and intertwining both hands above the table and feet below—Flair, who was feeling more than a little cynical, was going to have to ask them to go. She might have to purge the Wheel of Fortune, too. She'd just overheard someone loudly quitting their job by phone on the way out of the bakery. She found it nerve-racking enough to carry her family's tarot cards around without having to deal with how the real cards amplified the effect of every cookie she served. The Star, at least, seemed to provide mercifully quiet inspiration for the person tapping away at a laptop.

She'd wanted to leave the cards at home. She didn't need them here. Lucie had gone to school in a foul mood, muttering that a town that took Halloween this seriously ought to give them the Friday before off. David was in the woods with her mother, who'd decided to put his ability to follow instructions to good use.

But every time she tried to leave the cards behind, Flair found herself drawn back to them. If she put them in a kitchen drawer, an opened fridge would beep until she returned, and keep doing it no matter how firmly Flair closed the door until she put the cards back in her pocket. If she tried to leave them in her bedroom, Teabag would refuse to leave, and Flair could tell by the gleam in the little dog's eyes that if she left her alone with the cards, she'd pee on the bed.

So the cards stayed with Flair, and she had to admit their energy was better than coffee. They made everything feel easier, including serving tarot cookies with an outsized effect on their recipients and also—ahem—moving those recipients along.

At the sound of Flair's voice, the couple pulled apart and left quickly. Jude looked after them as he came through the door. "I'll have what they're having?"

Flair shook her head. "Here," she said. "Have a nice muffin." She stepped away from the pastry case, gesturing to Callie to trade places with her. The tarot cards had had enough fun for one day.

"I came in to suggest dinner," Jude said.

"Tonight? Halloween eve? Don't you have work to do, Candyman?"

"No, but you have accurately predicted my costume."

Flair thought about that for a minute. "Gene Wilder, Johnny Depp, or with a hook for a hand?"

"Depends on my mood," Jude said. "I vary it every year. So, dinner? The diner's open—I checked."

"I really shouldn't." She put the milk jug under the steamer and pressed the switch, then realized, as hot, damp air burst out around her hand, that she'd forgotten the milk. She cursed and dropped the pitcher and saw that Jude was smiling. "Stop it. You're distracting me."

She filled the pitcher with milk and pushed it under the steamer, then poured the milk over the espresso and handed the cup to Jude.

"You know I didn't order a coffee, right?"

Flair felt a deep flush wash over her face and chest. She snatched it back. "Well, someone did." She looked around, but the shop was quiet for the first time that morning, and there was no one besides Jude in front of the counter.

"Actually, I guess I made that for you."

"Thank you." He took it carefully. "Perhaps a good meal would help with your attention difficulties?"

She had to laugh at his mock pacifying tone. She wanted to go, but there was just flat-out too much to do before tomorrow and way too much to think about. "I have to go meet my mom, and yours, in the woods so they can brief me on the trail. And then there is so much to bake for the weekend." And there was David to keep under lock and key. One more night.

"I need to go to the woods and suss out my location, too. How about if I give you a ride this afternoon, and then we come back here and I'm your sous-chef for the night?"

"I want to," she said slowly, charmed by his willingness to put himself in her hands—and while he might be a huge deal in the candy world now, he must know the kind of grunt work that went into making a weekend's worth of pastries. If it weren't for everything else that was happening, she wouldn't hesitate to take him up on it. But as it was . . .

"That is less enthusiasm than I was hoping for."

"Sorry sorry sorry." He looked disappointed. They'd lost so much time already. To David. To the false ideas she and Jude both had about each other. To all the ways the cards and magic insinuated themselves into her life and turned it upside down. It wasn't fair.

Flair made up her mind. "I would love that," she said. She would, too. She wanted to give Jude her full attention, like the couple who'd just left—well, not quite like that. But she would much prefer to think about Jude than everything else she'd listed. He was wearing a different version of yesterday's checked shirt and probably the very same jeans, which made her think about him taking his jeans off and leaving them on the floor until he rolled out of bed and grabbed them again the next morning.

She should not be thinking about rolling out of bed with Jude. And she certainly should not be thinking about getting into one—she shook her head, distracted, and the way he was looking at her made her wonder if he might, just maybe, be thinking something similar. She blushed and pulled her eyes away from his.

"I will let you focus on your milk steaming," he said as the bell on the door jingled and Austin Powers came in, accompanied by Dr. Evil.

"Come back at three," she said. "I'll be done then."

She did finish at three, but she hadn't counted on Lucie finishing school at three, too, and being determined to see what her grandmother was planning on the trail. Her mood hadn't improved, either, and even Flair's frothiest mocha and the cinnamon croissant toast that she made only for Lucie didn't help. The happy, cooperative Dr. Jekyll–Lucie of last night was gone again, and Lucie's version of Mr. Hyde was back.

Lucie didn't even look up from her phone when Flair brought the drink and croissant toast over. "I'm not hungry," she said. "Just tell me when you're ready to leave."

When Jude pulled into the diagonal loading-zone space out front and waved, Not Hungry had managed to clean her plate and was licking her finger to pick up crumbs, but she was still salty at the discovery that they'd be riding with Jude. "I thought he had a different car," she said. Flair was confused until she remembered trying to pass off David's Lincoln as

Jude's. "This is probably Loretta's," she murmured as they left the shop.

Fortunately, Lucie was too busy conveying her general dissatisfaction with her mother to follow up, and she sat silently in the back seat as they drove to the parking lot that served the trails in the woods where Rattlebones took place. The lot was roped off by volunteers who recognized Jude but questioned Flair and Lucie. "They're with Cyn Starkley and her team," Jude said through his rolled-down window.

"Strict," Flair said.

"My mother takes trail secrecy very seriously," Jude said. He put an arm over the seat behind Flair and turned back to Lucie. "So no talking about anything you see, okay?"

Flair thought Lucie looked pleased by the prospect of being in behind the scenes, but she still crossed her arms over her chest and shrugged. "Whatever."

As they got out of the car on the passenger side, Flair grabbed her daughter by the arm. "You could be polite," she said. "He didn't have to bring us out here."

"You have a car," Lucie said. "You heard him. We're on Grand's team. We don't need him."

"Still. At least be nicer."

"How about you be less nice?" Lucie yanked her arm away. "You're still married. To Dad."

"You know your dad and I haven't been together in a while. And besides, this isn't— Jude is an old friend. And I wouldn't know where anything is out here without him. That's all."

"Why don't you tell him that?"

They'd been arguing long enough for Jude to have walked

ahead. He was waiting for them at the trail's entrance. Flair caught up, Lucie trailing behind, and if Jude had heard anything, he ignored it. "This isn't where the travelers will go in. That's up at the edge of our family's land. There's a bunch of tents there."

Flair knew this, too, but she stayed silent and let Jude explain for Lucie's benefit.

"Groups go in two or three at a time. It's a long walk, and the stops are spaced so there's a lot of time in between to freak yourself out."

Lucie seemed to be interested in spite of herself. "Do they have to pay?"

"It's a donation thing. And tickets are a lottery, because it's so popular and we only do one night."

"And your mom—Loretta—she arranges it all?"

"With my sister and a bunch of other people from Rattleboro. It's a nonprofit now. Very official. Our family's always run it."

"Cool."

They'd dodged around one group setting up what looked like coffins, and Flair could hear her mother's voice in the distance. Without looking at Jude or Lucie, she ran ahead. Cyn had finally answered her phone and had supposedly gotten David out of the way, but Flair wasn't sure her mother thought it was as important as Flair did.

Thankfully there was no sign of David. Instead, there were scaffoldings of two-by-fours going up into three oak trees around the tiny clearing. A tightrope stretched from one leg of the triangle to another, and on the other side, a trapeze dangled from wires that were nearly invisible even in daylight.

Jude and Lucie caught up to her, and Jude surveyed the setup, clearly impressed. "It almost doesn't matter what she does," he said. "Anything up there like that is going to scare the crap out of people."

Flair turned in a circle, taking it in, as someone began to manipulate one of the stick-figure marionettes, raising it up and beckoning with one of its twiggy arms.

Lucie took a step closer to Flair. "That's really creepy," she said.

"It is," Jude agreed. "I'm not sure that's what I was picturing, but I can definitely imagine seeing it in my nightmares." He walked over to examine the marionette more closely and fell into conversation with Alto, Cyn's chief of staff.

Flair was a gifted organizer, capable of creative flights, but her mother was a visionary. Cyn never hesitated to think big, which had come back to bite her a thousand times before, but it was clear she'd found her groove. Flair spotted her mother waving her arms around as she described how her production would work to Loretta, who, Flair was pleased to see, seemed to be appreciating it. They might need Loretta's help with David, but at least Cyn was holding up their side of the bargain with her efforts.

"They come in there," Cyn was saying as Flair and Lucie came up beside her. She pointed to a gap in the trees. "And there's a fire there, in the middle, that seems like it's all the light, although really we have lights set up to focus attention on the right things."

"Marvelous!" Loretta, with Pamela beside her, was looking up, down, and all around and shaking her head. "I've never seen anything like this."

"And then Danae comes out on the tightrope." Cyn pointed to a figure in harlequin tights, who waved. "And then the marionettes come up. Flair and Josie move in behind the travelers, so they go the right way. Or I might put Flair in the middle, kind of conducting."

Lucie was listening intently. "I could do that," she said.

Flair, behind her, began shaking her head intensely at her mother, who didn't seem to be rejecting the idea.

"Or not," Cynthia said, catching sight of Flair. Lucie immediately turned to glare at her mother.

"I know this is you," she said. "Grand would let me."

"You can't," Flair said, looking around and settling on Pamela as her best possible ally. "The high school does its own thing."

"I'm not even in the high school."

"Eighth graders do it, too," Flair said. "It's a tradition."

"Honestly, Annabel would kill to be out here," Pamela said. "But then I'd have to deal with her little brothers wanting to do the same thing."

"There is no way Lucie is doing this," Flair said, her voice louder than she'd intended and certainly angrier. It was the only thing Flair was absolutely certain about. Lucie, whose present—according to the cookies—might become increasingly frightening and whose future held the possibility that she would lose herself completely, wasn't going to be anywhere near whatever they ended up having to do out here to change David back, no matter how much she thought she wanted to.

Lucie put her hands on her hips. "Why do you only want me to do stupid kid things if you want me to stay here so much?

I don't even see why you care." She was clearly holding back tears. "It's not fair," she said. "You decide everything."

"You don't understand," Flair said, grasping for something, anything, that would convince Lucie that Flair was right. She wanted to give in to Lucie, desperately. But she couldn't.

Loretta put a hand gently on Lucie's shoulder. "I think this isn't your place this year," she said. "Will you trust that your mother and I will talk it over and see if there is something else you can do?"

Thankfully, Lucie still seemed somewhat awed by Loretta. She nodded, visibly subsiding.

"What's happening here?" Renee's voice, unexpected, made them all turn. She seemed to have come from the direction the travelers would take. "I thought this was going to be an inactive space, just decorations. What's all this?"

It was Pamela who answered her. "When your mom realized Cynthia was in town, she invited her troupe to perform. I don't think anyone else had any idea what she'd been doing, but it's perfect. It's like it was made to be part of the trail."

As she spoke, Flair realized that she was exactly right. Everything her mother did was like a smaller, Cynthia-specific version of Rattleboro.

It made her wonder if, deep down, her mother had ever really left.

Renee was clearly not interested in Cynthia. Her eyes had settled on the fire pit the crew had built in the middle of the clearing. "They're having a fire—here?" She turned to Loretta. Her voice, usually so flat and demanding, was almost plaintive. "This isn't what we planned," she said.

"It's better," Loretta said. "More is always better. Don't you agree?"

The question was addressed to Renee, but it was Cynthia who responded.

"Always," she said. "Flair and I are thrilled to be back and thrilled to be a part of everything."

Renee didn't seem to agree, which didn't surprise Flair, but her expression didn't hold the scorn that Flair had come to expect.

Instead, she was staring at the place where tomorrow night's fire would be, a look on her face that took Flair a moment to decipher, because she'd never seen it on the other woman's face.

Renee looked scared.

But before Flair had time to ask herself why, Loretta pulled her aside. Pamela swept the others into a spirited discussion of costuming, although only Cynthia seemed to be enjoying it.

"Bring David with you tomorrow tonight," Loretta said softly. Her tongue shot out to touch her lips. "After the final travelers depart, have your mother and the other performers follow them."

She gestured to the fire, a movement small enough that only Flair would see it and somehow large enough to encompass big plans. "You'll take my hand, and I'll give you everything you need. If that's what you want."

"That's what I want," Flair said.

Loretta clapped her hands together. "Excellent. Together we will ensure that David doesn't give you any more trouble."

Flair held back a nervous laugh. "That sounds ominous," she said. "I don't want to snuff him out. And won't we need Cyn? It was her spell. And Josie?"

"Cynthia's spell?" Loretta looked down and sideways at Flair, like a teacher reproving a disappointing student.

"And mine." Flair still didn't enjoy admitting it.

"You did something very powerful. You may not like it, but you should own it."

Loretta took Flair's elbow gently, but then her hand tightened. She turned Flair to face her. "You seem different," she said softly, releasing Flair's arm. "Something has changed." Her eyes searched Flair's face.

Flair's hand went to her pocket where the cards were weighing down one side of her dress. She shouldn't be surprised that Loretta could see that she carried the source of her family's magic. The cards had been the driving energy behind her too-successful spell, and with Loretta's help, she would use them to end it.

Josie didn't think she should tell Loretta about the cards—but there wasn't anyone else to ask. Maybe Loretta could help her to protect Lucie as well. "Something happened," she began, then hesitated, uncertain how to explain. "With the cards. Cookies. Cards."

"Cards?" Loretta sounded far more surprised than Flair would have suspected. "What cards?"

Renee seemed to hear her words. She abandoned her conversation so quickly that the others were left staring after her before recovering their manners and carrying on. She slipped in between Flair and Loretta.

"Has Flair been reading cards?" Her earlier fearful expression was gone, replaced by one of interest, and then dismissal. Flair had probably imagined the fear. "Or are her cookies getting ideas above their station?"

The wind picked up in the trees around them. The noise of the leaves, which Flair hadn't noticed before, grew louder. Any chance she had of confiding in Loretta was gone. "Just cookies," she said. "It was nothing."

Renee changed the subject. "We should get out of the way and let Cynthia's team keep working," she said. "I can see this is going to be spectacular, but not if it doesn't get finished."

At her words, Jude joined them, asking Loretta some question about lighting, and Cyn announced her intent to use Lucie to test out a few effects, waving at Flair in a way that Flair understood to mean that she wouldn't give in to any renewed pleas. At least she finally seemed to understand.

Flair moved to follow Jude and Loretta as they walked more deeply into the woods and found herself yanked to a stop by Renee. "I need to talk to you," she said.

Flair glanced after Jude and Loretta, then shrugged. "Talk."

"Alone."

"That's going to be difficult," Flair said. "Unless you've planted some clematis around here? Those seem very effective at keeping crowds at bay."

Renee ignored her. "What are you doing out here? I thought you said you were putting your full effort into your shop. I had the impression that when it came to Halloween, you weren't a huge fan."

"I'm a fan of my mother."

Let Renee say something dismissive about Cynthia. Flair was spoiling for the chance to defend her mother. In fact, there was a lot she wanted to have out with Renee, and she might just not care how publicly they did it.

But Renee's next words disappointed her. "Just as long as

you're not a fan of *my* mother," she said. "What did she tell you? What are you really doing here?"

"I'm overcoming my Halloween phobia," Flair said, annoyed. She looked over and saw Loretta watching them curiously.

"I don't think you want to do that," Renee said, holding Flair back. "There's something you need to know."

Flair thought the better of her impulse to take Renee on right now and pulled her arm out of Renee's grasp. "I know more about you than you think I do," she said. "And it's definitely enough."

She ran to catch up with Jude and Loretta and was delighted when Jude made room for her in between them. "What did Renee want?"

"Dire Halloween warnings," she said lightly. She wasn't going to let Renee get to her. "I've promised to pack my fire extinguisher and keep a close eye on my mother."

"I think it's your daughter you should be worried about," Loretta said, and Flair felt her mood waver as she glanced at the other woman sharply. She'd managed to put aside her worries about her daughter. But if Loretta, too, sensed that something was wrong—

"I'd be happy to talk to her about what the students do at the party," Loretta said. "There are one or two particular jobs the kids always enjoy. I could make sure she gets one, if you'd like."

Oh. That wasn't what Flair had been thinking about—though nothing would make Lucie feel better than to be singled out by Loretta. She brushed unexpected tears of relief from her eyes. "Definitely," she said. "That would be great."

CHAPTER NINETEEN

IT'S OKAY TO admit you're glad your mother and Pamela offered to get Lucie home," Flair said as they left the parking lot to pick up dinner before Jude's pastry sous-chef debut. "She really wasn't at her best today."

"She was fine," Jude said. "Not everyone has to be completely charmed by wonderful me."

"She's not having the easiest time adjusting to Rattleboro," Flair said. "I'm hoping this sleepover will help. Pamela's kid is kind of a queen bee."

"I remember Pamela from when we were teenagers," Jude said. "She was a little younger, so you probably wouldn't, but queen bee runs in the family."

Flair looked at the setting sun, far out on the horizon, and then, as they turned a corner, back toward the woods, where a faint sliver of the waning moon was still barely visible over the trees. "That seems like a better inheritance than what I have to offer."

"Oh, I don't know. Lighting fires and getting a good, strong breeze going might be useful for the average teenager."

"She doesn't— I didn't—" Flair spoke too quickly and had to stop and start again. "She doesn't do any of that," she said.

"Can't or won't or—"

"We just haven't gotten into it." She tried to laugh. "I'm sorry. I meant I'm not exactly a queen bee or a social butterfly. And I don't think Lucie knows what she is. By which I am not implying anything in the magical realm. She's just an ordinary kid."

"I can't imagine your kid is ordinary," Jude said. "But fine. Ordinary kid, ordinary Halloween sleepover. Truth or dare, Ouija boards, lots of giggling, very little sleep."

"Exactly." She leaned back in her seat, taking that in. In her relief at the idea of Loretta taming Lucie's anger over her lost trail opportunity, Flair had forgotten to think very hard about the upcoming sleepover. "I hadn't actually considered Ouija boards."

"Not a fan?"

"Not exactly." Her grandmother wouldn't have a Ouija board in the house. Josie and Flair had tried one once at a friend's and abandoned it almost immediately when the planchette, with their fingers resting on it, flew wildly around, making them laugh until Josie said Flair was pretending and Flair said, *No, you are.* But neither of them was, and they both knew it. The feeling that surged through the toy had been rough and grasping, as though something wanted to pull them through the board and hold them there.

In one shared gesture, they'd abandoned it to their seemingly unaffected friends. The next day, when the girls told Flair's grandmother and Josie's mom, both of the older women told them never to touch one of those things again.

Like picking up a hitchhiker outside a prison, Marie said, and Josie's mom agreed. *You don't know who you're going to get but you can guess it's not going to be anything good.*

Lucie wouldn't know to drop the planchette. Lucie might not—probably would not—come to Flair for answers. Flair bit at the corner of her lip, suddenly aware that Jude was watching her, and she'd been silent far longer than was justified. "I just think maybe that's not the best activity for . . ."

"Someone whose great-grandmother was known for her terrifyingly accurate tarot and tea-leaf readings? Whose grandmother writes stories about vampires and witches and whose mother . . ."

"You're really disturbingly blunt," Flair said. "Yes to all of that." They'd pulled into a lucky empty space on a Main Street full of happy pre-Halloween revelers. It was turning into a beautiful night, chilly but gloriously lit, and every restaurant and bar had as many tables and heaters out as they could fit into sidewalks and side alleys.

Flair pulled out her phone as they got out of the car. "I'm just going to send her a quick text."

"I'll go pick up the burgers."

Jude headed to the diner down the street where Josie had worked long ago, and Flair looked down at her phone as she walked. But after a couple of attempts, she realized she didn't know what to say to Lucie, probably because she was worrying about nothing. In the end, she decided to ask Josie, whom she'd already begged to help Cynthia with David for the evening, for another favor.

hey

Flair hesitated over how to word the next part.

worried they might get out a Ouija board tonight

yeah I could see that

could you . . .

pop over to your house and casually warn her

yeah

and say what??????

I don't know

Flair left her text bubble open so Josie would know she was still thinking.

tell her tarot readers don't do Ouija boards, she finally typed.
bc they like to stay focused on the people in front of them

not sure that's enough if other girls want her to do it

Flair didn't think it would be, either. *I know*

want me to scare her?

Flair hesitated.

yeah

done. David seems fine thanks for asking

sorry sorry sorry

yr #Notsorry it's fine. have fun

When Josie started to send a series of vaguely suggestive GIFs and emojis, Flair shoved her phone back in her pocket and went into the bakery.

She'd been making macarons earlier. Finished trays of the little sandwich cookies sat drying on one counter—the chocolate-filled ones—while trays of uncooked meringues waited on her tall rack for baking. She slid a few trays into the oven and set a timer, then straightened up the kitchen and skimmed her Instagram until Jude eased open the door from the alley and came in with their food, which she seized with embarrassing enthusiasm. She was starving.

And she was alone with Jude. Whom she'd kissed Wednesday night with equally embarrassing enthusiasm.

They sat across from each other at her battered wooden worktable. Jude ripped his bag open, then dumped the fries out onto the paper. "I figured we'd share a large."

"As long as they gave you mayo, we're good," Flair said.

"That is a weirdness we share," said Jude, opening the tiny plastic containers of mayonnaise for dipping. He brandished a mustard packet. "Spice it up a little?"

"Certainly, Chef."

They both preferred their burgers with cheese, lettuce, and tomato, no pickle. Jude liked a good thick fry while Flair preferred hers little and crispy almost to the point of translucence, making them, as Jude pointed out, fry compatible.

These topics exhausted, Flair found herself turning new possibilities over in her mind as she got up to take her meringues out of the oven and switch in a second set of trays. For example, did Jude have a girlfriend? Given Wednesday night, it seemed unlikely. How he got started in chocolate, which would mean pretending she hadn't read the profile on him on the James Beard website when he won one of their awards a few years back. Whether he'd asked Renee about that Halloween, or how long a lease he'd taken out on the space where he and his assistant had been making chocolate all week.

Minefields, every one.

It was possible Jude was having some of the same thoughts. He reached for another fry in the silence just as she concluded that a couple more fries were what she needed as well, and when their hands brushed, she glanced up and found herself staring right into his eyes.

She yanked her hand back. "Sorry."

"Sorry."

They were both apologizing for nothing at the same time. And neither of them had a fry.

It was time to try to be a grown-up. "I mean, not sorry about the fries," Flair said. "Fry competition is normal and worthy. But maybe I should apologize for the other night."

"Nothing to be sorry for," Jude said. He pushed the final fries toward her, then took one and ate it. "Not on either count."

"I think I moved us a little fast, though. We haven't even— I don't know if you're with anyone."

"Nope. Official length of longest relationship: eight months. There is a reason for that, though, as you know. You?"

She'd grabbed him and kissed him. He'd be excused for thinking her response would be similar. Lucie's reminder that at least one important person in Flair's life didn't see her as a free agent was fresh in Flair's mind.

"Separated," she said, and she thought she saw something she didn't like in Jude's eyes. She wanted to reassure him, but she also wanted to be honest. "Lucie's dad cheated on me. More than once. But I've never completely left, because . . ."

"Lucie."

"Yes, because of Lucie. But we are absolutely, completely done this time." He needed more—she could see that. And there was more, but she also had that one easy, if humiliating, explanation for why this time was the last time. "He had an affair with her babysitter."

"How very . . . clichéd of him."

She hadn't thought of it that way. She laughed, too hard, and then quickly ate the last two fries to try to make herself stop. "It was pretty classic. And it's history, as far as I'm concerned. But Lucie makes things complicated. So. I went too fast on Wednesday."

"And you want to slow down."

It was hard to read his face, even in her bright working lights. She nodded, and he started to push his stool back from the table. She realized he'd interpreted that entirely wrong. "But not stop," she said quickly. Without thinking, she grabbed his hand across the table. "Unless you want to, I mean."

She hadn't had a date in sixteen years, except the one ill-fated attempt to show David what he was throwing away, and it showed. She yanked her hand back and buried her face in her arms. "This is really, really profoundly awkward."

"I like it," Jude said.

She tilted her head up so she could look at him. He looked like he meant it.

"Okay," she said, returning to her burger. "Do you also love making buttercream macaron filling? Because that's tonight's project. And as much as I'm enjoying this conversation, I need to get going on it."

"You prep; I'll clean up."

They finished their burgers—Flair wanted to shake the salt and potato crumbs from the fry bag into her mouth, but she resisted—and then she set up. Eggs, vanilla, sugar. She pulled the butter out of the fridge and realized she should have taken it out earlier. It was hard as a rock.

She held it, considering. She could use the boiling-water hack. Or she could . . .

Not fire, she thought, shutting her eyes and inviting energy into her hand, then gently into the pound of butter she held. Just enough to move the molecules a little. Push them apart.

She opened her eyes to find that she could now press a finger into the butter, and that Jude was staring at her as though she'd just done something magic. Which she had.

And which felt pretty cool.

"Are you communing with the butter? Instructing it in proper creaming methods?"

"No. Warming it up. Feel."

Jude pressed a finger into the wrapper as well. "You're a genius," he said.

"Don't laugh. I've never tried this before. I learned to light fires, stuff like that. But I never did anything useful."

She was ridiculously delighted. Jude watched her, his expression somewhere between amused and tolerant.

"I suppose you do this all the time, Mr. My Witch Family Is Normal. But we were too busy being estranged and trying to make rent and stuff."

"I've never done that."

"So, not butter. But temper your chocolate, whatever. Warm people's hands in the winter." She couldn't help it—she was imagining him taking care of cold feet in a warm bed. "I bet you know all the tricks."

Jude shook his head. "I can't do any of it. No fires. No wind. I have to temper my chocolate one pant leg at a time like everyone else."

Flair's timer went off, so she had to express her surprise over her shoulder as she took out the final trays of meringues. "Seriously? Your sister tells you your entire love life is basically damned, and you can't even light a candle so you don't have to curse the darkness?"

"Fortunately, I like to curse."

"I bet you can do it." She slid the tray of meringues onto the rack to cool. "Come here."

How had her grandmother shown her? She remembered sitting on her lap . . . They'd skip that part. "Okay, give me your hand." She held out both her cupped palms and he reached out to take her hands. "No, not like that. Rest your hands in mine, palms up. Relax."

She looked up to find Jude's face bending over hers and started to feel a heat between them that wasn't part of the lesson, so she stomped gently on his foot.

"Ouch! What did you—"

"Because you can't do that. Don't look at me like that. That's not what we're doing."

"Okay, Maleficent. But I do think you liked it."

"I might," she muttered, returning her gaze to their hands. "But right now, I need you to pay attention. We're going to heat up your hand."

"Feeling warm is not really something I need help with right now."

"Shh. So, there's heat in the air around us. And water and fire, but ignore those. You want to call the heat. So—try."

"Call the heat."

"Or energy. But if you call that too much, you'll get flame, and you don't want that. You want the slower stuff. That's heat."

"Molecular chemistry meets puppy class."

"More like meditation. It doesn't have to come. But it will."

He closed his eyes. She waited until she felt Jude's breathing slow and sensed the heat he was trying to draw to himself beginning to gather, and then she ushered it gently into his hand, letting his be the force that was drawing it in, hers just amplifying it.

His eyes snapped open. "Do you feel that?"

Flair smiled, feeling a different flush in her cheeks. "I know," she said.

"How did you know I could do that? Can everyone?"

"Not everyone. Maybe not even everyone whose mothers—whose parents—can. But I knew you could." His delight made her grin so widely that her cheeks hurt. "I can smell it."

"As in literally smell it?"

"Literally smell it." The unique smell of magic was all around them right now, a yeasty scent of dough and dog paws with a hint of plum, peculiar and—at least in this moment—wonderful.

"Could I light a candle?"

"Maybe. It's the same thing, only more so. And you have to direct it." She looked around, as if expecting to find that the bakery kitchen had sprouted candlesticks. "I don't have a candle, though."

"That's okay. I'll warm something. Do you need more butter?"

"I really don't. Here." She held her hand out. "I won't help this time. See if you can bring the warmth to me."

He cupped her hand in his, and Flair realized she would hardly be able to tell if he succeeded. She turned her face up just slightly to see him deep in concentration, the tip of his tongue touching his upper lip, the pale red inside of his lower lip jutting out slightly, as if waiting for her teeth. Her breath came just a little faster, and she felt her chest lift closer as he bent over her hand.

Her very, very warm hand. "You did it," she said, and without intending to, it came out softly, like an invitation.

He lifted his eyes from her hand, and she couldn't take hers away or keep her lips from parting. He kept one hand under hers, and suddenly his other arm encircled her and pulled her fully into him, his body against hers, and she could feel the heat he'd gathered spill down between them, catching them both unaware as he pressed his mouth to hers, still talking. "Did you help?"

"I couldn't," she said into his breath. "I couldn't think about anything but you."

He released her other hand and she wrapped both arms around him, crushing him to her, but even as urgent as his hold was, his kisses were light, tender, dropping on her lips and cheeks and then down her neck. "I have been waiting to do this again for a very, very long time," he whispered, and she remembered how they'd kissed in exactly this way as the noises of the Rattlebones Trail faded around them.

That vibration against her leg, though, was not familiar.

They broke apart as Jude scrambled in the pocket of his tight gray corduroys. Getting the phone out took an amount of effort that made them both giggle. He kept one arm around her, lips pressed into her neck—*Don't go anywhere; I'll just get rid of it*—until it became clear that unless he used both hands, his phone was going to stay right where it was and it wasn't going to stop ringing.

When he finally tugged it free and saw the number on the screen, he stopped giggling. "John," he said. "My assistant." He answered, and his face changed completely as Flair tried to understand a one-sided conversation that consisted almost entirely of Jude saying "okay" in increasingly somber tones.

"He flipped an ATV out on the trail," he said. "That was the hospital. He's a mess—I have to get there. I'm sorry." He broke off and he looked at her, and in spite of the seriousness of the moment, an incredulous smile spread across his face. "I hope you know how sorry."

"I do," she whispered, feeling her expression echo his. "I hope he's okay."

"It sounds like he will be, but it might be a while."

"Let me know if you need anything?"

His answer was to sweep her up into a searching kiss, and then he was gone and she was locking the shop door behind him. She leaned against the closed door and took a deep breath and then another, tilting her head back against the glass.

That had been both more than she'd bargained for and exactly what she'd hoped it would be. She couldn't wait for more.

But first, macarons.

She headed back to the kitchen, to cookies and welcome solitude, and instead found Renee leaning against the table, munching on a meringue.

CHAPTER TWENTY

H E'S GONE, THEN?" Renee tilted her head to peer into the pass-through window.

Flair stared at her. Glanced at what she knew was the locked back door.

"What are you doing here?"

"I need to talk to you," Renee said, straightening. "Is Jude gone? I couldn't hear everything."

"He's gone," Flair answered automatically. She very much hoped Renee hadn't heard anything. "His assistant had an accident."

"Shame. Lots of roots in the woods."

"He rolled his . . ." Flair's voice trailed off as she realized that Renee already knew.

Renee pointed to the stool in front of her. "Sit. We need to talk."

Renee must have come from the night's festivities. She'd gone full Tolkien elf in a cream-colored leather suit with a quiver of arrows on her back, her hair loose under a circlet of woven twigs and leaves. She might very well have an elvish blade hidden somewhere, too.

And she was in Flair's kitchen, uninvited.

"Hell no," Flair said, striding past Renee to open the back door and usher her out. "If you want to talk to me, you can call me. Or ask me. Like a normal person."

Renee didn't move. "I am not a normal person. You aren't, either. Not anymore."

Her words stopped Flair, door open, her hand on the knob, but did not dampen her fury at the intrusion. She'd had a wonderful night. She had her plans set for tomorrow. She did not want to hear anything Renee had to say.

"I don't care what you are," Flair said. "I care that you go. How did you get in here?" Magic, she thought.

"Keys," Renee said. "We Oakeses are your landlord."

Of course. Flair should have thought of that.

"Not that I needed them." She shifted her eyes from Flair to the doorknob, and in less than a second it grew warm in Flair's hand, then hot—too hot to touch. Flair yanked her hand away.

Renee watched her. "Don't be more of a fool than you have to be, Flair. Shut your mouth, then shut the door."

Flair hesitated. Josie had poked her with a tiny shock and her mother had once blown a door shut in her face, but Flair had never known anyone to use magic to harm.

The calm she'd tried to find again in the front of the shop was gone, replaced by fear and a thumping of blood through her ears. Flair could run, she thought, get to Josie's; at least she wouldn't have to face Renee alone—

Renee sighed loudly. "I just want to talk to you." As if to

make her point, she walked past Flair, ostentatiously avoiding touching her, and pushed the door shut herself. "I'm not going to hurt you."

"Then why did you sneak in here?"

"Because you wouldn't talk to me in the woods, and I don't think you're going to welcome me into your grandmother's kitchen for a cuppa after I've been trying to get you out of here for weeks. So I'm going for the more direct approach. You said you wouldn't do the trail. Don't."

"But I have to," Flair said, determination replacing her fear. "Your mother—"

"That isn't my mother. What did she say, to get you out there?"

"What? I don't— She didn't say anything." Of course Loretta was her mother. Flair decided to focus on the rest of Renee's accusation. "You're right. I didn't want to do it. But my mother does, so here I am."

It was the truth. Just not the whole truth.

And Renee knew it. "That's not all," she said. "This isn't some PTO volunteer opportunity. There's some reason you have to do it, because even I can see you're not loving it. She has something over you."

"No," Flair said quickly. "I asked for her help with something, and she's helping. That's all."

Renee sighed. "Hers is the last help you need," she said. "I'm the one who can help you—the only one, actually—but you have to listen."

Flair, still angry over everything she'd learned about Renee in the past forty-eight hours, disagreed. "I don't," she said. "I don't need your help, and I don't want it. Just go." Flair went to open the door and push Renee out—then yanked her hand away as her palm burned again.

"Some people are slow learners," Renee said. "Fine. I'll tell you the truth. She plans to possess me, she's afraid she can't do it on her own, and she's going to use your power to make sure I can't stop her."

It was so ridiculous, so unexpected—and delivered with such dramatic gravitas—that Flair laughed in spite of her fear.

Renee grabbed her by the shoulders and shook her, hard, before releasing her with a little shove that sent her stumbling.

Flair tried to steady herself on the counter. Instead, her hand caught a tray of macarons, meringues she'd filled with chocolate earlier, perfect delicious little orbs, and she pulled it away, catching her breath—*No, no, don't fall; that's so much work*. The sheet pan slid to the edge, wobbled a bit, and . . . stopped.

Flair let out a sigh of relief in spite of her fear, and Renee's face tightened. Before Flair could stop her, Renee slammed her open palm down hard and fast on the unbalanced tray, crashing it to the floor, broken macarons all around it.

Flair shrieked in fury, and Renee faced her, unflinching.

"You. Have. To. Listen," she said. "That is not my mother. That is Rose Oakes, one of the original coven who founded this town, in her fourth physical iteration and ready for a fifth. It takes a lot of power to make that happen, and the black moon is the perfect time to move to a new body. She thinks she's taking mine, with your simpleminded help." She stared into Flair's eyes. "She's wrong."

In the silence that followed her words, Flair could hear the buzz of the big refrigerators, the drip of the cold brew straining in the corner, a reveler laughing outside, all at a distance, somewhere beyond this world where she had somehow ended up. The one where Renee could say something like that, and Flair was beginning to believe that she could be right.

"I can't imagine you're actually any match for me," Renee said. "But I can't take any chances. Halloween is not important. Making out with Jude is not important. Cookies are not important." She waved a hand in the direction of the laughter outside and kicked at the mess at their feet. "None of the rest of this matters if you don't listen to me now."

Flair looked at Renee, there in front of her. She was a little terrifying, intensity coming off her in waves, taking up all the air in the tiny kitchen. But she was also a little ridiculous, and suddenly Flair found this level of anger and fear and anxiety impossible to sustain. Fine—nothing else mattered. But the world outside had not ended, and tomorrow morning, people would still be coming through her door, wanting their coffee.

"Cookies are always important," Flair said, kneeling and beginning to pick up the mess. "I'm listening. But now I'm also cleaning. Give me a hand, or at least move your feet."

Renee took a step back, watching, her arms crossed. After a moment, she bent down, and Flair thought she might be about to help, but instead she picked up a macaron that had survived the carnage. "Five-second rule," she said, becoming human again. "Fine. You work; I'll talk."

Flair got a dustpan and trash bag and continued resentfully cleaning up the floor while Renee addressed her from a perch on Flair's counter, annoyingly close to another tray of finished macarons and the racks of meringues waiting to be filled.

"First." She slapped a place beside her. "Tarot cards. Get 'em out. They deserve to be here."

Surprised, Flair sat up to her knees, feeling the weight of the cards pulling the fabric of her dress to the floor. "How did you know I had them?"

Renee let out a tiny sound, almost a laugh. "I can see the box in your pocket," she said. "I'm a witch, not a psychic."

Flair took the deck from her pocket, hesitating. If Renee wanted to render her powerless, all she had to do was take the cards. Renee seemed to see her hesitation. "I don't want them," she said. "They do nothing for me. But we're going to give them the courtesy they deserve here."

Flair had stopped trying to figure out Renee. She set the deck on the clean worktable, then went to empty her dustpan into the trash. Renee looked at the cards and nodded as if acknowledging a fallen comrade. Something between them changed the moment the cards were on the table, and Flair knew the deck was safe. Renee wanted something, but this wasn't it.

"Fine. You should already know all this, but just in case: very short Rattleboro history lesson. This town was founded by five witches, all pretty powerful, but Rose Oakes, who is my ancestor, seems to have been in charge, and Alice Hardwicke, your great-great etcetera, was right up there, too. Everybody farms, because Kansas, but they all have their side hustles, practical arts. Basketmaking, weaving, carpentry. Teas, herbal medicine. You know how Rattleboro got its name?"

Flair shook her head. With the mess swept up, she moved on to buttercream, stirring egg yolks she'd separated earlier along with sugar, water, and salt in a double boiler with her back to Renee, although she remained intensely aware of the other woman's presence. And the fact that she was eating another meringue.

"It used to be called Rattlebone. It's a musical instrument. Ivory or bone, tied together or held together, probably came from the people whose land this was before the settlers moved in. Percussion. So by day they're these sought-after makers, and at night, they're supposedly dancing around a fire, shaking bones. Which was almost certainly highly exaggerated, but the women probably played the whole thing up, since they were safer if people were a little afraid of them. But eventually they changed the name to Rattleboro."

"Much classier." Flair glanced over her shoulder as she spoke and saw Renee eye her like a teacher considering a reprimand, but she dismissed Flair's flippancy. "However, I don't see what any of this has to do with me. Or you. Or your mother."

"Not my mother. And I'm getting to that. Think of me as the villain who tells you their whole plot before they kill you."

That made Flair pause, but she refused to turn around. "Are you planning to kill me?"

"Not if you stop interrupting. So they class up the coven by calling it the League of Kansas Craftswomen, and Alice gets herself to Europe for the big art tour everyone is doing and comes back with tarot cards, some she bought, some she painted. It's a big fad then anyway; everyone's into spiritualism and ghosts and things. Rose sees the possibilities, and she starts the very first Rattlebones Trail, which was more of an outdoor Halloween séance back then, and it grows from there."

That explained the similarity of the paintings in Loretta's dining room to Flair's tarot cards. Alice must have painted both. Flair glanced at Renee. "How did you figure all of this out?" It was an impressive history for a small-town bookstore owner to pull together in her spare time.

Renee shrugged, her legs kicking against the cabinets under the counter where she still sat. "I've gone down south where they came from, talked to people . . . Your grandmother knew some of it. And mine—I knew her a little." She shifted her gaze into the distance and pressed her lips together. "I'll come back to that, okay?" She took in a breath through her nose and went on, her voice a little less strident now that Flair had revealed her interest, and maybe her admiration.

"So there they all are, each of the five founding witches have families, usually one daughter each because that seems to be the way it works. They get older. Nobody wants to die, but Rose is really determined not to. She gets the others to back her up for some majorly intense spell she's come up with at the biggest Rattlebones Halloween festival yet. It's a blue moon, not a black one, and I don't know what she told the others, but the real purpose is to transfer her, or her power, or something, into her daughter."

Flair had stopped pretending to be only half listening. She turned off the stove and faced Renee.

"And apparently it worked. When they're done, they realize Rose is dead, and things were probably fine for a while. I don't know. An hour, a day, months. But eventually Alice, or someone, realizes Rose's daughter is different. Bossier, taking over everything, with powers she'd never had before, and it dawns on her. That's Rose. Rose took over her daughter."

"Like, she possessed her."

"Like, right." Renee imitated Flair's doubting tilt of the head. "Just listen. I think Rose admitted it, because she wanted Alice to do the same thing. Because if there are two of them, it's okay. But Alice is not impressed. Maybe she wants Rose to undo it, or maybe she just makes Rose feel bad, because I'm pretty sure Rose killed Alice off. But Alice was on to her, and instead of dumping herself and her power into her own daughter, she put it all into something else." Renee hopped down from her perch on the counter and set the tarot cards on the worktable as Flair came closer, drawn in by the story. "Those.

"Rose didn't stop there, either. She has Rattleboro, and her Halloween, all built up to give her everything she needs to keep going. She doesn't even need the coven anymore, just a willing descendant, and the longer she's around, the more she figures out how to make everything go exactly according to plan. Until here we are. The last daughter she took over was my mother. And the next one she's planning on is me."

It had occurred to Flair several times in the past few minutes that it was possible that witches, while capable of many things most people would consider crazy, were not immune to delusions. She put her hands on the worktable and leaned in to look directly at Renee. "You think Rose Oakes has possessed your mother."

"No, I know she did. I was there. I saw what happened."

Renee reached out and clamped her hand down over Flair's.

"I saw her take my mother. And kill my grandmother. And there wasn't anything I could do about it."

CHAPTER TWENTY-ONE

I WAS SIXTEEN," RENEE said, and although Flair had been listening to her for what felt like hours, Renee's voice was different now. She pressed her hand over Flair's, hard enough to be uncomfortable, and suddenly it was as if Renee's voice was inside of Flair's own head.

"We lived with my grandmother. Jude was little; our dad was still around. Things were pretty great. My mom and grandmother were magic—not in the way we're talking about, or not just in that way. Everyone wanted to be near them. The Rattlebones was a major scene. Witches from all over on one hand and hippies on the other.

"And then my grandmother got sick, just before Thanksgiving. Or at least everyone said she was sick, even though she seemed fine. Everyone told us she was dying but it would be okay, things would go on, she was moving to another plane of existence, that as the year turned, so would she—all kinds of stuff. She and my mom planned this huge winter solstice, like her last hurrah, everyone wearing white, all these rituals. My dad kind of put up with it. I think he wanted my mom back. I did, too, but at least I got to go with them. I don't know what he thought about all that, or what he knew. I wish I'd asked.

"They did a huge circle in the woods on the night of the solstice, but just as everything was getting going, I saw my grandmother take my mother's hand and slip away. It was almost like no one else could see them. They carried a torch from the fire, and they lit another fire farther away in the woods, and they threw things into it, and the smoke changed color and they held hands over it, and then I swear they were in the fire, both of them, and I wanted to run to them, but then—it was impossible—they weren't on fire at all."

Renee pressed her hand into Flair's with even more force, and suddenly it was as if Flair was seeing the scene as she had, from just at the edge of the forest, her hand clutching the rough bark of a bur oak, not quite hiding behind it but not wanting to be seen, either.

The fire, burning tall, flames peeking above the blackening wood, smoke streaming up into the darkness. Two figures, standing in the flames, holding hands, and then—it came as such a shock that Flair gasped—Loretta, because it was unmistakably Loretta, released the figure who stood across from her, flinging the other woman from the flames and to the ground where she collapsed with no sign of life.

Loretta remained in the fire, her face lit by flames and glistening with triumph. Then—impossible—her eyes met Flair's, and she lifted an eyebrow, tilting her head and acknowledging Flair across the years before stepping out of the fire, stretching joyously, and then approaching her prone companion. She flipped her over casually, peering down as one might examine an old canvas leaning against a wall, then left the older woman on the ground again before she strode off into the distance.

Flair pulled her hand out from under Renee's, stunned. She didn't want to see more, didn't know how Renee had stood it.

Renee went on, her voice hard. "She wasn't dead, my grandmother. I went to her, and she spoke to me, said my mother was gone now, that Rose would take her entirely. That I'd be next, or my daughter if I was dumb enough to have one." She stared into the distance, and Flair knew she was quoting her grandmother's words. "Don't trust her. Don't take her bargain, because it isn't a bargain. She'll steal your life—your whole life. And leave you with nothing."

Renee took a long, shuddering breath. "She wanted to live. I could feel it. Even then, I could feel it, a whole unlived life, thrumming inside her. It was like whoever she was, when Rose took her, was all still there.

"She told me to go to your grandmother and tell her the story. I wanted to move her, but she kept saying there wasn't time.

"She came back, my mother—Rose—with a sled. I hid before she saw me. She had a pillow—she smothered my grandmother and hummed the whole time. A song I remembered from when I was little—"

Renee shook her head, straightened, crossed her arms over her chest, visibly pulling herself back together. "So that was that. The end of my grandmother and my mother. But not of me."

Flair became aware that her mouth was hanging open. This was . . . this was . . . She came up with nothing. She'd reached capacity on emotions and was numb. She was going to have to run on practicality and fumes.

"Your ancestor possesses people. Mine went with tarot cards." She needed to at least try to put this into words. Clear, direct, impossible words.

"You could put it like that."

"Possessing people is not so great."

"Not so great, no."

"And all this runs in the family, so to speak. I get tarot cards. You get . . . Rose."

Renee nodded. The bright bakery lights cast odd shadows on her angular face.

"So you're saying you're a bad witch, and I'm a good witch."

Renee's eyes met Flair's, her expression flat. "I never did like you."

"Likewise," Flair returned. Her moment of seeing the dark humor in the situation disappeared, and suddenly she was furious. "You planted something in front of my shop that kept people away. You've been making everything harder ever since I moved back here. You broke up me and Jude before we even got started."

"Of course your grandmother and I didn't want you and Jude to get together. If you'd actually wound up with a baby—the product of two magical lines? Rose would have wanted that kid more than anything. It wouldn't have stood a chance."

"We weren't— You shouldn't have—" Flair didn't even know what she wanted to say. "Why didn't my grandmother tell me?"

"She would have. If you'd stayed. But you didn't."

"And all these years, you've been telling Jude—"

"What I needed to tell him. You don't understand what I'm up against. Rose made sure that the other families forgot what she did. There was only Marie and me. And then, after last Halloween, only me."

Flair took that in. "My grandmother—"

"Wasn't ready to go. Do I think Rose helped her along? I do. Can I prove it? I can't. And it doesn't matter. This isn't about proof. I have one chance to shut Rose down. One black moon, one Rattlebones Trail, one night that I've been preparing for for years until you came along and got in the way."

Renee stood up, scooping a handful of meringues off the nearest tray with a look that dared Flair to object. "So I'm asking you—no, I'm telling you. Tomorrow night, you stay home. No guest-starring role in your mother's Halloween carnival. No dancing around on the trail with my so-called mother or whatever she's proposed to you. You're a tempting little barrel of untouched magic just waiting to be tapped, and you need to get out of the way."

Flair strongly resented the image. And also, she had her own business with the black moon and the trail. She needed to unenchant David and get him to leave without taking Lucie. And she was beginning to realize that Loretta—Rose—might never have intended to actually help her, if what Renee was saying was true.

"Make this easier on both of us, Flair. Stay home." Renee tossed the quiver of arrows over her shoulder, preparing to depart. Flair watched, thinking.

In all their planning for Halloween night, Loretta had never mentioned Renee. Only herself and Flair. Renee was halfway out the door, not bothering to say good-bye, when Flair called after her. "Renee."

She turned.

"One question. Does it have to be her daughter?"

"What?"

"Whoever she possesses. Does it have to be her daughter?"

Renee met her eyes. "It always has been. But maybe not. I don't intend to find out."

"What would it take if not?"

"Someone with magic. Someone whose life she can take over. And someone who agrees to let her do it."

I'll give you everything you need, Loretta had said. *If that's what you want.*

And Flair had said yes. Without even realizing what she was doing, Flair reached out and took the tarot cards, still on the table, and clutched them to her chest.

Renee paused, her tall frame outlined by the darkness of the night outside. Then she looked from Flair to the tarot cards she held. "You're safe," she said, "as long as you stay out of the way."

CHAPTER TWENTY-TWO

Saturday, October 31

HALLOWEEN BEGAN WITH Flair hunched over the kitchen table, wondering if you could get a hangover from Sleepy-time tea. She'd come home to find that Cyn, taking advantage of Lucie's absence, had dumped David on Flair's sofa, presumably full of Josie's mother's stronger beverage. Truly the culmination of the evening. Flair's dream had been full of different versions of the woods and things that pursued her there, none of it coherent enough to be prophetic. Just her subconscious, vomiting nervously. Now she sat stewing in her thoughts, wondering if Lucie's sleepover had been a success, telling herself that if anything strange had happened, her daughter would have called. Or texted. Or something.

Last night, after finishing her macarons—because she was a professional and she had a job to do and she was going to do it—Flair had walked toward home through the most well-behaved, well-dressed Halloween crowd she'd ever seen. No

gory rubber masks or inflatable Frankensteins, no drunk Bad
Santas. Instead, the guests, like the streets, exuded Gothic
sparkle. All of it, from the shape of the streetlights to the wax
dripping from the candles on the restaurant tables, conveyed a
steampunk Victorian funereal vibe with Day of the Dead edge.

It should have been delightful. Instead, the tightly controlled
surroundings had only served to remind her that the whole
thing had been orchestrated by Loretta, far more so than Flair
had ever realized. Loretta. Or Rose. Flair wasn't sure what to
think. As had been true of every Halloween since its earliest
days, the fun served to mask the fear: of the growing darkness,
the approaching cold, the once-inexplicable changes in the season that might leave a puny solitary human alone and defense-
less and facing the unknown under a dark and moonless sky.

Flair could relate to the fear. She'd rushed through the
crowd last night, ducking past superheroes and vampires, sliding around aliens and fairy princesses. Somehow, the onslaught
of Renee's story had left her unable to barricade herself against
the potent buzz of pent-up desire and longing that vibrated
through the streets, an energy reflected in every fleck of glitter,
every sparkle. It was like a mass of storm clouds. Raw power,
waiting to be given form and direction.

By Loretta, or whoever she was. By Renee. And by Flair.

Her night's uneasy sleep had done nothing to ease Flair's
fears. Every certainty had vanished. Renee wasn't her enemy but
a cranky and dictatorial protector. Jude was everything she'd
thought he was at seventeen and nothing she'd believed about
him in the years after. Loretta wasn't Loretta but the newest
incarnation of Rattleboro's least appealing founder, her Rattlebones Trail a front for a form of magic darker than any Flair

had known and apparently threatening Flair's very existence. Meanwhile, the tarot cards Flair had stolen and hidden to keep them from destroying her life long ago were supposed to help her protect herself and everything she loved.

Or unleash a lot of pent-up, probably pissed-off hereditary magic.

Her mother's reassurances had helped Flair make a temporary peace with the cards, but after what Renee had told her about them, all she could think about was the chaotic nature they had always seemed to contain. The cards themselves sat, dark and brooding, on the table across from her.

As much as Flair would have preferred to disregard Renee's story, she was afraid of going into the woods with Loretta under the dark of the black moon, hoping for her help and getting something very different. But at the same time, staying home was not a choice. Those same woods, charged with the emotion from a night of delighted terror, were her only chance to both free David and, if necessary, use a little witchy intimidation to convince him that it was in his best interest to leave Lucie with Flair.

Today, she'd tell Cyn that the Hardwicke women—plus Josie—were on their own. She and Cyn had magicked David into this state, even if they hadn't meant to, and they were going to have to use magic to get him out. And she knew one other thing for sure.

If Flair had inadvertently given the spirit of Rose Oakes permission to move in on her, she was taking it back.

A soft tapping on the front door's glass window woke her up enough to scramble for something to cover the old gray tank top and pajama bottoms patterned in cakes and petit fours that she'd slept in. She found a hoodie of Lucie's that was too cropped to cover much and stepped far enough into the front hall to see who it was.

Jude, peering in the window. He smiled at the sight of her and held up two large coffees.

Damn. Flair wanted to see Jude, but with everything going on last night, she'd lazily left David sleeping on the living room couch. Opening the front door was bound to wake him. Flair pointed frantically toward the back, hoping he could see her through the window, mouthing instructions. *Go around back.* Was the door handle turning? She made her gesture bigger and saw Jude hesitate and thankfully step away. She ran to open the back door as silently as she could.

Flair meant to join him outside, but she stumbled over Teabag and Jude reached the back porch too quickly. He took her opening the door as an invitation and strolled in, holding one coffee out toward her. "It's the most witchiest day of the year," he caroled, hitting the notes of the Andy Williams holiday tune. "Callie made you your usual."

He stood looking around at the kitchen, once Marie's, now Flair's tidy perfect domain, white dishes and plain glasses on white shelves with the wall painted turquoise behind. Flair tried to decide what to do. She would love to sit down and have a coffee with Jude in this room. But for there to ever be any chance of that, she needed to get him out of here before he realized that her supposedly estranged husband was asleep facedown on her sofa in his boxers.

She set the coffee he'd handed her down on the counter but let go of the cup while it was only half on the surface and watched, frozen, as the paper cup turned over once in the air and hit the floor. The top flew off and a full large latte lightly laced with mocha syrup and cream sprayed everywhere. It spilled out onto the white floorboards, racing toward the spaces under the fridge and stove.

Flair cursed, and Jude started to laugh. She shot him a frantic look, which took him by surprise. "Lucie's asleep," she said. "She, uh, came home early. Her stomach hurt. I don't want to wake her."

Coffee was everywhere. Flair grabbed both kitchen towels off the hook and flung one at him, nudging Teabag away from the hot liquid with her foot.

They knelt, side by side, soaking up the coffee. Their hands met in the middle, and even that slight touch made Flair want to forget the mess and pick up where they'd left off last night. She yanked her hand away, exasperated with herself. This was not what she needed right now.

She looked over to see him smiling, almost as though he'd read her thoughts. He gently knocked his hip into hers. "Sorry," he said, his voice low. "I'm getting the idea that this is bad timing. The coffee, I mean."

"I would normally swoon over your bringing me coffee. But today's a madhouse. As you know. How's John?" She'd remembered his assistant's name just in time.

Jude sat back on his heels. "He's going to be fine," he said in a normal voice, and she shushed him again. He laughed, but softly at least. "I thought teenagers slept soundly."

"She's really grumpy if you wake her. Hang on—we'll go outside."

Flair ran a clean wet rag over the last of the mess, hitting the cabinet doors and table legs quickly, then stood up and tossed it

into the sink with the kitchen towels. She'd deal with them
later.

Jude went to the door. "Back porch?"

Flair nodded. Teabag perked up and followed them out.
She'd done it—no David. All she had to do now was get Jude
away from the house before David woke up.

Jude sat down on the picnic table's bench, and Flair was both
sorry and glad that he didn't seem ready to go just yet. She sat
beside him, both of them facing away from the table and stretching their legs out toward the house, keeping her focus sternly on
this moment and not on everything that was piled up beyond it.
It was going to be a gorgeous day, but right now it was chilly
enough for them both to glance down at her braless chest.

"You look great," Jude said, grinning. Then when she
glanced pointedly at the faded hoodie and the places where her
flannel bottoms were practically worn through, he laughed. "I
think I mean generally. You look great. And like you just woke
up. Which"—his expression grew mischievous—"is a look I
think I could appreciate if you gave me the chance."

She would. She absolutely would give him the chance. As
soon as Halloween was over and David was safely back in St.
Louis, without Lucie. She shifted, trying to think of something
to say that would both tell Jude how happy she was to see him
and get him to go away immediately. He spoke first.

"I have a brilliant idea," he said. "We blow this taco stand.
Leave Halloween for the wannabes."

"And neglect our witchy duties?" It felt good to try to joke
about it.

"Absolutely. By the time they're trick-or-treating here, we
could be halfway to the border."

"We'd just end up trunk-or-treating in some church parking lot, waiting for your car to charge."

"Fast getaways were not a thing I considered when I rented an electric."

Of course. It was a rental car. Because while she was sitting here trying to get him to skedaddle, he was probably going to leave for good soon.

But maybe not, she felt herself hope. He'd talked about his mother wanting him to settle in Rattleboro . . . his mother. The same mother that his sister was planning to defeat tonight in some big battle of the possessed versus the unpossessed, while Flair maneuvered around them trying to return David to his senses just enough to send him home without their daughter. She cast a worried glance back at the house, but other than Teabag's tail thumping on the back steps, it was quiet. "I don't think you can get out of your candy-distribution duties that easily."

"It's not too late to change your mind and join me."

Oh, how Flair wished that were possible. She didn't respond, and Jude went on.

"I've been meaning to ask you. What do the cookies do?"

She thought about it for a second. She was still working this out. The cookies did things, but not exactly like the cards. "If I give you a cookie—and it's the right cookie—it helps you make a choice. Hopefully the right choice. For you."

"But me, I get a muffin."

She smiled and tried to stop worrying about David appearing. "I kind of hoped you didn't need a cookie." She remembered Cyn's words about the tarot. *The cards aren't directions. They're possibilities.* That seemed true of the cookies, too.

"So you're not predicting the future? Foretelling our inevitable fate?"

Flair shook her head. "I think the future depends on our choices. It's not something you can predict." Or, at least, she didn't want it to be. Unless she, Flair, got to decide precisely what those predictions said. She couldn't help but remember the cookies she'd inadvertently given Lucie during their tarot lesson, with their air of fear and doom. No, she didn't believe in fate. Only possibilities. And some possibilities you crushed as soon as you saw them lurking in the shadows.

Jude sipped his coffee. "My mother's a big believer in fate."

She would be. "What about your sister?"

"Oh, Renee's definitely on the side of fate. But sometimes I think she thinks she *is* fate. I just wondered what you believed."

"There's no such thing as fate. Even the most obvious-seeming cards can hold a hundred different choices." At least, that was what she wanted to believe.

And what was fate, anyway? She and Jude were the perfect example. Had Renee interfered with fate or been its fickle hand? If Flair had been allowed to have what she wanted back then, maybe she wouldn't have what she wanted now.

Jude reached for her hand, but before he could take it, Flair heard a noise from inside, a kind of heaving and scrabbling. Teabag leapt to her feet and started barking.

The back door swung open, and David appeared, wearing nothing but boxer shorts and a blanket that he held around his neck like a cape. He should have looked ridiculous, but the anger that emanated from him sucked any laughter from Flair's throat as he stared them down, taking in her, Jude, everything.

"I want out of here, Flair," he shouted. "Out, now. I want

you to help me." He stumbled a little, as though the effort of getting himself this far without instructions had been too much. He hung on to the door frame as he managed one step down before he lowered himself and sat, holding the box of tarot cards that she'd left on the table in his hand.

"You can't have him now," he said, looking at Jude viciously. "You have me. You read my past and present. I want a future."

Flair glanced at Jude's face and saw betrayal. Anger. Disappointment. "That's David," she fumbled quickly to explain. "Lucie's dad. He's here. He's . . . been sick—"

"I am not sick." David made as if to stand but gave up. "Not sick. You did this, Flair. You."

Jude stared at David, who seemed to have used up all his effort and sat staring down at his bare feet, blanket still wrapped around his shoulders.

Flair grabbed at Jude's hand as he got up, following him. "Let me explain," she said.

She expected Jude to turn on her, yell, walk away. This was just unfair. If there was such a thing as fate, why couldn't it cut her just the tiniest bit of slack? Why did this have to blow up in her face now?

She hung on to Jude's hand, pulling him back. He looked over his shoulder at her and then back to David, his face unreadable.

"Please," she said. Jude's hand felt cold in hers. She gave it a gentle tug. *Please.*

Without meeting Flair's eyes, he pulled his hand from hers and sat back down at the picnic table, perched tensely on the edge of the bench. "Okay. Explain."

CHAPTER TWENTY-THREE

FLAIR CONSIDERED MAKING up a more plausible explanation, but only for an instant. Jude knew what she was and how things happened in Rattleboro. So she stood between Jude and David and told the truth, at least as far as it involved her, David, and Cynthia, and then she stopped and waited. She wouldn't blame Jude for being angry, or at least disappointed, but she hoped he would be willing to accept that she was doing her best to move on.

Jude took a long time before speaking. "I admit this is a little more tangled up with your ex than I hoped you'd be," he said.

Flair seized on what seemed like an openness in his response. "Me too. But it's not—I can see why it looks like I'm still more involved with him than I should be. But it's not about love," she said, finding the words with difficulty. "Or even wanting to be together. I got used to the way he was, even though it wasn't good for either of us. And as long as he was there, I didn't have to think about looking for anything else. That I might actually want."

She looked straight at Jude. "And might not be able to have."

Did he see that they were both in the same place? Neither had believed in the possibility of a real relationship between them. If that was going to change, they'd have to look at life differently. Their banter and undeniable attraction were a good start. But they were two pretty damaged people—and Jude didn't even know the half of it yet. Flair couldn't be the one to tell him. Even after they got through tonight, it wasn't going to be smooth sailing.

If they got through tonight.

"I'm sorry," she said when Jude didn't say anything else. "I could have told you earlier. Although it's not exactly the easiest thing to bring up."

Jude managed a smile, and relief swept through Flair.

"I did consider it," she said. "You know, like, hey, I've got my ex under a spell at my house; could you grab him a burger? But the timing never seemed right."

Jude rubbed the back of his neck. He didn't laugh.

"Too soon?"

"I think so."

"I would definitely rather have been helping you tonight," she said. "If nothing else, you're a better conversationalist."

Jude glanced at David, sullen and silent on the step. "Low bar."

"In this and everything else—I assure you."

Jude's eyebrows shot up, and Flair blushed. "Not what I meant. Just—never mind. So. The trail makes everything more powerful." She searched his face, looking for some sign that Renee had told him what she expected to happen tonight, and found nothing. "We're going to re-create the spell tonight and undo it. And then he's going back to St. Louis. Alone. You'll see."

Jude nodded but didn't speak, and Flair waited until she could wait no longer. "You will see, right? Give me a chance."

He met her eyes, and she knew immediately that she would wish she hadn't pushed him into responding.

"I've been waiting to get out from under all of this magic for a long time," he said. "I'm not sure how much more I can take."

He stood up again, then turned and walked off without another word.

Flair knew better than to call after him. Nothing she could do or say now would matter as much as whatever happened tonight, for both of them.

She walked up the porch steps and took her tarot cards back from David's unprotesting hands, shoving them angrily into the pocket of the hoodie. She stood back. "Up," she said. He didn't move.

"Up. Back in the house. Come on—you have to get dressed. You have to have figured out by now that this is the day we finally sort you out and send you home."

No response. No matter how many times she told him to get up and come with her, he continued to sit bleakly on the step. When she put an arm around him to haul him up, he was a dead weight. When they finally struggled through the door, she dumped him into a chair.

"Are you being like this on purpose?"

One look at his face told her the answer was yes. The spell, or some of it, seemed to be wearing off, but whether that would make tonight harder or easier depended more on David than Flair would like.

"You're such an asshole." She collapsed into the chair across from him, catching her breath. "Even when you're under a spell you're an asshole. Is it because I was talking to Jude? You can stick your tongue down our babysitter's throat, and I can't talk to a guy?"

She sat up suddenly, hearing the truth in her own words. "I'm right, aren't I." It wasn't a question. "You don't want me to talk to him, because you can tell I might care. And you haven't had the guts to really care about anyone in a long time. Including me. And maybe Lucie."

His face had gone blank again, but Flair kept talking. "And I just kept letting you slide, with Lucie right there learning how not to have a relationship. Damn it, David. I think I hate both of us."

He was about as responsive to hearing this while enchanted as he would have been if she'd ever managed to say it to his face. Not that she'd tried. Not that she'd even realized it herself.

Flair heaved an enormous sigh. "I think you want what's right for Lucie. I do. I just think that to you, what's right is whatever feels easiest. And I don't think that's going to work."

It was probably time to go upstairs and put on her witch clothes. It was definitely time to make David get dressed, and he'd better listen, or he was going to be wandering around the woods in his boxers. She stood up and stretched, arms high above her head, when suddenly she heard footsteps running up the front porch and the slam of the door.

Lucie was home.

Flair turned to David, frantic, but there wasn't time to hide him before Lucie was standing in the kitchen doorway, dropping her backpack on the floor, and then running at David with an excitement that she'd never shown for the appearance of Flair.

"I can't believe you came!" She threw her arms around him. "Did you see the town? I told you you'd like it. It's unbelievable, right? When did you . . ."

Her voice trailed off as she realized David wasn't responding. Her arms dropped to her sides and she backed away, tripping over a chair, and when Flair moved to catch her, she righted herself and yanked her arm away.

"What's wrong with him?"

She didn't look at Flair, staring instead at her father, who'd lost any of the occasional bursts of understanding he'd shown and seemed unaware of her presence. "What is this?"

She finally turned to look at Flair, her face full of confusion, misery. Betrayal. Fear.

The fear Flair had seen on the card. Lucie looked lonely, lost, hopeless, and Flair was why.

"What did you do?"

"It's okay," Flair said desperately. "He's sick—that's all. He'll be fine. I'm taking care of him. I swear. It's okay. It will be okay."

Lucie looked from Flair to David and back again, her breath coming in short, frightened gasps.

"Tell me what's going on," she said.

The sight of Lucie's frightened face brought Flair instant clarity. She had to protect Lucie from this. And to do that, she would have to lie.

"He's stoned," Flair said firmly. "I'm sorry, and I didn't want you to see this, but he came to see Halloween, and someone gave him something he couldn't handle." She didn't dare look at David, and she desperately hoped he didn't understand her, but if he did, well, she'd spent years not throwing him under the bus, but he was going now.

Lucie eyed her father, and then Flair.

"How dumb do you think I am? What's really going on?"

But Flair could tell by that slight hesitation that Lucie wasn't entirely sure of her ground, and Flair was going to ride that horse to the bank.

"I told you," she said in a tone of gentle condemnation. "This is what stoned looks like." She considered throwing a little antidrug speech in there but decided not to press her luck.

Lucie narrowed her eyes. "But I see you and Grand whispering. I see all that stuff with her and the candles, too. And your cookies—those are from real tarot cards. I know they are. I've seen them."

It was a confession, and Flair jumped on it, resisting the urge to check that the cards remained hidden in her pocket. "When did you see them?"

"I found them." Her guilty look told Flair she'd taken the right tack.

"You went through my things."

"The lid was off," Lucie said. "It fell on the floor. It was open."

That, Flair finally realized, was why her mother had gone to their apartment. What she and Lucie had been texting about. The cards had revealed themselves—to Lucie. Months ago.

Her anger at the cards, and her fear at what else they might be capable of, made her speak too sharply. "Still. You shouldn't have looked without telling me."

"Still." Lucie matched her tone, and Flair sensed her advantage slipping away. "You shouldn't be lying to me. You're hiding things."

Flair knew she'd made a mistake the minute the words were out of her mouth. "You have to trust me," she began.

Lucie's anger went from a three to a ten before Flair could even take a breath. "You're the absolute worst. Do you know that? The absolute worst. And now you've— I don't know what you even did to him. But it won't work. I don't care if he doesn't want me. I want to go back to St. Louis, but I really want to get away from you. You won't let me do anything."

Flair tried to be reasonable, to regain the high ground. "What do you even want to do?"

Another mistake.

"Everyone in this town does something for Halloween. Everyone else whose family has anything to do with the trail is in on it. But you won't let me in."

They were right back where they'd started the day before. "I'm sorry," Flair said. At least she only had to push this argument out for a few more hours. "Not this year."

"It's just like a haunted house," Lucie said. Then she gave Flair a sharp look that made the hair on the back of her neck prickle. "Or is it? It's not. That's what's wrong. That's what's wrong with Dad, too." Lucie glanced at David, then looked back quickly, as though too frightened to even take him in. "There's something real."

Flair started to shake her head again. To fill the room with more denial. But if Lucie had seen something else . . . She held her breath. "Why are you asking?"

"Because I know there's something."

Could she feel it?

Lucie kept talking. "At the party—we played a game."

"Ouija board?"

"No. Josie said not to." Lucie looked at Flair suspiciously.

Flair avoided her eyes. She waited, but Lucie didn't go on. Flair looked at her. "What happened?"

"It was the mirror."

Flair almost laughed. Bloody Mary. Of course. "That's just your reflection."

"You're right. It was my reflection." Lucie looked at her. Through her. "And it told me to ask you about the cards."

"The cards." Lucie's reflection had spoken to her. Lucie had powers. And the cards were calling to her.

No matter what Flair did, the cards would not stop making trouble.

"They're just cards. They're old, and you can use them just like the cookies we told you about. That's it." She took a breath and told another lie, one that she would make true. "And I don't even have them anymore."

"You don't have them? You got rid of them?"

"They were just old cards." At the start of the week, Flair had set out to destroy them. To remove their power to send her family careening into chaos. She would follow through with it tonight.

Lucie took a step closer and stared, without blinking, right into her mother's eyes. "You're lying," she finally said. "You don't trust me, and you never have. I'm going to find someone who will tell me the truth."

Flair took a deep, infuriated breath because she was right, and Flair hated it as much as Lucie did. Then she channeled all her parental authority. "You're going to your room, and then you're going out with the eighth grade tonight, and the next time you want to go through my things, you're going to ask me."

Lucie looked right at her and then turned and walked out the door.

CHAPTER TWENTY-FOUR

FLAIR RAN TO the door after her but saw only Lucie's back disappearing in the direction of Main Street—or, hopefully, Annabel's house. Lucie had friends now, at least. She wasn't running off into the darkness; she was heading into their small town in broad daylight. Flair could figure out where she'd gone; she didn't need to chase after her and make things worse.

Flair leaned against the door, taking deep breaths to calm herself. She knew, broadly, what was planned for Lucie and her classmates today. They would meet at Loretta's house. Uniforms would be distributed. They would be kept busy for the duration of the trail, offering trays of Halloween-themed hors d'oeuvres, distributing glow sticks, and generally keeping the excited travelers in line as they were sent, in groups of two and three, out onto the wooded trail while being firmly kept out of the woods themselves.

It would be the safest place for Lucie. And by the time they came home, there would be nothing to tell.

She went back to the kitchen and glared at David, the only person left to glare at. "You were no help."

Flair sat down at the table with him and let herself droop, arms in her lap until she felt the cards in her pocket and pulled them out, holding them in her hands. She wanted to blame them for all of this. The cards and David. And Loretta, too, or Rose—she should come in for her share of the blame. And Cynthia. And Marie. Renee. She could really spread that blame all over the place.

Lucie would go back to Annabel's, tell everyone about her crazy, awful mother but probably not her father, both because he was too embarrassing and inexplicable and because who ever ranted about their dad? Mothers were always the ones who were hung out to dry. Maybe Pamela would give her the nice reassuring hug of a normal mom and tell her things weren't that bad. Pamela was as nonwitchy as they came.

Flair would trade places with Pamela in a heartbeat. She leaned back and crossed her arms, ignoring David, ignoring the feeling that she should get up and make him a cup of coffee or something. If ever it was clear that her urge to take care of him was more about her than him, it was now. He wasn't asking her for anything; he didn't seem to want anything. He was just sitting there waiting, and it would be so much easier to make him a cup of coffee and blame him for not making it himself than to figure out what she really wanted to do, or do it.

She did not enjoy that particular realization.

The box of tarot cards thrummed with its own energy. Alice and her legacy might be pursuing Lucie, but Flair could protect her daughter. It was time for Alice and the cards to let them all go.

With her decision made, Flair felt a little better. Even the sight of David sitting across the table bothered her less. Loretta felt like a distant threat. Flair could see her way through to tomorrow, and for now, that was all she needed.

But the cards were still demanding her attention. As she'd taken the box from David, it had practically quivered in her hand, images shooting into the air around her like the stars around a cartoon character's head after the anvil struck. The Devil, the Empress, Pentacles, Swords.

She had to read them one last time.

Flair slid the deck from the box without letting herself think too hard about it and then, in once quick motion, fanned them out, faces still hidden. She spread her hands out on the table, pressing the tips of her fingers into the worn wood surface, then she clenched her fingers into fists, leaving only the right pointer extended, and pulled her hands slowly toward her body, her eyes on the cards.

Inside the fanned-out deck, one twitched. Flair kept drawing her hands back, and that one card slid slowly toward her, as though she were pulling it, even though she wasn't touching it at all.

She stopped. It stopped.

She pulled back again, and it followed, until it was fully separate from its fellows.

Flair flipped the card over. The Queen of Swords. Demander of honesty, ultimate deliverer of hard truths, with a blade meant for slicing through self-deception, here to end the pity party and insist that the big-girl pants be donned, the crisis faced, the battle fought.

Sometimes Flair hated these cards for other reasons.

She gathered the remaining cards and slid them through her fingers in a familiar shuffle, cutting them. Moving the bottom of the deck to the top and then shuffling them again until she could put it off no longer.

Cyn had always favored more complicated spreads, cards that crossed one another or formed an arch representing an entire series of events, but Flair rarely used them. Past. Present. Future. As her grandmother always said, if what you hoped to learn didn't appear in those three cards, it probably wasn't there.

The dealing was the easy part. The Five of Wands. The Five of Swords. Death. She took a deep breath. She hadn't expected to see anything good, but the slap of the memory of the Five of Swords and the appearance of Death as her future were still a jolt. She held herself away from the touch of the cards, trying to consider their meanings with detachment. Her past: the Five of Wands. Denial, refusal. Conflict, which she wanted to attribute to her situation. But under the eye of the Queen of Swords, she had to admit that this conflict was inside herself. She'd been pushing things off instead of dealing with them. For starters, the cards themselves—check. Here she was, doing that. Next, admit that she'd been part of the mess that was her marriage so that she could extricate herself and her daughter. *In process, Your Majesty*, she informed the card.

Her present: the Five of Swords. The card that had warned Cynthia, so long ago, that she was running headlong into danger.

But Flair was not her mother. She could see where she stood clearly: The magic that had dogged her childhood, now pursuing her daughter. David, and all that had to be done there.

Staying out of Loretta's way. The wild dance she'd be doing tonight to use the powers she feared without letting them consume her.

She would use what she knew to protect herself and everything that was important to her.

Her future: Death.

Was it possible to think that word without fear? But Flair knew the Death card had many meanings, foremost among them change. Transformation and closure, both of which, she reminded herself, were precisely what she intended. And there would be death, in a sense. The death the cards foretold would be their own.

There they were. The cards she'd been so afraid of. She leaned back in her chair, holding herself away, regarding the reading with an impartial eye.

And then she laid her hands over the cards and let the magic in.

She was in the woods; the cards were in her hands. Shouting, smoke, voices—this was her mind's eye, so why couldn't she see more clearly? Movement, running, and Flair was doing nothing. Standing in stillness, holding the cards and then letting the cards go, throwing them into the air, strung out like drops of water that swirled and coalesced into a figure, a person.

Lucie.

A Lucie made of cards, who held out her hands in acceptance, in welcome, to Flair, to something, to magic itself, and swirled, becoming a tornado of cards that flung themselves back into the air—

And disappeared.

With a sob, Flair snatched her hands back from the three cards on the table and swept them to the floor, the Queen of Swords sailing after them. David sat up for a moment, then slumped away from the table again. She spared him a mental curse before she huddled into her chair, drawing herself into a ball, arms wrapped around her knees, refusing to look up or give the cards another chance to invade her mind or her world in any way.

She sat there, face buried in her flannel pajama–panted knees, hearing only the sound of her breath and feeling only its warmth on her wet cheeks, for as long as she could and then longer. She might have sat there all day if she hadn't been startled by the slam of the front door, followed by Cyn's voice, and then Josie's.

"Kitchen," Flair called, her voice ragged.

It was Cynthia who saw the strewn cards on the floor and rushed not to the cards, as Flair might have expected, but to her daughter, coming up behind Flair's chair and putting her hands on Flair's shoulders while Josie made light of the moment, pretending to shield her eyes from David, still barely dressed and wrapped in his blanket.

"It's too early for that," she said. "I was hoping for coffee, not the aftermath of a bad rave."

"He does look pretty rough," Flair said, her voice still shaky. He looked like she felt. "I told Lucie he was stoned."

"Lucie saw him?" they said in unison, Josie sounding horrified, Flair's mother vaguely pleased.

"I told you you should tell her," Cyn said, patting Flair's shoulder. "Good girl."

"I didn't."

Josie took in her surroundings—Flair, the cards on the table—then took charge.

"David here needs to go put on some clothes. I know it's early, but big day ahead and all that." She bundled him out of the room, giving him clear and audible instructions like the mother of boy dragons she was. When she came back, Flair told all. Lucie seeing David and her fight with Flair. Jude seeing David this morning and her telling him the truth. His assistant's injury. Renee and her theory about Rose, which elicited an expression of doubt from Josie and thoughtful nodding from Cyn, who Flair could have predicted would adore that part of the story, with its big magic and high drama.

She left out the possibility that Rose might have targeted Flair instead of Renee. She might be wrong. And even if she wasn't, she didn't plan to get close enough to Rose to let it happen.

As they listened, Cynthia gathered the four tarot cards Flair had flung aside, looking at them thoughtfully. When Flair reached the end of her story without volunteering anything about the reading that had clearly upset her, Cynthia slid the four cards back into place and handed the deck to Flair, who tried not to reveal her reluctance to accept it.

"Did the cards tell you anything?"

Flair suppressed a shudder. "Only that Lucie can't be in the woods tonight. But we knew that." She didn't tell them about the way the cards had swirled around her daughter, consuming her entirely, or the way Lucie had disappeared at the end of Flair's vision. Because she knew what she had to do, and she knew Cynthia wouldn't like it.

She would hold the cards and play her part as the three of

them formed a circle around David, one so planned and simple and nearly silent that they could pull it off in between groups of travelers, before Loretta arrived at the end of the night. She would take the power that surrounded her and let go of David, because she was done holding on to that part of her life and ready to confront him and fight for Lucie if she had to, whether Lucie wanted to be fought for or not. They would stand by the fire that Cynthia's team had built in the woods and work their magic together.

And then Flair would throw the cards into the fire and watch them burn.

CHAPTER TWENTY-FIVE

Loretta's house would be crowded with trail-goers, its lawn filled with tented festivities. A giant party to be enjoyed until you were tapped for your time on the trail and then savored even more afterward. There would be people from town who walked the trail every year, the lucky outsiders who'd been able to score tickets to become "travelers," and then a long and excited waiting list—because you never knew.

Lucie would be there, part of the tribe of teenagers that oversaw the fun, a role Flair hoped she could relish. She'd responded tersely to Flair's midday text. *I'm fine.* And Pamela, whom Flair had sold a latte and a chocolate chip scone to around lunchtime, had laughed and said yes, they'd seen Lucie. She was heading to Loretta's house with the rest of the kids.

Town, like the pretrail festivities, would be a joyful madness, families and trick-or-treaters of all ages filling its streets, so many that Flair's neighbors had said you really couldn't afford to live on the residential streets around town if Loretta and her team didn't fund the candy. Flair, as instructed, had left a big bowl of chocolate miniatures under a leering ghost with a *Please Enjoy One* sign, and a friend of Josie's was enlisted to watch over both porches since Josie's boys would be out with their grandmother.

Josie herself was with Flair, holding tightly to her hand, both of them fully enveloped in black grim reaper–like gowns with hoods that included a mesh piece to drop down over their faces so they could—mostly—see out but couldn't be seen. Their stop was at the farthest stretch of the trail, which looped out from the edge of Loretta's fields as far as it could go in the unusually dense woods and then back again. Travelers might walk across the dark fields to return to the party or might be welcomed into a car as they emerged from what seemed to be the end of the trail only to find, once inside, that there were no handles on the doors and the driver had evidently bailed, leaving them seemingly speeding out of control into a dark night.

Overall, the experience was not one Flair would sign up for. But people did—hundreds of them. It was as democratic a system as possible. Those drawn from the lottery could not re-sell their free tickets or postpone to another year. If you got in, you showed up, made a donation if you so chose, and were sent with your companions to the entrance on a precise schedule, stripped of your phones and Fitbits and cameras and flash-lights and anything else, and then bidden farewell. A reporter for *Midwest Living* had once asked Loretta what Rattleboro would do once cameras in contact lenses became commonplace.

She'd appeared to think it over, the journalist wrote, and then leaned in close.

"We'll scrape them off your eyeballs," she'd said.

According to the magazine, it was the only quote from the interview that she approved for the final piece.

Flair and Josie stood on the edge of the clearing, away from the fire at the center of the trail stop Cyn had created, waiting for the black moon's all-enveloping darkness to fall.

Clothing stuffed to look like human figures, or possibly fallen scarecrows, lay scattered around piles of sticks that Flair knew would rise up into marionettes at the behest of the puppeteers now hidden on their platforms in the trees—all Cynthia's team. Travelers would look up to see the tightrope walker alone above them and then realize, as the sticks rose up into figures, that they'd been surrounded.

It was their job—Flair's and Josie's—to make sure that the now-terrified travelers ran in a particular direction, one that would send them to the next lighted signpost and so on down the trail.

They wouldn't all do what was expected, the trail minder had told them repeatedly. Graziella, Renee's assistant at the bookstore, had done this twelve times. She was the only one permitted to use a phone during the action and would get a notification when a group of travelers began the trail. Flair had been careful about Graziella not recognizing her, not wanting anyone to alert Renee that she was here.

Another trail minder, using a glow stick, would signal to Cyn's team that travelers were coming and then, when the performance was complete, would signal again to let the next stop know that new victims were heading their way. During the lengthy lull in between, the performers would be silent, so that their voices wouldn't invade the experiences around them.

It was a precisely timed operation, but one they rehearsed only once. Flair had asked Graziella why.

"Loretta's always thought it ruined the freshness of the experience if we were too prepared," Graziella said. "She likes it when people have to improvise. Other people," she'd added firmly. "Loretta herself has always got a plan."

Flair, Cyn, and Josie would have only one chance to enact their real plan. Loretta, if she appeared at all, would arrive after the last group. So they would have to act earlier, in between the last two groups of travelers, and they would have to be fast.

As the last travelers approached, Josie would pull the smoke and the darkness of the night tightly around them, masking them from Graziella and Cyn's team. Flair would rush David from his hiding place beneath one of the platforms and into the circle she'd already created, next to the bonfire but not around it, because it was simply too big for them to encircle together. Josie and Cyn would be waiting. They would clasp hands and Flair would declare her intent to undo what she had done, holding the cards and drawing in the energy around. Hopefully it would be all they needed.

If they were too slow and the final travelers arrived in time to view any evidence of real magic, they'd attribute it to the trail, and after Josie opened the circle, she would take over the job of moving them while Flair dealt with what would be the night's real unknown: David and his reaction.

But she'd handle it. The fear that had seemed overwhelming before had paled compared to the way the cards seemed to be pursuing Lucie. Flair would sort out David. And she would, quietly and without fanfare, rid her family of the unpredictable magic that endangered each of them, but Lucie most of all.

A sudden energy swept through the group as they heard Graziella's voice—"They're starting." A thrill ran through Flair. "Get ready."

CHAPTER TWENTY-SIX

For a while, nothing happened, and then Flair began to hear things in the distance. The stops were intentionally set up far enough apart that the sounds of another's experience shouldn't intrude, but they caught just a little. A snatch of organ music, a scream, the rustling of feet coming closer. Voices—*watch out, look out, come on*—and then three people appeared at the edge of the clearing.

They found only silence and stillness underneath the darkest of moonless skies. In the center of the clearing was the fire and around it the stuffed clothes, like fallen scarecrows.

"Something's going to jump out at us," said one.

"Shhhh."

They approached the figures, but cautiously. A shadow swept over the travelers from above—Danae on an invisible tightrope, sweeping a cape Phantom of the Opera style. The three people in the clearing stared upward, mouths agape, and then, in a smooth, coordinated motion, the scattered piles of tree

limbs around the edge of the clearing rose up into giant marionettes. They were nothing but stick figures, made from branches
and fishing twine, but their simplicity and the way they almost
blended into the surroundings made the fact that their movements were intentional all the more terrifying.

All three people screamed and clung to one another. Danae,
from above, called down to them, revealing that Danae was not
menace but protector, and pointed them onward. "Go."

Flair and Josie, in their hooded black robes, moved in, and
the tiny audience obeyed, grabbing one another's hands and
following the path that had been lit for them, and it was over.
The first of thirty-odd miniature performances that would be
recorded nowhere and remembered by no one but the actors
and their witnesses.

It was its own kind of brilliant magic.

As the evening drew on, Graziella began whispering up-
dates. "Ten groups to go," and then five and then three and
then two. At that point, Cyn slipped away from her sound-
board, where she'd been adding eerie music to coordinate with
Danae's appearance and the sudden cracking of branches as she
saw fit, and into the clearing.

The second-to-last group went through in relative silence.
Josie sent them on their way and cast her masking spell quickly
before she joined Cynthia. Flair grabbed David by the hand,
urging him up silently, rushing him into place. Only someone
who shared their magic could see or hear them now.

Josie closed the salt circle behind David, and Flair sat him in
the middle. The three women surrounded him, Cyn's back to
the fire, and took one another's hands. A tremor went through
Flair as they connected, and she felt it—the energy of the night

itself, coming up from beneath her feet, and all the tension and glee and fear and excitement left behind by the travelers who had already passed through.

The feeling was everything. It was the first time a candle lit at her command, it was her mother turning to her over the tarot cards, her grandmother applauding a reading. The cards answering her deepest desire. Meeting Jude's eyes across the crowd at seventeen. Her first successful éclair. Baby Lucie in her arms at last. At the same time, it was sensing her grand-mother's death and the call that confirmed it. David's betrayal. The cards, granting a wish she was ashamed to have made. Lucie, with her, and then Lucie, taken away.

She understood why people didn't want to let this feeling go—and why she had to.

It had been a still and quiet night, but now the wind began to pick up around them. Something seemed to move in the circle behind her, and Flair looked back quickly, but her eyes were dazzled by the fire and she couldn't make out anything through the mesh of the mask attached to the hood of her cloak. She pushed it back off her head—she'd replace it when they were done—and saw that Josie and Cyn had done the same. Flair turned her attention into the circle and began to speak.

"Three stalwarts live true," she began.

Josie and Cyn joined in. "Three ready and willing. Three in need, three in communion, ever prepared to embrace the power and take the journey."

"I have been granted what I sought," Flair said. Just a few words, short and powerful, the cards held between her and her mother's hands as they held on to each other.

They raised their arms as she spoke. The sound of the wind became a steady roar, like an overhead train, and in spite of herself, Flair wondered for a moment whether the last travelers were approaching. Where Renee was and what she was doing. What Loretta would say, when she arrived, if she arrived, and whether Flair would now see Rose looking out of her eyes. Whether Lucie, back at the house of the witch who had been a part of starting it all, would feel any of the power that Flair felt.

Whether Lucie would ever forgive her if she knew what the cards had once meant to their family, and what Flair was about to do to them.

She shook herself back into focus, reaching higher, feeling the power rising up through her, through all of them, as the spells that wound around David became visible to her again. "I have been given what was needed. Now I release what isn't mine."

The bright, thick cords of Cyn's magic loosened, snapped in the air around David. Flair felt her mother's fingers flex within hers and saw the threads dance in response. She clenched her own hands, concentrating, and the dark-red lattice that held David shimmered and pulsed. Flair bowed her head for a moment, and his head bowed as well. As she looked back up, their eyes met.

Here, in the circle before the fire, she could feel what she had created. She understood what she could do. Her mother's web was returning to her, and a quick glance at Cyn and Josie revealed faces flushed with success. Without moving, Flair pulled back on her own spell, lifting its power but not its sway, and the red threads thinned and deepened to a blood crimson, still there, invisible to everyone except her.

If she left things here, she and David would remain connected. He would appear restored, but his decisions would be hers whenever she so desired.

No one would know. David himself might not even realize. The web had become so fine, a faint mesh with a strong hold. Lucie would be safe. But neither Flair nor David would ever be free.

Flair kept her grip on her mother's hand on one side, Josie's on the other. She could snap the spell with the slightest of gestures, or she could leave it in place. She hesitated, uncertain, her eyes on David—until she felt a grip on her shoulder. Someone, or something, had breached the circle.

Flair wanted to whirl around, to scream, to push that touch away—they weren't finished—but, unable to resist, she took her eyes from David and turned her head to see a dark figure behind her.

Loretta.

And behind her—with a hand on Loretta's shoulder the same way Loretta's hand was on Flair's—Lucie.

At the sight of her daughter, Flair's grip on the cards and the hands she held tightened as she stared over her shoulder, furious, trying to twist from under Loretta's hand. "Get her out of here," Flair said into Loretta's face, so close behind hers. "Lucie. Go home."

Loretta shook her head, only a tiny bit, as though Flair's fierce demand was barely worth acknowledging. "She needs to be here," she said, and Lucie spoke from behind her over the sound of the storm.

"I have a choice, Mom," she said. "I want to be part of this." The pressure of Loretta's hand increased, and Flair felt herself being pulled backward, out of the circle. Her control over the spell that held David lessened, and the bonds between them swelled again until Flair saw that the web did not just ensnare David but covered her as well. At the same time, images began to unfold in her mind, a whole life unfurling before her in an instant. She saw herself, back in the house with Lucie, David at the stove, a different David, laughing, loving, extending a spoonful of something for Lucie to taste. She saw the two of them, her and David, taking over the culinary part of Rattleboro, running Rattlebones, Lucie glowing and thriving around them, their little family at the center of a safe and solid life, then David again, so much better than any version of him Flair had ever known.

All of those possibilities hovered in the air around her, and with them, a feeling of power and confidence like she had never known. Her web could extend farther, could encompass everything. She could seize it and make her vision real in an instant. Flair felt her hands release her mother's and Josie's as she began to reach up to gather it all in, Loretta's arms around her.

The weight of the cards dragged her down. She slid from Loretta's grasp and fell to her knees, the circle broken. The fire flared up with a roar and a snap as she clutched the box to her chest. The image of the Queen of Swords sprang up before her. Face reality. See the truth that's in front of you; do not be deceived by desires, not yours or anyone else's. Accept your life and your choices and all that comes with them.

The image of the Death card hovered beside them, hard and fierce and demanding to be heard. Death came in many forms, all of them final. Death was what Rose offered.

And death was what Rose did not understand. Flair's

grandmother had. Alice had. *We cannot outrun death, and we cannot outwit change.*

Death was everyone's future, and Death challenged you to accept what was coming for you and make certain it was your own.

Loretta's hands reached for her, pulling her back up, urging her to drop the cards, to whirl herself into the power around her—

Flair stood and broke free from Loretta's grasp. She would make her own choices. She reached for Loretta, intending to hold her in place, to call to Cyn and Josie, restore the circle, and draw them together to end Rose's power.

But Loretta had already turned back to Lucie, and Lucie, strangely, was embracing her, pulling her past Flair, past where their circle had been, ignoring David. Lucie's eyes glowed like stars and her entire being seemed to light from within. Her eyes met Flair's but slipped away, focused instead on visions that Flair could not share, and Flair gasped, but before she could stop her, Lucie—and Loretta—stepped into the rising flames.

Flair threw herself after Lucie but felt arms around her, holding her back as she fought uselessly against them. In front of her, Lucie held Loretta as one might hold a dying lover, clasped close until Loretta sagged suddenly, then slipped from Lucie's grasp to the ground.

The flames around them receded instantly. Lucie kicked Loretta's body out of the ashes, rolling it with her foot contemptuously before her eyes finally met Flair's with a look of revulsion and dismissal that shocked Flair into speech.

"Lucie!" Flair meant it as a cry, a plea, and yet somehow it came out in a corrective, ridiculous tone of reproval, as though

Lucie had failed at tossing something into a trash can and then walked away.

Lucie laughed, at Flair and at the fallen woman at her feet and at the world, with a smirk that Flair had never seen on her daughter's face before.

Because that wasn't Lucie.

It was Rose.

CHAPTER TWENTY-SEVEN

FLAIR SCREAMED.

But no one moved; no one reacted. Maybe the screaming
was only in her head. The heat of the fire pushed her back; the
smoke made her cough. Tears blinded her eyes. She was lurch-
ing toward her daughter before she even realized she'd moved,
but Lucie—Flair had to call her Lucie—stepped out of the way
and stopped Flair with an outstretched hand like an unexpected door. Flair grabbed at her arm and it felt nothing at all
like the familiar feeling of holding Lucie, as the girl in front of
her shook off her grasp.

Flair thought she'd experienced pain before. When her
grandmother died. When David betrayed her—and again,
each time she would have said, more awful than before. Every
time her mother yanked her away from something she loved or
wanted and demanded that she accept some new plan instead.

Now Flair knew those were nothing. Nothing. Because Lucie was in front of her, her Lucie, the same little girl she'd held

and snuggled and protected, the center of every thought she'd had and everything she'd done since she was born—and she was gone. Flair heard a sound come from her lips that she didn't know she could make, something between a moan and a cry. Josie grabbed her again and held her tightly. David still sat in the center of their broken circle, Loretta's body at his feet while Cyn stared, confused and frightened.

Behind her, Flair heard Danae shout "Go!" as the marionettes crashed to the ground around the last of the travelers, who stumbled out of the scene unguided by her or Josie. Josie's masking spell was gone, their circle revealed, its magic broken other than the power that now inhabited Lucie and stood in front of them, calmly watching as they stumbled into understanding.

"What happened?" Cynthia stared from one of them to the other and got no answer until Josie, understanding at least that no one else should be witness, waved her in the direction of her team and the trail minders. "Get them out of here," she said. "They have to go."

Cyn took in Flair's face and Loretta's fallen form and turned quickly, holding her hands out to keep the others away.

Lucie watched with a flat expression, then shrugged and ran an inquisitive hand through her hair, pushing the curls away from her face. Her eyebrows crumpled together thoughtfully, a very Lucie gesture, and then, in a horrifying instant, her tongue shot out in the tiny, familiar Loretta lip lick.

Flair pushed Josie's supportive arms away and managed a shallow breath but found herself unable to speak.

"I think," Lucie said, her voice slow and then picking up its normal cadence, "I think there's a party for the kids at the church. I can walk there from here. Yeah. I think I'll go." A knowing smile, very unlike Lucie, crossed her face, and she wriggled a little in the black lace dress and veil of Lucie's Lydia Deetz ensemble as if feeling out her new digs. "Give you a little time." She nodded slowly, then smiled again. "See you at home."

She turned on the heel of the black lace-up boots Lucie had chosen to accompany her costume, and Flair saw her glance down at her footwear and shake her head before she strode off in the direction of the parking area, her walk suddenly confident. Part of Flair thought, *But wait, she didn't ask, who's picking her up, hold on,* while the other part stumbled through what had happened. Lucie was out of sight before Flair could speak, and she realized that the wind had stopped and the woods had gone quiet except for Cyn's voice talking to her team, and then they were gone and Cyn was back, and Flair was still there in front of the fire, salt circle smudged around her, cards still in her hand. Frozen.

Josie knelt next to Loretta.

"We need to get her help," she said as she sat Loretta up.

Footsteps pounded down the trail as flickering lights appeared, powerful flashlights that could only belong to fellow haunters of the trail, and before Flair could say more, Renee was with them, Jude immediately behind her, swinging their lights across the scene until the beam of Renee's landed on Loretta, now sitting up with Josie's help. The light shook wildly for a moment before Renee handed it roughly to her brother and reached down to pull something from her boot. Flair realized, with a horrible rush of ice down her body, that it was a knife.

Everything in Flair's vision slowed except Renee, rushing toward her. Jude had stopped behind his sister, holding the lights, unable to see the knife until Renee grabbed Flair's arm and turned her around, holding her from behind with the knife under her chin.

Flair felt Renee look quickly down at Loretta and inhale deeply, but she held the knife steadily under Flair's chin. How good was she with that thing?

As if she'd heard, Renee replied. "Pretty good." She lowered the knife just slightly. "Don't move, Josie. I mean it. Flair. Is that you?"

"It's me," Flair said. "Um, how can I— What do you—"

"Never mind." She released Flair and dropped her knife on the ground. Turning to her mother, to Loretta, Renee dropped to her knees beside her, wrapping her arms around the other woman. "Mom?"

Loretta coughed and leaned on Renee as Josie pulled herself away from them slightly, giving them a little space while staying close enough to Loretta to help her if needed. Renee looked up at the circle of people around them.

"Where is she? Where is Rose?"

"Renee?" Jude's voice was deep and slow, as though he thought he might be dealing with a madwoman, and his eyes were fixed on the knife that had dropped from his sister's hand. She looked down at it as though surprised to find it there and then picked it up and slid it back into her boot. "Renee, what's going on?"

His sister ignored him. She looked at Flair and spoke slowly. "Where is she?" Flair watched her surveying them, calculating, saying nothing—*No, don't tell her; don't tell her until I can figure this out, please*—

"Lucie," Renee said, an exclamation as fierce as any curse. "Lucie. I didn't think—"

If Flair had thought she had any chance of getting away with it, she would have lied in an instant, but Renee knew so much that she did not. Instead, Flair felt her fury and terror spilling out as she screamed at Renee. "You didn't tell me she could do that. You didn't say—"

"I didn't know," Renee said, her own voice shocked. "I never thought of that—did you warn Lucie? Did you tell her?"

"No," Flair said, hating herself almost as much as Renee. This was her fault. She'd walked into danger and taken Lucie with her. "How the hell was I supposed to know if you didn't?"

"Renee," Jude said again. "Tell me what's going on. Mom?" He knelt at his mother's other side, replacing Josie.

"Yes," Renee said softly. "Mom." She wrapped her arms around Loretta, who had fallen against her, still not speaking, her breath harsh and rasping. "But it hasn't been. Not for so long, Jude. Since you were so little."

Jude stared at her, the only one present besides David who didn't understand, and Renee went on, although her attention was fully on the woman at her side. "Rose Oakes," she said. "The first witch to settle Rattleboro. She was in our grandmother and then she took our mother, and she's been in her, holding her. Possessing her." Renee's grip on Loretta tightened. "And now she's in Lucie."

Jude's mouth dropped open, and he blinked slowly.

"What are we going to do?" Flair pleaded with Renee.

"Nothing," Renee said. "It's over." She helped Loretta, who was standing up, one hand on Renee's arm and one on Jude's while Josie hovered nearby. Loretta's expression had been foggy, but now it cleared, and Flair could see her hands tense.

"No," Loretta said. Then again, more loudly. "No."

"Mom," Renee said. "It's okay. Let's just get you home." She was looking off into the woods, as if she thought there was danger. Flair remembered her description of how Rose had come back to finish off her grandmother. She knew what Renee was afraid of, and it all clutched at Flair's guts in a way nothing ever had before, because Renee was afraid of Lucie. And Renee had a knife.

"It's not over," Loretta said, and her voice was Loretta's, but the affect was different somehow, less demanding but still firm. "It's not over."

She turned to Flair. "Your daughter—Lucie—she accepted Loretta."

Not knowingly. She couldn't have. It was impossible. Lucie hadn't understood, didn't know— "No," Flair said. "She wouldn't—"

"She did. She would have had to. But she's still there, and right now she's still . . . close to the surface—I don't know how to describe it. You can still talk to her. She could—I think she could—change her mind. There's still time. If you can get her back here." Loretta seemed to wobble a little, and Flair saw Jude strengthen his hold, but her voice stayed firm.

Flair turned to the others, suddenly full of determination. "Then we have to get Lucie back here," she said. She shouldn't have let her leave—but if she hadn't, what would Renee have done?

Jude seemed to finally find words. "I don't get it," he said. "Mom? Is that . . . Are you—"

"Jude," she said softly. "You were so little." She touched his face, his hair, as if seeing him for the first time. "I've watched you . . . but to be here with you—"

She pulled her hand back and wiped her eyes, and when she spoke again, her voice was firm and devoid of emotion. "When you were a little boy, I let Rose—the spirit of Rose—into me. She'd been in my mother, and she raised me, and I thought I wanted it. She promised me great things. I didn't understand what it meant until there was no way to come back. She left me tonight, and Lucie took her. Or really, she took Lucie."

"She also killed our grandmother," Renee said. "After she left her and took Mom. The same night."

She wanted, Flair knew, to emphasize for Jude how serious this was, how very big a thing they were dealing with, but Jude's face was crushed into confusion, and Flair realized that to Jude, Rose *was* his mother. The tough, genuinely ruthless spirit had been with him since he was little, had doted on him and raised him, supported his dreams, pushed him to be more, driven him relentlessly, had—along with Renee—turned him into who he was today, good and bad. Renee was holding the arm of their mother, returned to her. Jude was standing next to a stranger who was telling him that his mother was a murderer, for all kinds of reasons, many times over.

That was going to take time to process. More time than they had. "So we have to get Lucie back here," Flair said, trying to pull him into the now. He was going to have to deal with this later. "Undo it."

"And then what?" Renee's face was grim.

Loretta spoke. "I'll take her back."

That got an instant response. "No," Renee said. Her grip on her mother intensified. "No. You can't."

"That's a thirteen-year-old girl," Loretta said. "We have to help her."

"You've been through enough." Renee turned to Flair. "Why were you even out here? I warned you—but no. You had to be smarter than me."

"You could have told me," Jude said, looking angrily at Flair. "You knew? You just told me that you had to deal with him." He glanced angrily in David's direction. "But you knew."

"It didn't feel like mine to tell. It was something you should have heard from her," Flair said, pointing to Renee, who had finally, it seemed, realized that there was another person in the circle.

"Who is that? What's wrong with him?"

"It doesn't matter," began Flair, who could only think of Lucie.

Cyn spoke over her. "He's Flair's husband. David. Well, her— They're separated. And he's . . ." She waved an arm to indicate whatever it was that David was.

"Cursed," said Josie. "We were trying to fix him."

Renee surveyed David. "Who did it?"

"Flair," said both Josie and Cyn.

"My mother," said Flair at the same time. Then, in a smaller voice, "And me."

"You were out here," said Renee, her voice dripping with contempt, "dicking around, trying to break some picayune little hex that you caused, when I told you—"

"This isn't important," Flair said desperately.

Renee shook her head. "You didn't have a chance," she said, staring at the ground around David. "You three were out here with your salt and your circle, and she was able to just waltz up and use you."

"She shouldn't have known we were going to," Flair said.

"She didn't know. That's why we did it before the trail was over."

"Do you think she couldn't feel it? I could feel it and I wasn't even looking for it. And she would have been. She knew something was up—I could tell."

"She's known you were onto her for almost a year," Loretta said to Renee. "That's why she brought Flair here. And Lucie was right there and so easy to bring along in case she failed with Flair. Lucie felt like she was on the outside of everything, and Rose promised to let her in. Tell her what she wanted to know, let her make all her own choices. She's so young." Loretta's eyes filled with tears. "It's so hard when you're that young."

Flair couldn't look at Cynthia. Her mother had been right. She should have told Lucie. Or she should have let Rose win, gone with her—except that Lucie would have been next. Because Lucie still wouldn't have known. It was still Flair's fault.

But it wasn't too late. It couldn't be.

Loretta took a deep breath and then held out a hand in a regal gesture worthy of her previous self. "We have to get her back here. To this place. It's where Rose made her change every time. They held their first rituals here, when the women first arrived. And their last. This spot is where she feels most powerful. And most vulnerable. And we have to do it soon. Every minute we wait, it gets harder."

Renee stood still for a moment, as though considering. Then she drew in a breath and spoke quickly. "Then Jude has to go get her," she said, turning to her brother.

"Me?"

"As far as she knows, you still don't know about any of this. If you show up to get her—as Lucie—she's still going to be adjusting to not being Loretta. She's still Rose, but she's in a kid who can't drive and who people aren't going to let just walk around and do whatever she wants. You tell her you're taking her home, treat her like Lucie. It will work. And then you bring her here."

"And what?" Jude seemed reluctant. "What if she won't come into the woods? I'm supposed to drag her? That's a kid . . . I can't—"

"It's not a kid," Renee said, and Flair couldn't help it. She put her hands up over her face, the box of cards she held pressing into her skin. She wanted to fling it away, to cry and run and leave all this, and the weight of it all made her hunch forward, drawing in a ragged, sobbing breath. She felt Jude step forward to catch her, but she didn't fall. She couldn't. She had to do this. She straightened and stood tall.

"Flair has to come with me," Jude said.

Renee shook her head. "She'll know," she said. She looked around, and her eyes fell on David. She prodded him with her foot, and he looked up. "Take him."

Jude's expression showed what he thought of that.

"Not like this," Renee continued. "Mom, wait over there. The rest of you, come on. We don't have much time." She took Josie's hand and nodded to Cyn, who pointed to the ground.

"The circle's open."

"Then close it."

"We tried this before," Josie objected.

"You didn't have me then. Flair. What did you do, and how do we undo it?"

"It isn't just me," Flair began. With so much magic in the air around them, she could see the faint traces of the spells even outside the circle, and both still held. Loretta had stopped them from freeing David.

Loretta—and Flair's own hesitation.

Renee's gaze brushed over David. "I can see that this is yours as clearly as if you'd written on him in Sharpie. Your mother's spell is tiddlywinks; yours is an iron maiden. What did you say?"

"This is taking too much time," Flair said. "We have to get Lucie."

"You said, 'I'm the devil, and I will crush him into submission and get him to do what I want for a change,'" Josie said, then shrugged at Flair's surprised look. "It was memorable. Not usually your style."

"But why?" Renee's voice was insistent. "You clearly weren't in it for a sex slave. And here he is, and you won't let him go for some reason."

"I can't let Lucie go live with him," Flair said. Even now, the words stung. "I just wanted to keep her safe."

"Well, now that ship has sailed, so you can let him go. Get in here." Renee stared back at them all, unrepentant. "It has. And the only thing worse than an untrained witch is one who refused to be trained, and that's what Flair is." She turned to Flair, not bothering to suppress her anger and contempt. "You had two choices. Marie told you. Leave it all and never come back or learn to control it."

"I didn't know what I was choosing."

"We never do. Fine. So, he's wearing basically all the magic you mashed up inside for years and what else?" She turned to Cynthia. "You?"

"My tiddlywinks?" Cynthia's tone was sharp. "He had the cards. I wanted them."

"So." Renee looked directly at Flair. "Everything you hated about him and feared for your kid plus all the magic mashed up in you for years. Plus Cynthia. Plus, the cards had been trying to get back here to warn you, which you also didn't listen to. Great. No wonder he's a mess."

David glared up at her as though he could understand.

"He was kind of a mess to begin with," said Josie.

Renee looked at Josie and then Flair. "This is not his fault," she said.

It is. If David hadn't threatened to take Lucie, none of this would have happened.

Renee stepped closer to Flair and spoke right in her face. "It's not, and it doesn't even matter if it is. You only get to be in charge of you, and you're going to be thoroughly unable to function until you understand this. But right now, you have to let him go."

"I know," Flair said impatiently. The only thing that mattered was Lucie. "Don't you think I know? Shut up and help me do it." She looked around. "We're four. It has to be an odd number."

"We're five," Jude said from where he'd helped Loretta take a seat on one of the folding chairs left by Cyn's team. He stepped into the circle and took Flair's hand roughly.

Renee looked at him as if to comment, then took his other hand as Cynthia took up a place beside her. "Flair," Renee said. "Start."

"Five stalwarts," Flair began, and the others joined in, Jude just a beat behind. Inside the circle, the web around David glowed again, pulsed, brightened, becoming visible to them all. Flair tightened her grip on the hands she held. The power throbbed in response. She felt it now, the way it surrounded and held her as well. Slowly, she drew the crimson threads up and away from David until only a few remained.

She hesitated. All of her anger was still with her. Her fear for Lucie was all balled up with it, and she couldn't find the end of the string, couldn't find the words to release her hold on him.

"Flair," said Renee, and this time her voice was almost kind. "You're going to have to let a lot of things go."

"What I have bound, I will release," Flair said slowly, and then repeated it. "What I have bound, I will release . . ."

That wasn't it. She couldn't release David, not fully—and it wasn't because of the spell. Lucie would always bind them together. But no matter how much Flair wanted to, she could not control how. She took a deep breath and reached behind her to join Cynthia's and Jude's hands and free her own so that she could shake away the crimson threads.

"What I have held tight, I will let go."

She repeated it once, twice, flicking her wrists each time. The cords around David swirled, swarming around him, rushing up over his head to join those Flair had flung into the air. The threads spun above them, a pulsing knot of bright light, until Flair lifted her arms farther, urging the others to follow with her gesture. Cynthia, too, had gathered her own spell, pulling its cords upward until David stood, unbound. The light above him disappeared as Flair brought all their arms down, hard.

Then David leapt from his place in the center of the circle and rushed at her.

CHAPTER TWENTY-EIGHT

JUDE CAUGHT DAVID with a single arm before he reached Flair. David stopped and took an angry breath.

"I'm not going to hurt her," he said.

"Seems to me like you haven't done much else." Jude had barely acknowledged Flair since finding out about his mother, had released her hand as soon as possible. But here he was defending her.

"She'd have to care about me before I could hurt her," David said, his voice rough from disuse. He looked around Jude at Flair. "Did you ever consider just talking to me?"

"You wouldn't have listened."

"You haven't said anything real in a long time."

Loretta rose from her chair to stand with Flair, brushing aside Renee's help.

"You should go with Jude," she said to Flair. "Not to find her—but be there once she's in the car. Concentrate on Lucie.

Don't let Rose distract you. Just be there for your daughter. Help her stay close. That's all you have to do."

"Fine," David said. "Let's go."

Flair couldn't imagine what he was thinking right now. "David," she began, hoping to explain, not knowing where to start.

"I don't want to hear it," he said roughly. "First you need to figure out how to get her back." Flair looked at him and realized that he knew far better than anyone what Lucie might be experiencing right now, if she was aware of anything at all—having the self she'd once thought was inviolable controlled by someone else.

Jude hesitated. "But what do we do if she won't come into the woods?"

"She'll come," Loretta said. "In her mind, the sooner she convinces all of us we're stuck with this and have to work with her, the better. She doesn't think anyone here is a threat." She put a hand on each of Flair's arms. "She's wrong."

Flair knew her panic showed in her face. Loretta gripped her elbows more tightly, and as fragile as Loretta seemed externally, Flair could feel a deep strength holding her up.

"Lucie wants to come back to you," Loretta said so softly that only Flair could hear. "You just have to let her."

David and Jude strode off into the woods, Flair behind them, her mother and Josie walking beside her. Flair was grateful for their support. Her feet seemed to find every root in the trail, and she was blinded by tears she couldn't shed.

"It will be okay," murmured Cynthia on one side of her.

Josie squeezed her arm on the other. "We'll get her back."

But Flair knew what she'd seen in the cards, and she grabbed her mother's hand. She wouldn't give up. But she didn't feel the hope she wanted to feel.

"I should have told her," she whispered. "I saw this. I saw magic taking her away. But I thought I could stop it."

She clutched her mother's hand tightly. "It was the same card as that night at Rodney's. You were leaving, and then I read for you, the Five of Swords, and I knew you would stay even though you should go. And you stayed."

Her mother didn't have to ask what night Flair meant. Cynthia put a hand to her own cheek, still faintly scarred. "That wasn't your fault," she said.

"I should have warned you," Flair said. "I could see what staying meant. I should have made you see it."

"You were thirteen. And I know you see things, baby. You always have. But only the seeker knows what's really in the cards. Every card contains all the possibilities. I stayed because that was what I wanted to see."

"I wanted to stay, though." Flair didn't want Cyn to let her off the hook. "Rodney—he gave me things. I liked our apartment. I liked staying there, the same school—everything. I wanted that. But not . . . not that badly. I promise."

"I know."

"I would have kept you safe. If I could."

"I know that, too."

"I just wanted to keep Lucie safe," Flair whispered. "And I couldn't do it."

Cynthia pulled her in close as they walked. "The Five of Swords is the mistake we make again and again," she said. "Whatever it is. I made mine. You make yours. But it's still a five. It's the middle of a journey. Not the end."

They'd reached the parking lot. Josie gave Flair a hug, and Cyn lingered over her hand, not letting go until Flair climbed into Jude's back seat. "You'll help Lucie," she whispered. "It's not over."

Flair wanted to believe her.

They were silent on the short ride to the church. Flair clutched the cards in her lap, then took them out of the box and held them. With a deep breath, she turned the top card over and looked at it in the fleeting light of a passing car. Was she reading for herself or for her daughter?

She couldn't be sure. She looked away for a moment, then down again, and saw that she hadn't turned the card at all. She turned it over again . . . to see, when another car passed, only the back again.

When they arrived, David ducked out of the car without looking at her. Jude gave her only a single unreadable glance before he followed David, and she quickly looked away.

She wished she'd told him. She wished she'd told everyone everything.

In the light of the church parking lot, she turned over the card again, and found the same. Only the back was visible. Another card, and another.

The cards were hot, nearly vibrating in her hand, and the design on their backs reflected the light and began to absorb it, until the eye within the triangle of vine glowed and stared back at her. She'd meant to destroy them, and instead they had saved her from herself. But they had not saved Lucie. She was so angry—with them, with herself, with everything. She had never felt so desperate.

But no matter how many times she turned the cards, she saw nothing but their backs. The cards wanted something. She could feel it. But it wasn't to be read.

She heard a sound outside the car, footsteps, chatter, and Jude and David emerged with Lucie between them. Flair pushed the cards back into their box, into her pocket. She didn't know what to do with them. She didn't know what to do at all, except follow the plan. As agreed, Flair sent her mother a quick text before the others reached the car. *We're on the way.*

The Lucie who climbed, giggling, into the back seat seemed like her Lucie until she saw Flair. She hesitated, and Flair heard Jude's voice behind her. "In you get," he said, sounding completely normal, and David got into the passenger seat, and Flair realized he'd resumed some version of his old, seemingly carefree self, and she wondered how much he was concealing and how much this hurt him, but only for a moment, because Lucie was sitting next to her, and she wasn't Lucie.

Rose knew Flair knew who she was, but Flair could tell she was uncertain about where Jude and David stood. She was silent, and Flair didn't mean to say anything, either, just to be there as Loretta had said.

But as much as this wasn't Lucie, it still was, and having her this close and yet not there felt as close to death as Flair had ever been. Before she knew it, she was crying as Jude left the parking lot, and she'd undone her seat belt and wrapped her arms around her daughter. She held her as tightly as she ever had while Lucie sat stiffly in Flair's arms and then, as Jude turned back toward the woods, pushed her harshly away.

"You fooled me," she called up to Jude. The voice was

Lucie's, but the tone belonged to Rose. "But you can't for long. There's no point, and you won't gain anything from joining them against me. Turn the car around."

"We're going back," Jude said, his eyes on the road.

David propped an elbow loosely on the armrest, as though he were perfectly at ease, and spoke gaily back over his shoulder. "Back to the scene of the crime, princess," he said. "Your mother and I want to talk to you."

"Talk," said Rose, and David laughed—Flair didn't know how he did it—and faced forward again.

"Lucie," Flair said, leaning toward her again, wanting to hold her daughter until she reached the part that was still Lucie, but Rose shifted in her seat so that her back was against the door and her knees toward Flair. She held out a hand to push Flair away even as Flair repeated her daughter's name, again and again like an incantation. "Lucie, Lucie. Lucie. Please. I know you're in there."

The tears dripped down Flair's face, off her cheeks and chin, but she didn't move to wipe them away. She couldn't take her eyes off the girl beside her, though her daughter had returned to facing forward, still as far from Flair as the back seat permitted, and was staring out the window, as though there were anything to be seen in the dark night.

Flair felt a huge sob catch in her throat and saw Jude glance back at her, and she realized there were tears running down his face as well. She couldn't look at David, because if he was crying, too, she would be totally undone. "Lucie," she said again, and she didn't keep the desperation out of her voice. "I love you, Lucie." She wanted to beg her to come back, but somehow she didn't. That wasn't what her daughter needed.

"I'm sorry," she said. She'd left Lucie on the outside, when she should have let her in. "I should have told you everything. I grew up so afraid of the cards, and my power. But I could have taught you to understand yours. I wanted you to trust me." Just as Cynthia once had wanted Flair to trust her. "But I never earned your trust."

That was the fate Flair hadn't been able to avoid.

Rose didn't turn back to face her. But Lucie's hand, the one closest to Flair, crept toward her, patting as though reaching without seeing.

Flair grabbed it. "I will now," she whispered, and felt her daughter's presence for the space of an intake of breath before the hand was yanked away.

Flair's eyes met Jude's in the mirror before she closed them and concentrated on holding on to that feeling, even if Lucie's hand was no longer in hers. She didn't know if she was still crying, or how long it took to return to the parking lot in the woods. In her mind, she was with Lucie, totally open to her, holding her there whether they were touching or not.

As Jude had predicted, Lucie—or Rose—refused to get out of the car. Flair wrapped her arms around herself and stood in the increasing chill, still holding Lucie in her mind and unable to argue with the voice speaking through her daughter. Cynthia and Josie came to stand next to her, silently. Jude held the door open.

"You're a thirteen-year-old girl," he said bluntly. "I don't care what else you are, and neither does the rest of the world. You can't do anything without us. I have your mother here. And your father. The control they have over what you do and when and how will astound you."

David, still in an agreeable tone that totally belied his words, joined in. "One of my friends wouldn't listen to her parents when we were kids," he said. "They paid a team of people to sneak in through her window one night and take her to a school somewhere. I didn't see her for years."

Flair had no idea if that was true. She would never do that to Lucie if it was and neither would he, but she pressed that thought away, not knowing how open her thoughts were to Rose and still holding on to something that felt to her like Lucie. Jude and David could handle this. Flair was just going to do her best to be here and hang on.

Rose got out of the car and slammed the door, then stalked onto the trail, not waiting for any of them. "This won't change anything," she said. "And I won't forget it."

Renee and her mother were waiting in the clearing. The fire still burned, lighting their faces, as Flair, followed by her mother and Josie, came out of the trees. Jude turned his flashlight off as Lucie stepped toward Renee. No, swaggered.

"You were never anything but a fool for your mother," she said. "You could have killed me a thousand times. But I knew you never would, and you can't change what's happened now."

"I can and I will," Renee began, but Rose interrupted her, looking at Flair.

"Flair knows," she said. "Lucie is gone. This was always going to happen. The cards saw it coming. It's fate."

Flair shook her head. "I saw something," she said. "But no one can know what it meant except Lucie. Nothing but fate is fate."

"That's where you're wrong," the person in front of Flair,

who was Lucie but could not be Lucie, said. "I'm fate. I always have been."

"No." Loretta stopped Rose's words with an imperious hand. "Let me talk to Lucie," she demanded of the figure in front of her.

"You are."

"Let her out, Rose."

"She's here," said the voice from within Lucie. "We're a team now."

Loretta took a step toward Rose-in-Lucie and seized her arm. Rose tried to pull away, but Renee's mother held her close, and the space where they touched began to glow, like a reflection of the fire that still burned nearby.

"Lucie," Loretta said. "You are not a team. You're here now, but you won't be for long. She'll take over. Within days. Hours. You can already feel it, can't you? You're getting further from the surface. You're saying things you don't mean to say. You've convinced yourself that this is what you want, that this is you, but you're lying, because you don't want to believe what's happening—but it is happening. It is. Soon, you'll have sunk into nothing but audience, and then not even that. You'll be there but not there. You'll be gone."

Rose tried again to pull away—and then, when she couldn't, Flair saw her grasp Loretta's arm instead and tighten her grip. Loretta winced, Flair saw it on her face, and without even knowing she was doing it, she stepped up behind her while Renee did the same, supporting the older woman while Rose's grip grew stronger and stronger.

This was why Rose didn't want to come back here. Lucie

was still close, and they were reaching her. She could hear them. And she wanted Rose out.

Flair thought Loretta would drop to her knees, but instead she seemed to grow taller, and the glow between her and Rose intensified, until it began to take form around Lucie, within her, so that they were seeing both Lucie and at the same time a ghostly form of Rose, still in Lucie but on the outside, as though Loretta was pulling her away.

It was working. Flair could feel it. Renee could feel it. Both of them stepped closer, surrounding Lucie and Loretta, looking for a way into their fight. Around them, Jude and David hovered—and then the figure of Rose sank back into Lucie again, pulling one arm violently free and reaching down to Renee's boots, her hand finding the knife Renee had replaced there earlier. A long, thin blade reflected the firelight.

Renee screamed while Rose lunged forward and, faster than Flair would have thought possible, plunged the knife into Loretta.

CHAPTER TWENTY-NINE

LORETTA COLLAPSED AGAINST Flair, and Flair felt blood on her hands, warm and thick and horrifying, making her gag and choke. Everything stopped. There were only her own hands and the woman sagging into them, her weight so much greater now, pulling Flair down and Renee beside her. She saw a flash of fear in Lucie's face before the glow that was Rose faded back into her entirely.

Flair leapt to her feet, leaving Renee to hold Loretta, and threw herself at Lucie, not caring about the knife or the blood. Nothing was going to happen to Lucie. Flair couldn't let it.

She felt it instantly. A different, vastly more intense coil of something, of electricity and strength. This was the hold that one person could have over another, the possession and power, but Flair didn't know who had who or why. She only knew that there were three of them here. Flair. Lucie. Rose.

And then there were four.

Cynthia stood behind Flair, her arms holding Flair tight,

and the two of them struggled to drag Lucie toward them, to force Rose out and away.

It wasn't working. Lucie—Rose—pulled out of their grasp triumphantly and stood terrible in the firelight, bloody, glowing. David, Jude, Renee all stared, powerless to help. Flair heard herself begging her daughter, found herself on her knees, the cards still in her pocket, still dragging her down, useless. "Please," she said to Lucie. "Please. Come back. I'll save you. I'll keep you safe."

As she heard herself say those words, Flair understood what it was that Rose had offered her daughter. She heard again what Lucie had shouted at her in the kitchen. *You don't trust me, and you never have.*

Flair didn't just want to keep Lucie safe. She wanted Lucie to learn to keep herself safe. She wanted Lucie to live her own life, and she needed Lucie to know that her life was hers to live. Loretta had told her what to do. *Lucie wants to come back to you. You just have to let her.*

She knew what to do now. This was her Five of Swords. The mistake she never stopped making.

But she would stop now. Flair struggled to her feet and stumbled toward her daughter, tugging the cards from her pocket, extending them in her hand. She had to give Lucie her own power. "Lucie," she said, and she grasped Lucie's hand with one of hers and then pressed the cards into it with the other. "Lucie. All the choices are yours."

Renee left a bleeding but conscious Loretta on the ground and threw herself at Flair and Lucie, but Cynthia pulled Renee away before she could reach them. Flair stood with her daughter, the cards between them both.

"You just played right into her hand," Renee said angrily, struggling in Cynthia's grasp. "If you give Rose the cards, she'll destroy them."

"Not Rose," Flair said. "Lucie."

Lucie would take the cards, as she was meant to. And Flair didn't care if she used the cards to leave Flair. As long as she was able to stay herself.

The cards in her grasp, Lucie stepped back. Flair couldn't breathe.

Lucie held the cards to her chest—and then lifted them above her head and threw them into the fire.

Cynthia might have screamed, or Renee, but Flair didn't hear them. She couldn't hear anything over the roaring in her ears, the burning in her eyes, the knowledge that she'd been wrong, that she'd thrown her family's magic and her chance of saving her daughter away screaming inside her head.

She saw Renee coming toward her and braced herself, knowing she deserved to be dragged to the ground, that she no longer cared what Renee might do to her.

But Renee didn't reach her. A flame burst from the air in front of her and a wind from nowhere swirled the flame in Renee's direction, making her leap back as Flair stared at Cynthia, who'd just done magic after the source of their magic had burned away.

With sudden fierceness, Flair turned toward Lucie, toward Rose, who was faltering, stunned, staring at the space where Cynthia's impossible flames had been. Suddenly everything was so clear.

"Lucie," she cried. "It's not the cards. You don't need the cards. You don't need anything or anyone else. It's you. You choose."

Rose—Lucie—faltered, reaching out to Flair and then snatching herself back, a fierce argument ensuing within her. Flair stood reaching out, offering all her will and strength and understanding. Cyn, her flames gone but still burning with the power that had produced them, stood beside her. Between them, Flair felt a third presence. Alice. The cards, their physical presence discarded and unnecessary.

Lucie had everything she needed, and Flair would make sure she knew it.

Lucie stumbled forward as though tearing herself from someone's grip, and this time, when Flair and Cynthia ran to her, she didn't pull away. Flair felt her daughter grasping her, holding her, clinging to her. She wrapped Lucie fully in her arms as Cyn held them both. Flair understood, as she never had before, that she had to both hold Lucie close and let her go.

Now, though, they were together, as tightly bound as any family could be. It was Rose whom they left behind, shimmering in the air, looking around her, her eyes landing on David, on Josie, on Jude, searching for a place to land as they backed away.

Then Renee ran forward, absorbing Rose in her arms and then into herself—but somehow in the same motion gathering up Loretta from the ground between them. For an instant, the three women were before them, a single entity.

And then Renee, holding the others with her, flung herself into the fire.

The flames rose, colors leaping out of it in turn, and Flair pulled Lucie back, sobbing, feeling Cynthia and Josie again beside her. Her family, safe. Jude ran toward the fire, looking for his sister, his mother, to pull out of the flames, and Flair's heart broke anew for him.

"They're gone," Lucie whispered, and Flair held her daughter close, turning Lucie away from the sight and dropping her own head on Lucie's shoulder, entirely caught up in the feeling of having her daughter back in her arms, until she heard Josie gasp and looked up.

"The cards!"

The tarot cards swirled out of the flames in a trail of color and light, a tornado of images emerging from the fire, carrying Renee and Loretta with them. Renee rolled forward, coughing, gasping, Loretta in her arms. Jude knelt to pull them away as the cards spun their way back into the fire and disappeared.

The flames leapt up, higher than their heads, higher than the trees around them. The wind picked up and the flames became like hands, reaching for the drying leaves still on the trees, snapping at twigs.

"They'll burn," Renee shouted, releasing Loretta into Jude's arms as she sat up and stared into the trees. "If they catch, the whole woods could go."

And all of them with it, Flair realized, straightening. She looked at her daughter, and the eyes that met hers were the eyes of the child who'd been by her side for so long and the woman she was slowly becoming.

"What should we do?" Lucie was still in Flair's arms, clinging to her.

The branches closest to the fire began to break off, and Flair realized it was Renee, using her magic to save the trees by releasing the limbs that would be the first caught by the flames.

But the fire continued to stretch higher, as though either it or Rose had to break free, and Flair didn't have an answer for Lucie.

"It's Alice," Flair said. "She's here—with the cards—"

"She pulled Rose in," Renee said. "And I felt hands pushing us out." Renee was still staring up, her eyes on the branches. "They're both in there. Fighting. And the trees are too close," she said. "I can try to hold them back, but I can't do anything else."

"I can," Cyn said. "I started the fire this afternoon; I can hold it back now." She reached for Flair. "Help me."

Flair released Lucie from her embrace, keeping a tight hold on her daughter's hand as she grasped Cynthia's. Josie caught Flair's eye and then took Lucie's hand on the other side.

Lucie looked from one of them to the other. "I don't know what to do," she said.

"Just hang on."

They couldn't encircle these flames, but this wasn't a ritual; it was the magic they had been born with. Flair lifted her arms, pulling Lucie's along with hers as the others raised theirs as well, and the fire rose in unison with their effort. They gathered it, fed it, reminded it that it was one of their own. Flames still scorched the trunks of the closest trees but their movement changed, slowed, the colors deepening. In the core of the blaze, a darkness swirled and struggled.

"Alice," Flair whispered.

"And Rose." Renee looked away from the fire to her mother, her shirt covered in blood, stirring in Jude's arms.

Flair felt Cynthia pulling at the heart of the flames, and

within them the familiar energy of the cards that had been a part of them both for so long. Rose had wanted to stop time. Alice had chosen to travel with it. But now both of their journeys would end.

Flair held tightly to the hands of her mother and daughter, felt Josie alongside them, Jude close by. Flair couldn't control what any of them did, or how long they were together. But she could be with them now.

The darkness in the fire roared upward, straining to break free. But Flair could feel Rose's power weakening, becoming thinner and smaller until, with a sudden flare that made them all jump, it disappeared.

Every one of them felt it. Rose was gone, and Alice and the cards with her.

Flair's shoulders sagged with relief but Cynthia still held their arms aloft, drawing the flames down, changing them until they became a fire of celebration rather than vengeance, sparks flickering merrily, sharing their light.

The instant their hands released, Josie rushed to Loretta, gently pushing Jude aside, touching Loretta's face and searching for the wound. "She's alive," she said, and they could see it—Loretta was moving, shifting herself on the hard ground, pressing against Jude's legs, trying to sit up.

Lucie flung herself into Flair, sobbing. "I did that," she said. "I didn't want to—"

David was there, putting his arms around them, and for once Flair didn't want to push him away. Lucie needed them both.

"We know, we know." Flair's voice was soothing, her hand

stroking Lucie's head, knowing Lucie was grieving her actions and trying to be there for that grief even while her own heart was singing. She had her daughter back.

Josie was helping Loretta to sit up. "It isn't even that bad," Josie said. "Either Lucie's or Rose's understanding of basic anatomy is gravely off. The heart is on the left." She looked more closely at Loretta's wound. "You somehow even managed to miss the lungs. Nice work."

Flair felt Lucie smother a sob on her shoulder and knew she wasn't up for jokes. "We can't all be trained EMTs," she reminded Josie. "And in this case, that was definitely for the best."

"If I had a first aid kit—"

"Wait," Cyn said, disappearing into the trees and returning with a backpack. "Always be prepared."

"You've become a Boy Scout in your old age?" The mother Flair had known never had so much as a Kleenex, although she could, and often did, produce things like corkscrews and party hats from whatever bag she was carrying.

"We had a tightrope over a fire." Cynthia handed the pack to Josie. "Things could go wrong."

"And a Band-Aid would definitely have helped," Josie said, rummaging around and taking out antiseptic wipes and bandages.

"Is that going to hurt?" Loretta spoke for the first time, and both Jude and Renee moved closer.

"On a scale of one to bodily possession by a displaced spirit, call it a three." Josie looked up. "I think you're going to be fine," she said. "I definitely recommend stitches, so you'll have to come up with some explanation for a doctor, but she really did miss anything important. It's not quite just a flesh wound, but it's not much worse. Maybe some antibiotics. I don't know how clean Renee keeps her daggers."

The look Renee shot Josie was as sharp as any blade, but she let her mother reply.

"I will be delighted to go in and get the damage I sustained while tripping over my too-authentic *Macbeth* costume seen to," Loretta said. "I've never been happier to bleed."

Jude helped her to her feet. Renee rose, too. David drew Lucie closer to him, and Flair found herself standing alone, face-to-face with her former enemy. She waited for Renee to say something. To apologize, maybe. Because even though Flair wouldn't change the past that got her here, it might be nice for Renee to own up to some of the less-than-magical ways she'd been trying to play the role of fate.

Renee gazed at Flair, and the faintest of smiles touched her lips before her face resumed its usual stoniness. "See you around, Hardwicke," she said.

"That's it?" Flair put her hands on her hips. "That's all you've got?"

"You might be less of a fool than I took you for," Renee said, then shrugged. "You want something else, find someone else."

Flair sighed. "Take care of your mother, Renee."

Renee permitted another tiny smile. "Take care of your kid, Hardwicke."

Flair turned to see that Jude was already walking toward the edge of the clearing, only his back visible in the waning light of the fire. He glanced over his shoulder at Flair and Renee.

Flair caught his eye. His face remained impassive, but Flair could see his anger simmering underneath his stoic exterior.

She'd kept him in the dark, exactly as his sister had, whether she'd meant to or not. And he wasn't going to forgive her for it easily.

Without changing his expression, he turned and walked away.

She would talk to him. Apologize. But not now. She turned away and found David looking at her over Lucie's shoulder. Before she could say anything, Lucie reached for her and pulled her in.

"I'm sorry," Lucie said. "I'm so sorry."

"No," Flair said, pressing Lucie in tightly, speaking into her curls. "I'm sorry. I should have warned you. I had so many chances. And I blew them all." She hugged her daughter even more tightly. "Well," she said, an enormous swell of gratitude filling her, "not all."

CHAPTER THIRTY

Saturday, October 31–Sunday, November 1

DAVID SEEMED SURPRISED to find that Cyn had driven his Lincoln to the trail parking lot.

"I didn't want the battery to die," she said, tossing him the keys. "Just looking out for you."

In spite of Josie's bright words, she and Renee decided to take Loretta to the hospital, and they left in Josie's car. David drove Flair, Cynthia, and Lucie home through a dark night lit by revelers of all kinds, passing at least one coven ritual, several groups of costumed partiers, and the occasional exhausted parent, child in tow, staggering home from festivities that had gone far too late. The closer they got to home, the more Flair realized that the time had come to sit down with David and Lucie and unravel what came next.

She tried not to dread it. When things were at their worst, you longed for your regular problems back. And then, when things were better, the regular old problems still sucked.

Cynthia's big tour bus was back in the driveway, Alto in the door, calling to Cynthia, asking what happened. Flair caught her mother's hand in a silent gesture of good luck and left her to it, and then she was climbing her porch steps, Lucie and David behind her.

She picked up the empty bowl she'd left for trick-or-treaters and brushed past the ghoul they'd left to keep guard over it.

Inside, on the kitchen table, was one single remaining bag of mixed chocolate bars and a note in Josie's mother's handwriting. *You don't have to share.*

Flair ripped it open and spilled it out on the table. Teabag came trotting down the stairs after what had probably been a long night of barking out the window. Flair let the little dog out and back in, then turned to find Lucie at the table and David taking mugs down from the cabinet.

"I would prefer Earl Grey to whatever you've been giving me, if that's all right with you," he said. "But I can make it myself."

Flair nodded, uncertain. She'd explained what she could about what she'd done to David as they drove home, but other than that, she and David had spoken very little.

Now Lucie stared down at the candy wrapper in her hands. "You don't have to tell me," she said to David. "I got your texts. I know you're not taking me with you back to St. Louis."

David looked to Flair, who nodded, feeling ashamed.

"Your mom and I don't think St. Louis is the right choice for you right now, and I don't think you really want to come. I know you blame your mom for bringing you here. But there's a lot you don't know." For once, it was David not throwing Flair under the bus, and she was grateful.

He looked over at Flair. "And a lot I didn't know. Even putting aside the whole witch thing."

Lucie slumped over the mug he placed in front of her, and Flair sat down next to her, then scooped Teabag up and set her, unbidden, in Lucie's lap, where the little dog nuzzled her face into one of her favorite humans.

"There's a lot we should talk about," Flair said. "But I promise—we're also going to listen."

Tears were slipping out of Lucie's eyes, and she'd already shed so many. Flair wrapped her arms around her daughter, and then, when she didn't resist, pulled both Lucie and Teabag into her own lap and rocked her daughter from side to side. "We're going to figure it out," she promised. "All of it. All of us."

Possibly it would have been kinder to the hungover Halloween revelers to open Buttersweet Bakery on the day after Halloween. And there might have been a fair number of them still interested in one of Flair's signature tarot cookies in honor of All Saints' Day.

But Flair couldn't face it, and she felt sure none of her helpers, all of whom had been out there ghouling it up with the best of them, could either.

So Flair, deprived of her witchy costume but perfectly happy in her worn flannel pajama bottoms and tank top again, was brewing a latte all for her very own self in her own kitchen when she heard the squeak of the porch swing. Teabag leapt to her feet but didn't bark. Instead, she gave Flair what Flair would have sworn was a knowing wink. Flair slid into the front room to look out the window, a hopeful flutter in her middle.

Jude was sitting on the swing, looking off at the street.

Quickly, she went back to the kitchen and divided her espresso in two—yet another reason to always make a double. She frothed twice the chocolate milk and added Lucie's squirty whipped cream and chocolate sprinkles.

She threw on Lucie's old hoodie again and started for the front door, then stopped, the sense of forgetting something tugging at her softly. She set the drinks down and turned back to the kitchen counter, where a bright-turquoise box of pastries sat. She opened it, already knowing what she was going to see, and then hesitated as a thought tugged at her.

It might not be a good idea.

But then again, it might.

She wrapped a pastry paper around a cookie and slid it into the pocket of her sweatshirt, took up her drinks again, and left the kitchen, Teabag following. She eased open the front door, hoping, for the second morning in a row, not to wake anyone. But she had a feeling that even if she did, David, Lucie, and Cyn, and even the occupants of the bus still in the driveway, would have the good sense to stay inside.

"Happy least-witchy day of the year," she said. "But caffeine never stops being helpful."

Jude looked up.

Her smile faltered at his expression, which was less welcoming than she'd hoped, but she didn't let herself stop.

He was here. That was where they'd start.

"Scoot over."

Flair handed Jude both coffees and hopped up on the swing. His feet touched the ground easily, hers dangled, and she could see him suppressing a small smile as she took her coffee back.

"I'm sorry," she said. "I should have told you everything yesterday."

Then she stopped. Because while she'd had her reasons and could probably go on for ages about how Renee had had years to tell him while she'd had literally hours, apologies that included the word "but" were not apologies.

And she did wish she'd told him, but then, she wished a lot of things.

"Thank you," he said.

He sipped his coffee. She sipped hers.

Flair wasn't a nervous talker. She could wait. If he wanted a nice silence, she'd give him a nice silence. A nice long silence, just sitting here, enjoying the morning, Teabag on the steps, looking out at the blissfully empty sidewalk.

"I should have told you but I didn't even know where to start and then David came out and I thought you'd be mad and you weren't but that was already one thing I hadn't told you and I didn't even know how to start with the rest. It didn't seem like it should be me telling you. Renee—"

Jude made a big show of looking at a nonexistent watch. "Ten seconds," he said.

"Ten seconds what?"

"Until you blamed Renee. I bet her you'd last at least five; she said you'd hang her out to dry before you even finished apologizing."

"Is ten seconds good or bad?"

Jude sighed and sipped his coffee. "Pretty good, I think. I do wish you'd told me. But even if you had told me, I still would have been upset that she hadn't, so probably it's mostly on her. Which she claims to be sorry for."

"This whole thing would have been a lot easier if she'd been more up front with everyone," said Flair firmly.

Jude laughed. "Okay, pot. Blame the kettle," he said. "You're a lot more like her than you think."

"Oh, no." Flair was nothing like Renee. Nothing.

"She thought she could fix everything by herself, too."

Flair sipped her coffee without saying anything. She was a lot nicer than Renee, anyway.

"We had a long talk last night," Jude said. "We haven't had much of a chance to be a family before, but we all feel like we're getting a second chance now. We're going to take it."

He took a deep breath and looked out at the sweet gum tree in the yard, the leaves at the top already a glorious shade of red. "Which for me means setting up shop more permanently here at Halloween Central. And asking around about anyone else who might be interested in a second chance."

Flair leaned against the back of the swing, making it sway slightly, and reached into her pocket. "Well," she said. "I don't know if you know this, but I'm kind of known for my fortune-telling tarot cookies."

He tilted his head to look at her, and now he really was smiling.

"Word is," Flair said, "if I give you one and it's the right one, they kind of help."

"Huh. Sounds interesting. I don't suppose you have one that's right for me?"

"There just happens to have been one in a box in my kitchen," Flair said, leaning toward him and angling her chin flirtatiously. "I'm not sure where it came from, but I think it might be just what you need."

He set his coffee on the porch rail as she handed him the cookie wrapped in the pastry paper. He opened it slowly—and then turned to her with a look of surprised outrage.

"That isn't what I was expecting," he said, holding the Fool in his hands.

"It's the card of new beginnings," she said. "Hurling yourself into the great unknown—but with all the optimism and hope in the world by your side."

He set the cookie down and reached his arm around her. "Is that my card?" Then with a sudden, coffee-sloshing tug, he pulled her closer. "Or yours?"

"I think it's for both of us."

"Ah. I do like that. One more question."

Flair was beginning to find the proximity of his lips very distracting. She reached up to take a little whipped cream from the side of his mouth with her finger, and he caught it in his mouth and licked if off before she finished.

Her entire body melted forward just enough that she was touching him everywhere she could and wishing she'd had the sense to put down her coffee. "Yeah?"

He plucked her coffee from her hands and placed it next to his on the porch rail before pulling her into his lap and whispering into her ear, sending goose bumps up her spine.

"Can I maybe get another cookie later? There was this one I had my eye on. The Lovers. Something like that."

"You can't choose," she said, looking him in the eye. "But yes."

ACKNOWLEDGMENTS

I have wanted the tarot to be a bigger part of my life ever since I did my first reading at age fourteen for a boy at my best friend's church camp, probably violating a dozen rules in the process. The inappropriate things we did at those camps were legion, but that tarot reading is the only one that stuck with me. I was completely inexperienced and totally winging it (with the help of a library book), but the spread I laid out on that dusty linoleum dorm room floor showed that kid a different way to look at his life. Suddenly, he was the hero of his story.

That was my introduction to the real magic of the cards. I've turned to them off and on ever since, and every time, placing myself along one of the journeys and among the universal symbols and archetypes the tarot contains reminds me that even when we can't control the plot of our lives, we still control the narrative: the story we tell ourselves along the way. Those stories matter.

But it wasn't until I began writing Flair's story that I finally had a chance to really immerse myself in the world of tarot. A great deal of my current understanding of the cards comes thanks to Michelle Tea and in particular to her book *Modern Tarot: Connecting with Your Higher Self through the Wisdom of the Cards*, and to Jessa Crispin and her book *The Creative Tarot: A Modern Guide to an Inspired Life*. Kim Krans's *The Wild Unknown Alchemy Deck & Guidebook* is my deck of choice and influenced many of the descriptions of the cards Flair fears and the cookies she creates, as did a lesser-known deck: *A Siren's Melody*, by Lauren Sleeper. I kept that deck, and the guide Lauren made to go with it, close by for months as I wrote.

My other guides to the world of tarot and witchcraft include (unbeknownst to them) Amanda Yates Garcia, author of the memoir *Initiated* and host of the *Between the Worlds* podcast; Stefanie Caponi, author of *Guided Tarot*; and Gabriela Herstik, author of *Inner Witch* and *Bewitching the Elements*, among many, many others.

My fictional witches were undoubtedly influenced by my thorough steeping in the work of Alice Hoffman, Deborah Harkness, Zoraida Córdova, Alix Harrow, Lana Harper, Erin Sterling, and other writers who've brought magic to life over the years, and everything I write has, I hope, the shadow of Shirley Jackson looming nearby.

Tara Singh Carlson at Putnam chose Flair, championed her, and worked tirelessly to make this story better (including one epic editorial phone call that wrung us both dry). When Tara believes in you—or the magic you create—you know you're on solid ground. Ashley Di Dio was the power behind the process (and Aranya Jain is doing a great job of filling her shoes).

LeeAnn Pemberton, Hannah Dragone, Emily Mileham, and Maija Baldauf do all the things to turn words into actual books, while Anthony Ramondo masterminds the way those books look on physical or digital shelves, with the help of a perfect cover from Vi-An Nguyen and a delicious interior from Tiffany Estreicher. Brennin Cummings, Emily Leopold, Kristen Bianco, and Ashley Hewlett make sure those books get out into the world and readers have a chance to find them, and the whole team and all the work they do help Ivan Held and Sally Kim make Putnam a house I'm so proud to be a part of. When I choose books, I actually do look for the Putnam colophon on the spine. I'm also delighted to be published by Titan Books in the UK. Thanks to Katie Dent for falling for Flair, Lucie, and the rest of the crew and for bringing us on board.

Thank you to Kristin Roth Nappier, whose copy editing saved me from myself countless times and also ensured that every cup of tea in this story (and there are many) had sufficient time to steep, and to Margo Lipschultz, still an occasional pop of support in my inbox and always in my mind. Natasha Leskiw and Jacqueline Ferrari, I appreciate you in ways that are too numerous to list.

Playing the Witch Card would not exist without the support of my fabulous fiction agent, Caryn Karmatz Rudy, and I would not be the writer I am without the encouragement of my fierce nonfiction agent, Laurie Abkemeier. Their team at DeFiore & Company never lets me down. And I would just be a sad shell of that writer without my own support team, starring Sarah Pinneo and Jess Lahey, Jennie Nash, Mary Laura Philpott, Christine Koh, Gretchen Rubin, Laurie White, Laura Vanderkam, Lisa Belkin (for SO LONG, friend!), Liz McGuire,

Susan Ellingwood (and Jake Not-Ellingwood, as he is known in my phone), Meg Ables, Amy Wilson, Wendi Aarons, Nancy Davis Kho, Kimberley Gorelik, and that's just a start at naming all the names.

Kendall Hoyt, Jen Schiffman, Mimi Lichtenstein, and Zion, Teddy, Sella, and Tigger provide much-needed woods-bathing breaks. Allie Levy at Still North Books supports both my writing and reading habits, which are also enabled by Lisa Christie and Julie Smith at every opportunity.

Judi Fusco, I dedicated the last book to you, but this one I wrote *for* you, which is different. May we find many, many witchy nerdy reads to love together.

Finally, huge thanks to Rob for full-on, all-in support in every way, and to Sam, Lily, Rory, and Wyatt for many variations on the same. I don't know if you know how much it means to me that y'all are honestly proud of me and say so. And to my parents, Jon and Jo, who never let me doubt for a minute that I could tell my own story.

PLAYING
the
WITCH CARD

KJ DELL'ANTONIA

———

A Conversation with KJ Dell'Antonia

———

Discussion Guide

———

**BOOK
ENDS**

PUTNAM
— EST. 1838 —

A CONVERSATION WITH KJ DELL'ANTONIA

You mention in your acknowledgments that you have a long relationship with tarot, and that you conducted extensive research on tarot cards and witchcraft while writing this novel. Did any of this research change your thoughts on tarot or inspire you to change something about your life?

The cards in the story don't foretell destiny, and they don't make things happen. They reveal possibilities. Because they're Flair's family's magic cards, with the spirit of that magic within them, they know a little more than most cards—but Flair still has to read her own story.

Figuring out the role tarot cards played in Flair's life—even though they're magic cards, and even though she's a witch—made me realize that what I love about the cards is the way they offer real-life readers that same possibility. We can see where we are in our own stories, decide what certain symbols—or events or people—mean to us. We can use them to open our minds to different paths forward. The Death card, for example, isn't necessarily the end of a story but might be an end to a particular way of viewing a situation. And when we try to force something—attach the Lovers card to a relationship that isn't working, for example—it doesn't help. We have to let the cards fall where they fall and read our story from there—even when we go to someone else to read the cards, we're always the only one who can really see the story.

Recipes are an important part of both Flair's and Jude's professions, and cooking was also a vital element in your novel The Chicken Sisters. *How do you think cuisine relates to intimacy and to family legacy?*

Food is so omnipresent in our lives. Whether we're eating with our family in the big bustling kitchen we romanticize, or eating with a roommate or lover, or alone when we thought we'd be with someone, it's the one waking activity that everyone does one way or another. Eating has rhythms, routines, expectations, and associations whether we mean to create them or not, and so when it does connect us to our people it's powerful. It's very challenging to control how our own history with food impacts us and our families, so I love exploring that relationship in fiction where I can watch it play out.

Which tarot card would you most like to receive at this moment in your life and why?

Is there a Taylor Jenkins Reid card? No, seriously—I'll give a real answer! I love the forward motion of the Chariot and the Wheel of Fortune. And Temperance gets a bad rap—it's really about finding balance, not giving things up. And who doesn't love the way the Magician tells us we are right where we want to be and invites us to do all the things?

But the whole point is that we don't choose. Choosing doesn't work (although it's fine to try to invite a card's energy into your life). We take a card we've been dealt and we ask ourselves what it says about where we are in our story.

What do you think draws Jude and Flair to each other? Why is their connection so powerful?

I think they're "fated mates" in Romance terms—everything about their history brings them together. No one else will ever understand how they became who they are. Which in real life could be good or bad (sometimes we need to become someone else), but because Flair and Jude both need to really lean into things they've avoided about themselves and their pasts, they're perfect together. They're not going to let each other off the hook, but they'll also be able to laugh about it.

Which was your favorite scene to write for this book, and why?

Probably the circle where they're trying to free David from his enchantment. They know what they're doing seems crazy and yet they also take it very seriously. I also loved creating the world of the Rattleboro trail, because we had, at our house, an annual outdoor "Spooky Trail," where parents haunted the woods to scare the pants off our children, and I could never get the effects as extreme as I wanted. There were always naysayers, insisting that we couldn't do things like dropping nets onto them, and my inability to get serious special effects out there was always disappointing. But when you're making it up, you can do anything!

Playing the Witch Card *is your third novel. How was writing* Playing the Witch Card *similar to or different from writing your previous books? How do the themes of* Playing the Witch Card *overlap with themes you've explored in your other novels?*

The Chicken Sisters was about how reality TV—or really, fame and external approval—never solves anything. *In Her Boots* was about how hiding your real self also never fixes anything. And in *Playing the Witch Card*, I was thinking about how even magic can't solve your problems. Nothing solves our problems. We have to do the work ourselves.

There are many unexpected twists and turns in this novel. Without giving anything away, did you envision all of these when you started writing, or did some of them occur to you as you progressed through the chapters?

Things changed a lot while I was writing. I always knew the deep town history and that the original founding witches very much disagreed about how to pass their knowledge to future witches (how's that for not giving anything away!). I also knew what Flair would have to confront at the end, both in terms of the plot and what's at stake, and in terms of her internal struggle with her own powers. But the details of how it happened definitely evolved. I changed the ending at the last minute, too.

What do you most want readers to take away from Playing the Witch Card?

I wrote *Playing the Witch Card* at a moment in my life when I was trying to come to terms with how little control we have over so many of the things that are important to us. I found myself realizing that even if you could control everything, you wouldn't want to, because in so many ways it's the unexpected that makes life interesting. Even the worst things at least give us an appreciation for the good stuff. I wanted Flair to realize that while she could control her own choices, she didn't actually want to control Lucie's—or Jude's, or David's, or even her mother's, even if that meant her life wouldn't go the way she planned.

I've finally realized that even if I could wave a magic wand and make everything perfect for everyone I love, it wouldn't work—because perfect for me isn't perfect for them, especially if they don't get to make their own choices. Which doesn't mean I don't still wish I could do it. But I've mostly accepted it, and I hope reading *Playing the Witch Card* nudges readers along that same path.

DISCUSSION GUIDE

1. This book explores themes of family and legacy. Flair is often known as "Marie's granddaughter" or "Cynthia's girl." Which identities have you inherited from your family, and what do they mean to you?

2. If you were to take over the line of work or the daily routine your grandmother was doing at your age, what would that be and how well would you accomplish it?

3. To what extent does believing in magic affect one's powers? Do you think Flair could summon up magic if she continued not to believe in it? How is magic a metaphor for female confidence?

4. The women in Rattleboro clearly believe magic is limited to other women. At one point, Josie suggests it's because men don't need magic. But in the final scenes of the book, Jude is showing signs of discovering his

own powers. How do you think his having magic will affect his relationship with Flair and with Renee?

5. Magic is often pitted against stability in Flair's mind. Did you think that these concepts were at odds at the beginning of the novel? Did your opinion change as you read further?

6. Why do you think Cynthia named her daughter "Flair"?

7. Multiple generations of mothers and daughters are shown in this novel. Compare these mother-daughter relationships: Marie and Cynthia, Cynthia and Flair, and Flair and Lucie. How do they contrast and inform one another?

8. Flair tragically underestimates Lucie at points in the novel. How might she have handled Lucie's tarot education differently? How do you think that would have affected the outcome of the book?

9. Who did you think was the primary antagonist of this novel at first? Did your opinion change as the story progressed?

10. There are very few men of import in Rattleboro, by design. How does this change the roles of the women running the town? Can you imagine the way your town would change under such matriarchal power?

11. Have you ever had your tarot cards read? Would you? Did this story affect your answer?

12. Do you think we each have a fate or destiny that could be "read in the cards"? Or do we control our own stories?

13. The book's dedication asserts that the all-important question is: "Are you a witch or not?" Having read the book, what do you think "being a witch" means in the context of the story? More important, are you a witch?

ABOUT THE AUTHOR

KATE SEYMOUR

KJ Dell'Antonia is the former editor of the *New York Times*'s *Motherlode* and the cohost of the *#AmWriting* podcast as well as the author of *How to Be a Happier Parent*, *In Her Boots*, and the instant *New York Times* bestseller and Reese's Book Club pick *The Chicken Sisters*. She lives with her family on a small farm in Lyme, New Hampshire, but retains an abiding love for her childhood in Texas and Kansas.

CONNECT ONLINE

KJDellAntonia.com
📚 kjda
f KJDellAntonia
▣ KJDA